A Dead Wizard's Dream

Book 1 of the Convent Series

Happy reading!

First Printing 2019
ISBN: 9781077280397
www.rosshughes.biz

A Dead Wizard's Dream

Book 1 of the Convent Series

A Fantasy Novel

By Ross C. Hughes

Cover and map design by Jeff Brown Graphics

Published 2019

Also by Ross Hughes

Secrets of the Ashlands

For my Dad,
For being my first reader and first fan

Acknowledgements

I'd like to thank my family for their support and for allowing me to daydream my whole life through. I'd like to thank my favourite English teacher from my school days back at Northamptonshire Grammar School, so thank you, Mr. Stanley, for all the inspiration you gave me. I'd like to thank all the authors who wrote such tremendous books that I was inspired to write one myself. Finally, I'd like to thank my cover and map designer, Jeff Brown, who brought Maradoum to life on paper. Thank you all.

White Wastes
The North
Chilblain Sea
Black Sea
Jaata Murgen
Skalda's Teeth
Northbane
Baldr's Saal
White Cliffs
White Woods
Crossroads
Justiqua
Port Hawn
Bellchob
Gynvul Lac
City of Justiqua
Pacia Castle
Mitteord
Great Divide
Fjellian Ocean
The Archipelago
Odendroth
Skeil Bay
Srejpoz
Najuzna
Anglasund
Boddle
Sol Top
Titan's Pass
Ban-Hodre
The Fringe
Fjelburg
Tchaipolis
Maradoum
The Parapet
Dragon Sea

N
E
S
Kiharaz
Temple of Celeste
Klundun
Humnumshibai
Lombonn
Shambot
Aegis Waters
Qabdara
Al Kutz
Jhando
Hevarre
Hanava
Shimyahein
Vuum
Harrukai
Eshimbranir
The Goblin Isles
Crysali
Babese Sultanate
Silent Straits
Lama Kului Desert
Calypra
Jungleside
Great Fissure
Lost Island
Swash Isle
Kauapunki Meren
Shala Hyddin
Ooa
The Ashlands
Quing Tzu

Prologue

The Fall of Convent

A pearl rolled down an arid tan slope. Chimmel wiped away the sweat on her brow. The sun withered her unmercifully during these hours she stood guard in front of the suburban outpost. Her lips were chapped and cracking, her mouth was cotton-dry, and an insistent throbbing had begun behind her eyes, which were constantly narrowed against glaring rays.

An image of a glistening lake filled with pure sweet water swam before her, and she smiled. The image faded as the dehydrated woman remembered that the lake was on the other side of the massive metropolis, but the smile persisted as her eyes came to rest on the beautiful spiked towers, spires and enormous otherworldly structures that stretched for leagues to comprise the city of Convent. Resembling a cluster of midnight black and sorcerous emerald mountains in the desert, the dark glass city gleamed under the beaming sun, surrounded by undulating dunes. To Chimmel, Convent was a symbol of what magic could achieve; rumour had it that the Sisters had built the glass of the city from the sand itself.

A group of men wandered down the crystalline street toward her; thin, wasted, dressed in rags, they prowled like wolves on the hunt. Their greedy eyes darted around shiftily, looking for opportunity. Chimmel clenched her staff and jaw tighter as they neared, looking straight ahead and trying to ignore them.

Her pulse quickened as unfounded theories floated through her mind. The men looked voracious enough to be rebels, and if so, then the outpost she guarded would be a viable target should they wish to undermine and sabotage Convent's rule. On the other hand, she reasoned, they appeared starved enough to be part of the general populace, in which case they might be thieves prowling for food. There were hundreds of rebels in the city now, and it made her nervous.

She did not know why there was such opposition to the Sisterhood's rule; the system had always treated her well. Although there were occasional food shortages, executions, imprisonments and disappearances, the Sisterhood – called Witches by the irreverent – kept the population safe from disease and outside harm. Best of all, they promised that, as long as the people followed their rules to the letter in life, the Sisters would welcome them with open arms when they died into the afterlife that Convent had created, the paradise named *Citta Pacia,* where they could live in bliss forever.

The men were close now, and eyeing her hungrily. Chimmel knew what they saw; a young, fair-haired woman in a coral robe tied with a blue sash, holding a staff. She was standing guard on the outskirts of the city in front of an emerald building that resembled a clump of crystal in that it was comprised of many adjacent, flat-faced spiked towers – some of which leaned out ominously over the street and yet, Chimmel was assured, would never fall. Behind her was an impassable doorway sealed by an eldritch lock, a sparkling green sheen that filled the otherwise empty space under the lintel.

Her hands shook with the effort she expended clenching her staff, and she involuntarily held her breath as the men drew up to her, but then they passed on and she exhaled heavily with lights dancing before her eyes. Whether they were rebels or not, it appeared that neither she nor the outpost were a target for them today.

A short while later, as blood seeped across the darkening sky from the fiery round wound, Chimmel noticed another figure approaching against the setting sun, this one cloaked and hooded. The figure's sinuous movements made her elongated shadow dance in and out of those cast by the sharp, spiky buildings that lined the street, so that at times it seemed she had no shadow at all.

"Sister Sandrea," Chimmel greeted the red-cloaked woman with a bow.

"Initiate Chimmel," Sandrea said with a nod. "Has there been any trouble?"

While the Initiate detailed the events of the day, including the men she had suspected of being rebels, she took the opportunity to study Sandrea's face. The Sister was immaculately beautiful, as was every Sister, thanks to their otherworldly arts. She had long hair like strands of woven gold, smooth and unblemished pale skin, long lashes, high, prominent cheekbones, and full, luscious lips above a soft jawline. Her eyes, however, were as hard as glass. Chimmel shivered as the other woman's aura of power tickled her senses, and longed for the day when she would command such arcane energies.

"We must be on the constant lookout for rebels," Sandrea was saying. "You did well in reporting. Now, I am going inside. I will not be long."

Summoning her courage, Chimmel spoke up, "You have been coming here a lot of late, Sister. May I know the reason for your visits?"

"You may not, Initiate," stated Sandrea, her tone glacier-cold and sharp.

Her voice had a lilting accent to it that the desert-girl could not place, but that was common to all Sisters of Maradoum. It was sweet to hear and yet too sweet, so that it felt bitter to the ear and, like a sickening dessert, made one feel ill to ingest too much.

"Perhaps I should report your unusual activity to Sister Marybeth or the Matriarch then, to be sure there is nothing amiss."

Chimmel wished she had remained silent. The Sister's eyes were no longer the eyes of a human, but smouldered with evil yellow flames as she glared at the desert-girl. Chimmel sank involuntarily to her knees and then to her stomach, pressing her face against the hard ground in forced reverence to the power she could feel surging through the Sister's body. She began to choke in terror, hyperventilating and panicking, fearful for her life. As her fingertips and toes went numb and her vision began to blur, the crushing feeling abruptly ended and Chimmel gasped for breath. She slowly picked herself up from the ground, dread still weighing on her chest and evident upon her face. Sandrea regarded the Initiate with dead eyes now, like she had no qualms about destroying this quarrelsome girl if she stood in her way.

"You will report nothing," the Sister hissed icily. "You have seen nothing. You know nothing. Never dare to question a Sister again or they may be less forgiving than I. Do I make myself clear, Initiate?"

"Yes, Sister."

"Good. Remain vigilant, Initiate."

"Yes, Sister."

With a wave of her hand, Sandrea dissolved the flickering, glowing shield of jade energy that veiled the doorway and walked through unimpeded. Once through, she waved a hand again, and the green sheen reappeared behind her, shining and impenetrable. By the time she had done so, she had all but forgotten the troublesome desert-girl.

Inside the outpost, Sandrea laid eyes on a spacious anteroom, from which led several doorways and staircases. Sconces in the green glass walls held torches lit with perpetually burning emerald fire, so that a lime haze filled the air. Choosing a staircase, she began to descend.

Crossing corridors in between, she plummeted down six flights of stairs until she was deep underground. There, in a vast empty vault, she gazed upon hundreds of stone rings lining the walls. Each was taller than a man and hollow inside of a thin band of stone. The seamless, grey masonry was carved with archaic runes, which pulsed with violet energy. In the forehead of each ring, a chunk of blue-purple crystal had been embedded.

"The prisons," she breathed, never failing to be awed by the scope of the room.

Walking down the right wall, she counted the stone rings until she reached number forty-seven. Up close, she could see that the air inside the band of stone shimmered like it was distorted by a desert mirage. Though the wall was visible on the other side of the stone ring, when she stepped into the swimming air, she vanished.

Sandrea reappeared somewhere else entirely as she stepped out of the other side of the ring. Again, a green sheen obscured her view, but she swiftly wafted it away and re-erected it behind her.

Instead of a setting red sun, a small pale one now flickered weakly, high in the grey sky above her. The hilly landscape that stretched out for leagues before her was wan, shadowy and ill-lit. Little colour could be seen thanks to the lack of light, so the Sister looked out over a black-and-white world.

She walked across soft grey grass, past a glistening black lake to the top of a hill, where she looked out over a monochromatic forest. Her hair, bleached by her surroundings, billowed over her face, blinding her with white wisps now that she had pushed her hood back. Walking down, she found a simple, thatched hut at the base of the hill, at the edge of the shadowy woods.

She knocked on the door, heard a scuffle inside, and then the door creaked open to reveal a tall man. He was middle-aged, thin, dressed in simple, poorly-stitched clothes and had unkempt silver hair. His handsome visage was marred only by a long black scar running down from just beneath his left eye, down the side of his nose, over his lips and chin.

His face lit up and he took her into his arms when he saw her. "Sandrea!"

"Besaleus!" she cried in return, kissing him long and deeply.

He pulled her into the hut, and they made love for a short while – experimental, passionate, at times rough sex – until both were exhausted, covered in sweat and fluid, panting like dogs. As Sandrea lay in his bed, in his arms, she felt warm, safe and comfortable, as she always did with Besaleus.

"Do you remember the first time we did this?" Sandrea stroked his chest with soft circular movements of her fingers.

"But of course, my love." The man's voice was strong and deep. His chest resonated with his words against Sandrea's cheek. "It was the greatest day I can remember."

She looked up into his scarred face and smiled. "For me, too. It has been so many years now since that day. It is a blessing in a way that this world keeps you young, is it not? For otherwise we could not have been together such as we are now."

"It is indeed, in a way, a blessing." Besaleus' smile faltered.

"What is wrong?"

"I have been here for as long as I can remember," he said with lonely eyes. "Year upon year, decade after decade. Do you think you can help me escape soon?"

The prisoners must not escape; that was the Sisters' mandate. Sandrea knew that if she was discovered here, she would be destroyed. She would likely have to kill the Initiate, Chimmel. The younger woman had not yet outlived her usefulness, however; she was the only one who knew of Sandrea's visits. Chimmel would never dare tell any of the other Sisters, would not dare to speak to them as she had spoken to Sandrea at the entrance. Sandrea smirked; she allowed the commoners and Initiates a great deal more freedom than did her peers, but they were still slaves to be used and discarded at will.

The Sisters ruled the world, and all others were expendable. This had been Sandrea's ideology for a long time, and yet Besaleus made her question everything. Looking into the eyes of this man made Sandrea feel as though she were standing on the brink of an infinitely deep abyss, trembling as she peered over the edge.

Now, however, as she gazed into his eyes, she trembled for a different reason. Her eyes swam, and her lip quivered. "There is something I must tell you."

"What is it?"

"After more than two hundred years, we are out of time! There is a great ceremony to be held soon, at the time of the eclipse. The Sisterhood is going to try to summon Gastar to Maradoum."

The silver-haired man jerked up to a sitting position, aghast. "Would they really do such a thing? Could they?"

"Yes, but … they need a sacrifice to bring him into our realm."

"A sacrifice?" Besaleus asked with widening eyes. "What are they sacrificing? Who are they sacrificing?"

"You," Sandrea whispered as tears leaked down her face.

"What will happen to me?" Besaleus' voice sounded strangled.

He hugged Sandrea to him as though he could prevent anything with his strength alone, she thought with a tiny smile, but she knew he could not.

"My Sisters are going to undertake an experimental feat of sorcery in which they hope that you will be …" Sandrea trailed off as her eyes welled up.

Besaleus grabbed her and shook her gently. "Tell me!"

"You will be possessed by the God. You will be his … mortal vessel in this world." Her voice cracked, and she looked up once more into Besaleus' face.

He was trying to remain calm, but his nostrils were flared with fear, and his eyes were round, showing the whites. "There must be something you can do for me!" he implored her, taking her hand and kissing it.

"I do not know what I will be able to do, my love," whispered Sandrea, her voice full of emotion. She traced his scar with her fingertip; the path of tears. "All my Sisters will be there, and they will try to prevent me from doing anything … If the spell goes wrong, the consequences could be disastrous. The energies we will be playing with could rip the world in twain. I do not know … but I will try."

*

Trumpets heralded an awed silence as the Matriarch of Convent, the absolute ruler of the Sisterhood and the people of all Maradoum, rose from her gilded throne. She was clothed in a black robe, to signify her pre-eminence among the Sisters of Convent. Her powers were vast, and as such, she appeared as the most beautiful woman ever beheld. Any man in her presence would weep at the sight of her divine beauty.

Besaleus was no ordinary man, however. The power that the Sisters had sensed in him, the cause for his imprisonment, made his will strong enough to gaze upon her splendour and yet be stony of face. Sandrea watched him as he was brought in to the centre of the enormous hall, in which the ceremony was taking place.

The round room looked like no other in Maradoum. It was the Grand Arcaneum of the Supreme Council of Convent, at the top of the tallest tower in the city, Cloudstriker; so near to the top, in fact, that its ceiling slanted up on all sides to form the crooked coned tip. It had been created using magical black and emerald glass; the same as that used to forge all of the Sisters' buildings, but Cloudstriker Tower was the oldest and first created.

When the original Sisters had reformed Convent after the Betrayer's demise, they had combined their colossal energies to mould the pyramidal fortress, and it stood for all the power they had used to create it. Their arts had been unrefined and barely contained, so the structure had hundreds of jagged edges, odd angles and vicious spikes erupting everywhere, even from the floor in the Arcaneum. Golden rays from the half-eclipsed sun shot in through the semi-translucent glass, and the room swam with dappled, refracted light.

Watching from the central dais, on which the Matriarch's throne was erected, Sandrea worried that the tiered ring of red surrounding the prisoner – the red of the cloaks of the hundreds of Sisters observing – must have been an unnerving constant reminder to Besaleus that escape was not an option. The only other platform was surrounded by vicious, green glass spikes like leaning stalagmites, as a result of the wild magic used to create it. Besaleus stood on this second podium, chained to the ground by his ankles, twenty yards from the Matriarch.

"Within moments, the eclipse will be complete and darkness will reign over Maradoum!" The Matriarch spoke with an ice-cold voice that frosted the far ends of the Hall.

Besaleus shivered at the sound and then jerked as hundreds of voices rose around him in unison, in cheer. There was no real mirth to the cheering, however; more a heartless acknowledgement that their will had been done. The Matriarch raised her hands slowly for silence.

"We have waited many, many years for this moment, my Sisters," she said when the women quietened. "For time near immemorial, we have ruled over the petty people, and now it is time for our ascension to divinity itself!"

Sandrea watched impassively; all the Sisters knew what was to happen today. This was an unnecessary speech to boost the Matriarch's own ego, she thought. Realising she had lost concentration on the ongoing rhetoric, she focussed her attention. She needed her timing to be perfect.

"Today, we experiment," continued the Matriarch, her eyes sweeping the room.

Each hooded Sister that met that gaze lowered their own in deference, but when the Matriarch locked eyes with Sandrea, the stare was continued in a test of wills for several seconds. Eventually, Sandrea smirked and lowered her gaze for but a moment, so that, when she looked up once more, the Matriarch had resumed sweeping the eyes of the remaining Sisters.

"We experiment with an entity with powers to match our own. You all know of whom I speak – the God of the Nether, Gastar the Wicked." Sandrea saw Besaleus flinch at the name. "If all goes as planned, our friend here," the Matriarch sneered at the lone man, "will be given the honour of being the vessel in which the great God will stroll our realm – under our thumb, of course."

The Matriarch smiled predatorily, her eyes boring deep through Besaleus' own, and he staggered back a step in horror. Sandrea could not watch him any longer. She felt her eyes watering as she neared a state of tears which would accomplish nothing but obstruct what she needed to do. She wiped her eyes and returned her gaze to the Matriarch's podium.

Reeling off a list of names, of which Sandrea was one, the Matriarch asked that these Sisters step forward to begin the spell. They were some of the most powerful women in the congregation; they would summon the

God. The remaining Sisters would concentrate their will on guiding the entity once it was in their realm. As Sandrea moved to her position, she reviewed all this once more in her head like an architectural design, the magic involved creating the sculptures therein.

"We will now begin the summoning! Prepare, Sisters, for what lies ahead," the Matriarch finished, turning away from the masses to join Sandrea and the others as they stood in a line by the throne facing Besaleus.

As they began to work their magic, Sandrea began to worry. She would need everyone's concentration to be elsewhere for her to succeed; there was no choice but to wait until the creature of the Nether was almost unleashed into their realm. She continued with the summoning spell and soon could feel the enchantment tugging at the fabrics of their world as it was forcibly and unwillingly brought into contact with another.

In front of the row of chanting Sisters, just in front of where their hands moved in unison to form occult signs, a purple symbol slowly took form, suspended in the air, shining brighter and brighter as the chanting continued. A second and third rune appeared, glowing as lustrously as the first, and then more took shape until the pulsing pictographs comprised a circle. The mantra wore on unabated, and within this circle, a shimmering began in the air as though a searing fire was obscuring their view with heatwaves.

This wavering soon turned into a vibration in the air as the image before the Sisters was warped. They chanted louder over the humming noise that it now produced, and Sandrea found that, though she had intended to stop before the spell was completed, she could not. The magic had hold of her now.

The swimming air in front of them slowly began to turn a reddish hue, and then, as the chanting grew louder still, the purple runes burst into flames with a heart-stopping boom. A scorching gust blew out from them, and a vivid vermillion light swept the glass room from the rune-ringed window.

The portal to the Nether was open, Sandrea thought, staring into it alongside the disarrayed row of Sisters, though little could be seen. The sun was eclipsed, and the room was dark. Unnaturally thick red smoke swirled around the chamber, blotting out what little light remained, reeking of death and decay. Besaleus covered his nose hurriedly, but still retched grotesquely, spewing up bile while the Sisters remained still as stone.

The entire chamber became unbearably hot as more of the crimson smoke leaked in. The magical glass construct in which all of them stood began to quiver and then scream as the two forces of magic collided. Besaleus, this time along with all the Sisters except a few by the portal, slapped his palms to his ears as the screeching produced an agony like the tip of a lance being jabbed repeatedly into his brain.

Sandrea struggled to maintain her focus as the feeling almost overrode her control. She could see nothing but the red hue of pain behind her eyelids, and her brain shrieked at her to give up, but she had to be strong for her love. She left her ears uncovered and ignored the screaming of the emerald glass surrounding her as she watched the portal intently with the Matriarch, squinting through the plumes, while the others in the line fell back.

Through the smoke suddenly emerged a figure, whose head stood three times as high as that of Sandrea. It seemed to wear the red smoke as a person would wear clothing. The smoke stuck to its body and thus, for the most part, it could not be seen and seemed to glide into the room. Its head was that of a monster with a bear-like snout flecked with gore and enormous fangs that gleamed gold in the purple-rune fire. Two ram-like horns could be seen sprouting from its temples, circling in on themselves. It had thick fur the colour of blood, and its eyes were the most vivid shade of red imaginable.

The congregation were now cloaked in the darkness of the eclipse, but the eyes of the being shone with demonic intelligence and seemed to light up the room wherever they gazed, as though they produced a beam of malignant illumination. It shrieked in outrage and hate when it was forced back from the unruly row of Sisters before it by the hundreds surrounding it, paralysed by their conjoined power.

Sandrea watched it being held, barely in check, by the combined powers of the Convent and knew that her time had come, but as she began to chant a new spell, her closing eyes saw the Matriarch turn towards her with a sickly sweet smile of recognition.

She knows! thought Sandrea wildly, her thought process faltering as she attempted to rush. Then, she felt herself blasted in the chest by a magical force. The Matriarch had blown her aside with a sweep of her hand.

Sandrea sat up from where she had landed, crumpled in a heap on the glass floor, snarling to see the Matriarch command the smoke-wreathed apparition.

"Possess this body, Gastar! We have done your bidding!" she cried, pointing her talon-like nails at the hapless Besaleus, who had fallen to his knees and begun incoherently babbling and begging for his life.

Sandrea rose and, in desperation to save Besaleus from possession, conjured and threw a spear of magical power at the bestial horror. The golden spear struck the smog and exploded in bright flames. The horror howled, but seemed more frustrated than hurt. The Matriarch turned her attentions to the errant Sister. Sandrea raised her hand abruptly and, with it, lifted one of the vicious spikes of emerald and black that ringed the hall, suspending it in mid-air with her will, before shooting her arm forwards, so that the stalagmite flew at the Matriarch's face.

The chorus of Sisters gasped as one of their own dared to make a direct attack on their leader. It had never before occurred in the history of Convent that a Sister should turn on her Matriarch. Although the spike was swatted aside by their black-robed leader, Sandrea began to see hints of doubt in her leader's eyes.

Magical attacks came from all corners as the Matriarch began to fight back, however; Sandrea defended herself and retaliated and the battle was begun. The infernal creature's power heating the chamber like a furnace, the magical tension of the Sisters all struggling to control the powerful beast and the unimaginable feats of offensive magic directed at each other between Sandrea and the Matriarch, but rebounding around the hall; all served to craft a charged, cacophonic tableau, in the middle of which Besaleus huddled up like a trapped bunny.

The Matriarch lashed Sandrea with a whip comprised of sizzling blue energy, leaving red welts across her skin, but the younger woman would not give up and the room shook with their exchanges of energy. In a flash of green and with a high-pitched scream of triumph, Sandrea finally managed to dispatch her sworn leader.

She turned from the Matriarch's smouldering corpse in time to see that she had ruined her fellow Sisters' concentration. The alien beast, sensing victory within its grasp, bellowed foreign words and the vile fog around it thickened further, spreading as though blown by strong winds to all corners of the room.

The Sisters were unable to maintain their control when the foul smoke permeated their mouths, noses and eyes. They doubled up, coughing, retching, even collapsing in places. The apparition then turned its flame-filled gaze on the man before it. It glided toward Besaleus slowly, malevolently.

Besaleus began to weep and sought to free himself from his chains through pure force, but to no avail. Sandrea summoned what remained of her power as she saw this and directed one last, monumental magical attack at the beast at the last second as it closed on Besaleus, even as the red fog obscured his image like the promise of the loss of his soul in but moments.

Time seemed to slow for Sandrea as she watched her burst of violet energy fly towards the creature. Her aim was true. The blast smote the monster in the back, and there was an explosion of gargantuan proportions. The black and emerald glass around the Sisters shattered as the forces of magic from Sandrea and the smoky horror conflicted with one another, creating a lasting conflagration of red and purple.

The sorcerous glass comprising the Arcaneum cracked, shattered and came crashing down with the din of a thousand cymbals, leaving the huge room open to the elements. Sisters were impaled by spikes and shards on all sides with nowhere to hide in the vast expanse of space. The air and the very sky seemed to reverberate with the force of the magical collision, and all within the chamber were blown backwards. Some were lucky enough to be thrown back to land on the floor, injured but alive, whereas some were not so lucky and were hurled from the Arcaneum to fall to their deaths hundreds of feet below.

As those remaining lay stunned upon the floor, a howling sound ensued. The runes vanished, and the portal snapped close with an almighty crack, leaving silence, smoke and scattered bodies amidst fragments of dark glass.

Sandrea picked herself up as precipitously as she could, but winced as she did so. She could feel that she had broken more than one rib and was badly wounded in several places. She would be able to heal herself once she had escaped with her love, she thought. For now though, she was drained. She hobbled with a grim expression to where Besaleus was chained to the ground, expecting the worst; that her beloved would have been destroyed by the blast, or that he would have been hurt by the crimson horror, who was now nowhere to be seen.

She looked upon Besaleus' body with a gasp. He was as gaunt as usual and looked frazzled with a sooty face and hair sticking up, but he did not appear to be hurt in any way. He seemed asleep and was breathing deeply and regularly. Sandrea quickly used what little power remained to her to magically sever the chains securing him, revealing cut ankles covered in sores.

"Besaleus! We must escape now!"

He stirred quickly and looked up into her face, confused and dazed. "My love! What happened here?"

"It doesn't matter. We have to get going now, while we can. I'll tell you on the way!"

"You're right – let's go!"

The two of them ran jerkily, as fast as they could in their conditions, to the depressed black door and out, before any of the other Sisters stirred from their unconscious states. They traversed some glassy stairs, and Sandrea led them to a cracked room on the floor below. There, they found portals encased in purple-rune-engraved stone rings. Stepping through one, they were transported instantaneously to the ground floor of Cloudstriker Tower.

As they left the tower through the grand glass doors, they found that standard procedure for explosions had already been taken in the city. Every soul had barred themselves in their own home, and the streets were empty and deserted.

Fruit, bread, vegetables and a wagon-load of timber lay scattered across the roads where there had been a panic to get inside when the blast had sounded, and there was even the body of a small girl, surrounded by her own lifeblood.

"Must've been trampled by the crowds," muttered Sandrea as she saw it.

Her eyes began to brim with tears, despite all the death she had seen in her unnaturally long life, and she clutched Besaleus tighter as he half-dragged, half-carried the Sister away from the tower, away from the city. Their escape was uneventful thanks to the deserted roads, but at one point in the suburbs, Besaleus stopped and demanded silence, swinging his scarred face this way and that.

"Shh! I hear something!" he whispered urgently. "Give me a weapon!"

Sandrea suspected him of paranoia, but supposed it was to be expected given their situation. She wordlessly handed him a knife from beneath her robe with feeble fingers as her strength waned. They swiftly moved on.

The two of them ran, albeit with a stagger, out of the unmanned western gate. Such was the fear the Sisters projected that even the guards hid inside when they heard arcane booms like the one that had ruptured the Grand Arcaneum.

Before the escapees was a vast, barren desert. They struggled on until finally they had passed several large dunes and were stood, breathless, in the penumbra of another. Sandrea slumped onto the sand, sitting and drawing ragged breaths. She looked back at the city of Convent, which was glinting in the sun now that the eclipse was over, and saw Cloudstriker Tower crumble and collapse like a washed-away sandcastle, raising a mighty dust plume. Besaleus walked past her and simply looked around, drinking in the fresh air of his home world for the first time in years.

"We can stop here for a moment," she panted. "We're outside my Sisters' range now. I can no longer sense them. We are safe, my love!"

She smiled as she rose and turned to face him. He smiled back, though the change in facial features caused the sun to reflect in his eyes, making them shine bright red. She reached out to embrace him, head tilted back for a kiss, seeing the glimmer of the blade in Besaleus' hand too late.

The blade swept up, plunging through Sandrea's ribs and into her heart. Besaleus stared into her eyes as her blood fountained over his hands and body in erratic spurts.

Her mouth formed a single word, "Why?"

Besaleus kicked her to the ground, and before he fled into the desert, he stared at her for a moment with malevolent red eyes whose glare lit her like a lantern.

"Stupid Witch."

1

The Plummet

A black chasm yawned like the maw of a sleeping Giant, and a fall into oblivion beckoned, its call a dire siren song.

Sir Raphael Fyrstsvard eased his foot down, but still his boot slipped in the wet. His heart punched his ribs, and his stomach leapt into his throat to cower. His leg scuffed the wall, and his armour clanged as it scraped rock. He grazed his hands scrabbling for a hold on the pitted surface in the dark and thought for a moment he would topple into the abyss.

Then, his fingers latched onto a jagged lip. The rock cut into his digits as it took his weight, but he managed to find his lost balance. His breath came quick and heavy, and his heart sounded louder in his ears than the waterfall that plummeted into unplumbed darkness down the opposite side of the slick crevasse.

"Phew, all is well!" he spoke over his shoulder, seeing his eight companions watching him in concern or expectation.

"Good, now keep going and *be careful!"*

He looked down at the rough-hewn, steep stone steps that slalomed down into the abyss in switchbacks, only wide enough for single file, their entire winding length constantly sprayed by the roaring falls.

"Oh, I will," he murmured.

Above them, thunder rang like war cries, black clouds roiled like stormy seas, and torrential rain hammered the earth like a thousand beating drums, for it was the height of summer; the wet season on the western outskirts of the vast and barren Lama Kulul Desert. Lightning stabbed the dark sky like spears, illuminating in golden flashes a glinting lake, which, overflowing, sent water cascading down into the wide fissure – the last definite water source before the dry wastes, where water could only be found by those who already knew where it was.

"Mind your step here. Keep going, chaps – and milady – we're almost there!" he cried.

The lowest figure of those descending, he cautiously placed another foot and tested the stone's strength for a moment before dropping his full weight on it. His voice was cultured and refined, belying his travel-stained clothes and scruffy blond hair and goatee. He wore a steel cuirass, pauldrons and plated boots, all worn and dented through years of use. The breastplate was embossed with an inverted V in white.

"That's easy for you to say, pretty boy!" bellowed back another of the climbers, struggling to be heard over the cracking thunder, pounding rain, frothing falls, flapping bat wings and the niggling buzz of the pervasive plague of midges. "I'm used to getting paid from the comfort of a seat at my age – you better believe it!"

This man was broad and wild-looking with unkempt ginger hair plastered to his head in the wet, a thick beard that covered half his face, beady eyes beneath bushy eyebrows, and a pot-belly.

"Teehee, you are not even fifty yet, pirate," chimed another of the climbers; an old, golden-skinned man, wrinkly as a raisin.

He climbed with the others with surprising dexterity for his age, though his back was as hunched as a rose-planter's, and he was dressed only in a ragged loincloth of animal skin. His eyes were filmed over with milky white cataracts, and yet he moved with confidence, feeling his way down the sheer rock face with a gnarled hand. His head was all but bald with only long wisps of white hair left to float about atop his pate. He carried an ash staff, curled at the end like a shepherd's crook, and small bones decorated his person, hung on strings around his wrists and ankles. Fangs adorned his throat on a necklace. A long, wispy, white moustache framed his mouth, hanging down either side like curtains.

A bat – one of a colony that blackened the crevasse – swooped near the old man, and he calmly waved his staff, giving it a gentle knock to set it going in the other direction.

"You are not old," he said, "just fat."

"You may be used to that, Heldig," retorted the leader, swatting at the midges and panting as he continued his slow descent, brown eyes piercing the veil of darkness below as best they could. "But you chose to be here, old boy! And you chose to do this because you will be handsomely paid upon completion of the job! So settle down and just think of all the wonderful and perverse things you will do with your reward, you stinking sea-rat!" He spoke with affection, and a smile tweaked his cheeks.

"Oh-ho!" chortled Heldig wheezily in return, looking downwards. "Don't think I won't make you eat those words when I get down there, Fyrstsvard! Knight or no-Knight, your arse is up for a tanning, boy!"

"You are Knight?" a similarly descending woman asked clumsily of

Sir Raphael Fyrstsvard. Traveller's Tongue was not her first language, and though she improved day by day, she struggled with its subtleties on occasion.

"Yes," Fyrstsvard answered, craning his fair-haired head back to bestow a rueful smile on the ebon-skinned nomadic woman. "I am a Knight of Justiqua, of the Order of *Pacia.* In fact, the men in my family have for generations watched over the Knights as Lord Protector – until me, that is."

"You still haven't told me exactly what happened to you, Svard!" shouted Heldig from above, his voice gruff and rough.

"What happened, Knight?" asked the nomadic woman of Fyrstsvard, flinching as a bat brushed her.

"It is a complex tale, milady. I will tell you the story one day, Kamilah, but perhaps not whilst one slip will bring about certain doom. Need my concentration and all that," replied the Justiquan, attempting to remain light-hearted as memories of his shame threatened to swamp him.

"I, too, should like to hear the tale," added the other Nomad with a voice of deep thunder, slapping at his skin to squash the buzzing insects alighting there. He had a gaunt, stubbly face, a hooked beak of a nose and dark, slitted eyes.

"It is a good one!" said the blind old man with a cackle. "Yes, yes – good one, good tale."

"It is a good tale," agreed Fyrstsvard sarcastically, glancing at the Quing Tzu native, "but one for another time, as I said, old chum."

"I'll hold you to that, nobleman!" Heldig assured him. "Or else you're buying the drinks when we get outta here!"

"A frightening prospect, given your high tolerance for intoxicants," Fyrstsvard commented. "Perhaps you'll get lucky and find enough hooch down below that I won't have to top you up at the end."

"Ha! You think there are hidden lakes down here?"

"Not for long if you find dem," muttered a cocoa-skinned man with dark dreadlocks hanging like tangled masses of rope from his head past his shoulders and gold flashing in his teeth. He ducked as he felt a bat flap past his face.

"Ahoy, I heard that, Jumal!" Heldig shouted over his shoulder. "What are you trying to say?" Before any reply could be made, he added, "It is important that you all know that I do not drink to excess. I merely drink because I like the flavour!"

"Yes," agreed a younger, mousey lad, and he snorted after adding, "and you like *so* many different flavours, don't you, Cap'n?"

"Why, you scoundrel!" Heldig roared with a big smile hidden by his beard.

The jokes helped to ease the palpable tension. Fear of the uncertain, as ever, was a consistency for mankind, and the group continued to step downwards without a word, the rumble of the storm, the gushing of the waterfall, the bats' whir and the midges' hum blanketing out all other noise, their dread of the unknown growing as they plunged into the bowels of the earth, one foot at a time.

After what seemed an interminable time of leg-numbing descent, Fyrstsvard's wailing voice once more echoed up to the rest of the group.

"Wargh!"

Caught up in plans for their escapade, the Knight had almost stepped off one step and into nothingness, for there was no next step. He scrabbled at the wet, mossy wall desperately, ripping away the soft green growth and cutting his fingers on the limestone, but finding purchase enough not to fall. He stood, panting at his boots for a moment, then squinted down. Below, when the lightning flashed far overhead, he could see in glimpses the water splashing from a dark surface. A foul odour wafted up to him, and he wrinkled his nose.

"Hey-ho, I can see the floor, chaps!"

The floor of the enormous cavern beneath them was some distance from the bottom of the steps down which they climbed, for centuries of deluges had carved out the rock into the wide expanse of underground cave that they could all begin to glimpse.

"Get down here quickly and hit in your anchors – we'll rope down there! And be quiet – we don't know what we might find."

The rest of the group hurried down with renewed vigour, knowing that their perilous climb was almost at an end. Once all had reached the bottom of the stairs, where the way widened, they used their weapons to hit small anchors into the rock. To these simple pieces of metal, they then tied long spools of rope which they had carried throughout their descent, wrapped thickly about their middles.

"Tar Feng!" Fyrstsvard whispered.

The small, wizened man with the golden skin and bone adornments turned his head toward the question. "Yes yes yes? What is it that you require of me, Fyrstsvard?" he spoke back quickly, his words hissing through the gaps between his few remaining yellowed fangs. His milky eyes stared past the Knight.

"Tell me, do you sense anyone down there, Wizard?"

In response, Tar Feng closed his eyes and hummed gently for a moment. When he reopened his unseeing eyes, he replied with a toothless smile. "No, no, we are safe, we are safe! For now, anyway. Yes, I detected no sign of any life in the cavern just below us. But we should be wary regardless, Fyrstsvard, for my spell was not wide-ranged, and there may be forces opposing us of which we are ignorant!"

"You mean you think there are Magicians down below us? Are we walking into a nest of Witches?" asked Fyrstsvard, his ignorance of the task revealed at last.

Heldig shook his head; how could he not even know what they were walking, or descending, into?

"Soon, we will see what we see," replied Tar Feng cryptically with a short cackle, hanging from the rope he had secured to his anchor, "and when we see it, we will know what it is we have seen – and not before!" With that, the old man climbed nimbly down with bats fluttering all around him.

"Helpful as ever, old boy," muttered Fyrstsvard, trying his best to ignore Heldig's meaningfully doubtful glances, before raising his voice slightly. "Alright – stay together, chaps! Let's move!"

He too swung out over the lip of rock and began to climb down his own rope after Tar Feng before more doubts could be raised.

"Bollocks," muttered Heldig with a scowl, shaking his head. "Rescuing a dead Prophet from a hole in the ground so he can save the world. It's all bollocks."

He looked to his left. Ratnik and Jumal, two of the most trusted men of his crew, had travelled with him on this mission when he had been summoned. Relatively young men both, Ratnik was less than thirty, Jumal maybe ten years his senior, but both had scars and pockmarks aplenty. Ratnik had fair though well-tanned skin, blue eyes and short brown hair and was as quick with a joke as he was with a blade. As for Jumal, there was no one Heldig trusted more than the dark-skinned, dreadlocked man from Chilpaea. They too looked increasingly agitated.

"S'alright, boys!" Heldig reassured them, an easy grin parting his bushy red beard. "Just think of all that gold Labogé promised us! Once we find that old Elf, we'll have riches, palaces and whores galore for the rest of our lives, me mateys!"

He swung down his rope after Fyrstsvard, huffing and puffing. Ratnik and Jumal eyed one another uneasily.

"Seems about as safe as covering yourself in honey and going bear-chasing," commented Ratnik dryly.

"Ha!" Jumal grinned. "Can't get da bear widout da bait, Rats!"

Greed and curiosity soon overpower reason and caution in a pirate, however, and they too shinned down, though with an adroitness lacking in their bulkier Captain.

Below the ropes down which the mercenaries climbed, there was a well, of sorts. In fact, it was simply a hole through the cavern floor directly underneath the great fissure that opened out onto the sable skies, through which the great curtains of water could pass whenever a monsoon chanced to come by. The circular well had a small but beautiful rim surrounding it, like a tiny wall that was fashioned of pure white marble and was etched with deft sculpting depicting tiny figures.

In a circle around the well, a series of great stalagmites rose up like unwelcoming spikes to ward off intruders, for not every spot of water dripped perfectly down the well, and over the centuries the droplets that had missed had formed the mineral sculptures that stood beneath the mercenary group now. Drops dripping from the cavern ceiling surrounding the aperture had formed a ring of huge stalactites that hung down like fossilised teeth, like they were climbing down into the mouth of some great subterranean leviathan.

Beside the well and the limestone formations, the rock floor was littered with guano, which had been the source of the aroma Fyrstsvard had detected from above. The dung looked to have been piled up into various heaps by some mysterious hand, however, in an effort to prevent the cavern becoming overcome. A soft crunching, wriggling sound could be heard emanating from the heaps, and the glints of cockroaches and centipedes skittering around could be seen in the ordure. The Knight controlled a retch with difficulty as he realised what he was looking at and what he was roping down into.

Dangling from the bottom of the ropes, there was a drop of several feet to the cavern floor, and most of the climbers dropped down easily enough, swinging slightly in some cases to avoid the reeking hills, the well and the mineral statues that ringed it. A man named Jerrat, however, dropped before seeing a stalagmite directly beneath him. He caught one of his legs on the pinnacle of mineral stone as he fell. The leg broke with a loud crack, and he was thrown to the ground in a heap.

"Argh!" Jerrat began to shout in agony, but even as he began he was cut off.

The ebon-skinned Nomad propelled himself violently at the crippled man, whipping out a small but lethal knife as he did so. He landed atop Jerrat, smashing his head back to the ground hard and stabbing him deep in the throat with the small knife, while clamping a hand over the man's mouth to muffle his death screams.

"What in the name of the Prophet was that, Izdaju?" whispered Fyrstsvard, furiously striding over to the brutal Nomad, his blonde beard bristling at the murder.

"A man with no legs is with no use," Izdaju stated quietly as he wiped off his little knife on the dead man's clothes. He stood to face the Knight. "Better he die while he remember being a man."

Fyrstsvard still looked enraged, and his hand gripped the pommel of his sword tightly, the knuckles white.

"He is right," said a robe-wrapped man, dropping to the wet floor from his rope with a splash.

The sandy-coloured robes covered every inch of his body apart from his hands and eyes. On his feet, he wore simple, leather boots, into which he tucked his sandy hose. His voice, though slightly muffled, was smooth and measured.

"He would only have slowed us down," he continued, "and he could never have escaped with his injury – and his scream would have alerted anything and everything to our position."

"You speak Traveller's well for a Sandman," responded Fyrstsvard, forcing himself to a façade of calm though he rankled at the killing. What was done was done, and he had to move forwards. He eyed the robed man for a moment. "I cannot recall – what is your name?"

"My name is Egobal, and I am of no tribe. You are Sir Fyrstsvard, once famed in the great city of Justiqua and now also a man of no tribe."

The Sandman – or *Serrici* as they called themselves – Egobal, unwrapped the cloth from around his face and rewrapped it about his head, uncovering his ageless features. His eyes were dark but warm, and he wore a tightly cropped dark beard in the middle of which his stark white teeth gleamed in contrast to his bronzed skin, for he smiled genially to assure the Knight that he meant no offense.

"That's right," said Fyrstsvard, sizing up the man.

The Knight looked around again, his sharp ochre eyes missing nothing. They stood beneath the great fissure in the earth down which they had climbed, and – though there was not much light since the moon and stars were smothered by dark, heavy wreaths of cloud – Fyrstsvard nevertheless took a moment to study his remaining band of fighters in the intermittent lightning flashes. It was a good group, he thought. He had worked with far worse.

The pirates, Heldig, Ratnik and Jumal, were savage fighters and friends even, for he had teamed up with them on missions in the past. The highwaymen of the seas would often be judged poor company for a Knight, Fyrstsvard knew, but they had proved themselves valuable allies, and he and the Lord Protector had always been satisfied with their results. Though they had no armour to speak of, they were good brawlers and could be relied upon in that they would follow him so long as they received their agreed-upon riches at the end.

Heldig was dressed in his usual blue jacket over a scarlet shirt, wide-brimmed sailors' boots and loose beige pantaloons. Wiry young Ratnik wore similar boots, a red bandana, calico breeches – chequered red, yellow, blue and green between lines of white – which left his shins exposed, and a loose white shirt. Sensible – if flamboyant – outfits, the Knight judged.

Jumal, on the other hand, sported a stylish, pointed beard that covered chin and cheeks. He wore a puffy yellow shirt with the sleeves rolled up, frilly in the style of Swash Isle, expensive, gold-trimmed black trousers and tall boots, and – until Fyrstsvard had strongly recommended that he remove them for the sake of the safety and subtlety of the mission – he had been festooned with more gold than Tar Feng was with bones. Fyrstsvard had tried talking sense to the old Wizard too, but to no avail.

Before being convinced to part with the majority of it, Jumal had worn half a dozen studs and rings on each ear, a ring through one nostril, tiny bars through his lips and eyebrows, false teeth, studs in his cheeks, clasps in his hair, necklaces, bracelets, rings, ankle bracelets and toe rings, all gold. Fyrstsvard suspected him of being avaricious.

"Dere is shit everywhere," the dreadlocked corsair commented, his upper lip curling.

"Goddamn bat droppings," agreed Ratnik with distaste, scratching a stubbly cheek.

The Sandman, Egobal, appeared unexpectedly precocious, given the rumours about those who dwelled under the baking sun of the Desert, and Fyrstsvard did not know enough about him to judge him further. Tar Feng would be an enigma if Fyrstsvard was not familiar with the eccentric old man; he had met him before on several occasions whilst undertaking various quests and knew that the Tzunese Wizard was highly placed in the new Lord Protector's esteem.

The Nomads he had never encountered before, but he knew of their ways. In comparison to the strict etiquette of his knightly life, they were utter barbarians. They looked the part of savages, certainly. The man wore nothing but warrior's sandals and a loincloth with a belt for his weapons, of which there were three – two scimitars and a dagger. His face was shaved, and his head was bald save for a strip down the centre of his dome, which continued down the back of his head and trailed down between his shoulder blades in the form of a long ponytail.

The woman, Kamilah, was garbed similarly scantily in a loincloth and sandals, but she wore thin leather armour over her torso, leaving her arms bare. She carried a dagger in her belt, a bow in her hand and a quiver over her shoulder. She had a skinny face with chapped lips, a button nose, and soulful eyes that seemed disproportionately large. The Knight could not help but admire the sleekness of her long neck and the graceful cascading curls of her jet-black hair, which she tied up as he watched. He forced himself to look back to her companion, Izdaju. Fyrstsvard did not know if he could trust him or contain the barbarity of the man. He resolved to keep an eye on him.

He spoke slightly louder so that all could hear him. "Everyone, spread out! Find a passage or a tunnel – anything that leads out of this cavern, preferably going down." He glanced at the roaring waterfall and the hole in the cavern floor through which it passed. "I don't think *that's* our best bet. Whistle if you find something else."

Tar Feng nodded enthusiastically and silently pranced on the spot, while the others swiftly disbanded around him into the buzzing black of the cave. Fyrstsvard took one last look down at Jerrat, and then stepped out of his pooling blood and left him where he lay, muttering the old Runic idiom, *"Reccé em Pacia." Rest in peace.*

A couple of minutes later, Kamilah whistled. The ragtag mercenary group hurried, as best they could whilst almost blind, to her side and immediately gagged at the horrific stench emanating from the area, which overpowered even that of the ubiquitous faecal matter. The Nomad woman stood to the side of a gaping ten-foot wide hole in the cavern floor. Several thick chains ran up from the corners of the square aperture and appeared to be attached to the ceiling in shadow high above them. Against a wall, mere yards away, was a great pile of black to match even the darkness of the cave.

"Eurgh! Tar sands!" exclaimed Heldig.

"Keep your voice down! What are tar sands?" whispered Fyrstsvard, choking on the fumes.

"Dunno!" replied Heldig more quietly, holding his nose. "I've heard about them from mining crew buddies and what have you. They call 'em tar sands – as in tar in sand – and it's some kind of toxic oil or something that they occasionally come across while mining. Cover your mouths with cloth – the Sandman has it right!"

He covered his nose and mouth with his sleeve, whilst Egobal stood by in silence, his face once again covered with only his dark eyes left free of cloth.

"Must be a pulley system of some kind – a lift for transporting people and supplies in and out," suggested Fyrstsvard through his sleeve, looking up at the chains.

"A lift, yes," responded Heldig gruffly, "but a lift with no controls! I don't see any – do you? How are we gonna use it?"

"Must be controlled from the bottom," muttered the Knight.

At that moment, the chains began to shudder and shake, and then they cranked loudly into action, some clanking slowly up and others down – presumably on loops, Fyrstsvard guessed.

"Something's coming up!" he whispered. He swiftly darted looks around. Nearby was a small ridge of rock that rose up from the droppings lining the cavern floor. "Hide behind this!" He gestured urgently, before ducking behind it and peeking over the lip.

With everyone hidden from immediate sight of the hole through which the lift would rise, Fyrstsvard drew his steel longsword from its sheath. The rest of the group followed suit in arming themselves, the smell all but forgotten; the pirates with cutlasses and knives, Izdaju with scimitars, Kamilah with a bow, Tar Feng with his staff, and the Sandman with twin daggers that appeared suddenly from beneath his gauzy robes.

"Technology like a lift – and so far underground to boot? Must be Dwarves!" breathed Heldig, hefting cutlass and hammer and lifting his eyes over the lip of rock to watch with Fyrstsvard.

2

A Brush with Dwarves

The chains continued to shake and clatter violently until eventually a wooden platform, complete with metal frame, torch-bearing brackets and side-railings to prevent falling, rose up through and filled the aperture. The chains were attached to its corners. On the platform were eight torch-lit Dwarves; two armoured and six wearing dusty work gear. They all wore cloth masks and with good reason; on the platform were several wide, wheeled trolleys, on which tar sands were piled in great heaps.

"Dwarves!" growled Izdaju quietly. "Let's kill these nasty little –" The Nomad began to rise, but was firmly shoved back down by Fyrstsvard, who almost received a disembowelment for his trouble.

"What are you doing, *pahr kong?"* hissed Izdaju through bared teeth, the tip of his blade still pointed at the Knight's stomach. "We have to kill them before they can raise an alarm!"

Fyrstsvard glared at the savage, his hand still clenched around the Nomad's arm. "A pale skin I may be," he whispered back forcefully, his longsword pointed away, "but I *am* in charge of this mission, and you *will* follow my lead! Although we do need to deal with them, we will not attack the Dwarves just yet, because that platform is heaped with toxic oils with potentially deadly fumes. We will wait for the Dwarves to clear the platform, because we need to use it to go down, and I for one would like to breathe some relatively fresh, albeit underground, air. So, you *will* wait for my say before you charge in like a barbarian. Understood?"

Such was the snarl on Izdaju's face that Fyrstsvard worried for a moment he was still about to be gutted, but then the Nomad nodded once, abruptly, and took his scimitar from the Knight's belly. Fyrstsvard relinquished his grip slowly.

The group resumed its silent vigil over the Dwarves' labour. Fyrstsvard watched them closely, for he liked to know at least a little of his opponents before he entered into combat with them. The Dwarves were short, peaking at roughly four feet in height. Their limbs too were short, thick and stubby, their arms ending in mud-stained squat digits, but their bodies were far wider than a human's. Muscular torsos and tree-trunk legs gave them indomitable strength.

They had adapted to live underground, too, in that their beady little eyes could see far better and further in the darkness than could any human's. Their skin was pale as snow, so long had it been since a ray of sunlight had caressed it, meaning that all the dirt – and there was a lot of it, for Dwarves apparently cared little for appearance – showed up vividly. All had thick tufts of filthy, dark hair about their head; curly, coarse and thick it grew, much like their beards. It was even difficult to make out facial features on some of the Dwarves, so overgrown with fuzz and smothered in muck were their visages.

The armour worn by the two Dwarves was typical by their standards, but appeared outlandish and bizarre to the onlookers. The armour was crafted of great white bones, strapped together and moulded around their short bodies, but what was so strange was that the end result of the individualising of the armour meant that each Dwarf had unique protrusions of bone, be it over their shoulders or off to each side of their legs like a fish tail minus the webbing. The thick bone armour did, however, appear to afford them formidable protection, and the pickaxes they bore were swung with the skill and strength that stems from a lifetime of mining.

The trespassing group observed silently as the six unarmoured Dwarves swiftly and heartily wheeled the trolleys off the platform and set to shovelling the noxious substance into the already vast pile by the cavern wall. So efficient, strong and synchronised were their movements that the small crew was soon almost finished dumping the mighty load.

Seeing that they were nearing completion, Fyrstsvard ducked behind the rock lip to escape the notice of the vigilant armoured Dwarves – guards, he presumed – who scanned the cave while they supervised the workers.

"Ready?" he whispered, flexing his fingers on his sword hilt.

The group nodded their readiness. The Knight peeked over the lip of rock once more, but at precisely the wrong moment. He was seen by one of the Dwarf guards, who happened to be looking in his direction.

The Dwarf hefted his pickaxe and screamed, his sharp voice cutting through the roar of the falls, *"Infava!"*

He spoke in the fricative dwarvic tongue, so the word was alien to the motley crew, but they all understood the warning in his tone.

An arrow punched him forcefully from his feet a heartbeat later, and the mercenaries decided as one that the shout was the perfect signal to attack. With no further directing needed, they swarmed over and around the rock lip to rush the dazed Dwarves with fearsome battle cries.

Izdaju was the first to encounter an opponent, and – quick as a blink – he lopped off the stout worker Dwarf's head, beard and all, with a mighty swing of one of his curved swords. Heldig joined the fray a moment later and smashed in the face of a second worker Dwarf with his hammer, saving Izdaju from the trouble of a shovel in the gut. The Nomad nodded his thanks to the blood-dotted pirate.

Kamilah – who still stood behind the rock lip, for she preferred longer ranged tactics – once again brought down a Dwarf with an arrow in the throat, shot from her powerful horn bow. By her side stood the crazed old man, Tar Feng, cackling, dancing and watching the skirmish with his blind eyes in glee, as if without a trouble in the world.

Meanwhile, the Chilpaean, Jumal, swiftly overpowered another of the shovel-wielding Dwarves with savage cutlass blows that drove him to his knees and then clove him apart at the collar. Fyrstsvard squared off against the remaining armoured guard. He parried one wild axe swing and efficiently ran the short creature through, the tip of his sword squeezing through a gap in the armour's midriff and protruding from the Dwarf's back obscenely, dripping with gore.

The buccaneer, Ratnik, was caught fighting the remaining two shovelling Dwarves whilst his companions were busy and was struggling with the odds against him, his cutlass flailing wildly, but then – like a ghost from between worlds – the Sandman, Egobal, appeared behind the Dwarves. He stabbed each of them in the neck with twin thrusts of his curved daggers, and they spurted pigment-less white ichor with stupid expressions on their faces before buckling and folding to the ground as if boneless.

The group then converged as a whole like a pack of starving wolves upon the one surviving worker Dwarf, who still stood atop the moving platform, desperately tugging at one of the chains that hung by the side, presumably to indicate a desire to be lowered back down.

Realising this, Fyrstsvard quickly ordered, "Everyone on the platform, now!"

The mercenaries leapt onto the platform just as it began to descend at the tugging of the chain's request. The remaining Dwarf was overwhelmed, and within moments his life was ended, his body impaled on the blades of two swords, his lasts shouts cut short.

As the wooden platform slowly clanged and clanked back downwards, conducted by the dwarvic pulley system, Fyrstsvard drew everyone together to posit a plan. He spoke quietly despite the din, which was exacerbated by loud clinking and tinkling coming from below.

When the lift had almost reached the lower ground level, the Dwarves standing guard below saw several small, hand-sized grey bags tossed from the platform, and where they landed, these bags immediately began to emit vast quantities of foul-smelling smoke. It stank like an infernal mixture of sulphur and rotten eggs, and it was so thick and copious that even the mercenaries wondered if there must be some sorcery to it.

"Nice work," whispered Heldig to Tar Feng, impressed.

"Thanks!" replied the shrivelled old man, showing his empty smile. "I call 'em smoke bags!"

"Great name!" approved the pirate Captain, grinning through his beard.

The dwarvic guards were caught in vast plumes of thick fog by the time the lift slowly trundled to a halt at the new level. With the beardy folk blind, coughing, spluttering, heaving and retching, it was no trouble for the small trespassing band to remain unseen.

The group had gotten a good look at their already smoky destination while the platform was slowly lowered and had seen a circular well, brimming full with water, surrounded by a ring identical to and directly beneath the marble one above them, so that water from the falls could pass through both unhindered.

The smoke they had initially seen had come from forges and smelting workshops, where the Dwarves worked the ore from the rock mined below and moulded it to their use. The next thing they had noticed was another platform, identical to the one that had brought them down, on the other side of an expanse of workshops. Since they had seen only solid rock above it, they had deduced that this other lift went down further to another level. Having decided this was most likely where they needed to go – further down – they had elected to make straight for it, while the smog from the Wizard's bags shielded them from dwarvic eyes.

They saw little of the level on which they found themselves while they hurried through the malodourous mist with noses and mouths covered with cloth. They had seen from above, however, that the level served as some kind of defence post for levels further down, for there were only a few abodes. For the most part, the whole level resembled one massive workshop. There were blacksmiths, bowyers, fletchers, smelters, tanners, factories creating wonders unseen and workmen of all kinds, as well as regiments of bone-armoured soldiers scurrying here and there before the smoke bags went off.

What shocked some of the mercenaries – those unfamiliar with the vicious little creatures known as Dwarves and their habits – were the Dwarves' pets.

The *Rodici* were a species not unlike the common rat in some ways, save that they lived solely deep underground and so had come to acquire a symbiotic relationship with the Dwarves, who also liked to delve deep by nature. They resembled rats in that they had similar long, pink, worm-like tails, small, pointed, rat-like ears and prominent front upper teeth. The shocking distinction from regular vermin was that the *Rodici* were many times bigger than a rat, standing as tall, if not taller on four legs, than the top of the Dwarves' hairy heads.

They could be further differentiated from the ordinary animal in that they were completely hairless. Their skin had no pigment due to the absence of sunlight, and so it was white and translucent-looking, allowing their thick, sharp bones to be seen shifting around beneath their thin flesh like a horror show. Their feet were huge like the paws of a dog, and the large claws on the end looked frighteningly sharp.

Lastly, the *Rodici* had no eyes. Through centuries of subterranean breeding, the need for eyesight had been slowly bred out as the creatures relied more heavily on their other senses in the pitch blackness. Above their long, pale snouts and huge, sharp teeth was an unusually long forehead of smooth, white skin with no trace that their race had ever had the ability to see.

The Dwarves kept the *Rodici* as pets, of a sort, and had done for as long as they could remember in order to eliminate the competition between them. They shared the underground foods, like the giant insects, fungi and worms that abounded, and lived in relative harmony. The *Rodici* had a need to burrow through rock every day of their lives to rub down the incredibly thick enamel on their teeth and claws to prevent them growing so large that the creature could no longer function. Such a daily need for digging meant that the Dwarves' desires to delve ever deeper into the world's core – the First Forge, as they thought of it – were complemented perfectly. The Dwarves directed the *Rodici's* mindless digging into aiding their own downward plummet, and when their pets died, the beardy little folk used their naturally tough bones to craft their armour.

Having glimpsed an insight into dwarvic culture, the ragtag group hurried past the hollering Dwarves and their shrieking *Rodici* in the smoke, making a beeline for the second platform and pulley system. Heldig went at the front of the single-file rush, so as to bowl over anything in their way – and bowl over many a Dwarf he did, running down a main avenue, elbowing and kneeing to force a path. The others followed closely and quickly, each with a hand on the one in front's shoulder so as not to become lost in the odorous fog. Although the toppled Dwarves squawked and bleated in alarm and anger, there was so much noise and confusion that it was impossible for the soldiers to identify the source of the mishap.

Luckily, the intruding crew made it to the second platform without major incident, and a sweaty Fyrstsvard quickly began tugging at the chain equating to the one he had witnessed the Dwarf guard pull on the previous lift to indicate their wish to go down. Again fortunate, the lift began to descend as requested before the smoke could clear, rendering the dwarvic defenders still oblivious to the group's passing.

As the lift descended and the clamour of the level above receded, Jumal shivered with distaste and asked anyone who could answer in his sonorous voice and wide Chilpaean accent, "What in El Vandu's hoard were dose rat-dogs? Dey were disgusting!"

"Ah yes, they are the *Rodici,* the Dwarves' pets!" answered Tar Feng. "Centuries of living underground will transform any race into such a monstrosity, yes yes!"

"Are dere likely to be more of dem?"

Tar Feng only laughed loudly and turned away – or rather, he laughed loudly for him, which meant that only wispy chuckles filled the air, not voluminous enough even to echo. Jumal shook his head, unsure what to make of the old man.

Turning back to his friends, the dreadlocked pirate held up a one-handed war-axe. It had a short haft with a blade on one side and a counter-weighing spike on the other. "I stole dis from dose beardy little swine as we charged tru dere," he said with a grin.

"First of all," replied Ratnik with a mimicking grin, "you are a greedy git. Second, in all fairness to ya, that is a nice axe! I didn't realise we'd have time for looting, charging through the little bastards at speed."

"Always time for looting, Rats. Just gotta be quick enough," Jumal replied with a wink.

"Let's have a look?" Jumal tossed it to his friend, who caught and twirled it, feeling the weight. "Beautiful weapon, man," Ratnik said, handing it back regretfully.

"Nice work, Jumal," said Heldig, waving for him to hand it over.

The Chilpaean passed it to his Captain, who took it eagerly and hefted it, giving it a couple of slow waves.

"Yeah, ruddy nice, mate," agreed Heldig, handing it back. "Sweet grab, but with luck there'll be plenty more opportunity for looting on the way, and more importantly there's the reward money when all of this is done, eh! Now, you two listen to me," he continued, placing a hand on the shoulder of each and bringing them close whilst he lowered his voice, "you are my crew and we stick together – we'll get out of here in one piece, don't you worry 'bout that, boys, we will. But I need you two to look after each other, yeah? You can't necessarily trust anyone else 'ere," he took a surreptitious look around, "but you can trust each other. So I want that to be the only concern on your minds, savvy? Keep each other safe, fellas, and we'll get outta this."

The younger men nodded sombrely, and Heldig gazed at them with affection hidden deep beneath his surly exterior, thick red beard and big, bushy eyebrows. Both were nameless orphans, who had been with him since they were small children, growing up on the docks of Kauapunki-Meren. Everyone there knew everything there was to know about the two lads, for they were the most open and honest of pirates.

Jumal loved money, specifically gold, and Ratnik – he loved to sail, that one, thought Heldig. The crew on their ship, the *Surfrunner,* had called him 'Rats', as much for his looks as for the fact that it shortened his name, but all had respected his knowledge of their turbulent mistress, the ocean. Quick in a fight, quick with a joke, quick to the drink, then quick up a lady's skirt, thought Heldig with an inner glow; he was fond of the two rascals.

"Good lads," he said gruffly.

Meanwhile, as the lift made its slow journey down through the redder rock of the deep earth, Fyrstsvard spoke to the wizened old man adorned in bones and rags about their next move.

"Tar Feng, do you have any more of those smoke bags? We're likely to need more diversions yet, I think."

"I do have one or two remaining, Fyrstsvard, yes," answered the old man, staring past the Knight, his eye twitching. "Yes, yes, I do have a couple more. But it will not be enough!" he began to jabber more frantically, his accent becoming more difficult to comprehend. "At some point, we will be discovered and seen and found and spotted and then, little Knight, then our luck will be up! Our game will be over! Our sparks will be put out, and our lives will be ended in a shower of shit! Is that what you want? Is it, Knight? Is it?"

"Alright, Wizard, alright!" said Fyrstsvard reassuringly, raising his hands. "Then I'll just leave it to your best judgement when to use the smoke bags, and we'll not plan on relying on them. Will that satisfy you?"

Tar Feng nodded quickly, his neck whipping back and forth and his fang necklace clanking loudly.

"Very well," said the Knight, taking a deep breath. "Now, before we make a plan for the next level, I think we should first see whatever's down there," he said, placing a hand on the smoothed sandstone walls that currently swaddled them and the lift, blocking their view of the level to which they descended.

"I hope dere are no more of dem rat-dogs," muttered Jumal, scratching a tattooed arm anxiously.

3

Dwarhummer

The lift continued to descend, and their destination eventually came into view as the walls enclosing Fyrstsvard, Tar Feng and the other mercenaries suddenly opened out to expose the subterranean world in all its mystery, cast in a reddish haze thanks to the sandy rock and clouding fumes.

Still far below the group on the platform, the next level could be seen. Dwarves and *Rodici* scurried back and forth like a swarm of insects in their view, for they were looking at the hub of all dwarvic underground activity.

The level below them consisted of a giant dwarf-built city, consisting of a labyrinth of squat, ugly sandstone houses on the ground amidst hundreds of strictly laid out majestic, white, alabaster-coated stone pillars in rows that held up the high flat ceiling for as far as the eye could see. Stunning, graceful alabaster arches served as raised walkways between the pillars, negating the need to return to floor level to travel.

Numerous braziers were scattered around the city to provide illumination on the ground, however the majority of the lighting was supplied by worms. The Dwarves had uncovered these tiny miracles in their subterranean excavations centuries before. Despite their tiny stature, the light they emitted was enough to brighten a room.

Thousands of silkworms hung from the ceiling, their tails glowing blue, their strands of dangling silk a million deadly gossamer filaments in which myriad insects were snared by the sticky trap. Even without the braziers, their radiance was enough to gift the city a soft glow, like that of stars.

A wide, bricked road ran around the vast perimeter of the city in a ring, interconnecting regularly along its trail with roads leading inwards, like spokes to the hub of a wheel. At the hub towered a monumental metal structure that reached to the very ceiling, wide at its circular base, narrowing to the top where it joined with the well that the group had seen on the level above. Fyrstsvard understood then why it had seemed that the level above had had a full well. It was because the colossal metal structure was a container, and it was full.

"A water tank," muttered Fyrstsvard. There were dozens of pipes leading from the tank all over the city to provide water to its citizens. "Ingenious."

To one side of the mountainous tank, a grand pillar, even thicker than its kin, aided in holding up the ceiling. It was even more breathtakingly beautiful than the rest. Inlaid with gold throughout, the pillar's alabaster was even sculpted lightly in places to depict scenes of glorious moments in dwarvic history. This great structure was the heart of the city, the residence of its monarch.

The pirates stood with mouths agape in awe. They had never seen anything so magnificent. The architecture was strikingly elegant; so much so that it was hard to imagine that the pretty cylindrical pillars and arching walkways contained greedy, violent Dwarves and their bestial rat-like companions.

Remembering the residents, Jumal looked away from the splendour of the worm-lights and the great water tank to the ground, where he saw the *Rodici* he dreaded so much wandering around by the hundred with their dwarvic masters.

"Merry's tits!" murmured the Chilpaean, his eyes wide.

"Dwarhummer," pronounced Tar Feng in his wispy accent, his eyes narrowed and his face dour. *"Dwarf Haven;* it is the legendary city of Dwarves. I feared that this might prove an obstacle."

"You knew about this?" demanded Izdaju wrathfully, stepping close to the old man and towering over him. His accent was wide, and he over-compensated for the unfamiliar words, but his meaning was clear and his fury transparent.

The group turned to regard the small struggle. Fyrstsvard did not step to intervene. He had been about to ask the Tzunese Wizard the same question.

"No, no, I did not *know!* I did not *know* anything – not for sure! So, back off, you barbarian!" The old man gave a shove, and the Nomad backed away a step, still snarling. "But," the Wizard continued, the word drawn out and almost apologetic, "it did seem highly likely by my deductions. Teehee!"

The old man giggled like a flirtatious girl, as though his lying to them and their current situation, which seemed more like suicide with every passing moment, delighted him. Izdaju had had enough and cocked back a heavily muscled arm to knock out the deceitful old foreigner, but the Wizard was gone in a puff of smoke before the blow could land. Appearing instantaneously in a second cloud of violet fumes behind the Nomad, Tar Feng quickly kicked him in the back of the knees and whipped his staff around the young man's neck, holding him there firmly whilst Izdaju's eyes popped.

"No more of this attacking your seniors, you hear?" Tar Feng said to the Nomad briskly, as if merely teaching him etiquette.

The rest of the group watched in stunned silence as the old man exhibited strength and celerity they could not have guessed at. Even Kamilah held her tongue in the face of his prowess.

"We are your betters, little boy," continued Tar Feng quietly in the younger man's ear, "and there is much you can learn from us – you and your lady with the funny coloured soul. But you cannot learn if your mouth is always flapping, flapping, flapping! So keep it shut. And when I want it heard, I will ask for it. Understood?"

He tightened the staff as he spoke, his wiry arms bulging with thin muscle, and Izdaju seemed incapable of escape. The proud Nomad warrior gurgled, which the Tzunese Wizard took to be an affirmative and released him.

Izdaju collapsed on all fours, coughing, choking and struggling to breathe, his puffy face as purple as the dissipating smoke. Kamilah dropped to her haunches to assist him, but he pushed her away, still choking and gasping, and she fell onto her rump on the platform unceremoniously.

Fyrstsvard helped the Nomad warrior woman to her feet, noting her earthy musk, and spoke insistently to the old Wizard. "What *do* you know of this place, Tar Feng?"

"Dwarhummer is perhaps the greatest and largest of all known dwarvic cities – known to those in the know, that is," Tar Feng responded, glancing around to ensnare everyone in his tale. His voice was soft and sibilant.

"And the Dwarves are a genius race. Not pleasant or kind, nurturing or fair, but they are cunning and innovative. Those monolithic pillars that you see holding up the high ceiling, which doubles as a floor for the level above, are not wasted space or needless building. The Dwarves think cleverly and use every inch of what they have. Those pillars are housing for their people. They contain hundreds, probably thousands between them, of levels of commode for hundreds of dwarvic families.

"And when the Dwarves that lived and worked down here eventually bred enough to run out of room for housing in their great pillars, they began to establish the ugly rock houses that you see on the ground. I am sure that it is a temporary measure. When they finish excavating deeper, they will create another hall like this, I should think, with its own pillars – and so on."

"How you know so much about Dwarves and yet told us so little, old man?" demanded Izdaju hoarsely, rubbing his throat. "What game you playing with us? I want no part! No part!" The Nomad swiped his hand aggressively to indicate his distaste for the idea.

"I play no games, savage," retorted Tar Feng, speaking slowly and carefully as though to a child. "I read and so know things, unlike you and your barbaric brethren!"

"Shut your mouth, old man!" growled Izdaju, clambering to his feet. "You will get us all killed! You cannot be trusted!"

"Enough!"

Fyrstsvard stepped in to calm matters down, for the Nomad's voice had been growing louder and louder. He looked from Tar Feng, who stood, relaxed and composed, to Izdaju, who wore a grimace, still massaging his bruised throat and staring daggers at the golden-skinned Wizard.

"We have to stick together on this mission," the Knight told them. "There are far greater odds than I anticipated against us already! If we add to that, then we are foolhardy beyond measure, and we deserve no better fate than to be slaughtered by those dwarvic runts as we bicker amongst ourselves! We must stand together! Only then can we succeed – and survive!"

Fyrstsvard, opening his arms beseechingly, looked again to and fro between the two combatants. They both nodded their agreement silently, though if looks could kill, Tar Feng would have dropped dead then and there.

There was no time for further friction, however, as Kamilah pointed up and said, "Look out!"

The mercenaries on the slowly-descending lift looked up and saw Dwarves sliding down the chains towards them from the level above, where presumably the smoke had finally cleared. The bone-armoured warriors could be heard shouting, *"Infava! Infava!"*

"Oh, we're up shit creek now!" Heldig supplied the perfect summary for their debacle, weapons in hand and scowl in place.

The Dwarves' roars as they came closer and the rattling of the chains made further conversation impractical. Ratnik and Jumal jumped out of their skin when a thrown axe landed in the wooden floor at their feet, and then their own angry hollers and the skirl of drawn steel echoed back up the lift passage.

Kamilah began to shoot arrows up at the descending Dwarves so as to filter their numbers before they could inflict any damage, and bodies began to drop on the platform with thumps, making the mercenaries scatter. One landed on Ratnik, laying him flat, and he wriggled out from under it with a sour face. The odd few Dwarves who did manage to reach the platform were, at first, quickly and easily bludgeoned to death by the awaiting mercenaries, but the hairy little folk kept coming, dozens jumping onto the chains to slide down, jeering and jibing menacingly. With all the commotion, the Dwarves below strained to see what was causing such a ruckus.

"Not good, not good," muttered Fyrstsvard as he hacked another Dwarf's face in half and tried to ignore the blood ruining his mien. He looked down, up and then down again. "What can we do? What can we do?" he asked himself frantically, his brain racing like a freed horse for an answer to their predicament.

As the platform touched down with a jarring bump at the next level, however, he had come up with nothing. As it rumbled to a halt, the Dwarves of *Dwarhummer* – who had crowded around the bottom of the lift in their dozens to find out the source of all the noise, some in the unusual bone armour and some not – charged the intruders, without hesitation but with unintelligible thunderous roars. The Dwarves from above, meanwhile, continued to drop down to join the increasingly confusing melee. Most of the *Rodici* on the ground – thankfully, thought Jumal – were held back from the skirmish, in case they proved more of a hindrance than a help in the confined quarters. A couple, however, escaped their handlers and hurtled forward with bloodcurdling shrieks, their great claws scraping at the ground.

"Pirates to the front, everyone else watch the ropes!" shouted out Fyrstsvard in clear, clipped tones, and he stepped to the front of the platform to greet their enemies as the lift landed.

Heldig, Ratnik and Jumal were beside him before he could take a calming breath, and – as he inhaled deeply – he could hear, comfortingly, the twang of Kamilah's bow, Izdaju's grunts of exertion, the swish of the Sandman's robes and Tar Feng's titter.

Then, he exhaled and, wishing he had his trusty shield, used his sword to deflect the nearest pickaxe into a second swinging his way, tangling the two Dwarves' arms and allowing him to puncture both their throats with lightning jabs.

At least, that was Fyrstsvard's intention. The second Dwarf moved when its companion died and so took the sword's point through the upper lip, up under his nose. Fyrstsvard's own lip curled at the sight of snot and blood oozing from the wound, and he kicked the dead Dwarf back with the toe of his boot, its body and that of its fallen comrade temporarily impeding those behind. Dwarves on all sides sought the Knight's flesh with the flashing steel of axe blades, but – fortunately for Fyrstsvard – none were able to overcome the pirates standing fast.

Heldig blocked blows from the Dwarves with his cutlass and bludgeoned the lead *Rodici* into submission with the hammer in his left hand. Where the Captain used his prodigious strength to his advantage, however, Jumal did not quite have the same luxury. With the consummate skill of a lifetime's experience, the Chilpaean instead wove glittering webs with his cutlass and lashed out opportunistically with his stolen axe whenever the opportunity arose to take a life. When the second *Rodici* came at him and leapt for his throat, however, he froze as if spell-struck, his dark eyes round. The moment before it could tear out his jugular with its outsized front teeth, a hammer flashed out from Jumal's peripheral vision and crushed the rat-dog's head with a hollow *bonk,* laying it flat. Bits of brain and splinters of skull spattered over Jumal, and he cringed and spat out the creature's rancid blood.

Heldig grinned at him sidelong, and Jumal, recovering himself in time to parry a dwarvic axe with the cupping bronze handguard of his cutlass, squeaked, "Tanks!" He ran the Dwarf through on the reverse stroke.

Ratnik, despite his wiry vigour, could not rely on brute strength alone to win his fights for him either, so he liked to use his opponent's strength against them, circling, tripping, jabbing and dodging like a persistent bee. In such confined quarters as the platform on which they fought, however, such tactics were inviable, and the pirate was smart enough to recognise the fact.

As an axe blade whistled down towards his head, he regretted that he could not even dodge lest his negligence allow the weapon to harm one of his friends. He set his feet wide apart, bent his knees slightly in as stout a stance as he could and, bracing himself, blocked the blow head on, holding his cutlass horizontal with his spare palm pressed against the flat of the blade for support. Despite the numbing jarring in his arms and the ringing in his ears, Ratnik held his cutlass steady against the biting axe blade and felt a brief flicker of pride, before the Dwarf twisted and barged him bodily.

The young pirate stumbled away, mildly winded, but fortunately he staggered into the back of Izdaju, whose sinewy frame was bulging with immovable strands of muscle as he ferociously battered with both scimitars at any foe brave or unlucky enough to drop down from above. The powerful Nomad did not budge an inch as the buccaneer was thrown against his back, but rather twisted and shoved out with his shoulder to propel Ratnik once more into the fray. Whether Izdaju knew he was helping out a comrade or throwing off a foe, the pirate was never sure.

Regardless, with momentum, Ratnik was thrown back into the fight so quickly that the Dwarf who had shouldered him had not yet had chance to act upon his intentions to cut down the pirate's friends. Moving too fast to bring his ill-placed cutlass to bear, too fast for his shocked opponent to swing back at him, Ratnik jumped, raised a knee at the last moment and felt it connect solidly with the Dwarf's rocky skull. The blow catapulted him back and knocked over a line of Dwarves behind him in a continuing tumble.

Lashing out with desperate speed, Ratnik clove down two more Dwarves on either side of him to make up for his lapse, realising as he did so that his face was set in a grimace, or perhaps grin, of rigour, breath hissing through bared teeth and flared nostrils, nose pinched and eyes narrowed to venomous slits. Such was the true face of man, Ratnik thought in that moment. Of all his masks, this was the one he felt wore him.

Egobal the *Serrici* sheathed one of his daggers and dipped his hand into a large pouch beneath his robes. In his palm, he pulled out a handful of sand.

"Look out, Ratnik!" he cried.

The pirate obligingly swerved to see who shouted and so allowed Egobal to step swiftly in front of the others, toward the charging Dwarves of the new level, and raise the sand clenched in his hand to his lips.

"Sihah Morohk," the Sandman whispered.

The sand he held turned red, and when he blew it from his palm at the enclosing dwarvic skirmishers, it flew from his hand as if taken by a strong wind and burned the Dwarves brutally wherever it touched as though superheated. Egobal stood at the front of the platform, duplicating his feat, spraying the red-hot sand again and again to hold the Dwarves and *Rodici* at bay. They crowded around the lift, unwilling to be burned by the robed man's foul sorceries, and paced back and forth angrily like predators that cannot quite reach their prey. Fyrstsvard and the corsairs, panting and impressed, stayed by Egobal's side lest any should slip through, but the sand scored them all.

"Tar Feng!" shouted Fyrstsvard throatily above the clamour of flesh-cleaving, screams and hoarse threatening.

"What is it, Knight?" snapped the old man, bashing a Dwarf over the head with his staff as it landed unsteadily on the platform. His head then whipped around to regard the swordsman with his milky eyes, his wisps of hair floating eerily above his mostly bald pate.

"Do you think he will be here in the city?" The Knight ran a Dwarf through, his sword screeching as it slid through a chink in the bone armour.

"No no," replied the Wizard precipitously, thwacking a foe in the legs with his crook and toppling it. "I sense dire energies amassing below us. We must go down, down, down!"

"Very well. Can you create a distraction, somehow?" shouted back Fyrstsvard, punching a Dwarf as it dropped down on him. "And then use a smoke bag so we can make a run for it? We have to get out of here – soon!"

Tar Feng – unexpectedly, given his earlier outburst – smiled almost sweetly and said promptly, "Yes, of course. No problem at all. Come along, varmints!"

He reached out and grabbed hold of both Ratnik and Jumal's shirts. The unsuspecting buccaneers looked around in anger at what they assumed to be an attack, only to see a smiling, toothless old Wizard. The three of them vanished in a mystical puff of plum smoke a heartbeat later.

Two Dwarves dropped down into the empty space occupied a moment earlier by the Tzunese man and the two Freemen, both snarling savagely at the Knight, their eyes wide, bloodshot and manic.

"Daft old man, he'll be the death of me," muttered Fyrstsvard, face morphing into a snarl as he leapt to the attack, his longsword singing out to deal death efficiently at a longer range than the Dwarves' pickaxes and axes.

The group felt like a blade being forged upon an anvil – hammered, bent and broken by the Dwarves – and yet, as even Egobal and his miraculous sand were about to be overwhelmed, the attention of their enemies on the ground seemed suddenly to shift in another direction. The pressure on the mercenaries lessened, and they could breathe a little easier, though every one of them was still engaged in a brawl with the short folk who continued to drop down on them from above. After a moment, like an uplifting clarion call, the group could hear Tar Feng and the pirates bellowing dissonant battle cries behind the mass of gathered Dwarves around the lift.

Cutting down a hairy face in a spray of blood, Fyrstsvard glimpsed through the throng the three who had vanished in a puff of smoke. They had attacked the Dwarf battalion ruthlessly from behind, the seafarers hacking at every dwarvic back they could see, while Tar Feng shot what looked like green globules of magical energy at the Dwarves, shouting the while, *"Banza'abas!"*

When hit by one of these sizzling emerald globs, the Dwarves were knocked back yards in the air like they had been jousted, their skin and clothing charred slightly. It made for an almost comical scene, thought the Knight – little Dwarves flying about above the skirmish, their chubby, hairy faces screaming with fear.

The pirates were dazzled by the magic of the staff, but Fyrstsvard, who had worked with Tar Feng in the past, knew that it was a relatively common staff by Quing Tzu standards and was wielded by most Magicians in that far-off land. It was a power staff. It used some sort of magical stones from Quing Tzu, which the Tzunese had kept very secret over the centuries, to create its own innate power. It was a tool of many uses, the most basic of which was to blast a charged magical force at a target, but it was hardly lethal. The force was enough to throw a person, or a Dwarf, a good distance, but it did no real damage, save to scorch and stun.

Still, it was effective in scaring the dwarvic horde, who thought they were being attacked by a far more lethal form of wizardry. Shouts of panic spread like a disease, and anarchy erupted as Dwarves fled this way and that like illuminated roaches, though many bravely rooted their feet to fight against the intruding mercenaries and the irksome Sandman, a spark-spitting blaze who burned them every time they ventured too close.

As the chaos spread, the fighting Dwarves became more desperate, and the mercenaries began to falter. An axe nicked Heldig's calf in a scarlet spurt, knocking him to his knees, and Fyrstsvard took a smack to the head, courtesy of a dwarvic pickaxe haft. The pirate and Knight both slew their opponents, but then felt their knees wobble and give way beneath them. Egobal, meanwhile, stood in a small clearing, for the Dwarves seemed petrified of going near the beige-robed man and his smouldering sand.

Kamilah, too, was relatively unhurt, as she had been protected by the rest for the most part, so that she could continue to wreak havoc with her horn bow, but her fellow Nomad, Izdaju, was covered in small cuts, since his aggressive technique left little in the way of defence.

With Heldig and Fyrstsvard momentarily out of the fight, the pressure grew too much. Just as the mercenaries began thinking up their last prayers, however, a foul-smelling fog filled the air in the midst of the Dwarves, and the group knew that Tar Feng had finally used another of his smoke bags.

Fyrstsvard, lying on the platform floor, turned his gonging head and saw the reeking mist creeping towards them. He closed his eyes for a moment and – swearing he could hear the crazy old Tzunese man shouting, "Run!" – staggered to his feet, protected by Egobal's incarnadine sand.

"We have to get out of here now!" the Knight shouted sorely, opening his eyes to a vision of concussed blurriness. "We have to break out under the cover of the smoke and make a run for it!"

"Leave it to me," said the Sandman, his voice smooth and placid. He reached into his pouch of sand and held it to his lips once more, but this time whispered a different enchantment: *"Sihah Alahehk."*

The sand glittered like diamonds for a second, before Egobal blew it in a high arc above the Dwarves' heads in one smooth motion. The sand seemed to hang in the air for a few moments, like dust in the sunlight, before the twinkling, infinitely small grains slowly fell upon the confused Dwarves and *Rodici*.

"Cover your mouths," instructed Egobal, indicating his face-wrap.

The sand slowly settled on and around the Dwarves, and they stopped fighting. They stared at the dust like children at their first sight of snow, and the mercenaries witnessed them breathing in the tiny, shining grains. All at once, every nearby Dwarf and rat-dog that had been caught under the crystalline rain began to sneeze.

A bout of sneezing broke out that could only be the work of magic or a sudden-striking plague, for every nearby Dwarf was irredeemably debilitated by their nose. Then, one by one, their eyes became blurry, stupid smiles spread across their faces, and they slumped heavily to the ground, each with a dull thump. Eventually, scores of them lay unmoving alongside their pets, splayed out, snoring loudly, fast asleep, with smiles still playing on their lips and slime from the sneezing decorating their beards.

The Dwarves that had not dozed off were raging loudly but uselessly, engulfed in the blinding, choking smoke, giving the mercenaries still on the platform a much-needed lull. They could see nothing of Tar Feng or the pirates though, and could only hope that the old Wizard would keep the young Freemen safe until they regrouped.

"Impressive," said Heldig to Egobal, after cutting down a dropping, fat Dwarf, wheezing through his sleeve from the effort of the brawl.

"Let's move quickly before that smoke engulfs us too," ordered Fyrstsvard, he too talking through a sleeve. "I figure the likelihood is that any platforms descending down further will not be nearby – perhaps they will even be on the other side of the cave. So, we will circumvent the city as much as we can, avoiding the centre and – hopefully – too many Dwarves and *Rodici*. Follow me!"

The area appeared unnervingly empty as the group ran away from the noxious fumes, which – as they spread – served to confound those Dwarves following from the level above, as well as those already caught in them. The Dwarves looked to have been scattered in fear as the group fled the smoke, for the troglodytes loathed and mistrusted magic; to them, it was far outside the norm, as it was for most men. No Dwarf had ever been recorded to have been a magic-user, Tar Feng knew, and any that had claimed such powers had been speedily silenced over the years. The Dwarves put their trust, faith and hope in technology and in logic.

Fyrstsvard set off at a light run, angling left so as keep to the outskirts of the massive metropolis. The Nomads followed like silent shadows, Heldig and Egobal behind them.

Seeing that they already laid foot on the bricked road that ran around the city like the rim of a wheel, and having decided that attempting to circumvent the majority of the Dwarves was their best chance, they sped off along the circuitous route, praying silently that the dirt-dwellers remained hidden long enough for the group to discover another lift to take them down.

"Lucky," commented Heldig about the lack of dwarvic attackers, running as best he could with his light injuries, sucking in rattling breaths along the way. "By the way," the ageing pirate continued between gasps, "those were some nice tricks you pulled with your sand, Sandman! How'd you do that? You just get any old sand and whisper in its ear?"

Egobal turned his equable eyes on the huffing pirate running next to him for a moment, his voice as phlegmatic and level as the desert hardpan. "No, seaman, it requires more than just any old sand. The sand I carry was scooped from the *Rosa Do Desier, the rose of the desert,* the secret oasis of my people, where we believe that all magic – and perhaps even all life – first began. Only with sand from that magical place and with the restricted knowledge lain down by centuries of *Serrici* forefathers can one achieve such an effect. But I am glad you enjoyed it."

"Certainly did, matey! Say, can I have some of that there magic sand?" Heldig eyed the pouch greedily.

"No, Heldig, you cannot," replied Egobal with indications of a smile about his eyes, whilst his lips were hidden by cloth. "And if you were to have it, it would afford you no magic, for you know neither the incantations nor the ways of my people. I will keep it, and I will use it to help in this mission; our mission, friend."

"Now, I am chuffed we are to be friends, don't get me wrong, Sandman, but about that sand … How 'bout if I bought some off you? Just a little?" puffed Heldig. "Gotta be worth a great deal, that has."

"I'm afraid not, seafarer."

Meanwhile, ahead of them, Kamilah attempted to calm Izdaju, murmuring in the clicking nomadic tongue, her voice husky, *"My intended, you must remain calm. You cannot destroy this group just because you dislike our leader – and he* is *our leader."*

"And that is how you would have it?" Izdaju looked like he was sucking on a lemon.

"I have seen how the others respect him and look to him for orders," responded Kamilah tactfully. *"They will side with him should you try anything, Izdaju! And you should not try anything. The orders he gives are the right ones! We must remain calm and follow his lead, otherwise we will never get our reward, and we will more than likely perish in this bottomless pit."*

"I could lead us, Kamilah! I could keep us safe!" retorted Izdaju, his pride wounded.

Kamilah sighed; some things had to be said. *"No, Izdaju, you could not. You are the greatest warrior I know, and no one can dispute that, but I believe that the decisions are best left to the Knight."* Ignoring Izdaju's glare, she ploughed on. *"He made the right call back at the top of the platform, in the cave. You did not. So please, can we just follow his lead and get out of here? Just think of what we can do with the reward, my intended! Put aside your ego, and worry about getting this mission done, please! I'm concerned that your arrogance will get you killed down here. Fyrstsvard is not your enemy. He is part of our group, and we must fight* with *him to survive, understand?"*

Izdaju nodded silently, his lips tight, though his swarthy face told of his fury.

"Keep up!" Fyrstsvard shouted over his shoulder in Traveller's, putting on a new burst of speed. "The Dwarves have been scared off by Tar Feng's magic, but they won't hide forever – and when they come out, I want us to be long gone!"

"Come," Kamilah said to Izdaju, and the two of them lengthened their strides easily to catch up with Fyrstsvard, for they were young and fit. Heldig groaned and tried to move his aching muscles faster.

Now that he was on ground level, Fyrstsvard noticed something a distance away that he had not from the lift. It must have been blocked from his view by a pillar or the mountainous water tank at the time, he supposed, for before his eyes, on the opposite side of the tank from the palatial pillar, squatted a huge and unique building. It looked to be crafted of a darker stone than any other structure in the city and stuck out like a cuckoo in the nest. It loomed, lording, over the houses and appeared to be completely circular.

"What do you suppose that dark building is over there?" Fyrstsvard called over his shoulder, but before any reply could be made, the place erupted with monsters.

4

The Terror of Port-Hav'n

"So it is true, then?" a mousey woman with tightly tied hair squeaked, wringing her hands anxiously.

"It cannot be!" a weathered old man in grey grunted dismissively.

"He has such pretty eyes ..." a young, beautiful and scantily clad woman mused.

"It *is* so!" a short, stocky man with fair hair and an overabundance of gold about his person, particularly on his stubby fingers in the form of rings, insisted earnestly.

"Hear me a moment!" interrupted a tall man with greying hair wearing chain mail, pauldrons, a tabard, greaves and gauntlets. "During the boy's absence, the skies and seas were relatively calm – the cattle too. And then there was the incident a week ago. Most of us here witnessed the atrocity, and all of us have heard of it by now, but for those of you who did not see, allow me to reiterate the events that transpired. Raised voices and smashing sounds were heard from inside Skallgrim Manor by its neighbours after dusk, and – fearing the boy's dark powers – the neighbours hurried to call the instance to the attention of myself and the guards: the right thing to do.

"When I and my colleagues arrived at the manor, the grand doors slammed open to emit Sir Horace Favorré, a retired knightly compatriot of Sir Skallgrim's, completely and utterly ablaze. Flames wreathed his body from toes to hair like a human torch! He screamed horribly as his hair cooked and his flesh began to melt, staggering back and forth in front of the manor while he burned alive. The fire was so strong we couldn't get within a yard of him without being set alight ourselves – we had to put out the flames on one brave Guard, in fact – and the blaze did not weaken.

"I was there that night, and I saw the expression on Skallgrim's face as he watched from the doorway with his son. He was stricken, his face twisted in sorrow and helplessness, as if he could not move a muscle despite wishes to the contrary. I have seen the two men together before, and they were as brothers! There can be no question of Skallgrim being the arsonist. He shed tears watching Favorré blaze. And when Sir Horace was long dead and all his flesh had been consumed, leaving only blackened bone … Only then did young Nighan – who had up until that point watched the entire affair evolve with nary an emotion on his cold, evil face – turn away and go back inside without a word, taking his father with him and slamming the doors behind them."

Gasp. "We are cursed! It is true!" the mousey woman exclaimed in a trembling squeal.

"Nay, I say the boy is cursed by the Gods!" This came from a bald, stern-looking man in his thirties with a shaven jaw and an azure robe.

"Aye, accursed!" A taciturn rumble from a mountain of a man ridged with muscle and speckled with dark stubble and soot.

"Witchson!"

The name was spat in a whisper that made the skin crawl and the spine shiver with ominous portent, spat like an insult or a curse with an accompanying angry thud on the thick cherry wood table. Around the room, heads bobbed and there were murmurs of troubled agreement.

A dog barked, rats scuffled, a crow cawed, the door creaked, the windows juddered as the wind howled against them, and the dimly lit trees outside rustled in private conference. The fire in the great stone hearth seemed to flicker for a moment, then rage back with a fury at the whisper. The shadows cast by its glare danced malevolently on the pale walls, and the dark corners of the room seemed suddenly all the more sinister.

The quiet, clandestine conversation was held in Roberts Manor by Lana Craffhile, the head spinner at the cotton mill; Trent Wetnout, the harbourmaster; Adele Norris, the Madame at the palace of courtesans; Bruce Frank, a wealthy merchant; Malcolm Bernard, the Captain of the town guard; Meinolf Sanders, the head priest at the temple of worship; Bran Cirrus, the town smith; and Able Roberts, merchant and Mayor of the harbour town, Port-Hav'n, on the western coast of the isle of Justiqua.

Mayor Roberts, resplendent in a gaudy yellow silken shirt and jacket and crimson hose from the east, looked down at his clenched fists on the table, then around at the awaiting frightened faces. "For too long have we suffered the derangements of his dark sorceries! It ends tonight! Terrence, Nod and Isaac are building a pyre for the boy as we speak. Are we all in agreement on this?"

There were again nods. Only a few had the courage to vocalise their assent.

"The Gods walk with you, Able. It is clear to us all now that, whether he is directly responsible for what has happened to us or not, he is cursed. The Prophet's will is clear," Meinolf, the head priest of the Order of *Pacia* in Port-Hav'n, bald and stern as ever, spoke up, his voice passionless, his face expressionless. With his hands clasped behind his back and his long robe covering him from neck to floor, Meinolf looked every inch the priest of *Pacia.*

That is to say he looked dreadfully dull, thought the flamboyantly-dressed Mayor, stroking a large green-dyed feather that stuck out of his stylish vivid yellow hat. The young priest was interested only in his prayers, in the Word of the Prophet and in the promise of his soul's eternal life in Elf-born *Citta Pacia, the City of Peace.*

"The boy has meddled in the affairs of the Gods for too long now," Meinolf continued. "The great All Mother, Gaia, will suffer this indignation no longer! For too long have the crops wilted, for too long have the livestock been spooked by his very presence!" The young priest nodded slowly, as though agreeing with himself. "It is time that the balance of nature was restored. Time that rule over the land was returned to rightful hands: the All Mother's hands. The Goddess will not be satisfied until the boy's dark influence has been removed!"

"Does the boy's father know about this?" a bark from the old harbourmaster, Trent Wetnout, showed he was not so easily convinced. He was garbed as always in grey trousers and a slate shirt with scraggly silver hair on his face and head that always looked wet and salty.

"Yes, he is at the manor now with the boy, to ensure that he will be there upon our arrival," Able answered smoothly, his voice gliding over his tongue like quicksilver.

Trent Wetnout looked around at the guarded and determined expressions of his fellows. Perhaps Able would never forgive him, for the wily merchant held a grudge like a lock-jawed mastiff bite, but the weathered harbourmaster felt he had to speak up.

"I cannot believe what we are discussing here!" he said, his voice loud, though hoary with age. "What *you* are willing to do!"

He looked each of them in the eye. Some, like Malcolm Bernard, shied away from his glare in shame, whilst others – such as the silk-clad Mayor, Able – flaunted their willingness openly.

"We are talking about a seventeen-year-old boy! A boy I have known for many years – and I know that you have, too! We have watched him grow since he was born. *I* have watched him run around town, trying to fit in with the other lads his age and never quite succeeding … He always seemed a nice enough lad. And I know that we have all seen the bruises. The father beats him something fierce after a night's drinking! Surely he deserves some sympathy for the harshness of his life?"

When averted gazes were his only response, still he ploughed on. “And I agree that there have been some mighty strange occurrences, what with the cattle behaviour and freak weather and his father’s friend’s … unusual … death – and that a rainy cloud seems to follow the sullen-faced little punch bag everywhere he wanders, but can we really condemn him to death ourselves? Shouldn’t we send him to Crossroads, at least, for a trial? His mother was a proven full-grown Witch, and yet even she received a hearing with the Governor before he torched her! Doesn’t her son deserve the same?”

Able smiled – somewhat cunningly, Trent thought, realising that the oily merchant was prepared for any line of argument. A silver tongue can still spoon shite, as his father used to say.

“Indeed he does, Trent, and I am glad you brought that to our attention,” he said slickly, giving the old man his best salesman’s smile. “As you say, the boy’s mother – the Witch, Samantha – was, at once, sentenced to death upon proof of her dark allegiances. That she was sentenced to death by the Governor is just, I agree – and in an ideal world, everybody would be fairly tried by Governor Peakes.”

Able paused expertly and looked around his dining room at the expectant faces. Trent remained frowning unsurely. “But the fact is that she was sentenced to death because she was a Witch. It was mere happenstance that she was near the Governor when she was discovered and, as such, was able to be tried by Peakes himself. We do not have such liberties with this boy,” he told the group firmly. “We cannot run the risk of ferrying him to Crossroads for trial. If he is as powerful as I suspect, we would be endangering a great many people by doing so. He could kill our own folk trying to escape.”

Able let the words sink in. “Furthermore, we *know* – know for a fact – that he is guilty. We have all witnessed it with our own eyes – even you just admitted to it, Wetnout!” The harbourmaster shifted uncomfortably in his luxurious leather seat. “We have all seen what that boy can do. As it happens, though, I have taken the liberty of compiling a list of all the known sorcerous practices of Nighan Witchson. If it will reassure some waverers,” he glanced pointedly at Wetnout, “then I will present it here as evidence of his guilt.”

Able looked from face to face, then back at the scrap of parchment between his pale, flabby hands. “Though some of these occurrences may seem vague or difficult to believe when read from a piece of parchment, know that there were eyewitnesses in each case who attest that the events happened, that Witchson was present and that he was undoubtedly connected to them.

“Ahem. As Wetnout so graciously reminded us but a moment ago, we have watched the boy grow for many years. And I put it to those of you with memories that extend back before the boy's birth that things have been different ever since he came into this world. No more can the weather be predicted. Sailors and farmers alike have struggled to make a livelihood in what should be a prosperous harbour town! Crops fail through lack of sunlight, because the sky we once knew is often hidden in grey haze even in the zenith of summer.

"Cattle bloat and die seemingly without reason in the boy's presence, and the old manor where he lives – which once flourished with life and greenery – now lies abandoned by insect or plant as if even they fear to make a home there! We have lied to ourselves for too long – we have all noticed these things, but we have been in denial because the cause for them does not seem possible! It is time to accept reality for what it is, good people; these occurrences – and their connection with the boy – cannot be ignored nor go unresolved!"

The wily merchant again pounded the table with a hammy fist to make his point, while the others exchanged knowing looks.

The priest, Meinolf, nodded sagely. "The boy unbalances nature with his dark ways. He meddles with powers best left for the divine, and the All Mother turns her face from him. He will prove our destruction if he is not dealt with at once!"

Able smiled at the priest – grateful for his help, though he could not help but find the man dull as dishwater – before clearing his throat and continuing in the same smooth, perfectly oiled pitch.

"Nighan was enrolled in the local school at the age of six, along with a great many other students, one of whom was my son. I believe others of you had children at the school there with him, too. So both our children and we, the parents, can attest to the veracity of these accounts.

"The first strange thing I have recorded here was told to me by my son and other children in the class. Everyone – including the teachers – noticed how incredibly fast Nighan learned. Anything he read, he could recite back perfectly. He quickly figured out the complexities of our own language, whilst others struggled with whole sentences. He could multiply complex numbers in his head the likes of which would leave an accountant with a migraine, and – as he grew – he began to study other languages, arithmetic, alchemy and herbal lore. Now, whilst it is not proof of his sorcery that he had such abilities, it is notable as paranormal. Moreover, the boy began to study anatomy."

There were a few confused looks and mutterings amongst the gathered council for a moment, before the Mayor deigned to shed light on the subject.

"Having read a book about the anatomy of animals at school," Able began again, his smooth rhetoric hypnotising the simple townsfolk, "the Witch's son disappeared from his father's manor home for two days. When he finally returned, much to his distraught parents' relief, he dragged a dead deer through the streets with him for the family to eat. Many eyes saw that carcass, and it had been gutted, turned inside out. My guess is that the boy opened it up and pinned back its skin on a tree so that he could examine its insides. While that sort of behaviour is not directly threatening to anyone, it is disturbing nonetheless and, in *my* opinion, is evidence of a rather sick and twisted mind."

"Ain't so bad," Wetnout mumbled. "They were gonna eat it anyway."

"It's horrific!" shrilled the head spinner, Lana Craffhile, the tight bun of hair atop her head bouncing slightly as she covered her mouth with her hand, aghast, and looked as though she might faint. There were murmurs of accord.

"I agree," grumbled Bran Cirrus. Always a happy soul that one, Wetnout thought sardonically. "My son, Brad, saw him dragging the thing back." He shook his large, dark-haired head morosely, the words coming out slowly and sounding sorrowful – or perhaps just drunk, thought the harbourmaster. "That a young boy could do such a thing is beyond belief. I mean, I'm all for killing the deer to eat it, but slicing away at its insides just for pleasure or curiosity's sake? Perhaps whilst it still lived …" That brought a small gasp from the women present. "That is sick."

Able nodded his thanks to Bran and Lana. "Indeed it is, Bran, indeed it is. Next is a much-discussed event about town; almost a myth now. During Witchson's first year in school – during that unusually hot summer when even old fish belly Wetnout over here got sunburn – we had weeks of sunlight, a placid, idyllic sea and almost clear skies overhead." He paused.

"And then one day we had a thunderstorm that blackened the sky! Its booms woke up the sea like it was a sleeping monster, and – with howling winds whipping it up into a frenzy – the waves roared up in response, smashing against the docks, destroying a pier and a dozen old buildings by the water's edge. Plants everywhere wilted and died, unable to handle the torrential rain that day." The merchant-turned-Mayor paused again.

"The next day, the beautiful, bountiful summer that we had been enjoying just two days earlier returned in full heat and vigour! I know you all remember it – especially you, harbourmaster! 'Twas the queerest, eeriest weather that any of us has ever known, without a doubt!"

A chorus of "Aye!" and "Tis true!" rang out from the council, while Trent averted his eyes from Able's uncomfortably.

"And what happened on that fateful day, I hear you ask," Able said with a smile, playing up to his audience like a troubadour, "after which, we began to suffer stranger and stranger weathers and happenings without so much as talking about it?"

Able had, in fact, talked of little else for years, Wetnout thought ironically. The fat Mayor had been spreading rumours about the boy all over town even before the mother was executed, and after, he was open in his hostility. Though he was half-right; no one else had dared voice their suspicions, even to themselves, for it had seemed like that route would lead to insanity.

It was well known that there was no more sorcery in the world, that all the Sorcerers and Witches of old had been eradicated hundreds of years ago by the great Lord Protector, Sir Barrett Heron, and his noble Knights of *Pacia* after they had overthrown the tyranny of Convent.

"I will tell you all what happened that day," Able told his audience in a lowered, foreboding voice. "My son got into a small ruckus with the Witch's boy. The way my son tells it, Nighan attacked him over nothing more than a book that young Abram was trying to admire."

Roberts paused to give his audience time to absorb his words, and when he began speaking again, Trent could tell that the words were no longer the young boy's, despite assurances to the contrary.

"My son told me that the moment Nighan spied him lay hands on the book, Witchson's face fell away – like a mask pulled from a performer – and all that remained was a monstrous ashen face with impending violence burning in his unnatural violet eye. He attacked my son with his fists and screamed until the sky itself darkened with a sudden thunderstorm. Strong winds whipped about the classroom – though there were no open windows – as if the boy's screaming was their source! When the boy finally got his book back from my rightly petrified Abram, his squealing ceased and so too did the mysterious winds. The sky halted bellowing its fury at the ground and ceased its lightning show – but remained as dark and sullen as Witchson himself thereafter.

"I believe that after that episode is when the mocking began in earnest. The children did not know that they were mocking such a demonic creature, and so they called him out on his differences, on his *strangeness*. And I now believe that they were right to do so, that they recognised, in fact, what we dared not. For Nighan barely smiled after that day, and the sky above us changed dramatically. Darkness, black clouds and lightning seemed to follow the boy about, everywhere he went, and so began the shunning." He looked them all in the eye again, knowing each person's guilt in the matter.

"We have had more freak occurrences than the rest of Justiqua put together, I warrant!" Able flowed on. "You all know I speak the truth now." Sadly, thought Wetnout guiltily, we do. "We have had hailstorms in summer, blindingly bright sun in the depths of winter, hurricanes, earthquakes, floods, raging fires in the town more times than I care to count, devastating plagues and infestations!"

"Come now, Able!" Wetnout interrupted, waving a disbelieving hand. "How can you possibly hope to blame the boy for fires, plagues and infestations? It is beyond ridiculous – they could happen anywhere at any time, and you all know that!" He tried to sweep the room with his eyes as the Mayor did, but his fellow councillors shied away from his glare.

"But they did not happen *anywhere,* Trent!" Able argued back as politely as he could, though Trent could see the fat man's eyes bulging in anger. "They happened here and they have happened a great deal more frequently than just about anywhere else!" The Mayor paused, took a deep breath and looked at the harbourmaster with more control. "But perhaps you are right. Perhaps these terrible debacles cannot be laid at the boy's feet, but perhaps they *can* be laid at the feet of his mother. A proven Witch!"

Wetnout clamped his mouth shut as Bruce Frank, a merchant who all but worked for the Mayor, grovelled nasally, "Good point, Mayor. We can never know now all that the Witch might have been responsible for."

"Indeed, the mother's role in this town's catastrophes will forever be a mystery," Able concurred, spreading his arms. "But I think we all know in our hearts that the mother's dark gift was passed on to the boy. Up until now, we have called these odd occurrences coincidences. But I believe, in light of the quantity of evidence that mounts against the boy, that we can now be *sure* that there is nothing coincidental about them."

5

Judgement

Able Roberts looked around the table, pausing to stare at each face. Trent could see that the rest of the council were completely under the Mayor's spell. Roberts was an insufferable leech who'd sell his own mother for a single bent Real, but he was a convincing public speaker. Wetnout stroked his beard, trying desperately to think of something that might help the boy in question.

"And then of course, there was Virgil Yngvar," said the Mayor. There were gasps as people remembered the eccentric old man and sombre nods as they recalled his fate. "The master storyteller. The one person in Port-Hav'n who did not shun the boy. He would tell the boy the old legends and myths of a time before Convent for hours on end in the dock tavern, the Sharkbite, pleased to have the audience. And the boy sought out the old man's company more and more, as the harassment from the other children increased.

"After a couple of months of this, in which the frequency of the boy's visits progressed to near daily, it became clear there was something wrong with Virgil. The boy had broken his mind somehow, until all Yngvar could do was tell senile tales that gradually dissolved into meaningless strings of words. He would not move, he would not eat, drink or sleep. He sat on his stool by the bar and drooled out words for days on end. Finally, when he was dying of starvation, he was taken to the hospice where they had to restrain and force-feed him just to keep him alive, whilst he writhed about and screamed out purposeless syllables. Such is the fate of all those who allow the Witchson to toy with their minds."

"Aye, he was a good man once," confirmed Wetnout quietly. Virgil had been his friend for decades. "No more than a drooling wreck now, though … Comes to us all with age." He looked hard at the Mayor's greedy eyes.

"It was not age, Trent," Able said softly, trying to wheedle his way onto Wetnout's good side. "It was the boy. You of all people should know that."

"It could've been age, Roberts," Wetnout said again, defiantly.

"A transformation like that almost overnight? I think not. In light of the rest of the evidence here, I think you must accept reason over this suspense of disbelief you have chosen. You will see that I'm right."

"Could be that Virgil too was cursed in punishment for not shunning the evil boy as he should have done!" Meinolf suggested gravely.

Wetnout grumbled in quiet frustration and waved a wrinkly hand for the Mayor to continue his tirade.

"Thank you for your input, both of you," Able said smoothly. "It is best to examine all possibilities – which is all I am trying to do here." He cleared his throat and looked down to his parchments once more. "Ahem, two years ago, when we received word that the boy's mother had been tried and executed for being a Witch, still we cowered in our homes," the Mayor continued darkly, as though disgusted by their behaviour and his own, "for we knew that the menace was not gone. Still the weather did not clear, still the skies were black, and still the feeling of unease pervaded the town. I know you all remember the night after we informed the boy's father of what had happened. After Sir Skallgrim went home and told his son …"

Wetnout remembered his dread at the cacophonic storm that had engulfed the town that night.

Able continued quietly, knowing they all remembered it with grief. Some had even lost loved ones in that fearsome tempest. "Darkness descended, so thick and so deep you could not see your hand waving in front of your face. The sky was torn apart by hundreds of streaks of forked yellow lightning like a great spider's web! Thunder so loud that you could not hear yourself shouting … Gale force winds ripped up century-old trees and tore apart wooden dwellings completely. I think near everyone lost their roof that night. I know I did. And so everyone remembers the downpour; queer, yellowish rain that hissed down from the sky so fast it stung when it struck.

"We were fortunate the entire town was not sunken to the depths of the ocean with the size of the waves whipped up in the squall that day – twice as tall as my own manor they were, come rolling in off the coast around the headland. When we awoke the next morning, our beloved town was a wreck. It has taken us years to repair that damage, and to be frank, we are not finished with the repairs even now. I know you, Bran, have yet to finish rebuilding your house and forge." The smith grumbled his sour agreement. "That storm cost us thousands of Reales, as well as the lives of a few treasured citizens."

There was silence for a moment as each reminisced on what was probably the worst night of their lives.

"I believe," proffered Able, still in low tones, "we all know, deep down, what caused that storm. We may tell ourselves that it was merely nature or coincidence, but I hope we're past fooling ourselves at this point. It can't have been the boy's mother, because Samantha had just been executed. A storm seems to build about the boy every time he does not get his way and, that night, after he heard what had happened from his father … I believe the boy's emotional turmoil and his rage were so great that he could not control them, and his sorcerous powers eked from him, like water from a leaky jug, to destroy everything around him. Sir Skallgrim's manor was desiccated come sunup, surrounded by dead plants and grass, glass shattered, roof caved in, with a tree leaning on it."

There were nods as people remembered the state of it. Even Wetnout could not argue. The boy *was* at the centre of every storm.

"After Samantha's execution, Sir Skallgrim began drinking in earnest – as any who have been down the ol' Mermaid and Sailor can tell you. Many are the nights after the Witch's execution that we would witness the boy's father drink himself to oblivion, before staggering home to beat on his disappointment of a son. As Trent has already reminded us," he gave the old man a deferential bow of the head with a slight mocking smirk, "we have all seen the boy's bruises. And we have all felt the sudden gales, seen the lightning and heard the downpours and thunder after the boy's father gets through that door. That is no coincidence. I cannot believe it anymore." He spoke slowly. "It is the boy."

Wetnout glowered at his boots. I set the oily bastard up perfectly, he thought bitterly.

"When the boy turned sixteen," Able ploughed on, the list beginning to seem interminable, "his father took him to that same tavern for his first drink as a man. There were many witnesses to the outing, among them my son, Abram, and your son, Jord, too, I believe, Malcolm?" He gestured and raised an eyebrow to Malcolm Bernard, Captain of the guard.

"Aye, Jord saw it," the Captain agreed, though he could not quite meet the Mayor's expectant eyes.

He too feels guilty about this, realised Wetnout.

"He saw the whole thing." Captain Bernard nodded his head and looked up to the Mayor's face for just an instant, before turning to stare off into the fire wordlessly.

Since it was evident the Captain was more than happy to let the Mayor tell the tale of the night, Able resumed his damnation. "After drinking near on a barrel of mead between them, from what I hear, Skallgrim and his boy began to argue with one another. Abram tells me that this rowing escalated until they were on their feet, screaming at one another, flushed red in the face from both mead and anger.

"Eventually, Skallgrim knocked Nighan to the ground. On the floor, the Witch's son began to moan; a low, rasping, depressed noise that meant nothing and yet contained all of the boy's sorrow and fury, the witnesses tell me. This noise continued on, spooking the regulars, until the tavern itself began to vibrate as though it were in a localised quake. It shook more and more violently, the stones in the walls scraping against one another loudly, until the very timberwork began to splinter and snap on the ceiling, the walls, the windows …

"When it seemed the inn would crumble to the ground completely, the father broke a clay mug over his son's head to cease his sorceries – and cease they did, the instant the mug shattered over the boy's head. The father picked up the unconscious boy, slung him over his shoulder and walked home without a word to anyone, leaving a lot of scared and curious folk behind. Moreover, when my son turned to get a drink to calm his nerves, the innkeeper – Siegbert, a close friend to us all – was gone. Vanished! And nobody has seen him since."

Again, irrefutable, thought Trent sadly. Nighan was doomed.

"The boy has been beaten in the streets by terrified townsfolk five times that I know of since the incident at the tavern – and there are doubtless more of which I am ignorant. Each time, the sky cracks with thunder even when it is blue, and the very ground beneath the townsfolk shakes with warning, and they soon give up the beating for fear that they will be the boy's next victim. It is clear that we have the community's support." Able looked smug now, victory all but in his clammy grasp.

"The last event on my list is, of course, the cattle escape. Were Nod here," Able indicated a vacant chair on which usually slouched the merry farmer, Nod Glenning, "he would back me up on this one, because he himself witnessed it with several of his farmhands. They told me the story; it happened last year in autumn. One of the young'uns spotted Witchson leaning against the fence of one of their enclosures, staring hard at the happily grazing cattle. The young lad went to fetch Nod, unsure of what to do.

"Nod and the young lad returned to the enclosure just in time to see the cattle stampeding their way free, smashing down a fence in their haste to be away from Witchson, who still stood watching – and laughing. One particularly powerful bull gored a young farmhand during the mad rush, an innocent lad named Douglas who was only trying to placate them. The farmers were forced to chase after their runaways, and Witchson slouched safely back to his wrecked manor."

Wetnout wanted to argue that anything could've spooked the cattle, but Witchson's presence there was inexplicable. The boy had signed his own death warrant many times over.

Head bobs of agreement. "Need I say more?"

There was no need for him to say more, but he loved the sound of his own trumpet, thought the harbourmaster sourly.

Able did indeed continue. "Throughout his life, whenever Nighan went away with his father for a few days, *all* of us," he glanced meaningfully at Trent for a second who could not disagree, "noticed that things were a lot calmer during his absence. The winds were gentler, the seas calmer, the sky brighter, the people happier, the livestock content – even the birds seemed to sing more gaily! I hyperbolise slightly perhaps, but you all know of what I speak. Things were much improved during the boy's absence. And *that* is our proof. When the boy returned, dreariness and greyness seeped into our skies, our lives and our souls once again. And I, for one, wish to be rid of it! Forever rid of it!"

"Aye!" rang out from several council members.

"To summarise, through purposeful and malicious sorcery or through a curse placed on the boy by the Gods, Nighan Witchson has brought near obliteration on this town with devastating tempests the likes of which were never seen before his birth! He has brought hurricanes and earthquakes down upon us, caused people to be killed even! He can be linked to the disappearance of one man and the sudden insanity of another, and now – with the testimony of Captain Bernard of what he saw last week with Sir Horace – I believe we have proof of Witchson's dark powers. There is no other explanation but the sorcerous murder of Sir Favorré. What you have just heard is my complete list of evidence against Nighan Witchson, and I have already sent a runner to bring a copy to the Governor in Crossroads to notify him of our discoveries and intent. "

Able looked to Trent, prepared for his last-ditch effort.

Trent tried it anyway. "There could have been a rational explanation for Sir Horace being set alight!"

"Coincidence only stretches so far, Wetnout," Able said condescendingly, "and not as far as my imagination in this case."

Trent bumbled on. "But, what if – what if he isn't *consciously* responsible for these things? What if he doesn't even *know* he's doing them? They could just be highly unlikely coincidences still! You said yourself, Mayor, that the catastrophes that have befallen this town seem linked with the boy's emotional turmoil. What if he's completely unaware of the effect you say he has on his surroundings?"

Able shook his head slowly, sorrow and regret wrinkled in his expression, victory gleaming in his beady eyes.

"I'm sorry, Wetnout, truly I am. But even if that is the case, he cannot be allowed to live. Magic is the province of the Gods, is that not so,

Meinolf?"

The priest nodded sombrely. "I need hardly remind you all of the centuries of darkness and oppression that we knew under the rule of Convent. Magic must be forbidden from man, for he cannot control it and it will ultimately lead to his downfall all over again. That must be avoided at all costs."

The Mayor looked Trent in the eye once again. "It is the boy's time," he told him. "We must do the right thing, as Terrence, Nod and Isaac hope we will. They have already let us know their decision by building the pyre. Now, it is our turn. Let us vote."

By a vote of ten against one, Nighan – dubbed Witchson – was sentenced to death.

6

Release the Mutants!

After tossing the smoke bag into the midst of the Dwarves crowding the stationary lift, Tar Feng shouted thinly, his airy voice sounding like a loud whisper, "Run! Run, sea-dogs, run! Get out of the smoke, or they will release the *Rodici* on you!"

That was enough persuasion for Jumal. On the fringe of the stinking, smoky ruckus, he parried a pickaxe blow with his newly found axe, before reversing the flow and swinging it backhand, spike-first, into the side of the Dwarf's wide, hairy face with a wet thud. Jumal kicked it back viciously into the smoke-obscured crowd of its own people, disengaging with haste to join Tar Feng behind him as the smog encroached on his position. Ratnik gutted his opponent with his cutlass – a low blow for their stomachs were close to the ground over their short, stumpy legs and their big, wide feet – and joined his comrade in falling back.

As he retreated, back-stepping so as to keep an eye on the crafty Dwarves, Jumal suddenly leapt with fear as a green glob of energy whizzed closely past him, sizzling the hair on his arm as it went, to smack into a body within the smoke, sending a Dwarf hurtling.

Jumal spun hastily as more of the jade globules zapped by him and saw Tar Feng shooting the magical attacks from his wooden shepherd crook. More scared now than he had been when fighting the Dwarves, Jumal hurried to the demented old man's side, wondering how in the seas the old man could see well enough to aim with his blind eyes. He knew the answer, though. Magic, he thought, and his skin crawled. Truth be told, the magic shook the pirate more than the Dwarves in many ways.

The Dwarves were simple flesh and blood enemies. Wizardry made his skin crawl, and Jumal had believed, until he had met Tar Feng, that it had been completely eradicated from the world, as he had been led to believe all his life. Every story he had ever heard involving magic, growing up among the pirates and sailors on the docks of Kauapunki-Meren – sometimes known as Swash Isle – concerned an evil Sorcerer, who usually ended up killing himself through his own insanity and wild, uncontrollable magic.

So, the Chilpaean found himself growing more and more concerned about the presence of the Tzunese Wizard. Jumal could not bring himself to trust the old man, though he began to wonder if he should, since they were on the same side, undertaking the same mission, and since it was evident Tar Feng was trying his best to aid the young men's escape, covering them every step of the way with magical blasts.

When he reached him, Jumal slapped Tar Feng on the shoulder – an easy task, for the Tzunese man was short and wizened – and said with a slight pant, "Tank you, old man."

The Wizard beamed back at him like a delighted child and rested a hand on Jumal's arm for a moment. Then, he turned to business. "Alright, scoundrels, a job well done I would say, hmm? What say we get out of here now?" The Freemen readily nodded their agreement. "Yes, yes, well then, let's go!"

The Wizard set off at a run that was barely faster than a brisk walk for the younger men, but they followed him at his own pace, at his side every step of the way, wondering at their choice of direction. There were houses and pillars on all sides of them, and the water tank in the city centre reared up in front of them, but the area was clear. As the others in the group had discovered, the Dwarves were currently cowering in terror from the magical blasts, sand and smoke. Still, the Wizard and pirates hurried, their own fear driving them on.

After a short time, Tar Feng raised a wrinkled arm to point, the bones around his thin wrist clacking against one another as they swung. Jumal flinched at the sound, but then followed the Wizard's finger. It pointed to a huge building to the side of the monumental water tank in the centre of the city; something they had missed whilst coming down the lift. The building nestled among the houses was like an oak amid acorns, and – whilst it did not have the same height as the pillars – it stood plenty tall in the dwarfed corsairs' eyes. It was made of a different rock than the houses, darker in colour, and the whole thing was circular in structure.

"Look there, boys," said Tar Feng in his unnerving, whispery voice.

"What is that?" asked Ratnik, gaping in awe.

"What is it?" Jumal repeated his friend's question, keeping his voice quiet.

"I believe, cads, that it is an arena!" the Tzunese Wizard answered in a dramatic whisper. "Come!"

The old man hobbled off swiftly in the direction of the grand arena of *Dwarhummer,* and the buccaneers quickly followed.

Once in the shadow of the enormous structure, the trio spotted two dwarvic guards brave enough to remain at their posts, despite the word of magic afoot spreading through the subterranean city like wildfire. As they jogged closer, Ratnik pulled ahead to study their foes and adjusted his assessment accordingly. The two guards were sweating, licking their lips and visibly shaking at the knees at the thought of facing a Wizard.

So, on impulse, Ratnik put away his cutlass as he drew near and slowed to a purposeful walk. He threw back his head, thrust forward his chin, looked down his nose with wide mad eyes at the Dwarves in his path and began to gesticulate wildly with both arms and hum mumbo jumbo in a deep, foreboding voice that rose and fell like the ages of time themselves – or so feared the dwarvic guards, who took to their heels in mortal dread, while the trio in their wake shared a good chuckle.

"Brilliant, scallywag!" complimented Tar Feng warmly.

"What can I say," responded Ratnik modestly. "Spur of the moment."

"Spurred dem away, alright," grunted Jumal with a golden grin.

Tar Feng led the boys to the huge metal door, which the guards had heretofore protected, where he turned to face them.

"Listen closely, curs. I need you to remain out here now and guard this door against all-comers, so that I can escape when the time comes. I will not be gone long – and when I return, be ready to run, for I will not be alone in fleeing this place."

A mischievous grin crept over his golden face as the eccentric Wizard did a bone-jangling little jig, before turning to the great door to the arena.

*

Upon seeing the monsters that looked like giant *Rodici* break free from the great circular arena, Fyrstsvard's group of mercenaries cursed almost simultaneously – though with varied inflection, tongue and content – and quickened their step until they were in a flat out sprint around the perimeter of the city, along the smooth-bricked road.

The freed beasts were, in fact, a mutant race of *Rodici* that had developed even deeper underground. The Dwarves had come across them during excavations and had, at first, been terrified and repelled by them. They had decided not to tangle with them head-on again, for many lives had been lost in that brief encounter, but – with a new goal in mind – some Dwarves had later been given the mission of luring one such beast away from the others and somehow capturing it.

With a great deal of rope, trickery and an unseemly amount of sedative, the seventeenth group of Dwarves tasked to this had been able to succeed. After that, they had captured more over the years, so as to hold bloodletting shows for their own people, wherein the starved *Rodici* mutants would fight against one another for the Dwarves' entertainment. It had become a popular tradition over the years in *Dwarhummer* culture.

The mutants varied in height from eight to fifteen feet, Fyrstsvard guessed, glancing at them. They had the ability to stand upright on their enormous, clawed feet, unlike the smaller *Rodici.* Their equivalencies of hands were smaller than their feet, though still had deadly claws. Their stunted snouts were full of long, pointy teeth and culminated in many pairs of protruding pink, fleshy appendages that wiggled like fat little worms where a nose should have been.

These fleshy appendages served as an extremely sensitive touch organ to help them dig through the underground that was their home. They had grown to need such specialisations over the years as a species, for – like their smaller *Rodici* counterparts – they were eyeless. Most had rat tails, though a few did not. Some were hairless and white like the *Rodici,* but some had mottled, patchy fur over their frames. It was apparent that the beasts had virtually no intelligence or group mind, for each one set out from the arena in a different direction, looking for nothing but revenge and food.

The monsters bellowed and screamed so loudly that the mercenaries flinched. Upon hearing the raucous bestial roars echoing around the city, the Dwarves began to poke their heads out of their stone houses to find the source of the ruckus. Fyrstsvard swiftly unsheathed the blade he had put away whilst running, just in time to smack an unsuspecting Dwarf out of the way on his mad dash.

Hundreds of bearded dwarvic heads could be seen looking out of windows from their abodes in each and every pillar that the group ran past, but it was those living on the ground that were the primary problem, for – as the group smashed and hacked their way past the emerging Dwarves at a sprint – more and more appeared from their dwellings ahead of the band. It was becoming clear that there would soon be too many for the mercenaries to run past, and then they would be in real trouble.

The great beasts unleashed by Tar Feng from the arena, however, were having an effect of their own. They had begun a savage rampage throughout the city, destroying houses in rage tantrums, raking the monumental pillars with their great claws and taking their vengeance on their captors by scooping up and devouring each and every Dwarf upon which they could lay their giant claws.

Whole parts of the city were soon in ruins, and dwarvic screams could be heard echoing from every sepia wall of the grand cavern as their lives were torn apart by the monsters that they themselves had brought into the centre of their city.

As fortune would have it, one such hairy *Rodici* mutant came screaming and crashing through the city toward Fyrstsvard and his remaining group, perpendicular to the path they trod.

"Halt!" shouted the Knight, holding up a clenched fist upon seeing the beast out of the corner of his eye.

A bare heartbeat after the group stopped, the mutant creature tore up the area into which they would have run. They stood stock-still in the centre of the path and watched the nightmare barrel into the wall to their left before their eyes, crushing against it a litter of bodies and debris. Luckily, it turned its monstrosity of a head to its right and so never noticed the intruders. Instead, it began a violent massacre of the Dwarves, who had only a moment before threatened to block the way of the mercenaries. Bellowing, ripping, smashing and shredding, the great beast made its destructive way through the ancient city of Dwarves, leaving only carnage in its wake.

The mercenaries with Fyrstsvard surveyed the scene in shocked silence. Nothing stirred in the vicinity now, except death twitches and the slow pooling of pale blood. They watched the furry back of the *Rodici* mutant wordlessly as it stormed away from them.

Finally, into the stillness, Heldig said, "Ferrymen's nuts, that was close!"

The group heaved a sigh of relief as one as the danger receded.

"We got lucky," responded Fyrstsvard briskly, mind turning back to business. "We must remain wary – especially now that those things are wandering around in here." He looked around for a moment, before spotting a likely-looking smashed house, where the debris looked as easily climbable as a staircase.

"Kamilah," he pointed, "could you climb up there and see if you can get a look around? See if we can avoid more of those monsters and whether we're getting any closer to another of those lifts."

She started up the pile of refuse, and he called after her, "Look out for Tar Feng and the pirates, too." He turned to Heldig, whose brow had creased with worry at mention of his comrades. "I'm sure they're fine. I suspect that crazy old kook had something to do with the release of those beasts, and I'd love to wring an explanation out of his scrawny little throat!"

"Heh, well if he is responsible, he just saved our hides!" observed Heldig.

"Yes," Fyrstsvard admitted grudgingly, "but the day is not over yet, and that is unlikely to be the last we see of those monsters."

"Don't be so gloomy, Svard," Heldig rebuked him, putting his hands behind his head and stretching his back. "Life is a carnival, don't you know? Filled with games of chance. It doesn't matter whether you win or lose, 'cos we all lose eventually. It's about how you play."

"Knight!" Kamilah distracted them by sliding down the debris of the house she had just climbed, smoothly reaching the floor in a cloud of dust. "I see no Wizard, no pirates," she said first of all with an apologetic look around. "Monsters all spread out over the city. One we saw cleared a path ahead of us – and I saw chains!" She said this last excitedly, and it took Fyrstsvard a moment to understand her meaning. As comprehension dawned on him, she clarified, "Chains, Knight! Chains for lift platform!"

"Where?" he asked, relieved.

Kamilah pointed along the path they already followed. "Ahead!"

The group raced forwards with renewed vigour, their goal in sight once again. After a short while of running along in the bloody, corpse-strewn wake of the uncaged monster, the companions rounded a bend in the path and were at last rewarded with the sight of a lift at the wall's base to take them on to the next stage of their mission. It was not just one platform to the side of the road, however; instead, there was a row of a score of lifts. Since this was the control centre of dwarvic life, they evidently had numerous mechanisms to take great numbers of their people to and from their work deep in the dark bowels of the earth, Fyrstsvard figured.

The platform closest to the fast-approaching mercenary band was clear of activity; however, the same could not be said for all the lifts in the row. In many, desperate Dwarves tried to barrel their way in to escape by the dozen, only to be confronted by the enormous, hairy mutant creature that had cleared the way for the ragtag group earlier.

The mutant *Rodici* stood, blocking the way to several lifts, clawing and devouring the torrent of Dwarves that surrounded it and hacked at it manically with their axes. Some of the Dwarves noticed the mercenary group, but it was clear they had a great deal more on their minds than the sudden appearance of mysterious intruders, and no Dwarf paid them any heed.

Fyrstsvard and his companions took advantage of the situation, hastily getting on the nearest platform where Egobal began to tug at a chain by the side of the lift that looked to be the counterpart to that which they had used to descend earlier.

These lifts, however, were controlled from the top rather than the bottom, since this was where the majority of the dwarvic population lived and, as such, was where they had centralized control as much as possible. The group deduced this when they saw one brave Dwarf run to a control panel on the other side of a metal railing, opposite the row of platforms. The panel was a metal structure as high as a Dwarf, running parallel to and as long as the row of lifts opposite, with levers poking out from the inner mechanics at even intervals, each lever opposite a lift.

The brave Dwarf cranked back the heavy lever opposite the platform on which his friends were crowded, and with a jump and a clank, that lift began to descend. The brave Dwarf, however, was not so lucky as to escape with his friends. As he ran and tried to jump onto the descending platform, the *Rodici* mutant skewered him mid-air with its long claws and, with one bloody flick of its wrist, shook him loose like an unwanted parasite.

"El Vandu deals a terrible hand!" cursed Heldig, eyes wide at the display. "One of us needs to get over there!" He pointed at the control panel, where the levers were.

Izdaju happened to glance the opposite way, back the way they had come, and his eyes almost popped out of his skull in shock and fear. Another giant beast was approaching from that direction; huge, hairless and white, with slavering jaws and a long whipping tail. In moments, they would be trapped between the two mutant creatures.

"Look to the rear!" cried the Nomad, brandishing his scimitars.

Seeing the peril, Fyrstsvard did not hesitate. He vaulted the rail surrounding the platform and sprinted for the levers. His quick movements, however, attracted the attention of the hollering hairless monster that approached. As the swordsman reached the panel of levers, the mutated beast turned toward him, intent on eating the quick-moving man.

The remaining Dwarves crowded around the platforms, having also noticed the approach of the second *Rodici* beast, redoubled their efforts against the furry legs of the first. Though they could reach no higher than its waist, dozens of them cut at it until its legs were nothing but bloody ribbons over bone, and the great creature was brought to its knees, where it was soon swarmed and sliced to bits by the grim and desperate Dwarves.

Meanwhile, as the hairless mutant newcomer closed in on Fyrstsvard, Heldig leapt to the rescue, running from the platform out into the open, shouting and jeering with every step.

"Hey, you! Yeah, you – you lousy, stinking, hairless sack of filth!"

The beast growled malevolently as it turned its eyeless face toward the lone pirate.

"The Dwarves over there took care of your buddy," shouted Heldig mockingly, "which makes me think you're not so tough after all, are ya? You scummy, rat-faced fuc-"

The hairless monster roared defiantly and cut off the pirate's tirade by spinning surprisingly quickly and smacking him back into the crowd of Dwarves with a whip of its wormlike tail.

Heldig's distraction, however, had given Fyrstsvard the time he needed to find the correct lever and pull it. He did so as Heldig was knocked from his feet, and the platform, where the rest of the group was waiting, began to descend with a clunk and a rattle of chains.

"Hurry!" Kamilah shouted to them.

She shot a few arrows into the crowd of Dwarves to help out, though all too quickly the lift had dropped too far for her to do so any longer. Izdaju watched with sword at the ready, though his eyes were directed towards keeping back any Dwarves that might hinder their descent. Luckily, the city's residents were well-distracted by the ruination of their homes.

With the red-bearded pirate down, the hairless mutant turned once again on the Knight by the levers. Heldig got to his feet amid a pile of concussed and confused Dwarves, whom he had barrelled into, leaning on several of them in the process despite voluble protest, though in the scuffle and tangle of bodies none could reach or swing a weapon.

Then, with a gruff, "Sorry, lads!" he staggered off, leaving them bewildered. They had no interest in following the old pirate Captain, however; only in escaping from the freed monsters that they had caged for so long.

Heldig limped back to confront the raging creature that was so intent on eating the Knight and shouted at it again, more tiredly this time.

"Hey, arsehole! Remember me, eh? Guess what – you can't get rid of me that easily, you limp-pricked git!"

It worked. The pirate's booming voice visibly irritated the great beast, as though it understood the slanderous nature of his words. It turned on him, long pink tongue lolling out to drool in anticipation.

Fyrstsvard – disregarded by the huge mutant as it turned away from him towards his companion – abandoned the lever panel, ran up to the beast and, with one smooth swing of his shining longsword, lopped off the *Rodici* mutant's long pink tail just as it was about to disembowel Heldig.

The creature shrieked horribly in agony and threw itself flat. Its whole body writhed violently as it sought a way to ease the pain, but there was no such way. Wriggling around, it tore down several dwarvic houses, and then the beast began to roll aimlessly, screaming like a banshee, crushing everything beneath it and spraying pigment-less blood from its tail stump everywhere it went.

Fyrstsvard ran to help the injured Heldig stumble toward the platform where the others had descended, for the giant creature was rolling towards the injured pirate. The two cumbersomely staggered to the lift and looked down. They could still see their comrades, but it was a long drop to the platform. The Knight looked up to see yet another mutant approaching to the side of the one destructively rolling around in pain. When he looked back, Heldig was already sprawled on the platform below.

"Time to go!" he muttered and leapt from the ledge after the pirate. He landed staggeringly on his feet, before falling on his backside. "Oof," he exhaled, rubbing his legs.

The others helped him up, whilst Heldig sat down in the corner of the platform, leaning against a rail. The ageing sailor looked worn and haggard, his face red and his breathing heavy.

Seeing Fyrstsvard's concerned look, he coughed weakly and said, "I'll be alright … don't worry. Just need a … minute or two to catch my breath."

"We should get that leg bound up before we go any further," replied Fyrstsvard, taking a deep breath to slow his hammering heart.

He tore off a strip of his tunic and handed it to Kamilah, who was hovering over Heldig's outstretched leg, examining the wound.

"It is not deep cut. You should be good," she announced, after sniffing it. She began to bandage the leg with Fyrstsvard's tunic strip. "I would advise rest, but no can do, eh?" She smiled slightly as she tied the knot around the corsair's leg.

Heldig returned the smile wanly. "I'll be fine," he repeated. "Thank you – Kamilah, was it?" She nodded. "Thank you, Kamilah."

"Not as young as you used to be, eh, Heldig?" Jumal teased him with a wide grin.

"Hey, shut it, you!" Heldig retorted, coughing heavily afterwards but smiling at his comrade. "I've still enough vigour in me to show you young pups how it's done!"

"How what's done – falling on your arse?" asked Ratnik innocently.

"Oh, you dolts!" Heldig scorned them affectionately.

This platform descended faster than those before, and the band silently prepared for whatever lay below. With luck, they thought, it might be an end to their downward travels, if they found what they were looking for.

Eventually, after a long descent, the lift reached the bottom of its journey. The group emerged onto a wide sandstone ledge, which extended off to either side of them and looked out over a steep slope leading down to an unfathomable hole in the earth, only vaguely lit by the silkworms and their glistening threads hanging from the ceiling above like tiny icicles.

"So, this is where they came from," Fyrstsvard muttered, stroking his beard, thinking of the mutant *Rodici.*

He looked off to each side. There appeared to be nothing of value on the left, but on the right was a narrow stone staircase, which led down the steep slope, doubling back on itself again and again as it led deeper into the crevasse.

Fyrstsvard pointed to it. "Looks like we must plummet down another godforsaken hole, my friends." He sounded less than enthused. The Knight enjoyed the daylight, he now realised, and hated being stuck underground, further and further away from it.

The ragtag group, which seemed to grow smaller with each level it descended, set off down the treacherous, winding staircase, the worms' luminescence growing dimmer with each step.

7

Drowned

Ratnik's blood pulsed alarmingly loudly in his ears – its volume matched only by the sound of his own harsh, ragged breathing – drowning out all sounds of pursuers, though he was still confident they were there and dared not slow to be sure. The taste of metal filled his mouth, his lungs burned, his arms pumped furiously, aflame with ache, and his legs weighed like lead as he sprinted after Jumal and the foreigner, Tar Feng.

How the little Wizard was suddenly so much quicker than him, he would never know, he thought, his vision narrowing to a pinprick in which the old man cavorted. He could not bring himself to hate or be mad at the old kook who had found some way to free the giant rampaging monsters from their cages in the arena, but he was not at all certain that liberating the beasts had been a wise move, for they had barrelled out of the arena, shattering the doors and thresholds as they went and proceeded to behold everything that moved with indiscriminate hate and hunger.

Their long, vicious claws scooped up Dwarves in droves, tearing them apart like unruly children with toys, only to drop them again into unmerciful maws. When the pirates had witnessed Tar Feng sprinting, screaming, from the monsters' midst, missing the myriad scooping claws by some miracle, they had hardly needed his encouragement to run.

The young pirate had always hated running, had always preferred the smoothness, luxury and ease of sailing. He had been sailing for as long as he could remember, though the boats in which he did so had thankfully grown larger over the years. He had been sailing under Heldig's Captaincy for fifteen years now and had enjoyed most every minute of it. He even enjoyed the dirty and foul jobs which most people avoided, for he knew they needed doing. Heldig was a great Captain, in his opinion, and had done right by him and Jumal so far.

He wondered how his Captain was getting on, but then he heard the bestial growls and barks of the *Rodici* thundering down on him from behind – the fact that he could hear them over his own din indicating their proximity – and fear lent him wings.

He wondered then if any of the giant mutant monsters that the insane little Wizard had unleashed were following them, for he feared that if they were, the small group of three was certainly doomed. He could not risk a look behind though, for it would cost him valuable time and speed, and so he prayed silently, whilst his feet pounded along the dwarvic path.

'Merejulanna,' he invoked the Goddess of the Sea, whom he had always considered to be his patron Goddess, as did most sailors. 'I know I am not currently in your domain, but I had always hoped that I would meet my fate in your cool, soothing waters. I beg of you, Goddess, if you can hear me, don't let me die down here! I want to see the sun glinting on the ocean many mornings more before I rest, so please keep me alive! Don't let the monsters eat me!'

Horrific, gory images of his own death at the hands of the grubby little Dwarves and their monstrous pets plagued Ratnik's mind as he ran. He was barely able to see through his own veil of terror save enough to follow his companions.

Tar Feng shouted reedy instructions to Jumal who ran in front, directing him as though he knew the layout of the city by heart. The Chilpaean followed the orders unerringly – diving down this street and that, zigzagging through the metropolis – putting his life in the old man's eccentric hands, for he had not led them astray so far.

Soon, the Tzunese Wizard had them back on the road that ran around the outer rim of the city, albeit on the opposite side of the subterranean civilisation from Fyrstsvard and the others. Once there, they had but to run until they came across the series of lifts as had Fyrstsvard's half of the group.

Jumal shouted for joy when he saw the platforms ahead of him, but as he came closer – his long, hope-bolstered legs eating up the distance with ease – he saw that every one of the lifts had either been lowered, as in most cases, or else destroyed by the giant mutants. A giant rat-like carcass with a severed tail lay on one of the wrecked lifts amid dozens of bloody dwarvic bodies. It looked as though it had rolled there in its death throes and mangled the platform beneath it.

"Gastar's balls!" yelled Jumal angrily with a stomp, seeing his way blocked.

He took a step nearer to the beast with the tail stump, only to discover it was not dead when it suddenly swung its head around and tried to take a bit out of him. The Chilpaean sprang back with a cry, but lashed out reflexively with his dwarvic axe and sank its blade deep into the pink, fleshy appendages wiggling on the end of the mutant's snout. The beast screeched again and again, high like a wounded eagle, and the pirate guessed the nose must be especially sensitive. Striking there again seemed to paralyse the creature, so – leaving his axe embedded in its snout for a moment – Jumal took his cutlass in both hands and rammed it down through the mutant's skull with a grunt.

Panting and shaking, dotted with hot, white ichor, Jumal turned to see how his companions were faring behind him and took an involuntary step back with wide eyes. They were catching up quickly, but it was what ran after them that scared the Chilpaean.

Chasing his friend and the Wizard were three huge, hairy mutants – as well as a hairless one – bellowing like thunder as they came. Beside them raced a veritable swarm of the smaller rat-dogs, slobbering as they hunted their next meal without the restraint of their masters' leashes for once. An avalanche of *Rodici* savagery was descending upon Jumal at a violent pace with a deafening din of howling, barking, roaring and snarling. Now that the young pirate was stood still in shock, he could actually feel the ground beneath his feet shaking with the pounding of clawed feet. All he could think was that he had better be paid handsomely when this job was done, because no amount of gold was worth this.

Tar Feng's wispy shouting reached Jumal through the fog of fear that held him frozen.

"Jump in the hole!" the crazed old Wizard was shouting desperately, his skinny arms flailing and his bones clanking loudly as he ran. "Jump in the lift hole! Jump in the nearest hole!"

He repeated his instructions time and again until Jumal made his decision. There was nothing else for it; a bestial horde the like of which he had never dreamed possible came pelting toward him and there was no escape, save to trust the old man who wore bones for jewellery. Jumal was starting to wish he had never left Swash Isle.

He turned around once more, stepped past the mutant he had killed and set off toward the rest of the lifts with Tar Feng not far behind. Ratnik brought up the rear, his feet flying with stamina and speed he had never known before, but which circumstance had forced upon him. He was almost certain he would have a heart attack if he did survive this. Then, he heard the Wizard shouting for them to jump down the hole where the lift had already descended, which would – in all probability, he thought – lead to certain death after a fall of a few hundred feet. That was when he knew for sure he would have a heart attack.

"Fantastic," the buccaneer grunted. The taste of blood in his mouth seemed to be building, and his limbs burned as if on fire, but he did not slow.

It was as the three of them hurtled toward the empty lift-space – and as Fyrstsvard and his companions carefully traversed the narrow steps leading down deep into the ground on the level below – that a small contingent of enormous *Rodici* mutants was able to tear through the thick metal lining of the enormous water tank at the heart of *Dwarhummer* civilisation with their huge claws in a concerted effort.

The great concentration of water contained within sprayed from the sudden leak with such force that it ripped the tank asunder. It mangled the metal, bowled over the great mutants that had set it free and set about rampaging and ravishing the city it had once nurtured. It tore through the streets, destroying everything in its path, unstoppable in its vastness. It wrecked houses, Dwarves and giant mutant *Rodici* alike, taking them up into its watery maw to be engulfed and carried off to distant corners.

The deadly cleansing water chased after the three companions like a beast on a hunt, frothing at the mouth as it anticipated swallowing its meal whole. Its roar as it stormed over the hard ground rivalled that of any creature. It deafened the trio hurrying towards the lift, until its swishing, bubbling bellows were all they could hear, growing ever louder as it drew in for the kill.

Ratnik – terrified at first that the ear-splitting roar signalled the arrival of some new, horrible, gurgling monster – chanced a look back at the doom that breathed loudly down his neck. He quickly looked forwards once more and pelted on, faster than he had known he could, though his straining muscles screamed at him to just give up and embrace the watery death that pursued him. He had seen it devour the enormous mutants chasing them like they were aperitifs, and now the surf was looking for its main course.

Looking up from his numbly pounding feet, Ratnik beheld the Wizard gesturing and pointing wildly as he ran, chanting in a voice unlike his own. In cadences increasingly deep and rumbling like a rockslide, the old man repeated words known to no man or woman in the mercenary band, for they were spoken in the language of magic, a secret heavily guarded by his teachers at the Chi Academy in Quing Tzu. The mantra rose in volume with every arcane syllable he uttered in his shockingly robust voice, until it felt like it pierced the pirates' eardrums with its intensity and drowned out even the gushing roar of the following flood.

"Herathrea lampini-hrellel!"

Jumal had almost reached the first open gap in the middle of the row of lifts. He eyed the square hole unenthusiastically as he drew near it. He too risked a glance behind him and saw the wall of water threatening to engulf them all and Tar Feng screaming vehemently.

"Jump in the blasted hole, seadog!"

Jumal reached the empty aperture in the ground where the middle lift in the row had already been dropped, but he could not jump. He teetered on the edge of the precipice for a moment, and then the flood came and swept them all up in its embrace and dragged them down into the deep, hesitation be damned.

*

Darkness grew with each step, leaving to the imagination the sinister scuffle of feet that broke the eerie lifelessness of the echoing caves. The silkworms were distant specks of light overhead now, like far-off stars. The stone steps underfoot crumbled into powder around the edges with age, making every footfall delicate with hands rubbing along the rough, sandy walls for support.

With a raised fist and a low shout, Heldig halted the group's slow, careful treading down the narrow steps leading into the bottomless, musty depths of the dark world beneath *Dwarhummer.*

"Wait!" he said, a confused look on his face. He glanced at his arm and then looked up. "I'm sure I just felt a couple drops of water! How in all the oceans can that be?"

He looked up in time to witness the deluge unleashed by the *Rodici* mutants in *Dwarhummer* crash down on the band from above with torrential force. It swept the entire group clean off their precarious perches on the escarpment where the narrow stairs wound their tight way down, drowning their screams. Some of the mercenaries were scraped and rammed against the steps brutally by the flailing water. They hollered incoherently in panic – those that could get their heads above water long enough to draw breath – but the water cared nothing for their fear and dragged them down with ungentle arms. Bumping, bouncing, grazing and spluttering, the comrades made their way down to the bottom of the pit.

Fortunately for them, myriad ugly and enormous *Rodici* mutants had assembled at the bottom of the long descent with dumb curiosity as to what caused such a bestial roar in their caves. The dim-witted, fleshy creatures provided ample cushioning for the group to survive their fall from the stairs; the monsters watched their demise drop upon them and did not move for the wonder of it, even after it crushed them.

The mayhem of the water ride did not stop there, however; the mercenary crew was swept away into the mutants' labyrinth of tunnels. Luckily, the entrances for the tunnels were, at first, so large that the group was not separated further during their mad swim at breakneck speed.

Soon, however, no one in the group was able to keep track of anyone else's progress or position, for they could barely keep hold of their own breath as they were buffeted about like ragdolls underwater, their world having become a bubbling realm of despair. They were slammed into the walls and the rocky floor by the pounding surf and were only occasionally and unexpectedly swept up to the surface to draw desperately needed breath.

The situation worsened, although how it did so was more or less unknown to the mercenaries themselves. They were swept from the open-topped passages into the underground warrens dug out by the giant *Rodici*, where the flood could fill the tunnels, and air became a luxury of better days gone by.

Every one of them genuinely considered that his or her demise was at hand as the water kept them in the dark of its shifting depths, where it could batter at each of their resolves individually, picking them apart and making them feel more alone, closer to death than ever before. Their bodies ached and bled, and their lungs burned as if on fire, especially the armour-laden Knight.

Fyrstsvard – barely able to reach the surface for breath at all throughout their watery escapade – could hold his breath no longer once they were dragged underground, and he gasped in what felt like painfully hot liquid. His lungs filled, his eyes swam, his head spun dizzily with pain, and darkness overcame him. The surge dragged him along the rocky floor in its wake like a ritual degradation; its final humiliation for the once-honoured Knight.

Eventually, the band shot out of the seemingly endless underground tunnels. They were suddenly aware of something other than bashing and buffeting water, and as they flew into open air, they gasped in much-needed breaths before plummeting immediately into water again.

This time, however, the mercenaries were soon washed up on a dirty, rocky subterranean shore. Kamilah was the first to emerge from the water and scramble onto the rock. She sat for a moment, shocked and ecstatic to have survived at all, and took never-before-known pleasure in breathing in the dank, musty air. She had always pictured living out her days in the vast expanses of the desert, beneath the sun, close to the Gods. Death down here in this hole was anathema to her.

Once the shock had worn off, she looked around in wonder. The expanse of water into which they had fallen from the tunnels looked to be an underground lake, whose waters glowed ethereally with all the colours of the rainbow reflected in shimmering spangled patterns upon the sandy walls and ceiling, lighting the massive cavern quite clearly. Staring hard at the colourful water, Kamilah spotted shining, darting movements in its depths and smiled in childlike fascination.

The lake's fluorescence was produced by luminescent fish, all of whom glowed vividly with a different colour to the next. She wondered how such beauty had come to exist in such a dark place and recognised that, somehow, the marine life shone *because* of the pall. The two – light and darkness – had evolved side by side, inseparable.

The others in the group, propelled by the spurting of the water that had dragged them down so far, were washing up on either side of the young Nomad woman as she ogled. Kamilah was pleased to see that her husband-to-be, Izdaju, had survived – though he was proving troublesome on this quest, she thought, giving him a small smile.

Jerking, awkward movement from the far left of the shore caught her eye. She turned from Izdaju, who was dragging himself out of the water, to see Egobal, the desert man, struggling mightily with a heavy weight of some sort. As Kamilah ran closer, she saw what it was: Fyrstsvard's limp form.

"Knight!" she exclaimed without thought.

She ran and helped Egobal drag the armoured body up out of the water onto the rock, but as she knelt by him and rolled him onto his back to look at his face, she saw that his cheeks were deathly white and he was not breathing. She clapped her hand to her mouth before she could utter any further exclamation.

"He's dead! Knight is dead!" she said with a breaking voice after a moment, removing her hand from her face.

She caught Egobal's eye. He looked miserable, his robes and beard dripping on the rock, but more than that, he looked saddened at their loss. She looked back to the waxy, yet handsome face of the Knight.

Suddenly, Kamilah was grabbed roughly from behind. She instinctively tried to turn and break free from her aggressor, but the hands that clasped her were large and strong and she could do nothing from her kneeling position.

The young Nomad woman was thrown easily aside, for she was not the target. Heldig, the perpetrator, swiftly knelt by Fyrstsvard's side. His thick fingers struggled to unbuckle the thick straps of the Knight's cuirass, and he removed it as fast as he could. With it off, the pirate began to beat the dead man's chest with his fist rhythmically. Then, he locked his lips on Fyrstsvard's and, holding the Knight's nose, blew air into the man's lungs repeatedly. Then, he returned to pounding the Knight's sternum.

Kamilah watched in fascination, for drowning-related resuscitations were not common in the desert where she lived.

Fyrstsvard lay still and white, until finally Heldig gave out an anguished bellow, which would have frightened off a bear, and hung his head to hide the tears. Kamilah's dropped unnoticed.

"Dammit, man!" said Heldig hoarsely. "We were supposed to get out of here together! Goddamn honourable bastard – just wake up!"

With his last shout, the old corsair thumped the Knight's chest with all that he had left to muster. Fyrstsvard's body suddenly convulsed. Water spewed from his mouth with violent coughs and retches as he doubled over and then rolled onto his hands and knees to expel the rest of the liquid from his lungs.

"Fyrstsvard!" exclaimed Heldig gratefully, a wide smile appearing beneath his beard.

"Knight!" Kamilah whispered.

She closed her eyes and sighed with relief. Though she had only met the man some two weeks before, she had come to respect both his leadership and what she saw as his knightly oddities.

The Knight's insides burned as they heaved, his head throbbed abominably, and his blinking eyes could see so little he worried he had been blinded, but he was alive. He could feel cold, wet, uneven rock beneath his fingertips and knees, and strangely it was the most wonderful sensation Fyrstsvard had ever experienced.

Once the painful coughs abated, the Knight rolled tiredly onto his back and glanced up at the relieved and waiting face of his companion, Heldig.

"I wasn't sure I was going to be able to bring you back there, you crazed lubber," Heldig told him shakily, clasping his hand.

"I'm glad you did," croaked Fyrstsvard, his voice weak. "Thank you."

"It is good to see you in the land of the living once more, my friend," offered Egobal from nearby.

"Thank you," the Knight murmured again, before coughing sharply and laying his head back on the ground.

His mind spun like a whirlpool, whilst waves – created by the propulsion of the water surge that had brought them down to the lake – lapped placidly at the rocky shore by his feet.

He did not have long to rest, however. After a minute of quiet recuperation, during which the mercenaries took a moment to marvel at the miracle of shiny fish, Izdaju appeared from behind them, where he had gone off to search the cavern. The group turned to regard him. He appeared indifferent to Fyrstsvard's improved health and flashed Kamilah only a brief glance from under heavy eyebrows.

In a deep, foreboding growl, low despite the roar of the water still gushing out of the warren into the lake, the Nomad told them, "You will all want to see this."

8

Baldr's Safe

"Ha, take that!"

"Ow, you big –"

"Ooh, temper, temper, little brother!"

"I'll show you temper!"

"Haha! Gotta stay calm in battle, you know. Hyah – or else someone will get you just like that!"

"Ow, my bum!"

"Shouldn't have left it unprotected then, should you?"

"That's it! You're going down!"

"Big words, little man. Show me what you've got."

The rap and clatter of wooden swords echoed loudly in the brisk morning air as two brothers sparred together with lead-weighted training weapons in a granite courtyard high up in a tiered city.

Both were powerfully-built young men with bull necks, thighs like tree trunks, broad shoulders, and thick arms banded with muscle on either side of barrel chests tapering down to narrow waists. Both had wide, flat faces and beards trimmed close to their jawlines, but one had bright red hair and blue eyes, and the other straw-blonde hair and green eyes. The chestnut-haired, older brother wore woollen trousers, fur-wrapped boots, and a black linen tunic marked with an eye beneath a jagged peak – the insignia of a member of the King's elite bodyguard – over which the beige fur of a great cat hung over his shoulders and down his back, while the younger wore only a pale tunic, breeches and leather boots.

"Ha!" the red-haired brother laughed at the other's expense, having rapped him about the head with the wooden sword. "Too slow, Saul!"

The blonde brother, Saul, grinned ruefully as he rubbed his head. "You just got lucky, Rork, don't get cocky!"

So saying, he levelled his wooden sword at his brother and jabbed it at his torso. Rork dodged to the side, laughing as the other swung to chop at his legs. He stepped back and then kicked his brother's swiping arm, overbalancing him.

"Careful," Rork warned, chortling. "Don't overcommit!"

Determined, Saul sprang up and charged his older brother with a flurry of fierce strikes aimed high and low alike, but Rork, having taught him the patterns, blocked them all. On attempting to block the final blow, though, his sword found nothing but air, and he realised too late that Saul had altered the pattern on the last blow, ducking low instead of striking high.

"Oof!" Rork wheezed as his brother's sword smacked him in the stomach, and he doubled over while Saul cheered and waved his sword in the sky. When Saul had finished taking a single spin, he was staring down the length of a wooden sword at his brother's stern face.

"Do not give up the battle until you know it is won," Rork warned in a deep, mock-ominous tone, and Saul gulped. Then, the red-haired brother grinned, relaxed and lowered his sword. "That was a nice move, Saul. Well done. Let's go again."

The sun shone ghost-pale in a cottony sky above them. It was summer in the Highlands of Fjelburg, and it was as warm as the country ever became, though still folk circumventing the courtyard wore wool and fur.

The brothers sparred on the highest tier of the city, at eye level with snowy peaks and clouds. The tier was commonly called the King's Bastion, and the city had been known for all time as Baldr's Safe. It was the hereditary capital of the Stonebrows, the Kings of Fjelburg; a vast fortress containing a maze of metropolis, nestled in a crook in the mountains, carved into the rock between the great ranges, the Great Divide to the east and Skalda's Teeth to the north. The city was home to King Aodh, his twelve wives and some of his twenty six sons, as well as who knew how many daughters.

Beneath the sparrers, the half-moon-shaped city fell away to the south with four tiers spread out beneath theirs, like a massive set of stairs that grew larger as they descended, at the bottom of which a tall, thick, grey wall curved from mountain range to mountain range, encapsulating the city. The tiers allowed those at the top to see not only everything in the city beneath them, but also the picturesque vista looking out over the rugged, rock-pocked fields of the Highlands to the south, for Baldr's Safe was the second northernmost fortification in the country, hidden far away from the Lowlanders and outsiders that lay beyond Titan's Pass and the Great Divide.

The courtyard in which the brothers trained stood on the edge of the tier, so that a single slip could prove fatal. Behind them, set back into the rock of the mountains, was a fortress within a fortress; the seat of the monarch. Grey, granite, squared and relatively unadorned – save for waving banners, patrolled parapets and murder holes – it was an imposing structure and a forbidding prospect to invade.

The tier beneath the fighters was called the Pantheon Level and was filled with colonnaded temples dedicated to all the Gods of the Pantheon. The tier below that was the Warriors' Level, where soldiers who had survived long enough to attain rank took their retirement in luxury. Below them was the Lower Level – sometimes called the Dump – where the most numerous folk lived in close quarters, slime, crime and poverty. The outermost tier of the city was the Garrison Level, where the warriors on duty were posted. This level barred access to the upper city to protect those inside, just in case a foe ever passed the giant, granite wall.

Their father, King Aodh, happened to walk past the sparring brothers, going about his kingly duties, chatting with his attendant. The monarch was even more powerfully built than his sons, though with grey hair. He wore simple garments; a white tunic, dark trousers, boots, and a golden fur mantle speckled with dark rings. His attendant was an ancient, stick-thin man, dressed all in grey. Aodh was busy from dawn till dusk with the tedium of responsibility, but he loved nothing more than to spend time with his boys, and so when he saw them fighting playfully, he stopped to watch for a moment.

Despite his stern, flat face and heavy brow, the King's heart glowed with warmth to see his offspring living life. "Keep your knees bent, Saul! Rork, stop flailing – precision!" he barked at them.

"Yes, father!" they shouted back as one, both fighting more carefully and fiercely under Aodh's watchful eye.

After witnessing a few furious exchanges, the King smilingly stepped in, ignoring his attendant's quiet reminders of his duties. "Let me show you how it's done, lads!" he said in a voice like a hammer on rock. "Saul, fetch me a sword."

Once equipped with a wooden blade like his sons, King Aodh crouched in a fighting stance and grinned at the two of them. "Come on then," he taunted them, "let's see if you can beat your old man!"

Grinning wolfishly back, the two brothers spread out and closed in on their father, knees bent and swords at the ready. Aodh sidestepped a jab from Saul and shoved him away with his free hand, turning to block a low blow from Rork and shoulder-barge him back.

"Come on, lads, don't hold back now!"

Saul sprang up like a cat and Rork steadied himself, and they came again. Aodh blocked an overhand chop from Rork above his head, twizzled his body to the side to dodge a stab of Saul's sword, kicked the younger brother away and pushed Rork back with a show of strength.

"Just because I'm old doesn't mean I'm weak," he said, enjoying himself. "Come on – make me proud and hit me."

Aodh parried a wild swing from Saul and diverted his charge with a nudge, sending him hurtling past, and then jumped back from a body swipe from the older brother, only to step back in with remarkable speed for his bulk and smack his son on the elbow with his sword, making Rork drop his blade.

"Careful, Rork," said Aodh, still smiling. "You are overconfident today."

"As are you."

Aodh was thankful for the cryptic warning, for it meant he turned his head in time to see Saul's swing coming. He ducked and punched his younger son in the stomach, pulling the blow. As Rork picked up his sword and Saul coughed for a moment, leaning on his knees, Aodh stepped away and began to pace around them.

"Don't play with me now, lads," he said cheerfully. "I'm all warmed up, and I don't want you going easy on me. You won't learn anything that way – now, come get me!"

Aodh parried a leaping strike from Rork and spun away from Saul's slash to find space, but they pressed him, Rork chopping at his face, while Saul repositioned himself. Aodh kept moving to keep Rork between them, but the younger brother darted around and almost pronged his father in the belly. Aodh barely swerved his gut enough to avoid it, and then he had to spin away again, or be struck on the head by the elder brother.

Panting slightly now and still smiling, he beckoned to them. Saul charged in more carefully this time, slowing to swing faster and more accurately, and Aodh was pressed back by the ferocity of the assault. The King managed to shove Saul back in time to block a swing from Rork, but then the older brother barged his father as had been done to him, and Aodh staggered back toward the edge of the tier a few scant feet away, beneath which a fifty foot drop ended in hard granite.

Rork's eyes widened in fear as he realised what he had done. He cried and reached out for his father's flailing hands, but he had pushed him too far and – as Aodh stumbled, trying to regain his balance – he drew further away with every step. Time slowed for Rork as he helplessly watched his father backing away towards his doom; his muscles bunched to help, though he knew he could not in time. Suddenly, there was a blur of movement, and Saul lay on top of Aodh in the courtyard, on the edge of the precipice, panting and grinning.

"Got you!" shouted Saul victoriously.

Rork dragged his brother off their father and then tugged the latter to his feet too, his eyebrows meeting in the middle of his face in consternation.

"Are you okay, father?" he asked. "I'm so sorry! I just got caught up in the fight and forgot about the edge – you know I didn't mean for that to happen, don't you? I would never –"

"I know, I know," Aodh interrupted, brushing himself off ruefully. "You would never hurt me on purpose, laddie, I know. Don't beat yourself up; it's fine. It all worked out for the best, thanks to Saul here." He clapped them both on the shoulders and grinned at them, before drawing them in closer to hug the big men, one under each armpit. "I didn't think you'd be able to beat me yet, Saul," he said jokingly. "Maybe I should make *you* my bodyguard."

"Maybe you should!" Saul enthused, and the King laughed.

"Maybe one day, laddie, but you've a ways to go yet. You'll be making your pilgrimage soon," Aodh said, releasing them from his hold and indicating the fawn fur wrapped around Rork's shoulders. "At least I know you'll be ready for that."

"You think so?" asked Saul, starry-eyed.

"I'm sure of it."

"Thank you, father, I won't let you down."

"King Aodh?" the attendant continued to try to attract the King's attention, sidling closer and increasing his volume a little to be audible. "King Aodh? We really must press on, my liege – the armourers are waiting for us, and –"

"Aye, alright," Aodh snapped at the thin man. "I hear you, Breckish." He sighed. "Curse responsibility! Who in their right mind would want this bloody crown?" He touched his fingertips to his grey hair and then remembered he wasn't wearing it. He rarely did, save for on official occasions. "But you are right of course, someone must do these things … and I guess that someone is me. I'm sorry, lads, but it looks like that's all I have time for today. Teach him well, won't you, Rork?"

"Of course, father."

"Good lad. Train hard, my boys; your country needs you."

"Aye, father!" they said together.

"I will see you at dinner tonight. Let's go then, Breckish; mustn't keep the armourers waiting. Come on – keep up!"

After his departure, Saul and Rork stepped back from one another to pant for a moment, sweat trickling down their faces. "You are much improved since I left, little brother," Rork said with a smile. "You must have had a great deal of practise."

The older brother had recently returned from his two-year tour of Fjelburg; an initiation ritual that Saul would soon have to undertake, if he was ever to take a place among the King's guard.

"You're a lot better, too," Saul returned the compliment, his chest heaving. "I take it you had a lot of practise with the Crawlers and Elves?"

"I did not see many Elves actually, which was strange … Word from the Elfguards is that they've been quiet these recent years. But yes, I had a great deal of practise against the Crawlers at Jaata Murgen. Horrid creatures they are, with deadly spiked legs and pincers in front of their mouth to snag and shred their victims … But, of course, you'll see for yourself soon enough!" Rork grinned, while Saul gulped. "You'll climb the mountain, get your fur, then you will have to endure the boredoms of the Flatlands, and finally it is the icy ravages of the north for you, little brother!"

"But I will come back here eventually, like you, won't I?" Saul asked.

"Oh yes – if you survive."

Saul shook his head; Rork had changed. Only two years older than Saul at twenty years of age, he had nevertheless lignified, become more callous. "Yes, if I survive. So tell me, how was your tour? Were you injured at all, or did you fight heroically at all posts?"

The older brother looked out pensively over the lush green fields to the south. "I must admit that I was wounded by a Crawler on the first night I encountered them. Still, by staying alive, I did better than a dozen others. After that, I could not fight for a few nights, in which time the Crawlers came every night … I could hear the screams of my brothers up on the ramparts above my room … So, as soon as I could move again, I rejoined the others on the wall. I thought if I was going to die, it would be better to do so with sword and axe in my hand than lying beneath blankets, protected by fitter men."

"Of course. Baldr would have smiled upon you," Saul nodded, invoking the God of War.

"Indeed he did, little brother, for that night I slew no less than eight Crawlers myself! We threw them out of Northbane like rabid dogs!"

"And they did not come again?"

Rork looked at him wistfully. "They come every night throughout winter, killing and dragging men off to be eaten … They have no remorse …" Seeing that he was unnerving his brother, Rork clumsily changed the subject. "Enough about my tour. Tell me, Saul, how goes it with the ladies?"

Saul's heartfelt laughter echoed around the top tier, infectious as a disease, and everyone who heard it smiled.

9

Crashing the Crèche

Jumal was sure he was going to die when the flood swept him from the edge, down into the hole where the lift had already descended. Fortunately for Ratnik and him, Tar Feng was not completely insane; there was method in his madness.

Once he was falling in the vertical tunnel, the shrivelled Wizard shouted out his incantation in as voluble tones as he could muster, while the water battered and flowed over him.

"Herathrea lampini-hrellel!"

In the starry skies in the world above, a cloud heard the Wizard's call. The cloud twitched like a dog that hears its master's cry, then it broke free of its celestial constraints and tumbled earthward. Soaring with purpose, it flashed down the crevasse, past the waterfall, zipped through *Dwarhummer* and threw itself into the lift-hole down which Tar Feng plummeted. It flew underneath the Wizard and Freemen, and then flew up again more slowly to catch all three of them on its soft, cushiony surface. Surprised and winded, the pirates lay gasping for a second, sprayed by the falling water, which was now hitting the cloud and splashing over their prostrate forms.

They heard Tar Feng mutter, *"Hankampano'fia."*

After a few moments – during which time his eyes were squeezed shut and he was certain beyond a doubt that he was dead – Jumal looked down with wonder upon the cloud that had saved his life. It was black as night, like those he had seen hurling down rain like javelins in the skies, before the company had descended into nightmare. It was as fluffy as a sheep's coat, and yet despite its soft squishiness beneath his fingertips, it appeared to hold his weight with ease.

It struck him then that he should not be able to see a black cloud in the dark pits beneath *Dwarhummer* at all, but the cloud was lit with a whitish hue. Jumal looked up from the arcane marvel to witness another. Tar Feng had gotten to his feet already and had summoned a small, shining white bird – translucent but bright as a star, like the ghost of a hummingbird – to light their way. The little bird circled noiselessly above them, its little wings flapping, its glow illuminating dark rust-coloured walls. Jumal felt a bead of sweat break out on his forehead as his unease at the sorcery all around him reached tangible levels, but he was growing surer and surer that he was not, in fact, dead. He saw Ratnik lying flat beside him, looking as shaken as he.

Finally, overcoming his fears, unable to contain his excitement at not having died, Jumal whooped with relief and ecstasy. He stood up carefully, pleased and reassured when the cloud held steady.

"Wizard!" he exclaimed happily, hugging the old man. "I could kiss you, you blind old bat you! You are a goddamn genius – I never should have doubted you. I cannot believe we are alive! Oh, Gods be praised, tank you, tank you, tank you! If we get out of here, Tar, I swear by Gaia's tits I am going to buy you da nicest bone necklace you ever did see! Maybe a bracelet, too!"

"Don't you want to know how I did it? How I summoned a cloud?" asked Tar Feng, clearly excited to reveal his secrets.

"No," Jumal said simply. "I do not give a rat's arse, old man. Just tank you!"

While Jumal gave his prodigious thanks to the still-panting old man, Ratnik lifted his head but then slumped back down on the soft cloud. He kissed and drank the water that flowed over his face and mumbled his own gratitude, "Oh Merejulanna, thank you Goddess, thank you for delivering me. Bless you for your gift. Watch over me still."

"That was unbelievable!" Jumal was saying as Ratnik got to his feet. "Did you see that, Rats?"

The younger pirate stood, wobbled and nodded with a nervous smile, which faded as he looked down and shifted his feet slightly. It was an extremely odd and worrisome feeling, standing on a cloud. It made him feel slightly nauseous, and – not for the first time – he wished for the deck of his ship beneath his feet. Taking a deep breath, he looked up at his two companions.

"Hmm, the clouds are still black. It must still be raining outside," Tar Feng commented banally, stretching his back with a satisfying crack. "Everyone okay?"

"Yarr," answered Jumal, looking down at himself. "All is good here."

"Dunno about that ..." muttered Ratnik, looking at Jumal as if he smelled something foul.

"Shut it!" warned the Chilpaean, though he could not hide his smile.

"Tar Feng? You all good, mate?" Ratnik asked.

"Yes, yes, no needs to worry about … ooh … old Tar Feng," the Wizard said, breathing heavily between words. "Just out of breath he is, that's all, yes, that's all."

Ratnik nodded and looked down at the eerie magic that provided their footing, but the eccentric old man was not done.

"But that's not all is it, Tar Feng?" the Wizard suddenly snapped at himself, startling the two buccaneers. "No, no, no, not by a long shot, that's not all, no! There's also the problem that you're blind, yes, don't you see? No, I don't see very well at all actually, because I am *blind!"* He ranted on, whilst Ratnik and Jumal watched, unsure of what to do.

If the Wizard lost concentration, there was a good chance they would fall to their deaths, and so they stood silently and listened as he argued with himself. "And you're old! You're an old, old man, Fengy, yes you are, there's no point in denying it! Denying what? That you're old, you senile old bag of bones! I wear bones. Yes, you do, you forgetful sap of warts and liver spots, you most certainly do. Crazy old bat. Focus up now, or you'll get us all killed. Crazy or not, bone-wearing or not, blind or not, old or not, you are one clever little chap! So get it together, and let's go down. Down we go!" he shouted, raising a bony arm up.

As he did so, the cloud suddenly dropped at an alarming rate, the magic bird whizzing down after it.

"Ahhh! Slow it down, old man! Slow it down!" Ratnik roared, hugging the dark fluff of the cloud.

Jumal, terrified of heights, simply cried out, "Make it stop! Make it stop!"

"Oops!" said the Tzunese Wizard, waving an apologetic hand. "Sorry boys, one second … there!"

The cloud began to descend at a much more leisurely rate, as did the white bird-light, though the falling water spattered the cloud-riders as much as ever. Getting to their feet for a second time, the pirates muttered their thanks, but they looked at one another nervously, both thinking the same thing. This insane old man might be magically powerful, but he could well be the death of them.

Despite the few drawbacks, the rest of their descent beside the newly created waterfall was smooth and uneventful. Tar Feng's wizardry did not waver, even when he started a second argument with himself halfway, as to whether they were halfway down or halfway up. This led to a philosophical debate of some length, a debate that was completely lost on the clueless buccaneers lucky enough to hear it.

"Halfway down, halfway up, either way's fine as far as I'm

concerned. He's just splitting hairs," Ratnik mumbled at one point, covering his ears in case the inane babble infected him with an equal eccentricity.

After a relatively short time – in comparison with their other lift rides – the tense trio on the cloud floated down free of the constraints of the walls that surrounded the lift tunnel, and were able to see what this next level in the subterranean maze had been, before the flood had nigh obliterated it.

As they hovered above the water that flowed over the rocky ground, Ratnik noticed something by the soft luminosity of Tar Feng's bird-light spell.

"Look!" he said to the others, pointing to the wall by their side, careful not to get too close to the edge of the cloud where there was nothing to prevent his falling off.

In the red wall were crevasses, dozens of them. As they passed one such niche, the two young sea explorers craned their necks to peek. The hollow looked relatively large, and inside the pirates could just about make out tiny, infant *Rodici* on beds of dead insects and worms.

"Eurgh!" spat Jumal, pulling his head back like the sight had burned him. "Dis is da rat-dogs' breeding ground!"

It did indeed appear that way, for in every one of the crevasses was at least one infant *Rodici,* and in some that Ratnik spotted after Jumal looked away, there were as many as six. He opted not to tell his friend that – the older pirate looked worried enough, he thought. In the water below them too, Tar Feng noticed adult *Rodici* swimming for their lives against the current that threatened to drag them away from their young. There was no chance of swimming against such a torrent, however, and they were soon dragged away, far in front of the levitating cloud on which the three men stood.

"Let us follow the water, boys, yes yes; we will pursue that water unto the depths of the world, teeheehee!"

With a wave of his hand and a manic laugh, Tar Feng indicated he wished the cloud to move, and accordingly it whooshed gently forwards, following the flow of water. Jumal's stomach grumbled uncomfortably at the unnatural movement beneath his feet. He spread his legs and bent his knees to maintain his balance, while the wind created by their motion pushed against him.

The cave they passed through now was simple. The snowy bird revealed it to be wide and tall with hundreds of holes in the walls – and presumably in the drowned floor, thought Jumal with a shudder – where the *Rodici* young could safely be spawned. It was a long, meandering, vast passage that the *Rodici* had dug out for themselves, but eventually the trio reached the far end of the breeding grounds and saw the destination of the water flow.

"Fantastic. A shit hole," said Jumal sarcastically upon seeing it.

His shoulders drooped in sadness at the prospect of traversing it. It was indeed a simple dug-out hole that dropped through the rock floor to another level, and it seemed highly likely from the stench and all the floating brownness the three saw that this had indeed been the waste removal centre for the *Rodici* for many years.

"At least the water should have cleaned it out a bit," muttered Ratnik, trying to reassure both himself and Jumal, though he could not help but imagine that the hundreds of *Rodici* who had been swept away by the flood would be waiting for them at the bottom of the drop.

"I just hope I don't get any on me," replied Jumal, who – being fastidious about appearance – was beginning to look positively green at the prospect of being smeared with *Rodici* faeces.

"Teeheehee!" Tar Feng giggled and wheezed at their trepidation. "Boys, boys, boys, boys, in life one must always get dirty to get the job done! I would think you sea-rats would understand that, but I guess you've been mollycoddled and coddlemolleyed since you were first born – little arse-naked babes all swathed in linens and hugs and kisses! Heh!" He barked with laughter at them, while they turned on him defensively.

Before they could defend their good names, however, Tar Feng continued sibilantly, "Or … maybe you are hardy, tough Freemen of Kauapunki-Meren! The time now comes to prove this. So, into the breach, gentlemen?"

Ratnik and Jumal eyed one another uncertainly, but neither was eager to appear a coward or a prim and proper lady of court before this crazed old man. With their pride on the line, there was nothing else for it.

"Yarr. On tru da shit," agreed Jumal, reluctantly.

"Into the breach, old man!" stated Ratnik defiantly, chin held high. "But wait a minute first, so all the rat-dogs are swept away before we go down."

"Good idea!" the Wizard approved. So, the cloud hovered and they waited, while the flood scraped out the cavern and carried dozens of whining *Rodici* away through the waste hole.

Finally, the cave was clear of *Rodici,* save for those clinging on in niches high up. When the water flow had slowed to a trickle, Tar Feng flew the cloud forwards until they were hovering over the hole. He was positioning them carefully directly above it, when the cloud began to lighten in colour and his snowy bird began to fizzle and sputter, its radiance dimming.

The wizened Tzunese Wizard looked at his two companions, who looked stuck somewhere between concerned and terrified.

He smiled at them – somewhat mischievously, mused Ratnik in that split second. Then, the Wizard said, "Sorry boys, storm must be clearing up."

The magic bird's white light winked out like water-fed flames. The cloud beneath their feet dissipated into nothingness without a sound, and the trio were left floating in mid-air for another split second, in which Ratnik thought, but had not the time to verbalise, 'You crazy old bastard!'

The three of them plummeted, like lemmings from a cliff, straight through the gaping hole below them to land in a watery mound of faeces, surrounded by rocky, dung-smeared walls on three sides. The pile was unsurprisingly squishy and vast, though they could all see a wider expanse of water in front of them at the end of two long parallel rock walls, into which the rat-dogs and some of the waste had been washed away by the deluge. They could still spot an occasional eyeless, white face break the surface and witness paws scrabble for air for a moment, before the beasts re-submerged and drowned. The stench was the worst part, however. Since they were all saturated, the stomach-wrenching smell was unavoidable and the two young pirates gagged a multitude of times in the first few seconds and spat up bile.

As Jumal regarded himself and his formerly elegant, unstained clothing with horror, Tar Feng, also brown from head to toe, chuckled quietly at the look on his face.

"Teeheehee, it's only poo, young peacock! Now, don't get agitated," the old man continued precipitously, seeing the shouts building up in the two pirates, "because we don't know what might be down here. For example, there could be packs and packs of *Rodici* or giant mutants ..." Jumal shuddered. "So, let's try being a bit sneaky, shall we?" The Wizard lowered his voice to a whisper. "Don't fret, miladies! We are in water – poo will wash off. Teehee!"

"Crazy old bastard," Ratnik muttered, moving to wipe his face with hands drenched in faeces. He changed his mind at the last moment. Jumal simply looked dejected, disgusted by himself.

"Shush now," Tar Feng told them genially, seeming unaffected by the awful stench, "and follow me, quiet like a dormouse. Quiet as mice in doors ... scurrying around ... squeaking ... eek eek eek ... Oh yes, yes, quiet, quiet! We are being quiet! Shhh!"

The young corsairs regarded him worriedly down noses wrinkled at their own stench. They waded slowly and carefully through the knee-high water after the old man as he set off from the dung pile, dunking themselves and washing as quickly and quietly as they could.

"Do you hear something?" Tar Feng asked suddenly, cocking his head to one side.

The young men made no reply for a moment, for it was not clear whether he was speaking to them or the voices in his head.

Then, Jumal ventured, “I hear nutting.”

“Hmmm,” the Wizard hummed pensively in response.

From the cul-de-sac filled with *Rodici* filth, the three ventured forwards between the two parallel sandy walls, toward the great expanse of water they could see at the end. Light shone from those waters, illuminating the walls and ceiling of the cavern in its fervour; varicoloured light coming from glowing fish. Mouths hung open at the exquisite sight, though none said a word. As Tar Feng reached the end of the small passage, he could see that the wall to the left continued around the haloed lake, while the right was merely an outcropping.

The old man looked slowly to the left, and then, as he turned to the right and peeked around the rocky protrusion, his stomach dropped away at the vista laid out before his eyes. He stumbled back noisily, splashily. He froze and held his breath to hear if he had been noticed, but no alarm was raised. The Wizard then turned to his companions.

“This is not good, rapscallions,” he began in a whisper, stroking his droopy moustache. “Beyond that rocky crag on the right, there is a ledge on higher ground. On the ledge, there is a small army of Dwarves and a demonic-looking figure with big horns growing out of his head.” The pirates started to gasp, but it was not yet time for that. Tar Feng ploughed on, “And he’s talking to a giant worm in that lake right there.”

The pirates gasped.

“Be quiet!” the Wizard breathed irritably. “I’m going to the edge to try to listen. Stay back.”

10

The Demon and the Worm

Tar Feng inched up to the edge of the outcrop, hands against the sandy walls, and peeked around the corner of the rough rock with eyes glazed over with cataracts.

Not far away, lit by the luminescent waters, on a higher level than both the lake and the Wizard, a Demon stood on the edge of a red rock ledge, wearing only dark trousers torn below the knee, and black boots. The lower parts of his trousers looked like they had been ripped clear of his frame simply by his own expanding muscles. He bore no weapon, but behind him waited a large contingent of bone-armoured, axe-wielding Dwarves.

The Demon resembled a man – to an extent – with wide shoulders, narrow hips and flowing silver hair that glimmered in the eerie nebula of the waters. His bulging muscles would have been the meridian of human aesthetics, save that the image was awfully distorted.

Thick red veins pulsed across his pale visage, crisscrossing his entire creamy body and interlinking to form a complex pattern of circulation that was grotesque to the eye, for the capillaries were obviously working frantically with a great deal of tainted blood. The effect looked mildly like blood-webbing, thought the old Wizard. The fiend's face could have been handsome if not for the engrossed arteries and the long black scar coursing down his cheek from beneath his eye, over his lips, ending at his chin.

The Demon's two horns were long and black and looked as though they had erupted through gouged skin at his temples, growing out of his skull. They were cruelly pointed at the end and each grew curled like a ram's – just like any picture any child would ever draw of the dread Lord of the Nether, Gastar, Tar Feng thought in wonder. The Demon's eyes were a bright, fiery red; the old man felt sure he wanted to avoid that gaze. The horned man's mouth, when he spoke, contained large yellowed fangs and an unusually long, dark, slithering tongue.

Tar Feng could not see the features of the giant worm that spoke with the Demon, for he saw only the side of its tubular segmented body, which was covered in short dark bristles. It was a vast creature, though. While the old man could not see the full extent of its long sinuous body, he could deduce by the long expanse of neck he could see – which was thicker than the trunk of the oldest oak trees – that the rest of the body had to be of enormous size. Its skin was the same lightless creamy white as the *Rodici's,* and as it turned its vast lump of a head to the right, Tar Feng glimpsed that it, like the rat-dogs, had no eyes. He did not see ears or a nose either; what he did see was a lobe poking out above a circular mouth which opened like a sphincter to display radial, serried sharp teeth.

Behind the worm, Demon and Dwarves was a lift; a far wider and more smoothly dug-out entrance to the cavern than that which the Wizard and pirates had used, which answered Tar Feng's unspoken question as to how Demon and Dwarves had gotten down here. The only way from his position up to the Demon's level that the wily old Tzunese man could see was a narrow, curving path that led from the upper level down to the lake shore, just the other side of the outcrop behind which the Wizard and pirates now hid.

To wander beyond the rock now would be a fatal mistake, for all eyes were on the worm, and any movement would be noticed immediately. Tar Feng resolved to hold his position and bide his time. With good fortune, he thought, an opportunity to ascend would present itself soon. The Wizard settled against the rock, listening closely. When all was still, when he and the buccaneers had ceased the slightest sloshing, he was able to attune his ears to the speech above him. He craned his neck for better hearing.

"She is well, Sirraesutha," the veiny Demon was saying in a language that Tar Feng recognised, fortunately, but had thought he would likely never hear spoken: the tongue of the long-dead Builder Races from the legendary crystal city of Vayloraheim.

The horned man's voice rang out deep and hollow, like an empty crypt, croaky like he had never tasted water. Luckily, their conversation was purposefully slow, so that they did not misunderstand one another. Worms are likely not always the most comprehensible in a conversation, Tar Feng thought with the idea of a chuckle, holding perfectly still and silent.

"She is pleased with the progress made in this realm – with you, in particular, Sirraesutha. You have aided and cooperated with these dirty little creatures," the Demon jerked a thumb over his shoulder, toward the mass of ranked, armoured Dwarves, "with great grace. Fear not, however; the time for chaos and consumption will soon be upon us."

"Thank the moon for that!" the worm, Sirraesutha, replied. Its voice hissed, like a pranged cat's, with a definite female quality, Tar Feng thought. "I tire of being surrounded by meat on feet when I cannot eat! The puny morsels that they provide me with barely sustain me and are becoming more infuriating than satiating. I would have waited little longer before I needed to be free!"

"Well it is that the time has come, then," the Demon responded lightly, clearly unworried by the worm's impatience. "When last we came face to face, my powers were tiny and insignificant, for I was as a new-born to this realm in this accursed vessel," it gestured towards its muscular body, "but now, at long last, my energies cascade about my being like encaged stars and I am ready to unleash my plague upon the world. But first, the vessel must be refilled. So please, would you fetch us that which you have protected for so long, so that we can get started?"

The worm bobbed its enormous head once in a nod and then swiftly turned to swim away. The old Tzunese man ducked back and pressed himself against the wall as it passed by, holding his breath until it had completely submerged. Then, he stared at the water where it had vanished and saw the bright pulse of a deep-sunken purple circle.

*

Fyrstsvard's group slowly got to their feet, the Knight managing it with only a little unsteadiness. His face was pale and wan, but his mouth was set in a determined line. After strapping on his cuirass once more, he rested a hand on the pommel of his longsword in its sheath at his hip and took a deep breath. The smooth golden sphere that served as a pommel and the leather wrapping the hilt were familiar and comforting to him, like a favoured memory. Many were the times he had stroked the magnificent hilt of his heirloom blade. The others looked back to him, waiting for him to catch up.

Exhaling, he nodded. "Let's go."

The group followed the grim Izdaju, who led them to a tunnel through the rock wide enough for two abreast, by the side of the lake. As they neared the tunnel's mouth, the giant worm that Tar Feng had witnessed suddenly swam into view of the Knight and his companions, its great head moving from side to side high in the air above them as it went. Like the Wizard, the mercenaries saw only its hairy neck and head, but they could see light coils of vast proportion furling and swishing in the glorious waters, sending gleaming fish scurrying in all directions, hazing the wonderful nimbus in which they stood and which they could see dancing upon the ceiling.

Upon seeing the worm, the group flinched to a man and backed into the darkness of the tunnel, pressing themselves to its walls in silence, but the great creature passed by without noticing them, and when it reached the wall furthest from the Demon, it dived beneath the water smoothly without a single splash.

"That was close," muttered Fyrstsvard, anxiously brushing a hand through his golden hair.

"Too bloody close," grumbled Heldig, shaking his head.

"What was that creature?" asked Kamilah, clearly shaken. She grasped Izdaju's hand tightly.

"We must get out of here," stated Izdaju, looking to Fyrstsvard.

"I agree," the Knight responded, coughing gently. "Let's see where this tunnel takes us. That thing could come back at any time, and I don't wish to be its meal. Egobal, go on ahead; let us know what you see."

They waited whilst Egobal, whom Fyrstsvard had noticed to be silent as a ghost, padded forward and out of the tunnel. He returned after a few minutes and told them, "As you can see, the path runs parallel to the lake, and up ahead there is a jumble of boulders that is easily climbable with a level plateau at the top."

"Did you climb and take a look?" asked Fyrstsvard.

"I did take that liberty, yes. On the plateau above those boulders is a gathering of over one hundred armed Dwarf warriors. They were all facing away, so none saw me as I risked peeking. They stood still and silent, in ranks – like soldiers on parade. I do not know if they guard something, perhaps, but here is something interesting. At the head of this Dwarf force, there stands a distorted man – a man with horns on his head, like Gastar, and horrible veiny protrusions all over his body! He too was facing the other way, thank the Gods. Fyrstsvard, I think he must be a Demon."

Looking out over the lake, standing by the slight shelter the tunnel mouth provided, the Knight absorbed this news without comment for a moment. Then he spoke, his words unexpected.

"Does that look like Tar Feng over there to you?"

Egobal glanced across the lake of light and saw a small inlet on the far side where three figures could be seen lurking. One of them was a golden-skinned, little old man with a crooked staff.

"Why, yes it does," replied Egobal, with a slight smile beneath the cloth around his face. The eccentric old man amused the Sandman and was clearly as tough as an old boot to have survived this far. "I was wondering how they fared."

"Thank Gaia's mountain-sized titties for that!" Heldig added, hearing their words and waving vigorously at the three on the opposite side of the lake. "I take it we can't get to them, though, with a bunch of Dwarves on lookout up there?"

Fyrstsvard nodded slowly, his expression distant. Heldig had seen his contemplative look before and shut his mouth, backing up a step to let the Knight think. After a moment of collecting his thoughts, Fyrstsvard gave voice to his ruminations quietly, but loud enough for the gathered group to hear.

"We have seen no sign yet of the Elf for whom we search, but these Dwarves and this Demon … They must be waiting for something, I suspect," he spoke slowly, as if savouring each word on his tongue. "It could be that they wait for the worm to return for some kind of ritual … I think our best bet is to wait and see what they're up to. If we attack now, we interrupt whatever ceremony they have going on here. With any luck, they will lead us to the Elf – I cannot believe it is pure coincidence that they are gathered here right now, just as we are. It *must* be for the same purpose! I believe this Demon is after the same thing we are. Keep your eyes open, for if I am correct, we must rescue this Elf from its clutches."

The mercenaries nodded determinedly, but each thought the same thing: fighting a Demon would be far from easy. There were stories of Demons having been killed before, but not many, and far more were the stories of loved ones lost to a fiend's grasp in the night. The abominations were supernaturally powerful and fast – could chop off a head or rip out a heart easily with their claws – and legends said some had powerful dark arts at their disposal that helped them tear their victims apart to get at the juicy meal inside.

The band did not have to wait long before the unusually large worm returned from the depths of the still waters. Its huge, white head emerged glistening, and – looking on from the safety of the tunnel – the Knight from Justiqua noticed something: its mouth was open and shining brightly.

"There's something in its mouth," murmured Fyrstsvard pensively. "Egobal," he leaned in close to the Sandman, not wishing to be heard now that he knew a hostile force was so close nearby. "Climb back up those boulders there and keep an eye on what is going on. Holler if you need our aid. Signal if you've something to report. The rest of us will prepare and join you up there soon."

11

Witchson's Execution

The manor of the ageing Sir Skallgrim of Justiqua had once been the home of a beautiful young couple, well-loved and admired around town and beyond.

The young Knight, Nestor, had dashing good looks and a wide smile, and his wife, Samantha, was a true beauty in her day. Everyone in their pretty little town of Port-Hav'n had been thrilled to hear that Samantha had been blessed with pregnancy. After an unusually long trip away during the pregnancy, the couple had returned with a baby boy and many well-wishers had come to pay their respects to the infantile addition to their community.

That first night after they had returned, the town had been shaken by a freak summer storm. Crooked forks of lightning had lit up a cloudless night sky, rain had smitten the earth, and thunder had pealed so voluminously that the zealous might have believed the Gods themselves made ready for war in the celestial dome. So began the rumours about the boy, Nighan.

Seventeen years later, a riled mob was ascending a small grassy hill to the manor of the once great and well-respected Sir Nestor Skallgrim, slightly south of the town proper. The manor, on which the masses – including the town council and a dozen of the town guard under Captain Bernard's supervision – now descended, however, was no longer the picturesque home of tranquillity it had once been. Now, it was decrepit and rundown, like a poor artist's rendering of the splendour it had once possessed.

At its base, where there had once been a lush lawn and impressive gardens, now the manor was encompassed by dead plants strewing sad brown leaves across yellowed grass and patches of dirt. The roof was makeshift, for the retired Knight in residence had lost a number of roofs to the tempests that seemed to congregate about the small hilltop. One half of the second story had been rebuilt after a tree had caved it in, and the newer stones looked incongruous next to the old, well-worn ones. On the opposite side of the second story, there were large, black scorch marks on the walls where lightning had struck multiple times.

Windows had to be replaced so frequently at the manor that the glassblowers sent a man daily to scout out the place for work. It was easy to divine the reason behind the rumours around town about the vortex of freak weather surrounding the manor when a passer-by viewed the structure for the first time.

It was such rumours – and others, such as the ones Mayor Able Roberts had described to his privy council – that the townsfolk talked openly to one another about now, for the first time above a frightened whisper, as they stormed through the night and up the small hill with pitchforks, knives and lots of torches, and it was with such rumours that they had been incited to do so by the Mayor and the council on their way to arrest the Witchson.

The panicking people had been easy to whip up into a frenzy, once they had understood who it was that was the root of all evils in their pleasant little town. Once they had a small crowd, more were eager to join, as is the way of sheep and men. They muttered to one another and grew uneasy beneath the sullen skies, however.

A freak summer storm, just like the one at the time of Witchson's birth, hovered over the hilltop now, threatening to engulf the entire town. In light yet saturating rain, with thick grey clouds ominously obscuring the great dome overhead, the mob squelched up the sodden hill to arrive at the solid oak doors to the manor, loudly shouting curses and threats at the building. The Mayor puffed up his chest authoritatively, like a mating bird, and rapped his pasty knuckles against the wood.

"Noble Sir Skallgrim!" Able shouted over the coarser cacophony surrounding him, his voice as cultured and polite as ever. "Sir Skallgrim, it is I – the Mayor, Able Roberts! Come out and bring your wretched son with you, so that justice can be done!"

To Trent Wetnout's surprise, the oaken doors opened immediately and Nighan Witchson was shoved stumbling out into the open. Wetnout gulped as he watched the two emerge. The father, dressed in crimson woollen trousers and a yellow linen shirt, was lit by a lantern in his hand.

The boy was clothed in its shadow. He was short, thin-shouldered, hunched and skinny to the point of gauntness, with pallid ill-looking skin and bags under eyes deep set in dark sockets. A cream shirt and linen olive trousers fluttered in the squall, hanging loosely off the scrawny youth's frame, and his shoulder-length earth-brown hair rippled in the wind.

The boy looked sickly, like he was wasting away, and yet there was a certain vitality about the odd-coloured eyes; one a dark blue partially hidden behind a lazy eyelid, the other a round, bright violet that flared up sometimes like Saint Elmo's fire – a weather phenomenon well-known to sailors, discovered by the revered Saint Elmo, where pointed objects like ships' masts glowed with a vivid blue or purple light because of all the lightning in the atmosphere during a storm. The boy's mother had been guilty of one violet eye. There had been rumours about that, too. Once upon a time, a sighting of Saint Elmo's fire had been considered good fortune, but now the people of Port-Hav'n were not so sure.

"Get out there, boy!" the father growled as he pushed his son from his home. Nighan, slipping slightly, turned to regard his father with daggers in his eyes.

The old harbourmaster shifted from foot to foot miserably as he beheld them. Why was Skallgrim giving up his son so readily? Trent wanted to go home and hide under a pillow and pretend none of this was happening, but he was a part of the council that had condemned the boy to die. He felt he had to be there.

The father looked worn out and haggard, with tufty grey hair, thick stubble and red-rimmed, dimmed eyes, as though he had not slept in days – like a shadow of his former self in his old self's fashionable, colourful garb. A slight totter in his step informed the harbourmaster that the boy's father had been drinking heavily, as usual. Strapped to Skallgrim's belt was his gaudy, ceremonial sabre, granted to him upon his honourable retirement from the Order of *Pacia*.

Wetnout felt the boy's stare fall upon him and the gathered crowd and could not meet that gaze. He stared wretchedly at his muddy shoes.

"Nighan Skallgrim," the Mayor intoned pompously, reading from a prepared document. "You are hereby charged with sorcery and with all the damages that your dark powers have inflicted on this town – from loss of cattle, to loss of human life, to loss of property in storm after freak storm!" He lowered the document and walked in a slow circle with arms spread wide as the mob cheered its approval. "We, the good people of Port-Hav'n, have enough proof to satisfy ourselves of your guilt in this matter," the Mayor said, giving Skallgrim a knowing look, "as well as to convince your father."

The boy, Nighan, glanced up at his father sharply at that. Trent wondered sceptically if the boy had expected his father's protection after nightly beatings.

"It's for the best, boy," the harbourmaster heard the old Knight mutter whilst looking at the ground by his son's feet.

It was surreal. Trent felt sure there was no way this could possibly be happening. He had children himself and would never, ever give them up to anybody – least of all the Mayor. Skallgrim must truly be afraid of his own son, the old man thought, feeling nauseous to the depths of his stomach.

"He will be given a trial?" Sir Nestor Skallgrim asked the Mayor quietly, his voice slurred.

"His trial is over, Skallgrim, I am sorry. His guilt *is* determined and his punishment is set."

The ageing Knight hung his head pathetically and looked like he might break down in tears.

Tears of relief or sorrow? Wetnout could not help but wonder.

"You know me, many of you!" cried out the cursed boy of a sudden, stepping away from his father toward the mob.

He looked almost normal, Wetnout ruminated, dressed simply as many boys are in rags covered in brown splotches of adventure. He could never be ordinary, however; Wetnout began to see that. He was set apart by the darkness of the one eye, the violent intensity of the other and the angry, scraping voice that seemed to rake the mind with its sound, like nails on a chalkboard. He stood out like a raven amid swans.

"How can you do this? How can you believe this?" the boy cried out plaintively, his voice sounding like it emanated from the slow grating of two swords in his gullet.

His unnerving eyes darted around to meet only averted or hate-filled gazes. Trent had known the boy for many years and could tell that he was trying his best to appear friendly and reassuring. Somehow, though, he did not fit the role he tried to portray. He was a poor actor. Despite this, his outburst elicited a response.

"How can you just give up your son like this, you cold-hearted bastard?" someone cried out at the resigned father. A moment later, Trent Wetnout gasped aloud in horror as he realised he had recognised the voice. It was his own.

Skallgrim turned to regard him with hatred burning in his eyes. "*You* know his guilt as well as any!" he hissed through gritted teeth. "And so do I, *old man!*"

Such was the sudden fury that seemed to descend upon Skallgrim that his hand curled around the leather-bound, golden-wire-wrapped handle of the sabre at his belt and – with a mad gleam in his eye – he advanced a step on the old harbourmaster, who held only a torch.

"Hold it right there, Skallgrim!" the Mayor bellowed, pointing a stubby white finger at him and, surprisingly, freezing the retired Knight in place, though still he snarled like a wild dog at Trent. "Wetnout is not to blame here! You said it yourself. We all here know the boy's guilt! Beyond that, there is no one else to blame!"

This brought stillness and silence for a moment, in which Skallgrim seemed to almost recover from his madness for a second, but then Able continued in a malefic sneer, "Other than you, I suppose, for marrying that poxy Witch in the first place, you honour-clad imbecile! Honestly, are you completely brainless?"

The entire crowd gasped as one, and the Mayor's already waxy, chubby face was leached of its remaining warmth as he too realised he had spoken his thoughts aloud. This brought a secondary sort of stillness, a sort quite different to that which his earlier remarks had brought about. That had been a calming, commanding stillness. This was the still before the storm.

The great and respected Knight, Sir Skallgrim of Justiqua, slowly turned his fiery gaze on the fat Mayor, who was visibly trembling with fear. A feral roar tore from Nestor Skallgrim's throat as he ripped his sabre from its sheath. He ran and leapt downhill – etched in ebony silhouette for a moment against a bright lightning streak, with animal rage given voice through bared teeth – at the oily merchant Mayor, who stood with wide, hopeless eyes, paralysed by fear.

Fortunately for the unarmed Mayor, the man stood next to him was the town smith, Bran Cirrus, who had spent some time training to be a Knight before choosing his current profession. He had some experience of fighting pirates and Goblins, as well as the thick bulges of muscle associated with pounding an anvil for more than a decade.

Bran swiftly shoved the Mayor aside with his bulk, knocking him to the ground and taking his place. His smith's hammer, short and unwieldy with a heavy iron head, swung up with both hands clasped to it firmly to block Skallgrim's vicious chop. The gleaming cavalry sabre – silver-hilted with swirling ornate quillions that swept back to cup the hand of the wielder and a three-foot curved steel blade, issued only to the honourable – bit into the thick wooden hammer handle with a dull thud and proceeded to fasten there.

The ageing Knight's haggard face was horrifically twisted in a vindictive snarl, so as to be unrecognisable as he stood, stuck, for a split second. He snorted loudly, like a raging horse, with gritted teeth behind which Bran could hear feral gurgling.

Then, the battle-trained, veteran Knight thoughtlessly took on the bloody mantle he had worn in his earlier years, when every Goblin or marauder he saw could be put to the sword without hesitation or fear. His mind drifted back to its old friend, its comfort place. From cohesive well-thought out arguments, his thoughts became choppy and jarring, ordering him this way and that, and his body responded reflexively.

Letting go of the sabre, Skallgrim smashed his fist into the smith's chest to back him up a step, then swung a vicious hook under the aloft hammer to cripple Bran's left bicep, forcing him to let go of the hammer with one hand. The heavy weapon slumped downwards as the grip was lost, and the smith's other hand was at the far end of the haft from the heavy head, meaning he had not enough leverage to swing it at all.

Bran dropped it to the ground as blows began to rain down on his soon-battered visage, stepped back a couple of paces and lifted his arms before his head to protect himself. The blows halted, but the middle-aged smith could see nothing for the blood in his eyes and his swollen skin for a moment, nor hear anything other than the fast drumming of his heart in his chest and the slow wheezing breaths he consciously sucked in to stay alive.

The powerful smith's vision cleared just in time for him to witness his impending doom. His own forge hammer smashed his skull to a rotten-fruit-like pulp, raining gore on those nearby. As Bran's body folded in on itself, Nestor wrenched his sabre from the hammer haft with a crazed grin and laughed murderous mirth at the sea of frightened faces that beheld him.

The mob – as if awakening from a dream or realising that they were not, in fact, watching a theatrical show unfold, but real events – cried out in a dissonance of different voices as hatred suddenly swamped their minds, tearing down the dams of reason and civility. Like a demented parade, they sang their death-hungry marching song as they descended on the lone Knight with a steady tramp of squelching stamps.

"You're a dead man, Knight!"

"How could you, Nestor?"

"What have you done?"

"You'll pay for that!"

"I will tear you apart with my own hands, you filthy murderer!"

These were just some of the cries from those under the pouring black skies. Such threats were accompanied by more primal ones, such as "Die!" and simple nonsensical roars of inarticulate wrath.

"That's it!" the Mayor screamed manically, his round, chubby face warped into a gleeful mask of sadism by the flickering torchlights bouncing up the hill. "That's it! Get him – get the Knight! Kill the murderer! Kill the Witchson! Kill them both!"

The town guard, who had come up the hill on either side of the council, now closed in on the retired Knight like pincers.

Howling like a wild beast, the veteran Knight leapt to meet the guard – most of whom were callow youths, who hadn't experienced half as much combat as a true Knight. Puncturing the lungs of the first man to come at him, Skallgrim then sheared off the face of the second with his razor-sharp blade before anyone could come close to landing a blow on his powerful frame.

Before long, however, the wary guardsmen began to encircle him, and the Knight spun and spun in the slippery mud, lashing out wildly like a cornered stag making a final stand against the wolves that have hounded it for so long.

Skallgrim severed one arm jabbing a sword hesitantly at him and, with a hefty pommel smash, caved in the sternum of another who tried in vain to set the errant Knight aflame with a torch. As he did so, though, one gutless guard darted in behind him and, with as much force as he could muster, stabbed his sword into the once-noble Knight's back. Sir Skallgrim shifted as the blow landed, so that the blade stuck high in his right shoulder. The garish yellow of his shirt slowly darkened radially outwards from the weapon like a colour-consuming red ripple.

Skallgrim cried out in pain and swung around, his only thought to deal death to those that sought his. The sabre in his hand whistled around and beheaded his stabber in a spray of blood. The man's head landed upside down in the dirt, where it stared in surprise at the gathered mob. Many a woman, and a few men, gave vent to a yelp of terror at that.

"Stop!"

The mind of the harbourmaster, Trent Wetnout, snapped. He could take no more after seeing his friend and one-time sailing companion crumpled and inert in the dirt beneath the Knight's wild eyes. The Captain of the guard, Malcolm Bernard, who had been about to skewer the Knight with his sword, stayed his hand at the harbourmaster's cry. The murderous mob halted their crow-like cawing for blood at the old man's shout too, but for how long he was not sure.

"Stop!" Wetnout screamed again at the top of his lungs as he shoved and elbowed his way to the front of the surging crowd that ringed the Knight.

"We are not mindless beasts!"

Wetnout stepped over the lifeless body of his friend into the muddy circle in the midst of the mob, in order to position himself between Skallgrim and the rest of the townspeople. The Knight, glad of the respite, simply stood, gleaming with viscera, shoulders and chest heaving as he drew in great shuddering breaths. He managed to wrench the sword from his shoulder and clasped sticky, red fingers about its handle with his free hand.

Skallgrim was spattered with mud heaved up in the scuffle, but he took no notice. Indeed, his eyes seemed vacant and only half-aware. Trent knew more than a sliver of fear that the once-honourable man had been completely unhinged by his son. He had known Skallgrim for many years, though, and put his faith in those years of peace rather than this night of horror.

"Nor are we murderers!" the harbourmaster continued quickly, seeing that the bloodlust in the eyes of the mob was slowly diminishing, that their weapons were gradually lowering in their hands.

"I have known most, if not all of you, all my life," the old man told them, his grey hair and liver-spotted skin testimony to his years amongst them. "You are all *good* people! I do not believe that you want this on your conscience! Nestor Skallgrim too is a *good* man – a Knight of the noble Order of *Pacia*, who destroyed the soul-sucking evil of Convent for the benefit of all not so many centuries ago! It is because of men like him that we have our freedom at all, or have you forgotten?" he demanded, hoping that the good acts of the thousands, centuries ago, would outweigh the vile acts of the one, moments before.

He turned to Captain Bernard. "You! Malcolm, I *know* you! You are a good man, and I cannot believe that you would take part in such fearful, over-zealous murder! Let us stop this bloodshed now, before it is too late! Skallgrim *has* done wrong here, but we *can* forgive him." Some of the people began to nod thoughtfully. "And whilst his son, Nighan, may appear to us to be the centre of a hurricane of evil, I don't think we have fairly considered the possibility that this poor young man is just as petrified as us! Surely it is not possible that he is soulless nor that he has made a pact with dark forces unbeknownst to us! Such nonsense belongs in fables – not in our pleasant little town! Paranoia must not triumph over common sense!"

The crowd was stumped momentarily. The bewildered townsfolk began to mutter amongst themselves yet again, once more analysing and reanalysing the evidence they had witnessed in town or that they had heard from neighbours and friends. Trent was pleased and relieved to see a few lower their weapons and torches and give the old harbourmaster a gesture of respect and agreement. The boy for whom all were there – still stood apart from his father and the mob, by the manor – nodded to Wetnout when the old man turned to regard him and even shouted out to those who had, seconds before, bayed for his blood.

"Trent is right!" he told them, though his raspy voice still caused a few winces and ear rubs. "I am just as scared as you! I cannot explain these unnatural occurrences any more than can you! My father *is* a good man, and he deserves your respect and loyalty!"

Pleased with the boy's bravery, Trent turned back to the waiting townspeople, some of whom had evidently been moved by the boy's words and had dropped their torches and makeshift weapons entirely. Even the Captain of the guard had lowered his sabre a jot and was looking thoughtfully at Skallgrim.

"He has such pretty eyes," contributed Adele Norris dreamily from the fore of the crowd. As if this helped some to make up their minds – as if evil can never have a handsome face – a few more muttered shamefully and dropped their weapons.

"Thank you, my friends," Wetnout began to say, when he was loudly interrupted.

"How can you all listen to such drivel?" demanded the head of religious authority in the small town, Meinolf Sanders. The priest walked around Wetnout while he spoke, his voice clear, powerful and swaying. "To such utter nonsense as this old man spouts, I say faugh! The Dark Lord of the eternal Nether reaches forth his omnipresent hand to sway this weak old man's judgement, to claim his soul for his own! This man has been corrupted by Gastar himself into lying to us all!"

There were nods, grumbles and confused murmurs. Seeing that he was getting through to them, Meinolf continued more loudly, slowly wending his way through the muck until he was behind Nestor Skallgrim and Malcolm Bernard and could point easily at the silent boy atop the hill.

"The boy is cursed! The boy's father is cursed! And this old sailor *is* cursed by the All Mother! She demands justice! And she demands death! As the Word says, 'unbelievers will be punished with death and eternal damnation.'"

The priest spun to face the guard Captain's back, and Malcolm hissed in a deep breath, his muscular frame becoming stiff and his eyes wide and frightened.

"If this man is too weak to carry out the Mother's will," Meinolf pronounced morosely, "then he too is accursed and deserving of death."

From behind the lanky figure of the guard Captain, out stepped the sky-blue-robed priest, only now his robe was stained with crimson and his right hand looked to be gloved in the same colour. In this hand, the priest clutched a small silver dagger, from the tip of which slowly dripped drops of the same hue to blend with the dark earth.

"May this man find peace and forgiveness in the life after this one. *Reccé em Pacia,*" Meinolf prayed, gazing up at the hidden stars for a brief moment, while Malcolm Bernard slumped in on himself like he was hollow. Landing heavily, he further stained the priest's once-immaculate robe with splashes of wet mud.

Wetnout was so shocked and disgusted he could not even gasp. He stared at the priest of *Pacia* with unblinking, uncomprehending eyes and a mouth hanging open gormlessly.

Meinolf turned to the guards, who stood as aghast as Wetnout, completely unsure now of what to do.

"Finish him," the priest ordered them, nodding toward the blood-drenched Knight.

Though Nestor Skallgrim stood still as a statue, seemingly worn out and making not one threatening or defensive move, the remaining guards closed in on him like a pack of wolves and tore at his flesh with iron teeth until he too lay in the sludge; a mashed reminder of what nobleness he had once stood for. The beautiful silver sabre lay with him in the muck, wallowing in the dirt and the rain like the rest of them.

Nighan watched his father's demise with something akin to glee, any eye that cared to witness could see. The boy's nostrils flared excitedly, his lips parted, and his eyes widened to drink in the tableau. Thunder boomed, and lightning crackled above his head like a fireworks celebration.

12

Hates and Furies

"What have you done?" a grieving bellow sounded from the midst of the stunned crowd.

Jord Bernard – Malcolm's teenage son – charged to the van of the mob, where he halted with a choking sob as he beheld the dirt-smeared corpse that was all that now remained of his father.

"What have you done, priest? You are a murderer! Murderer! Murderer!"

Screaming the accusation in an increasingly crazed manner each time, Jord swept a pitchfork from an unsuspecting farmer's hands and, hollering uncontrollably, charged the priest with the makeshift weapon as though it were a lance.

"You will die for what you have done!"

The guards saw the bulky youth coming at them and the priest. One sliced open the boy's chest with his blade as he dodged out of the way of the levelled pitchfork, and a second impaled him through the gut, but neither stopped him. Jord's mad rush carried him through the guards' attacks, and – though the priest slashed open the boy's face with his silver dagger, roaring, "Heretic!" – still Meinolf Sanders was skewered on two prongs out of a rusty three, before the old pitchfork snapped under the priest's sagging weight with a dull, rotten crack. Young Jord toppled to a muddy grave a heartbeat later.

By now, the townsfolk did not know what to think. There had been more murder and death in their peaceful town in the last few minutes than in the whole of live memory. Some had dropped their weapons and torches, whilst others clung fiercely to theirs.

"Hehehehehe!"

Low, grating laughter caught the people's attention. Atop the hill, Nighan Witchson chortled hideously. Other than the hiss and splash of the rain, there was no other noise. They had almost forgotten that there could be. Witchson's laughter consisted of quick, wheezy exhalations. It reminded Trent Wetnout of the repetitive scraping back and forth of a saw against a tree trunk – the same quick, sharp noise. It was a gruesome sound, containing too much mirth and madness for such a macabre time of murder and betrayal.

"Hehehe!"

Eventually, the sawing chuckles gave way to barking coughs that wracked the young man's whole body painfully. When they ended, Witchson spat heavily on the ground and then looked up to his fellow townspeople of Port-Hav'n, Justiqua.

"So much hate!" he shouted at them, a smile snarling his pale face. Looking from face to silent face, he leered at them malevolently as thunder pealed loudly overhead. "There is *so* much hate in this town! In *you* people! Do you know that?" He singled out a frightened woman with a finger. Then, he pointed at a man. "Do you? And not only hate – but greed and jealousy, lust and anger! *So much anger!* It pours from you every moment like a ceaseless rain!"

He threw his arms wide and his head back and spun on the spot manically, pounding the wet earth with his feet in a mad little jig. As if in agreement, the rain hissed down more sharply until it did not seem like rain at all; it seemed like web-thin pillars connecting earth to sky all around.

"In each and every single mind present, there is anger! I see it! I *feel* it every moment of every day, surrounded by you people! It gnaws away at your insides, eating up all your other emotions until only hatred is left – hatred for all and sundry! You all go around every day, *pretending* to be friends, family, fellow workers, soldiers, husbands and wives, but every single one of you *hates* – every single one of you has untended grievances! Adulteries, thefts, insults, offences, extortion, bribery, shame, guilt and rage!

"I *feel* the rage building up inside you all … and I cannot take it anymore! Paranoia and spite run amok in Port-Hav'n, and every one of you is guilty. You all teach your sons and daughters about selflessness and virtue, helping the less fortunate and making the world a better place … But how many of you can claim to follow your own teaching, d'you think? I will tell you – none of you! There is not an innocent here, and you all know what you did wrong! I see it in your faces and in your minds! Cheaters, thieves, hypocrites, liars, killers, rapists! I am sick of you all!"

Witchson counted off his fingers, then swiped a hand acrimoniously in front of him, and lightning flared and crackled about the manor at his back.

"And when you die," he continued more quietly, a haunted look in his eyes, "I feel that, too. I feel your anger at the Gods, and I feel your dread swelling until it blots out all else, until panic overturns your mind like a tidal wave. I feel that horrible asphyxiation as you struggle and fail to breathe. I feel your energy wink out like a snuffed candle as you leave this world. All of you are the same at the end. I had nightmares for weeks the first time I sensed somebody die." He gave a mirthless bark of laughter. "Even sleep is no escape. I have felt it countless times since then."

He took a deep breath.

"You come here to take me by force of arms, to unburden your hatred on me! To cut me and prod me and burn me at the stake! Is that not so?" he demanded roughly, swivelling on the fat Mayor, whose chubby lips quivered haplessly.

His bright eye burned with violet flame, casting an eclipse over his second orb. "Is that not so, *Mayor?"* A violent crack in the sky echoed his demand. "All of this hatred you've built up against me – against each other, against the Gods and against the fates – is *all* I feel! All day, every day. From all of you – including my father. Fear and hate is all I felt from him. And when I close my eyes to hear myself think in peace, it gets even louder! Until I can barely remember my own cursed name! All I can think is *hate!"*

He bent at the knees to bellow the word at the sloppy mud beneath him, and the ground shook and cracked open, so that a chasm like a dark snake slithered from between his firmly planted feet toward the appalled mob, which backed away in fear.

"For that is where I live. I *live* in your hatred, in your greed, in your anger, and when I finally break and lash out, I cannot control it! And *this,"* he pointed to the dark chasm at his feet, "is the outcome!"

His furious, gesturing arms slumped to his sides as his energy dissipated. His violet eye cooled perceptibly, and his head hung as if pounded down by the pummelling shower. Still, he glared at the crowd from beneath dark eyebrows. "How does a man escape his own mind? There is nowhere else for me. Nowhere to flee."

Witchson took several deep breaths.

"You come here to string me up in hatred. You call me Sorcerer, you call me Witchson, and you blame *me* for all your problems. Well, you know what? You are right."

Lightning cracked portentously, and there was no surprise. All gathered were now convinced of the truth.

"I am a Sorcerer, like my mother before me. I can *hear* your thoughts – can barely block them out, in fact! And perhaps I *am* the source of a great many problems in Port-Hav'n. Perhaps I *do* cause freak weather and instil dread into your lives. But know one thing; it is all of *you* that have driven me to this! Driven me insane with your inane mind-chatter, your hateful incessant drivel! Your hatred has infected me like a disease, and I can create nothing but from what you have supplied me as material! Hates and furies are my inks, and carnage is my written word. You are all fools – *fools!* – to have created me so."

His gaze scored their faces, his voice raked their ears. "I am your worst nightmare, Port-Hav'n. You may think you have wounded me by slaying my father, but I did not even consider the old brute kin. You have done only *my* will. You have found me out at long last, good people, hehehe!" He applauded them with his grating, sardonic laughter, punctuated by ominous rumbling in the dark clouds.

"You are my pawns and I your puppeteer! I *use* your grievances and hatreds to sway you this way and that for my entertainment. And now you come to *my* home to threaten *my* life and wonder why you suddenly begin killing one another? Because *I* will it so! Watch, good people," he told them forebodingly, raising his arms like a showman. "Watch."

Witchson's evil glare, one eye lit with feral rage and the other cloaked in shadow and mystery, bored deep into the skull of Nod Glenning – the farmer representative in the town council – seething through his eye-sockets to burn alight his mind and expose the darkest corners therein. Witchson's voice – sounding to the farmer like the slow scrape of a whetstone against a blade – rolled resonantly out over the silent, ensnared crowd, despite its unearthly grating.

"Nod Glenning," his growl was like a purr in its softness, *"I* sent fear into the minds of the cattle that gored that young man. *I* made them stampede! *I* caused that boy's death. Douglas, I believe was his name."

Nod's face contorted in a heavy grimace of pain and anger, and he hefted his pitchfork higher. "Shut up, Witchson!" the farmer shouted, his voice cracking ever so slightly.

Witchson smirked at the man cruelly. "Your bastard, was he not?"

Nod exploded. His muscles clenched tighter than ever they had and then released in a fount of energy as he rushed the young Sorcerer. A tenor rumble began in his throat and soon escalated into a full-blown bellow that vied in vain with the thunder for loudest roar. His sensibilities screamed at him to kill this exposer of his secrets, this defiler of his mind. A haze, like the blood for which he lusted, veiled his vision as his heavy feet pounded up the hill.

"Kill him!" Witchson's voice grated against the air.

As Nod Glenning came abreast of the mute, bloody guards who stood over the fallen dead, one of them stepped toward him slowly – dazedly, as if in a dream – and stabbed the farmer through the heart. Nod crumpled to the ground as if the sky had fallen on him.

"Aaaah!" the offending guard screamed, his voice high pitched with a manic, unhinged note. Leaving his sword in its fleshy sheath, the guard turned to his comrades with a look of utter horror on his face, his bloody hands held out before him, as if for manacles. "What happened? What did I do? *Why did I do tha-"*

The raving man was cut short by a fellow guard, who beheaded him with one grim swing of his sword. This second guard – the decapitator – immediately dropped his sword thereafter and raised empty palms in an unthreatening gesture, for the rest of the guards eyed him with the utmost of suspicion with swords in hand, not knowing whether they could trust one another. They all opted for wary stillness, afraid of both their comrades and themselves.

"Hehehe," Witchson quietly laughed his abrasive, scornful laugh, outlined against the dark shape of the manor by the flicker of lightning. "Unlike my mother, I refuse to be taken, refuse to be restrained and refuse to be punished for who I am. You will never stop me. I *dare* any of you to test me. Come get me, if ye be brave enough!" He beckoned to the array of statuesque figures mockingly. "The moment you step foot from the herd, the others will see you for a stranger and stab you in the back! That is your way, people of Port-Hav'n, and that is *my* will."

Silence reigned once more supreme. So still was the grisly, lightning-lit scene that Wetnout could easily count his own heartbeats as they thudded in his ears.

"Guards, finish him!" the Mayor broke the silence, croaking hoarsely at the hesitant guards, pointing a stubby finger at the boy who stood still by the manor doors.

The boy's face was pallid like an albino's, but his violet eye burned brighter than ever before, lighting up his bloodless face with a creepy glow. The guards turned to behold him, but none moved.

"Very well, *I* will finish it!" the Mayor shouted with cracking voice, furious at the cowardice of his people.

Able snatched a sword from a statuesque guard and marched purposefully up the hill toward the manor and the terrifying young boy before it, the longsword clasped in a pudgy fist, the knuckles white with strain. He stomped through the squelching slush slowly, but with surety in his step; surety that the world would thank him for ridding it of this demonic filth.

Nighan Witchson stared him down unflinchingly. His right eye was incandescent with violet fire. "Turn back now, Mayor, or you will regret it."

"Shut your mouth, boy!" Able snapped. "Your reign of terror ends today!"

As Able Roberts, pillar of the community, tramped nearer to the young son of the Witch, a fancily – albeit scantily – clad woman threw herself in protest upon his back.

Adele Norris, Madame of the courtesans, wrapped her slim arms partway around the Mayor's portly abdomen and cried out in sobbing epithets, "No, Mayor, no! Able, please – you mustn't! You can't! Able! Stop, please! The boy has such pretty eyes! No! No! Stop, Able! Please, Mayor!"

Mayor Roberts tried in vain to disentangle himself from the obstinate grip of the clinging woman, but she held on tenaciously. She dug her delicate long fingernails into his silken garb like a cat and dragged along behind him, smearing her beautiful client-bought dress in the mud and calling to him over and over. Roberts tried to ignore her cumbersome weight, but could barely move another step. He tried to pry off her arms, then he tried pinching them, and then he tried beating them with his free hand, but to no avail.

Finally, without thinking, Able drew in his second hand to help extricate him from the feisty woman. The sword, forgotten in his grip, plunged easily between the crying woman's ribs, for the Mayor lurched about with quick, frantic movements.

Adele's moon-round eyes widened further until it seemed they would swallow the Mayor whole into glistening portals.

"Oh!" she gasped faintly as her blood welled and bubbled out.

Able quickly withdrew his sword in horror, jaw agape, and the blood gushed faster.

"I am so sorry!" he whispered, lowering her gently to the dirt, sickened to his stomach by what he had done. The blood was barely noticeable on the scarlet of his suit, he thought dazedly – perhaps he would still be able to use it after this.

When the light faded from Adele's eyes, he rested her beautiful head gently on the ground and, with sword still gripped tightly in his now-bloody hand, turned again to Nighan Witchson.

"*You* made me do that, Sorcerer!" he bellowed loathingly, tears meandering over his fat cheeks.

Witchson smirked. "Oh no, Mayor, it was by your hand that this beauty died. Look out now, I warned you that you would regret this choice."

A garbled yelp of anguish, fear and hatred ripped forth from the throat of Trent Wetnout at the sight of the beautiful courtesan lying slain.

"Nooo!"

Before he knew what he was doing, the old harbourmaster was charging up the hill after the Mayor, empty handed. A thick red veil of hate obscured his vision and cognizance.

The old harbourmaster sprinted, skidded, slipped and stomped his way up the hummock after the adamantly advancing avaricious merchant and tackled him bodily to the mush of mud at Witchson's feet, spattering the boy's shoes with wet dirt.

"What in the Nether …?" Able demanded savagely as he hit the ground.

The Mayor – his round face distorted by mud and unrestrained anger – writhed and spun under the older man like a cobra, slathering his fancy clothes in grime, twisting round so that he faced his attacker. He could not bring his sword to bear in such cramped conditions, and so he abandoned it in favour of punching the body atop his own, yelling incomprehensibly and spraying spittle from his slapping lips. Trent only grunted and clamped down harder as the Mayor's fists knocked the wind from him, pounding his abdomen.

While Able continued futilely trying to bludgeon his attacker, Trent got his slimy hands to the other man's face. He jammed his thick thumbs into the other's eye sockets and shoved down with all his strength, sinking the wailing head into the brown slop that lay beneath. The Mayor tried to fight back, but could do no more than hit at the harbourmaster weakly amid soul-chilling screams.

Trent could feel an unpleasant squishing gooeyness underneath his thumbs, like jelly, but he did not stop pushing until the majority of his thumbs were inside his victim's skull, until the body beneath him ceased its howling and fighting and jerked and jolted in death spasms. Only when it lay still and unmoving beneath him did Trent release the deadly pressure on the crushed orbs and retrieve his gory thumbs from their gruesome hollows.

He looked down at the plump, lifeless face over which he knelt and at his own stained hands, which began to shake violently. He retched and vomited on the dead Mayor's face, but could not tear his eyes from his horrible handiwork.

"What have I done? What have I done? What have I done?" the bloody old man moaned over and over again, slipping off the corpse to sit in the mud. He wrapped his arms around his knees then and rocked back and forth slightly like a babe in a crib, numbed and stricken to his very core with grief and self-loathing.

Nighan Witchson stared on without words, his violet eye as bright and hard as an amethyst.

Nobody else had moved. They could not accept what they saw. It had happened so fast they were convinced they had imagined it. Silence controlled the death-riddled tableau with an iron fist. The people's dream-like reverie was broken only by the crying skies and the soft, incessant moaning of the wind and of the old man that so many of them had called friend.

The attention of the surviving mob eventually returned to the boy they had come to claim. As the young Demon's glare lit up their colourless faces, however, they turned and fled with all haste down the treacherously muddy hill, slipping and sliding and trampling more than one unfortunate to death, to a man never to return.

Witchson slowly turned his tired eyes on the one man who yet lingered in the darkness, lit by sporadic flashes of lightning; the mayoral murderer, Trent Wetnout, who sat next to the plump figure still, oblivious to the world in his self-hatred.

The old man clawed at his own eyes with stained fingernails until, over the corrugated topography of his wrinkled face, tears of blood coursed like undulating rivers. All the while, he moaned in tune with the wailing wind.

"What have I done?"

13

Rebirth

Seeing his companions on the other side of the phosphorescent lake taking up position to surprise the Dwarves from behind, Tar Feng held up an open hand to indicate that they should wait for his signal before they attacked. Fyrstsvard waved in recognition, then swiftly ducked down behind a boulder as the huge worm rising out of the iridescent subterranean lake turned its eyeless face towards him.

Turning his attention to the second approach of Sirraesutha, Tar Feng noticed her open mouth and the purple glow it emitted. The worm did not spot either half of the mercenary band and proceeded calmly back to where the Dwarves and vascular Demon waited patiently. The horned man looked on wordlessly as the slithering creature's vast, dripping head loomed over and lowered towards him.

Sirraesutha gently laid her head down on the platform beside the swollen, veiny figure, her enormous, circular mouth wide enough to be a doorway for him, horns and all. The Demon looked into her maw in triumph.

"At last!" the figure of evil said to no-one in particular, raising a victorious arm whilst his deep voice boomed about the cavern like the beginning of an earthquake. "The time has come to wring what information there is to be had from this sorry wretch – and then, ohhh, that's the sweet part!" His voice rose in a crescendo of his own delight at the prospects of torture and murder. "But first, we must awaken the sleeping beauty! Get the portal out of there!" he ordered the nearest Dwarves with a wave of his hand.

The bearded folk complied, reaching with consternation between the rows of lethal teeth and dumping what appeared to be a large stone ring onto the rocky ledge by the Demon's side. Tar Feng could not observe it clearly, for it was too high above him, but he could see its top half once it was set down upright; a curve of grey stone inset with pulsing purple runes. He could smell the magic emanating from it in pungent waves. He felt certain it had to be connected to the Elf they were searching for.

With the stone ring out of the worm's mouth and on the plateau, the Demon announced, "At last, the time has come, then. Await me, Sirraesutha. I will return with the vessel in no time. It's been a long time since I travelled between realms. This ought to be interesting."

Tar Feng had to rub his eyes then, for he thought he saw the Demon's head and horns approach the stone ring and then vanish completely from sight as the veiny figure made to step through the circle's holey centre.

"What the –" the Wizard squeaked, before clapping a hand over his own mouth, drawing back and hiding with a hammering heart for a few tense seconds until he was sure he had not been heard or seen.

He peeked around the crag again just in time to witness the Demon's head and horns reappear through the fluorescent ring, and though he ducked back lest he be seen, he did first spot that the veiny figure held something large, swaddled in a red blanket, in his hands. Despite the risk, Tar Feng spied again and gasped as he saw what looked like a skinny, snow-white man dumped from the blanket onto the ground.

"The Elf!" he whispered.

The Demon turned its back on the Wizard and jerked violently, and Tar Feng was certain he had kicked the comatose figure lying prone on the rock.

"Well, that failed!" the veiny figure declared, seeming delighted with himself nonetheless. "I guess we'll just have to try something else, won't we?"

Without further ado, the Demon knelt at the side of the pale body and began to chant, his words a guttural, bass growl that left the Tzunese Wizard's bones feeling hollow, his mind frozen and his gut clenching in panic just to hear it.

The old man knew he had to move, however, for now was the time. The great worm had not raised her head back into the air, apparently content to rest and watch the Elf, and the demonic figure was kneeling with its back to the lake and the Wizard. Tar Feng only hoped the Dwarves would be intent on watching the display with the Elf, too.

He turned slowly, without a single bone jangle, to face the young buccaneers.

"Follow me, *silently!*" he breathed.

The three of them moved through the shallow water slower than they had ever moved before, each foot carefully placed without raising it high enough to drip, hands against the wall for support the entire time. As they waded out of the shelter of the outcropping rock wall, Tar Feng signalled Fyrstsvard and the others to wait again lest they get the wrong idea.

The three circled around the rock as silently as they could, the pirates crouching instinctively when they caught sight of the back of the horned Demon and the giant worm. The buccaneers were quivering with terror, but they showed no unrest in following the fearless old Wizard. Once around the rock, they padded silently onto the path that meandered its steep way upwards. They crept up with a degree more speed now that they were back on dry land, for ahead they could see that they would be hidden from the view of the massive maggot, should she lift her head once more, by the rock wall that held up the plateau to which they ascended.

They crept cautiously to a point near the top of the path, where it rounded a bend and would bring them out onto the plateau. Tar Feng put out a low hand to tell them to stop, before tilting his head to listen. Ratnik and Jumal longed to see what was going on just above them, for the Demon's mantra was growing louder and seemed to fill the cavern with an aura at the same time tangible and grotesque, as if the air had turned slimy with the oily attar of a thousand rotting fish.

The stench seeped into their nostrils, their mouths, their eyes and their very skin, and the buccaneers hardly dared to breathe. They looked at one another with noses wrinkled, pulses racing, knowing they could be killed at any moment should they be discovered. Their legs shook and began to ache from their positions on their haunches, but they accepted the muscle burn and the gut-churning aroma, preferring them to the alternative.

The Wizard from the faraway lands of Quing Tzu could feel the horned figure's dark energies building in the air, could taste them upon his tongue. They tasted of powerful magic, of soul magic. The shimmering water of the lake shifted and swirled out of balance, then it began to bubble, boil and writhe as if in agony as the sorceries cast by the Demon permeated the cavern. The light patterns scattered on the wall became frantic in their temperamental flickering as the fish fled the surface, dimming the nimbus that had imbued the cave with alien wonder.

The foul aura that pervaded the area thickened until the air felt as heavy as treacle, weighing the Wizard and Freemen down with the rank and cloying odour. Breathing came only heavily and raggedly, and the reek was such that – if it had been optional – respiration would have been abandoned altogether. The minds of the crouching trio seemed dampened by the sorcerous effects. The pirates could barely remember their own names under the guttural chanting that absorbed their psyches.

Tar Feng could feel the atmosphere begin to swirl out of balance around them, just as had the waters of the lake. The air eddied with arcane energies and crackled as though so much sorcery abounded that it almost caused it to ignite. Ratnik and Jumal could barely see, for the air was distorted as if a heat wave blurred their vision, and their nostrils were clogged by the foulest of bouquets, like decomposition. The Demon began to roar even louder, his volume growing until his words boomed and reverberated around the cavern and it shook as if in the grip of an earthquake with the force of his words.

Stalactites fell by the dozen to land in the dimly glittering lake. Some landed among the ranked Dwarves, crushing some of the hairy little folk, and some even landed on the waiting worm. Most appeared to do no great damage to the colossal creature, for her hairy skin was tougher than leather; one large spike, however, jabbed her where the segments met and pierced the side of her neck, gouging a bloody dent.

Sirraesutha shrieked in pain and raised her great head from where it rested. The worm queen, as Ratnik thought of her, did not spot the three on the path nearby in her fright, such was her hurry to duck beneath the relative safety of the tumultuous water to hide from the projectiles from above. Behind the Demon, the rock above the lift – which the dwarvic army must have used to gain access to the cavern – cracked loudly and visibly. A second later, it collapsed in a noisy shower of rubble, sealing off the way completely, crushing a few Dwarves and making a few more jump hastily out of the way of falling debris.

Holding deathly still, Tar Feng and the pirates were fortunate to escape unscathed from the cavern's fierce response to the dark magic practised within, though stalactites crashed down all around them. The Demon ignored the carnage his chanting had caused – lucky enough to escape its effects himself – and increased in volume still, until the mercenaries on the path below were buffeted with preternatural winds howling from his maw and scouring the entire cavern. The corsairs hunkered down close to the ground, so as not to be blown from their position, and closed their watering eyes against the gale, while the Wizard held his ground, crouched immaculately immobile like a golden statue.

When the young buccaneers began to imagine that either their eardrums or their entire bodies would erupt from all of the dark words and foul forces that filled the very air about them, the despair-inducing invocation came to an abrupt halt. The air and the waters slowly stilled, though there was a tangible aftershock and a lingering smell about the cavern, like the aftertaste of something burnt beyond recognition. Tar Feng knew the place would never be the same again.

Ratnik and Jumal looked down at themselves, for they both experienced the oddest feeling like their skin was frazzling, their hair was on end and their entrails were as cold as ice. They felt lighter than the suddenly stilled air one moment; the next, their lungs felt crushed, like there was nothing to breathe.

While the pirates struggled for a moment to draw breath, Tar Feng heard what he had been listening for; a sudden and desperate inhalation as the Elf came back from the dead. Though he had been waiting for it to happen, the thought of reincarnation chilled the Wizard when he heard that breath. Powerful forces were at play here, forces beyond his ken.

"Water!" ordered the Demon, and the wizened Wizard heard the shuffle of dwarvic footsteps in response. After the Elf had managed to gulp down some water – only a mouthful or two, from the sound of it – the crimson-eyed figure set to with the interrogation.

"Elf!" he barked at the newly reborn figure lying naked on a blanket on the rock out of sight of the Wizard. "You are alive only because of *my* mercy, which stretches only so far as you tell me what I want to know. Should you prove resistant," he lingered on the word, "you will once again be cast from this world in death, and you *will* know eternal torment in the pits of the Nether!"

Tar Feng then heard a quiet croak, no louder than a whisper, from the Elf.

"Gastar?"

The Wizard gasped; it seemed he had been right.

"I am pleased to be recognised so quickly," the demonic figure purred. "It means both that you understand the plight you are in and that your brain has not been turned to mush by the rebirthing process. You remember me. Now, Elf, do you remember who *you* are?"

There was slow gulping as the Elf drank more water. Tar Feng awaited the answer with bated breath.

Eventually, it came. "Yes, Gastar," whispered the quiet, wheezy voice – a voice like one gets after a long sleep when their mouth has become extraordinarily dry, thought the Wizard, and this Elf had been asleep for longer than most. "I remember. My name is Amhrahil Serenpitua, the most powerful of the *Vaylorici*. My mother's name was Ehelema and my father's was Sitorro. I was born in a village named Hjem-Kodur in the land then known as Holoi and was murdered, age nine hundred and seventy three, by a man I should not have trusted."

"The most powerful of the Vaylorici," Gastar repeated mockingly. "That might have been true once, but not anymore, eh, you hypocrite? Oh, that's right. I know all about your little squabbles with the Betrayer and your *dirty* little secret! I know there is *nothing* you can do to stop me, and more importantly, I know *why!"*

Tar Feng was surprised to hear a small sound like a sob then.

The Demon laughed cruelly. "So, Amhrahil, now that you realise just how helpless you are: do you know why you are here?"

The Elf's voice regained a small semblance of strength. "I am the Prophet, the creator of *Citta Pacia,* the haven for all in death. I don't know how you have brought me back, Gastar, but I know why. Your greed for souls to torment in that little rat-trap you call the Nether is insatiable. You will never find *Citta Pacia!"* So vehement was the weak Elf that he coughed and gasped for air after his vituperation.

"Oh, I think I will find it," responded Gastar, his voice louder, deeper and more menacing, "for you are a puny sight, little Elf – like a new-born calf that can't even stand on its weak, little legs – whereas *I* have power you cannot dream of! It has been almost a millennium since your timely demise, and I have used that time well!"

"A thousand years? How – why have you kept me so long? And why bring me back now?"

The demonic Lord of the Nether, Gastar – figment of every child's fevered nightmare – stared daggers at the Prophet he had awoken.

"I will ask the questions here, fool! Now, tell me where you hid *Citta Pacia!"* roared Gastar, his patience clearly wearing thin. Tar Feng heard a meaty smack that could only have been the Lord of the Nether's hand striking the vulnerable Elf. "Tell me!" He struck again.

"Never!"

Tar Feng heard a crackling like lightning, followed by the sound of the Prophet screaming. A faint whiff of burning flesh reached the old man's nostrils.

"Tell me, Elf, or I will teach you pain such as none has ever known!" Gastar demanded.

"*Citta Pacia* will live on," Amhrahil mumbled, drained and weak. "Magic or no magic, I will never betray the souls of my followers."

The Dark God growled angrily again and leaned close to spit his words loathingly in the Elf's face. "You *will* betray your people, Prophet – it is only a matter of time! And I have nothing but time on my hands down here; time in which to pick you apart, piece by piece, shred by shred, and then put you back together to do it all over again, over and over, until you tell me *everything* you know! And then, you can die, content in the knowledge that your life's works will come to nothing, that I will eviscerate your *followers'* souls, that I will find your blasted haven and I will *drain it dry!"*

Tar Feng suddenly stood up from the crouching position he had maintained, which had hidden him out of sight of Gastar and the army of Dwarves, and waved his arms to and fro frantically. The little bones about his wrists clacked furiously. Ratnik and Jumal looked on, paralysed by shock for an instant. The horned figure's back was still turned to the old man, but the army behind him saw Tar Feng in an instant and whipped out their axes in a blink.

Before the Dwarves could advance more than a few paces on the old man, however, Fyrstsvard, Heldig and the other mercenaries – who had manoeuvred themselves atop the slope of boulders and debris, behind the Dwarves on the raised plateau, to await Tar Feng's unsubtle signal – pounced up and attacked the bone-clad army from the rear with distracting hollers. In the first few moments, Kamilah shot one Dwarf in the neck with her bow, Izdaju lopped off the head of another, and Fyrstsvard impaled a third. The rest of the company were hot on their heels.

As Gastar turned to see what had alerted the Dwarves to unsheathe their weapons, he was knocked from his feet by a searing green blast from the Tzunese Wizard's power staff. Tar Feng got his first decent glimpse of the Prophet as the Dark God toppled. The Elf was sitting on the rock with a faded red blanket wrapped around him for warmth. His long hair was white as fresh snow, and he was thinner and taller than most men, like a willow wand. His scholarly face looked human, for the most part. His nose, however, was too slim to be human, his cheekbones too prominent and delicate, his chin too slender and sharp, and his ears too pointed at the top. He reminded Tar Feng of a fragile, hollow-boned bird. His piercing, pale blue eyes slowly opened, reinforcing his already wintry aura. He sat still, gathering his strength.

Suddenly Jumal, the first of the two young buccaneers to respond to Tar Feng's blast and the shouts of his comrades' attack, leapt onto the plateau in front of the surprised Wizard and set off determinedly to help his companions fight the Dwarves. The rune-inscribed stone ring and the downed but uninjured Gastar lay between the young buccaneer and the developing skirmish. Jumal ran straight at the God and then – before the dumbstruck Wizard's eyes – straight over him, even going so far as to stamp down on the demonic figure's abdomen as he passed, inducing a grunt. He was past – though Tar Feng could barely credit his eyes – and he clove into the Dwarves heroically with both cutlass and stolen axe, but it was clear he needed aid.

Then, Ratnik too leapt up onto the plateau, and though Tar Feng put out a grasping hand to hold him back, he broke free and ran after his friend. Gastar was not to be trifled with twice, however. As the younger pirate sought to follow his friend's footsteps and jump over the still prone horned figure, the God of the Nether stretched up a clawed hand and clamped it firmly around the young man's ankle. With a violent wrench and a bloodcurdling roar, the Lord of the Nether brought the young corsair smashing down, face first, to the ground, where he lay still until Gastar wrapped his hand around the young man's throat and lifted him up so that the swashbuckler's limp legs dangled a foot above the red rock floor.

Tar Feng was unable to shoot at Gastar with his staff again then, for fear of hitting the wounded Ratnik – whose face, he could see, was smashed and bloody – and Jumal was unaware of his friend's plight, with his back turned, busy fighting for survival against multiple short, hairy opponents. Gastar held Ratnik in the air effortlessly – like a bloody life-size doll, rather than a man – squeezing the last dregs of life from him.

Heldig, able to see easily over the short Dwarves' heads, witnessed the plight of his crewmate and bellowed like a wounded bull, "My son!"

The ageing pirate lowered his enormous shoulders and charged forward into the array of armed and aggravated Dwarves with all the speed his bulky frame could muster.

The first Dwarf in his path was batted aside like a pest with Heldig's hammer, the second was shoulder-barged to the ground, the third torn open by his cutlass in a white spray. Seven more Dwarves went down in similar fashion on Heldig's rampage. Several of them scored hits on the pirate's body as he barrelled past, however, and his blood began to litter his trail.

Jumal glimpsed his Captain rampage past him like a bear with a headache from the corner of his eye, sending blood and Dwarves flying, but he was too entangled in a web of steel to lend a hand.

Despite the cuts, stabs and bashes that he received on the way, Heldig never slowed and every Dwarf that stood between him and Ratnik was bowled over, cut down or knocked aside until the old pirate reached his crewmate.

Fortunately for the red-bearded Captain, Gastar was facing away from the skirmish, holding Ratnik aloft and watching him wriggle as feebly as a bunny held by the scruff. Heldig tackled the horned figure to the ground with all the momentum he had built up and landed atop him on the rock, though his cutlass was lost on impact. Ratnik, too, was thrown clear to land with a dull thud on the rock by the silent Prophet.

Heldig roared incoherently as he beat at the figure beneath him with his hammer, but the blows had less effect than bee stings on Gastar. Where the hammer struck, it did not even bruise or break the skin. The Lord of the Nether quickly slid out from underneath the pirate and cuffed him over the head with an open palm. Such was the force of the blow that Heldig's head was smashed down onto the rock with a sickening crack. Before blood from the wound could even begin to pool, Gastar picked up the old seafarer's hammer and, with the other hand, wrenched the bulky pirate up by the neck just as he had done to Ratnik, hoisting him into the air so that his feet hung above the ground. Heldig struggled against the vicelike grip, but it was clear the blow to the head had done its work.

Tar Feng shot several more of his magical, green globs at Gastar while his back was turned, but to no avail. The Dark God was prepared for such an attack this time, and they did little more than stagger him. Then, just before the Wizard's last splotch struck, Gastar spun with inhuman speed and held Heldig's squirming body before him as a shield. The scorching globule struck the old pirate in the back, singeing his blue coat, and he groaned, not having the energy to shout out in pain.

"Sorry!" apologised Tar Feng with a superfluous wave, abandoning his energy globs tactic. Instead, he closed his eyes and began to incant as precipitously as his thin lips could move. *"Sith'eshu zam'beamber!"*

He felt his energies begin to respond to his will as his spell took effect. The moment after it was cast – and his concentration was no longer required to hold at bay and command the magical forces he manipulated – Tar Feng opened his eyes once more. He was just in time to witness Gastar raise a clawed hand over his head and form in its palm what looked like a shimmering crimson spear comprised of energy, scintillating, crackling, as jagged and luminescent as a thunderbolt. The God snarled vindictively, his arm shot forward, and he cast the magic spear at the pesky Tzunese man.

Luckily, Tar Feng had opened his eyes just in time not only to witness but to dodge; he dived to his left, off the edge of the plateau on which they stood and into the lake of light below, though he did avoid the red energy bolt.

The spell the wizened old man had wrought took effect on Gastar as the Wizard hit the water with a splash. Large, scaly red snakes emerged from the rock at the Dark God's feet, though the bottom of their serpentine forms never left the red rock, but rather seemed to flow unceasingly from it like waterspouts. Two of the snakes swiftly wound around Gastar's legs, binding them tight, while two slithered up his body, seeking to encircle his arms, hissing and coiling around him.

The Lord of the Nether seemed constrained for a moment as he struggled to move against the snakes, but then he ceased struggling and, before he was completely tied up, used the pirate's hammer to smash the snake wrapping its way around the arm that gripped Heldig to bits of fragmented rock. He then pummelled the serpents that encircled his legs and the final one on his arm viciously, as if running out of patience for disruptions, and they too turned into shattered stone in death.

Clear and free of distractions, Gastar turned his attention back to the once-great sea Captain clasped in his mighty grip. This time, the Dark God had no intention of slowly draining the life from his victim.

Instead, he brought Heldig's mottled face so close to his own that the pirate could clearly see the scar on the God's face peeling back to reveal the blackness within. Then, he spoke scathingly in his abyssal voice, "You are brave, fat man, I will say that for you. As your reward, I shall eat of your still-beating heart while you watch and drink my fill of your soul! You will have the honour of being the first of my *Thakshir!* The Lord of *Thakshir!* What's that?" Gastar asked, seeing that the dying pirate was trying to mumble a few last words.

"Do it quickly then," the old pirate wheezed. Blood flowed from his temple down his face, sealing one eye shut, and his face was red and puffy from the punishment he had taken. "'Cos I can't stand to smell your putrid breath a moment longer!"

Two barks of laughter from Gastar were swiftly followed by the God ramming his claws deep into the Freeman's abdomen, rupturing skin and ripping through flesh. Heldig groaned in pain, but could do nothing more. The Lord of the Nether reached up through Heldig's body until his bloody fingers found the man's heart. Elbow-deep in the pirate, Gastar wrenched out the heart with one quick, gore-splattering motion.

Dropping Heldig's twitching body carelessly, Gastar bit into the heart with sharp teeth, sending its juices squirting over his face to drip from his pointy chin. He ate slowly, making sucking noises, savouring it as though it were the finest of delicacies and he had all the time in the world in which to enjoy it.

14

Goading a God

Fyrstsvard and the mercenaries, witnessing Heldig's end while trying to fend off the blows of the surrounding Dwarves, felt the fires of fury fill their gullets and swung their weapons with mounting wrath.

Fyrstsvard and Izdaju, both expert swordsmen, were able to scythe through the dwarvic attackers like a spear through flesh, their swords flashing with such grace and precision that no enemy could stand before them long, darting around axes and between gaps in the bone armour to unerringly seek the hearts of those beneath. Steaming dwarvic blood pooled on the plateau, making it slick and slippery, and dwarvic screams rent the air – bass cries of pain – whenever one of the swordsmen could not find a killing blow and opted instead to lop off an appendage.

Steel skirled against steel, and feet pounded the ground as Dwarf and man pitted themselves against one another in a gory heaving contest. Fyrstsvard wished he had his shield with him, but had judged it too bulky for stealth. He was glad of his armour after the first dent in it and was vowing never to take it off again by the time three axes had scored it. From the corner of his eye, he could see Izdaju mowing down foes like a farmer does wheat at harvest and was at a loss to explain how the Nomad, with no shield and no armour, had taken no major wounds. The Knight was one of the finest blades in Justiqua, but he feared he would have died numerous times by now if not for the steel plating swaddling him.

His arms burned with the effort of two-handed swings of his longsword, his shoulders felt beaten and his wrists numb, but – as fast as he moved – he could not keep up with the pace of the Nomad's twin scimitars.

Fyrstsvard stabbed a bearded fellow in the eye, leaned back from a pair of axe swipes and then crashed forwards again, chopping at one Dwarf and punching at another. The punch with his off-hand connected with a bulbous nose, but did little more than stagger the recipient, while the sword hit a bone shield with a dull thud and fastened there.

Yanking his blade and the shield to which it was attached to the left, the Knight jerked one Dwarf off-balance and into the other, retrieved his weapon with a twist of the wrist and clove the thrown Dwarf's skull in two at the cheek, the blade whistling through the nose and out the other cheek in a fountain of bloody screams.

The second opponent, whom the first had been thrown into, managed to throw his companion's corpse off him and hack vengefully at the Knight. Fyrstsvard sidestepped easily, however, and jabbed him in the forehead, making brains squirt out.

As more foes stepped up to take the place of the deceased, the Justiquan parried an axe and slashed at its owner, but his sword glanced off the Dwarf's armour and he was left overbalanced and vulnerable for a second. Fyrstsvard cringed as he saw an axe blade drawn back, ready to slice into his unprotected midsection, but could do nothing to stop it. By lucky happenstance, however, Izdaju had torn apart six opponents in the time it had taken Fyrstsvard to overcome three, and as the Nomad's scimitar came crashing down on a dwarvic head, blood from the wound spurted out violently, some of it spattering in the eye of the Dwarf swinging at the Knight.

Blinded by hot blood, the Dwarf let out a garbled cry, swung wild and wide with his axe, slipped in the viscera around his feet and tumbled onto his back, where he wriggled – not unlike an upturned turtle, Fyrstsvard thought. The Knight was grateful to still be breathing, but he was not sure Izdaju had even noticed what he had done in saving his life. The Nomad did not look sideways or acknowledge the Justiquan in any way, only kept whirling his blades so fast that they hummed, even when passing through somebody.

Fyrstsvard threw himself back into the fray and, determined to repay the favour, threw himself on top of two Dwarves at great risk when it appeared they were wearing the Nomad beside him down. Although he felt like he saved Izdaju in doing so, he also knew he would not have been able to escape the situation without the Nomad's help, so the act did not fully assuage his conscience.

Despite the swordsmen's prowess, though, they were soon pushed back once more by force of numbers.

The group could make no headway as the battle-raged Heldig had done, for the Dwarves swarmed them too tightly now that they were all aware they were being attacked. Egobal flung his scorching sand in the faces of his attackers – burning their faces and eyes – until they got too close and he was forced to resort to his twin daggers as a method of protection. Kamilah, at the rear of the mercenaries with her bow, was quickly becoming frustrated as her arrows bounced off bleached bone shields and armour.

Jumal stood like a lone rock against a fuming tide of bearded opponents on the other side of the dwarvic contingent from Fyrstsvard and the others, but he was unable to reach his comrades as they began to falter. It was all he could do to stay alive himself, for at any one time at least three Dwarves were trying to kill him. The Chilpaean had given up conscious control of his body. His instincts and reflexes kept him alive as his brain functioned on a far more primitive plane than usual; kill or be killed.

He was fast and strong; good at ducking and dodging the attacks of the relatively slow, muscular little Dwarves. This was fortunate, because the stout little warriors did not go down easily. With all their armour, it was difficult to deliver a killing strike without first having to deliver punishing blows to the armour to create an opening. For the most part, Jumal tried to stab at their unprotected hairy faces with his cutlass, but they used their shields well.

Jumal hacked down one shield with his axe and stabbed a Dwarf in the mouth with the point of his curved cutlass, swiftly dodging to the right to avoid a downward hack from a Dwarf to the left. He kicked the offending Dwarf in the leg, and the stout fighter was forced down to one knee. Jumal smashed in his teeth with his fist, before turning quickly to parry a blow from the right with his cutlass. His brain whirred at wild speeds as it tried to keep up with his movements.

After parrying the blow, he kicked the Dwarf to the ground, smashed another shield aside and stabbed the Dwarf who held it, rolled to the right, hacked at another shield, blocked a blow, delivered one himself and was finally shield-barged to the ground by two Dwarves working in concert with one another. He rolled backwards before they could chop him up, and their axes struck the rock floor awkwardly with loud clangs.

As those clangs rebounded amidst a cacophony of others about the cavern, Amhrahil Serenpitua's icy blue eyes snapped open and came into focus on a small golden man, who was dripping wet.

Tar Feng had crept back up to the plateau, unnoticed. "Hello, Elf!" he whispered, waving a bone-jangling arm. "Can you move? Can you walk?"

"Yes, I think so."

Tar Feng looked up to where Fyrstsvard and the others fought. Taking a deep breath, knowing it would bring unwanted attention, Tar Feng shouted at the top of his airy lungs, "The Elf is fine! He can move – we have to go now! Everyone, over here!"

All activity ceased for a split second as every being in the cavern heard the Wizard's plan, then Fyrstsvard yelled, "Now, Egobal!"

The desert-dweller ducked back from the fight as Fyrstsvard took up the slack by booting the Sandman's foe away. Egobal spoke to his sand and cast it in a high arc above the heads of the remaining dwarvic force. *"Sihah Alahehk!"*

The tiny granules drifted down lazily, and – just as before – the Dwarves beneath began to sneeze helplessly. Their eyes watered, their eyelids became heavy, and their muscles were subtly weighed down with lead. First, one Dwarf fell to the ground with a thump, snoring blissfully, then another and another until every Dwarf lay on the bloody floor, all snoring like contended children.

Jumal, on the other side of the pile of sleepers from Fyrstsvard, nodded to the others thankfully, but could find no words, panting through his shirt, with which he covered his mouth and nose. He turned to look for his friend, Ratnik, and then, seeing him lying crumpled by the side of the Prophet, he ran over.

Fyrstsvard, Egobal, Kamilah and Jumal ceased attacking the Dwarves when they dozed off, but Izdaju – caught up in bloodlust and an excuse to uncage his animalistic side – continued to cleave them apart like a butcher, his slashing swords mesmeric to him in their rhythmic rise and fall as he rained gore and bone fragments down on himself and the others.

Fyrstsvard stepped up behind him and shouted to him sharply, "That is enough, Izdaju! Put away your weapons!"

The orders had no effect, and the Nomad scythed at the prostrate Dwarves like he was cutting weeds; bent at the knee, swinging low. Fyrstsvard – much as he disliked the grubby, beardy people – could not bear to see any sentient creature treated so cruelly and unfairly, and so he shouted again, louder, "Enough, Izdaju! Put away your weapons right now – that is an order!"

When Izdaju did not stop, Fyrstsvard tapped him with the back of his hand on the man's back, and the Nomad whirled like a surprised tiger and pounced at what he perceived to be a new threat. Izdaju lashed out with one scimitar virulently, which Fyrstsvard – taken by surprise – barely ducked, and then the Knight had to back away from the flash of a second blade. He stumbled over a Dwarf body and fell to the ground. Izdaju raised his hand for the killing blow, but Kamilah's voice pierced the cavern.

"Stop!"

Izdaju stopped, his bloody scimitar raised high above the Knight who lay with upraised hands. A sense of self, of reality, of civilisation and of circumstance returned to the Nomad, and he realised guiltily he was about to kill his own companion – though part of him still longed to, he had to admit.

He stepped back, tucked the raised scimitar under his arm and offered his hand to the Knight. "Sorry. Guess I got carried away."

Fyrstsvard nodded slowly and took the proffered hand gingerly, retrieving his dropped sword on the way up.

Gastar – having finished his meal – was aghast for a moment at the sight of his force put to sleep, but then he turned on the oblivious Prophet with a menacing throat rattle. Tar Feng held him back by firing blob after magical green blob at the God, which served only to distract and infuriate, for he was unharmed by the scorching energy pulses.

"Enough, little man!" Gastar bellowed, fury wrapping its fiery fingers around his brain.

His arm shot out toward the old Wizard who bombarded him with sizzling magical globules, and grey smoke poured out from his clawed hand. The smoke coalesced into a mimicking hand to match Gastar's own, and then it flew through the air, seeking its target.

The mystical misty hand seized Tar Feng by the throat as Gastar clenched his own hand on thin air. The Dark God lifted his fist up, and at the same time the foggy hand hauled the little Wizard up off the ground to dangle like a puppet in the air.

Before the Lord of the Nether could do more, however, Fyrstsvard and Egobal enacted a quick plan. Having snuck up on Gastar from behind – for the *Serrici* can move as quietly as a night breeze – Egobal suddenly wrapped his arms around the God's mutated, vascular legs and heaved him up off the ground as high as he could.

Fyrstsvard had taken a running start. He leapt into the air with all of his built-up momentum and smacked Gastar in the back of the head with his blade with as much force as he could bring to bear. As he had expected, his simple steel sword was not enough to do any real damage to the God – he was not even sure it broke the skin, and it felt like hitting the trunk of an ancient, hardened tree – but the force of the blow catapulted the Dark Lord's unanchored body off the edge of the plateau and into the water below. With Gastar's concentration broken, the misty hand was robbed of its power and vanished without a trace.

Tar Feng fell through the air with a yelp to sprawl in a bony heap on the ground. *"Tai woon!"*

Jumal helped the shaken and bloody Wizard to his feet, and the mercenaries regrouped around the naked Elf, who sat motionless on the scarlet blanket with his hand lying gently on Ratnik's head.

"Everyone alright?" asked Fyrstsvard quickly.

The injured young pirate, Ratnik, sat up slowly, groaning and holding his throbbing, bloody cranium. "I think I'm gonna be sick … what happened?"

The rest of the group nodded, looking around at one another. Most had scratches and bruises and were spattered with blood, but none felt like complaining, having beheld Heldig's fate.

"Dat Demon … tore out Heldig's heart, Rats," Jumal told him hesitantly, resting a hand on his shoulder. "Cap'n is dead." The Chilpaean's eyes swam at the words.

Tears burned tracks down Ratnik's bloody cheeks. He gulped and said thickly, "I know. I saw – I – I thought it was a dream – or a nightmare – but I saw …" Jumal squeezed his shoulder, and further words got stuck behind lumps in their throats.

"Tar Feng, is this him?" the Knight asked the shrivelled old man, who was leaning on Jumal.

The Wizard could only cough, wheeze and wave in response. The fall had knocked the wind out of him.

"Better be him," Kamilah asserted, thinking of the long way they had come to get here.

Fyrstsvard knelt at the Elf's side with a clank of armour. "Are you alright?"

"Yes, thank you," responded the Elf haltingly in Traveller's Tongue. His slanted eyes looked sad, Fyrstsvard thought. "Help me up, please?" The Knight grabbed the Elf's arm and gently lifted him to his feet. The Elf picked up the red blanket and wrapped it around himself to cover his modesty. "I will be fine, but we must leave before Gastar gets back."

Fyrstsvard was shocked to hear that the demonic figure they had fought was none other than the Lord of the Nether, Gastar, but there was no time for more than one other question.

"Are you the Prophet who created *Citta Pacia*?" he asked the Elf straightforwardly.

Amhrahil smiled sorrowfully, looking weak and frail as a new-born calf wrapped in his old blanket, and said, "I am."

Before anyone could say another word, a plangent splash caught their attention and all looked out over the lake. With stalactites falling on her from above and her mission presumably completed, the worm, Sirraesutha, seemed to have decided it was time to leave. The group could see her long form slithering hastily toward the inlet by the lake where the Wizard and pirates had hidden earlier and, they guessed, on through the hole in the roof leading to the *Rodici* pits, through which Tar Feng, Ratnik and Jumal had descended so hastily.

"Follow me!" commanded Tar Feng wheezily.

He waved his staff like a baton and stepped off purposefully down the twisting slope that he and the buccaneers had ascended earlier. As they rounded the bend, they saw Gastar waiting for them at the bottom, Sirraesutha's trail still sliding out of the water foot by foot behind him.

"Just where d'you think you're going?" demanded Gastar in

outraged incredulity, his eyes manically wide like volcanoes about to erupt, his scarred visage split by an evil grin.

Tar Feng wasted no time when he saw his adversary, but pointed his staff and barked, *"Hachak'hithi-iriscamae'glit!"*

From the end of his crook exploded thick, clinging webs that looked to have been spun by a spider the size of a horse, which engulfed the Dark God in a cocoon of whiteness in an instant, smothering both him and his attempt to cast an energy bolt. Mummified by the webs, Gastar was blind and impotent to defend himself for a short time, and the wily Wizard – firing off globs of hissing green energy at the God to keep him distracted – began to incant a quite different spell under his breath.

"Shihass'sa-mae-lin'sifluba!"

The Lord of the Nether, however, was not easily constrained, and in a matter of mere moments after Tar Feng ceased his emerald bombardment, Gastar had clawed and ripped his way free of the white veil that incapacitated him, tossing its ragged remnants from him and stamping on them in ire, before turning his attention to the Wizard who had ensnared him.

Seeing that the Dark God was readying to cast a spell, Fyrstsvard – who had up until now been standing at Tar Feng's side, protectively in front of the Prophet, whom he had regrettably but necessarily pushed to the ground out of the way – stepped up and shoved the emaciated Wizard to the side, much as he had done the Elf, breaking Tar Feng's concentration as effectively as any spell.

The attack that Gastar conjured – a hastily thrown glob of yellow energy intended to snap the Wizard from his trance – spattered over the Knight, spinning and felling him. It singed his shoulders, neck and beard and blackened his gleaming steel breastplate, tarnishing the mark of the Order of *Pacia*. Fyrstsvard, the world spinning above him, was thankful to be alive as he fought back the nausea that invaded.

"Tits!" muttered Ratnik, his gonging head still sticky but his cutlass at the ready.

Amhrahil, Fyrstsvard and Tar Feng – who was downed, but not harmed and had already restarted his interrupted incantation – were all sprawled across the path in front of the young pirate, who wondered what good he could do where a Knight, a Prophet and a Wizard were not enough. The path down which they walked – narrow now between two walls – was not wide enough for anyone to pass them, and so Ratnik and Jumal looked at one another helplessly.

"Ready, mate?" asked Jumal, hefting his weapons and rolling his shoulders to loosen them.

"That's it!" Gastar leered. "Come and meet your doom!"

"Yarr, let's do it," replied Ratnik, clenching his jaw.

Together, they advanced on Gastar and ran the last few yards between them, roaring with weapons held high. Ratnik swung first, his cutlass whistling in an arc towards the horned fiend's neck only to be firmly blocked by the God's left arm. The blade's reverberation made Ratnik's hands feel numb and his arms ache like he had hit a steel wall.

Jumal, less than a step behind, swung at Gastar's midriff with his cutlass and received a similarly sound block, except the lower blow meant the God's right arm had dropped, pointed down, and his left was still blocking Ratnik's cutlass. So, when the dwarvic axe in the Chilpaean's right hand came hissing down towards Gastar's unprotected head, Jumal was certain he was going to land a blow – and a decisive one, too.

The strike never landed. Before it could, Gastar opened his mouth wide and emitted a deep, guttural, skull-shaking sonic vibration so potent that it threw Ratnik and Jumal back before the the latter's axe could fall. The buccaneers landed prostrate on the red rock, while the rest of the group were blown onto their rumps, if they were not already there.

Izdaju was up again in a flash and bearing down on the veiny figure a snarl later. He bounded over Ratnik before the prone pirate could recover and leapt again to bring his twin scimitars humming around and down on the Dark God, forming a keyhole shape between them. Before the blades could cleave, however, Gastar met the Nomad's running leap with a prodigious jump of his own and punched Izdaju in the face, straight through the middle of the keyhole. The blow flipped Izdaju backwards in the air, and he sprawled hard on his face, winded and seeing stars.

Landing lightly, Gastar stepped forward and raised a foot over the flattened Nomad, ready to crush his skull under heel. Before his foot could fall, an arrow twanged from Kamilah's bow and struck the Dark God in the face. The force of the strike broke the arrow and failed to pierce the warped, veiny flesh, but it did snap Gastar's head to one side and send his body staggering two steps after it.

"Knock him back to the water!" Tar Feng's shout resonated around the cavern, and the water of the underground lake began to bubble and froth behind the Nether's overseer as the Wizard resumed his invocation.

Ratnik and Jumal – back on their feet, despite cuts and bruises – leapt to the attack once again while Gastar reeled, both landing solid blows on the God's head and torso. Their opponent did not stagger for long, however, and when he recovered, the pirates' blows were like bee stings to a bear, leaving no dent or mar.

Batting aside Ratnik's cutlass, Gastar backhanded the young pirate soundly across the face, knocking him down without a noise. Then, he ducked a swing of Jumal's axe, sidestepped a cutlass jab and cuffed the

Chilpaean around the head. Jumal crumpled like a sagging sail. Fortunately for them, Egobal was yet to engage himself, and he did so with aplomb.

While the pirates had attacked, the Sandman had calmly shifted forward, and now – barely noticed yet by the demonic figure they faced – he stood almost within striking range. By the time the Lord of the Nether registered the Sandman's presence, he was too late to stop him.

Grabbing a large handful of the fine white sand in his pouch, Egobal whispered to it as he walked and, when he was close, cast it all toward Gastar's ugly, red-streaked face, which instantly lit up with bright red scalds and emitted high-pitched howls. Blinded by the burning sand in his eyes, Gastar slashed madly in front of him with fingers like claws ending in sharp, black nails. He was knocked back by an arrow buzzing from Kamilah's bow, however, and Egobal had time to step back out of harm's way. He did so gracefully, but then darted in close again to blow more sand in the God's face, this time whispering the sleeping enchantment. As he had expected, though, it had no effect on the powerful being.

"Push him into the water!" Tar Feng yelled, before continuing his low mumbling mantra and gesticulating frantically. *"Shihass'sa-mae-lin'sifluba! Shihass'sa-mae-lin'sifluba!"*

Ratnik and Jumal leapt forward again, smashing at the sightless God with axe and cutlass. Gastar roared in anger as he felt the blows, and though again they made not even a dent, he staggered back two steps closer to the water, once more swiping blindly at his foes dangerously fast. When he snarled, his scar bunched up like a black worm wriggling across his face.

The Freemen took it in turns to attack, and therefore – though they were swatted back almost every time with a new welt or graze – they held the God in check, giving him no time to launch his own offensive between assaults. Though they yelped in pain at each new wound, Gastar could gain no ground nor concentrate enough for a spell while his eyes stung so fiercely from the sand.

By the time the buccaneers were finally clubbed down by waving fists, Egobal had heard Tar Feng's calling and put his own plan into effect. While the pirates had distracted the Dark God, Egobal had murmured his own incantation, *"Sihah melifluo'chiavellima! Sihah melifluo'chiavellima!"*

He upended his pouch of sand, emptying all of it, and yet not a grain made it to the ground. Before gravity could take effect, the Sandman waved his arm in a wide, theatrical circle above his head and his spell took hold of the thousands of grains of sand. Instead of falling, they adhered to Egobal's body like iron filings to a lodestone, save that they whirled around him like a tornado in response to his hand's twirling and coated him evenly across his entire body. In seconds, the Sandman was sporting a suit of sand armour that glowed like grainy gold in the light of the lake, covering him from neck to toe.

He leapt over the fallen corsairs and grappled with the God of the Nether. Fyrstsvard had seen the God's strength first-hand and had felt what it was like to strike him with a steel blade – it was like hitting stone. So, he had never expected to see anybody manhandle Gastar, and yet he saw it now to his stunned disbelief. He wondered what kind of eldritch strength and protection that sand armour afforded the Sandman; clearly, the powers involved were prodigious. God and Sandman grappled, arm to arm, face to face, with snarls deeply etched, grunting and spitting. Neither seemed able to take the upper hand at first.

Egobal did not overpower the God, but he did eventually manage to shove him back the few steps necessary so that Gastar's feet sloshed into the edge of the lake. Then, most surprisingly of all, thought Fyrstsvard, the Sandman held the God there. Gastar strained and hissed, his tendons standing out and his face turning red, and the Sandman staggered from side to side precariously.

"Hurry, Tar Feng!" Egobal gasped, wrestling to regain his balance. "I cannot hold him much longer!"

Tar Feng's voice rose to a crescendo. *"Shihass'sa-mae-lin'sifluba!"*

The lake water writhed, crashing and splashing, swelling and caving in again – like lungs breathing – and the light patterns on the walls fluctuated dizzyingly.

"Shihass'sa-mae-lin'sifluba!"

Tar Feng finished his incantation and cast out his hands towards God and lake. For a moment, nothing happened but the water boiling at the Dark Lord's feet. Then, from the bubbling froth emerged two figures, one on each side of the horned fiend.

Both were six feet tall and made of water, with sloshing, ill-defined adumbrates that were only vaguely humanoid. The companions could see through the glowing, translucent figures; inside them, streams of bubbles rose up their centres like spines until they reached the tops, where they foamed – white like surf – before crashing down the sides of the watery domes to form thick arms with no neck or shoulders in between.

Nevertheless, they exhibited some strength when they reached out their watery limbs to grab and hold Gastar's muscular arms, taking some of the pressure off Egobal. Tar Feng knew his water elementals were flimsy, simplistic creations. If Gastar had not been preoccupied, the Wizard did not doubt he could have smitten them down with his little finger, but as it was they proved helpful in subduing the God. Trapped and unseeing, Gastar hollered his rage at the ceiling, cursing them all to the Nether. The water elementals gagged him with watery hands and began to pound the pinioned God of the Nether with their flowing fists rhythmically and mercilessly, each punch punctuated by a splash and a gurgle from Gastar.

The Prophet, Amhrahil, shook Fyrstsvard, whose breastplate was still black and smoking, and said, "Get up! We must flee at once!"

The Knight, who had been watching events unfold in pain and nausea since the God's power glob had hit him, twitched an arm and decided he could perhaps try to move again. He did not for a moment take his eyes off Egobal and the God wrestling between the two watery, blue figures, however.

Weakened and gagged by the elementals, Gastar could not resist or even cast a spell as Egobal slowly pushed him away from the shore, deeper and deeper into the garish lake. God and Sandman sank up to their chests in no time, the water elementals by their side every step of the way, beating the God with liquid fists.

"All of you – go!" Egobal screamed, his voice strangled from the effort he was expending. "Get out of here while you can! I can't hold him back forever and I can't kill him, but I can give you time to escape! Go, Knight! Take the Prophet back to the surface world once more! Flee, my friends, before we all die in this nightmarish cave!"

Fyrstsvard's heart panged, beating fast. He barely knew this man – he was not even clear on his motives for coming on this quest – but the Sandman's sacrifice touched the Knight.

"No, Egobal!" he cried. "He'll kill you! We will not leave you behind! You're coming with us!"

"No time!" Egobal hollered. "I can only hold him back so long … Please, Knight, do not let my sacrifice be in vain! Use the time I am giving you to fulfil your mission! Escape! Live! I beg you!"

Tears stung the Knight's eyes, and his words came out husky. "Thank you, Egobal! We won't forget you!"

Together, the four figures drifted out into the middle of the lake, where opposing waves clashed like cymbals in white surf all around them, whipped up by Tar Feng's energies. Not wishing to take any chances, the sly Wizard from Quing Tzu lobbed his last two remaining smoke bags out over the lake. Within a minute, fog had wreathed the entire body of water in thick, grey, reeking swirls and God and Sandman were lost to sight.

15

The *Thakshir* Lord

Ignoring Gastar's garbled, gargled threats, Tar Feng turned to the others and panted, "I can't believe that worked! Run!"

"Wait, we must help them!" replied the Elf, gesturing to the groaning warriors scattered across the floor.

The two pirates sat up groggily, moaning, clutching their heads and inspecting cuts and bumps. After a quick shake from Tar Feng, Izdaju climbed to his feet, his nose bloody but his jaw set angrily; he did not like to lose.

Helped up by the Prophet, Fyrstsvard was able to stand unaided after a minute. Before that, however, he was half-carried as the group hurried away from Egobal, the screaming God and his waterborne gaolers, heading into the faecal inlet and on towards the jagged gap in the ceiling through which Sirraesutha was still slithering so innocuously.

"Not da poop shoot again," griped Jumal under his breath, probing his bloodied head with a finger and wincing.

"You want to get out of here, don't you, fish-brains?" Tar Feng snapped back.

"Yarr," said the pirate resignedly, wrinkling his nose.

"And you know that the other entrance up on the ledge is blocked off, don't you?"

"Yarr."

"Then shut up and head for the poo!"

"How are we going to get past da worm?" Jumal asked sardonically.

"I was thinking we would use the worm as a ladder," Tar Feng answered brightly, reaching the behemoth's side.

The others stopped in their tracks. "What?" they said.

"Come now," said the old Wizard, beckoning to them. "Get a running start with me, and we'll be up the worm and out of here in no time!"

So saying, he stepped back and began a run parallel with the worm's slithering form, though the creature's girth was only slightly less than the man's height. With surprising agility, he leapt onto its back and even managed to run forward a couple of steps before he slipped and fell off to land heavily on the rock below.

"Ooooh!" he moaned, clutching his back.

The others shook their heads at his stupidity, only to turn back and see Ratnik – bloody and sore as he was – wiping his face and readying himself to repeat the manoeuvre.

"What are you doing?" cried out Jumal in surprise.

"Well, we *do* wanna get outta here, don't we?" asked Ratnik with a shrug.

"Yarr, but you will never make it, man – da worm will shake you off!" the Chilpaean protested.

"Such little faith in my skills," teased Ratnik, drawing in a deep breath and beginning the run-up.

If anyone could do it, Jumal acknowledged, it was Ratnik. The young pirate was the most surefooted sailor the other had ever known, able to run along the yardarms in the middle of a thunderstorm without slipping, able to climb the rigging in the heart of a whirlwind as fast as a monkey does a tree.

Finishing his run-up and leaping onto the great worm, the young corsair swayed to and fro drunkenly as the creature writhed and twisted to shake the puny man off its back. Ratnik had peerless balance, however, and would not be shaken. Clinging on as though the soles of his boots were glued to the cylindrical, slippery hide, his feat seemed almost impossibly agile at times.

He ran, scampered and climbed up Sirraesutha all the way to the *Rodici* breeding level, where the stench was just as bad as he remembered, and there made his way along the worm – for it had pulled itself a fair distance along the tunnel – all the way up to its head, ducking in places to avoid stalactites. Once there, he unsheathed his cutlass with a clear ring of steel.

Hearing this and feeling him almost atop her head, Sirraesutha twisted desperately to shake him off and crush him once and for all, manoeuvring her body all the way around so that her face pointed up towards the pirate and his feet slipped in the ordure over which she had slithered. Still, Ratnik did not fall and, stepping back from a vicious bite from the circular mouth, he drove his blade into the worm's tubular body beneath the sucking, gnashing maw all the way to the hilt. The worm went berserk, smashing her head and body into the walls and ceiling in her death throes.

Ratnik clung on to his sword grimly, flung around more than by any storm he had yet encountered, his pained body flopping around on the shit-slick worm. Soon, his arms felt stretched to breaking point, his head was aching abominably again, and rubble was raining down all around him from Sirraesutha's fit. When she finally stilled, the pirate pushed himself up with a sigh, grimacing at the stink and the feel of the worm's gross slick skin and harsh bristles against his hands, and gruesomely sawed at her belly until he had opened a cavity wide enough to hide in. Now sure that she was dead, Ratnik walked back along her limp length lackadaisically, trying to breathe shallowly through his mouth.

When he reached the hole leading down to the lake where the others waited, amazed by what they had seen, he shouted down, "What in the name of the Ferrymen are you waiting for? The worm is dead – let's get outta here!"

Ratnik's face dropped as he looked behind them, however, and the group quickly spun about, fearing the return of Gastar. There was no sign of the God, though. At the end of the inlet, in front of the smoke-wreathed lake, the fallen pirate, Heldig, stood knee-deep in water and regarded the companions with malevolent crimson eyes and an expression of hatred and hunger.

His head was caved in at the right temple. It looked wet and sticky still, and skull showed clearly through the blood. The hole in his abdomen through which his heart had been torn out still trickled with gore, though its edges had begun to blacken, for the dead man's skin was as grey as rotten fish. Like Gastar, engorged vermillion veins stood out all over the ambulant corpse's body, bulging above and beyond the constraints of mortal flesh.

Ratnik recalled then what Gastar had said to the brave pirate: "You will have the honour of being the first of my *Thakshir!* The Lord of *Thakshir!"*

It was true then, he realised woodenly, the horror of the situation building in the back of his mind for later ventilation. The Dark Lord had transformed Heldig into a Demon, a creature of the night whose bloodlust for the living knew no bounds.

"Beware of Heldig!" the young pirate cried out, the crack in his heart mirrored by the crack in his voice. "He is a Demon, a *Thakshir!"*

The others surveyed the new threat for a moment, but Heldig did not move; only skewered them with his scarlet eyes.

"Hahaha!" Gastar roared with watery laughter from the depths of the stinking smoke, spitting out words between splashes. "Yes, you see your fate now in his eyes, meddlers, and the fate of your entire realm! Heldig is only the first! Soon, my army of *Thakshir* will sweep the land like a plague and consume each and every life in their path, and there is nothing you can do to stop them!"

Jumal wrenched free of restraining arms and stepped away from the company, back toward the lake, toward Heldig. He ignored all the shouts and pleas for him to stop, to wait, even those from Ratnik, whose pulse went into a paroxysm at the sight of his dreadlocked friend approaching the scabby, grey fiend his Captain had become.

"Heldig?" Jumal crooned as he closed in on his old comrade. "Heldig, it is I, Jumal. Do you remember me, my friend?" The pirate Captain only groaned loudly and splashed nearer. "Remember me, Heldig! Remember Ratnik and da *Surfrunner* and Kauapunki and all da good times we – yargh!"

When Heldig reached Jumal, he seized the Chilpaean by the arm and – in a show of surreal strength – hurled him effortlessly with a flick of the wrists into the wall, where he slumped down like a slug, moaning torpidly in pain.

"Jumal!" Ratnik cried out from the top of the worm, knowing he could not descend in time to help and wishing he had slid down already, despite all his injuries.

The rest of the group exclaimed at the sight, too, except Kamilah, who strung an arrow to her bow and shot it through Heldig's throat so that it hung gorily out of his nape, felling him like an ox.

"That stopped him," Kamilah commented calmly, recalling Gastar's bragging.

"Let's move! Everyone, after Ratnik, now! Prophet first!" Fyrstsvard quickly decided, running back, hauling Jumal to his feet and supporting him as he stumbled back to the group.

The mercenaries turned away from the cavern, the lake and Heldig and hastened to Sirraesutha's carcass. At the top of its segmented, white form, Ratnik cleared his throat, brushed a hand over his eyes and then readied himself to help the others climb up. His heart was beating at his ribs to escape at the sight of his Captain coming back to life and dying all over again.

Heldig's words – "my son" – echoed in his brain as though resonating in a stagnant temple and he felt as empty as a hollow tree trunk, like part of him had been pecked away, never to return. He absentmindedly reached down and helped the Prophet scamper up the dead worm, and then caught the blanket that was thrown after him, all the while feeling the void beckon. The Elf rewrapped the blanket around his shoulders and thanked the pirate, but Ratnik did not hear him, oblivious to all for a while but the sight of his dead Captain.

"Who is next?" asked Jumal at the base of the worm. He was bruised and sore from his encounter with the rough, sabulous wall, but not incapacitated.

There was a dull boom, and the cavern shook violently before any could respond. Looking over their shoulders, they saw water sploshing high into the air while the walls shook and any reticent stalactites now fell to join their brethren. The reason for the ruckus was not hard to divine.

Invisible in the smoke, eyes wide with insanity, Gastar was delightedly directing blast after magical blast at the lake with his pinioned hands; a simple attack at the only target he could reach. A deepening crater began to grow around him, and he laughed madly as he sought to bring down the entire subterranean empire. The group could only imagine what had become of Egobal.

"You will all die down here!" the God's chilling shrills reached them, muffled by the banging crescendo.

"Oh, put a sock in it!" Tar Feng told him dismissively. Turning to the others, he whispered urgently, "We must leave now! Those elementals will not hold the Dark Lord for long!"

"Can't you just kill him wid magic?" demanded Jumal.

The Wizard shook his head gravely. "I know no spell powerful enough for that, I'm afraid, my friend, no, no. He is a God, after all. I don't even know if he *can* die! The best I could do was hold him back – and I could not have done that without the Sandman's help. Now, please, hurry!"

The others nodded and set about scurrying up the worm's back as best they could. Jumal reached the top without incident, but once there he heard Tar Feng below exclaiming, "Sif's life-giving bosom! He's still alive!"

"Gods above, what *is* he?" whispered Ratnik, his face white as a sail.

The Chilpaean spun to behold Heldig emerging out of the rubble and bubbling surf, new wounds from the falling detritus decorating his suppurating skin and forcing him to limp.

Kamilah gasped and covered her mouth when she saw that her arrow was still poking through the *Thakshir* corsair's neck. She felt like swooning when he snapped off the fletches in front of his neck and then reached around, pulled the shaft out of his nape and cast it aside. Undeterred, he tottered toward them like a drunk, reaching out for them with sickly hands. He gnashed his teeth wordlessly like he might be trying to talk, his skin flaking as he went like ash blowing off a fire, his hair falling out, his eyes unholy incarnadine.

"No way," murmured Jumal, round-eyed. "It cannot be!"

There was no denying it, however; now that he was dead, Heldig refused to die again. Although all of the companions, especially Ratnik, wanted to believe that it was a miracle and that their friend had been returned to them, they knew in their dread-clenched hearts that he had become an abomination. They could see nothing in his eyes of the man he had been, nothing but the desire to kill.

"Go! Go!" Tar Feng urged the others who had yet to make the climb, levelling his staff at the red-eyed pirate with the shedding red beard.

Biting back a whimper and a flinch at the thought of touching the creature, Kamilah laid her hands on the worm and began to haul herself up it like it was a massive, hairy rope, using the indents between its segments as footholds. Izdaju ascended so fast behind her that he got kicked in the head and hands a few times.

Meanwhile, Tar Feng hissed, *"Banza'abas!"* and pelted the oncoming Heldig with hot green splotches from his crooked staff that sizzled when they struck and jolted the rotting pirate like he had been stabbed or electrocuted. The Nether creature yet made no sound, save for the quiet swish of the water as he waded forwards, slowed to a crawl by the constant patter of the globs, but never stopped entirely.

"Hurry! Hurry!" Tar Feng kept prompting as the dead man drew closer and the Wizard began to weaken from his never-ending assaults and the spell he still held in effect on Gastar.

Soon, the Nomads were nearing the top of the worm and the stinky hole there and Fyrstsvard and Tar Feng were all that remained in the inlet, along with the *Thakshir* corsair, who was closing in by the second, now only ten paces away.

The Knight stood by the Wizard's side with his blade drawn, but the old man barked at him, "What d'you think you're doing, you nincompoop? I'm trying to hold this monster off so you can all escape – so escape already!"

"But –"

"But nothing – go!"

"What if –"

"Get going, you farce!"

"Right, sorry," Fyrstsvard said, frowning, but sheathing his sword and rushing to Sirraesutha's corpse.

The Knight was halfway up the horribly bristly worm – smearing his skin, armour and clothes with its innate slime, as well as dung, and hating every minute of it – when he noticed that the Wizard had started a new incantation; one that rang bells of remembrance in the Knight.

"Sith'eshu zam'beamber!"

Fyrstsvard pulled himself up to the top of the worm, through the excrement-rimmed aperture, and was hauled up to the breeding level by Ratnik's strong hand. By the time he got there and swivelled to look back, Heldig was all tied up by stony red snakes coiling around his body, limbs and head, completely immobilised. Tar Feng was shimmying up the worm like a sloth up a tree. When the old man neared the top, Fyrstsvard and Ratnik both reached out, grabbed him and yanked him up to the wet, rocky floor of the *Rodici* breeding grounds, where he and the pirates had flown on a cloud not so long ago.

"That was amazing, Fengy!" said Ratnik, leaning against Sirraesutha and clapping the Wizard on the shoulder. "D'you think you could teach me how to do stuff like that?"

Wheezing and red-faced, Tar Feng panted, "I could if you had a staff like mine, but it would take many many years, skunk, oh my yes, many many years! Why, you would be as long in the tooth as old Fengy when we were done, oh my yes!"

Ratnik pursed his lips in thought and resolved to ask the old man what he meant at a more appropriate time. With all the companions having escaped the lower cavern, however – and with reverberations abounding, bringing down boulders all around them – he opted to flee presently.

So, with Gastar's splenetic, hollow cries ringing in their ears, the companions turned and fled.

"I will get you, Amhrahil, and your paradise! You hear me, Elf? You are dead!"

"We should hurry," advised the Elf.

Once at the base of the shaft that led up to *Dwarhummer,* Tar Feng glanced at his staff, the source of his power. Focussing the crook's energies, Tar Feng again called out to the skies for help, *"Herathrea lampini-hrellel!"*

Once more, a cloud – white this time – abandoned its fellows in the sky far overhead and dove down the deep fissure in the earth. It swooped through *Dwarhummer* and down a lift passage in seconds to arrive – floating back and forth, eager as a puppy – next to the Tzunese Wizard at the base of the shaft.

Staring at it askew, Ratnik said, "Can't you just *poof* us out of here like you did with me and Jumal in the Dwarf city?"

Tar Feng shook his head. "I certainly could not *poof* so many so far. The effort might kill me!"

The sere old man politely asked them all to climb aboard, and though there was considerable confusion, the others' doubts were assuaged by Ratnik and Jumal's assurances and by the fact that the entire subterranean complex was collapsing around their ears. With no other means of escape, they soon all stood clumped tightly together on the cloud, clutching one another for support. Without any warning, Tar Feng had the cloud sweep them up through the squared passage, causing a good deal of stomach-churning disorientation and unsteadiness in the rest of the group, some of whom cried out in fear.

The Wizard started off going slowly at first, dodging rocks and debris that fell from the level above and keeping away from the crumbling walls as best he could. He looked strained, though. Sweat beaded his brow, his tendons stood out, and his fists shook with effort.

"I cannot keep this up for much longer!" he gasped out between breaths. "Everybody hold on tight – we must get out of here *now*!"

All at once, he sped up the cloud until it was flying upwards at a frighteningly fast pace. Everybody, save the Wizard, screamed and flattened themselves against the fluffy base, partly in fear and partly by necessity as the resistance above them suddenly grew in strength and wind seemed to buffet them from above. Ripping out of the top of the rock-strewn lift shaft amid a shower of dust, Tar Feng sent the cloud whizzing across the desiccated city of *Dwarhummer* at face-numbing speeds.

The mercenaries could not see a great deal whilst soaring at such incredible velocity. Flying debris clogged their vision too, but what little the band could see informed them that the once-beautiful dwarvic city was in ruins. Half of the squat little dwellings had been flattened, and gone were the majority of the monumental and elegant pillars that had housed the smelly little Dwarves, all destroyed by flood and mutant *Rodici.*

The Dwarf King – crowned, heavily bearded and resplendent in gold and crimson – shook his hammy fist at them as they flew overhead from where he stood in front of the pile of stone, gold and alabaster that had once been the proud palatial pillar of *Dwarhummer.*

"I hope you boil in the fires of the First Forge!" they heard him curse them in Traveller's.

Then – seeing that the giant monsters were still rampaging around the city, destroying the remaining Dwarves and houses alike – the King promptly hid among the wreckage of his home.

The mutant beasts halted their killing spree to stare in awe at the speeding cloud that bore the intruders up through the air, but they only paused for a moment. After that, they returned to their mission of carnage.

Seeing the mess the dwarvic city had become, Tar Feng muttered, "Oops."

Sending them hurtling up the shafts down which they had descended only hours before, the little Wizard's fluffy white cloud bore the amazed group up through falling debris and rocks and past collapsing caverns until there was only starlight above.

16

Zibeltor's Temple

Saul's hand slipped, and he cursed through numb lips as a cascade of small rocks shot past his dangling body to clatter loudly down the sheer cliff face to which he clung, now with one hand. He could barely see anything. His world was white, wet and frozen, and it had been ever since he had ventured out of Baldr's Safe and up into the mountains of the Great Divide three days ago with a few rations, a spear, a piece of flint, borrowed furs and a knife.

The Prince of Fjelburg had turned eighteen a few months ago, and as was tradition among Stonebrow sons, he was now beginning his manhood rites at the height of summer; first of which was to climb the tallest mountain in the Great Divide to Zibeltor's Temple, there to be blessed by the Thunder God with fur to survive the freezing temperatures at vertiginous altitudes.

He managed to find a firmer handhold for the hand swinging over the abyss, and then he clung to the escarpment with scuffed boot tips and fingers scraped raw, shivering and chattering his teeth as the wuthering wind sought to pry him loose and cast him down. His straw hair, though tied back in a ponytail, was being tugged loose and was billowing in his eyes. His beard had grown out, and its tufts now wafted. He dared not move while the gale cut across him so viciously, and so he held still, praying his strength would not give out before the wind did.

He thought of what his father might say if he failed, but shoved the thought aside; such ruminations were less than helpful. He forced himself to remember instead what his father had said before he had left. At the Garrison Level, at the sole entrance to Baldr's Safe, his father had taken him outside the grand gates alone and given him his food, spear, flint, furs and knife. Legend had it that the first Stonebrows had made the pilgrimage without food or furs, but such extreme practises had long since been abandoned after too many princely deaths.

"Do me proud," his father had said, "but, more importantly, do yourself and the Gods proud, my son. They will be watching you."

"Are you sure?" Saul had asked sceptically.

Aodh had smiled. "Oh yes."

"How can you be so sure?"

"I see the doubt in your eyes," his father had said, "but I see something else too, which makes me believe. Have I ever told you Baldr's story?"

"Only a hundred times," Saul had replied with a grin.

"Okay, okay, I'll tell you again – if you insist. At the beginning of time, at the dawn of creation, hot and cold were the very first forces in the universe. Sensing each other and using their differences to forge identities, hot and cold became Fire and Ice. Fire and Ice named themselves Surtr and Skalda and were the first of the Gods. When they clashed in the void, as was their nature, a third God was born from the clash itself: Baldr, the spirit of violence, the God of War.

"Able to wield six different weapons in his arms at once, he was a whirlwind of death on the battlefield. Every time the Gods sought to come together to make peace over the millennia, he would interrupt and attack them wildly without cause, just to remind them of their own base natures. They had created him, and he would never let them forget. One day, to keep him busy, they ordered him to build the most impressive fortification he possibly could, and he carved Baldr's Safe out of the rock of the mountains themselves.

"Upon completion, however, the Gods took the name too literally and locked Baldr inside his own strongbox. Having built it, though, the God of War knew every nook, every cranny and every secret way out. He escaped in no time and now makes the Gods war with one another through stealth and subterfuge to get his revenge, for they still think him locked away in his creation."

Saul had continued to stare at him long after he had stopped talking. "So?" he had asked. "What, in that story, makes you believe in Baldr?"

"Oh, it's not what's in the story," Aodh had replied with a laugh. "It's what's in your eyes. I see the spirit of violence in your eyes. I see Baldr in you, my son; a man capable of fighting *many* kinds of wars, and *that* is what makes me believe. You'll find all kinds of wars out there, my son, and you'll need to be ready. You'll war with nature, with the elements, with the cold, with the beasts and with the mountain, but most importantly, you'll war with yourself out there. That's how a man finds out who he is. Be brave out there and know that the God of War will watch over you. And if you should die, die with the spear in your hand or you will never reach Valhalla.

Understand?"

"I understand."

The screaming squall eased. As soon as he felt its buffeting lessen, Saul looked for a new handhold through the sleet and snow that drenched him, finding one and hauling himself up as fast as he could with a grunt. Then, he could find no handhold; only a ledge, above which was a vertical crevasse. Pushing with his feet and stretching his arm up, he shoved his hand into the fissure and clenched it into a fist, trapping it in the hole. Then, ignoring the sore scraping on his knuckles, he used the arm to pull himself up to where he could reach another handhold.

He forced himself to keep going, but the climb was beginning to tell. His shoulders burned, his arms ached, his legs trembled, and his fingers bled. His breath was ragged, and his skin was frozen. He could not feel his toes, his lips were numb, and – perhaps worst of all, in the Prince's opinion – his stomach would not stop grumbling. Despite all this, he did not allow an ounce of discomfort to show on his hard, flat face, save to bare gritted teeth against the taste of iron as he jostled his fiery shoulder sockets into movement. The spirit of Baldr was inside him and the God of War could not be defeated, he told himself.

No ordinary man could have made the climb to Zibeltor's Temple, and it was perilous for a Highlander. Saul, however, had a will stronger even than his bulging muscles. He never stopped forging ahead, and he made it to the mountaintop in record time, little did he know it. Half-starved, frozen half-solid, completely exhausted, Saul dragged his body unceremoniously over the clifftop and rolled onto his back on the snowy plateau, sucking in great lungfuls of thin, cold air.

When he had enough breath, he laughed. "I made it!" he shouted to the white sky, his words reverberating off the mountainsides around him.

He rolled onto his side and looked around at the clouds, peaks and snow. For a moment, he panicked, not seeing the Temple, but then he forced himself to calm. Fear helped nothing, after all. He knew the Temple was here; now, he just had to find it.

Hauling himself to his feet in the whipping wind and blistering cold and stamping his feet to try to pump some blood into his toes, Saul squinted into the blizzard. He was white from head to toe with slush now, just like the surrounding landscape, and saturated to the bone. He slogged through calf-high snow over uneven ground, often bumping and scraping his shins on hidden rocks, testing each footfall carefully lest he inadvertently step off the peak. Such a slip would lead to a fall of hundreds of feet now.

Though he walked across a plateau, his sight was partially blocked by small crests jutting up from his level. He was sure, however, that all of these were too small to support the Temple. He was proven half-right when he staggered past one such wall of rock and beheld behind it a snow-capped round roof held up by a semi-circular colonnade, while the back half of the roof was attached directly to the sheer rock face of the jagged peak he had just passed.

The granite structure was huge, and its frost-veined columns were rugged with uneven edges, like the whole thing had been hollowed from a larger crag. Saul whooped and punched the air tiredly, but then the reality of his situation set in and he chuckled and cursed quietly.

There was scant shelter to be had from the deadly elements in the holey Temple, and he knew that if the Storm God did not deliver him fur soon, he would freeze to death. He had barely enough rations for the return journey, so he could not afford to wait on the mountain for too long. The prospects seemed bleak, but he gritted his teeth and ploughed on through the snow, reminding himself that he had already conquered the Great Divide and found Zibeltor's Temple. Surely, he thought, the hard work was already done.

Tripping on a rock hidden in the snow and falling flat on his face just before the Temple, Saul groaned and dragged his body through the slush up onto the wet granite inside. He crawled, shivering, to the back wall, where the roof met the sheer rock. The stone there was dry and he curled up in a sodden, shaking ball, trying to recover some body warmth, but still the wind stung him like ice.

It was no good, and the thought crossed his mind again that he might die up here, alone, in the silent white world. He was starving, but too cold and tired to eat. He raked the simple Temple with crazed eyes, but it was completely empty save for a rough-hewn stone shrine and crude artwork on the back wall, against which the Prince cowered. Saul sat up and shuffled back from the wall, so that he could see it in its entirety.

It depicted the acts of the Gods, he realised, telling a linear story from left to right. The first image – carved deep into the wall – showed eight stick-figures standing in a ring around a spoked wheel with no hub, with their hands outstretched towards a separate ninth figure. Saul was not certain who the ninth figure represented, but from the skirt, breasts and flowing hair, he knew it was a woman.

The other eight – he was confident – represented the Pantheon of Gods, for they were often represented in ancient artwork as eight of the major Gods conglomerating around a spoked wheel with no hub, which symbolised prayers flowing to the Gods from the empty centre; the sentient races. It was the motif of the Pantheon, an emblem of the many Gods and Goddesses of Maradoum.

There were four women in the group – the most famous Goddesses, Saul presumed. One had a fish's tail and likely represented Merejulanna.

Another, who held up a mountain teetering on the brink of a precipice, clearly represented Sif. Skalda was characterised as a sharp-edged, ice-made woman, and Celeste stood in the clouds. The remaining four figures were men. One, stocky with flat edges, like a simple statue, delineated Crag. The second, Baldr, had six arms and each of them wielded a weapon. The third showed Zibeltor himself with a spear of lightning, and the fourth, Surtr, looked like he was on fire.

Now that he had some context, Saul looked on the image afresh and saw the Gods welcoming with open arms a new member to their number. He looked on to the second scrawling, where the Pantheon was shown again, huddled around their symbol as though they were conferring conspiratorially.

The next image depicted the Pantheon with their arms outstretched to the mysterious ninth God again, but this time they were drawn with fists and pointing fingers, and it looked to Saul like they were angry at the ninth figure. His suspicions were confirmed as his eyes swept right to behold the ninth figure holding sword and shield, where before she had been unarmed. She was attacking the Pantheon, illustrated in mid-leap with sword raised, while Baldr brandished his own array of weapons at her. Saul was confused now, for he had never heard of any evil God attacking the Pantheon, not even Gastar.

His gaze was drawn on to the following image, where he was shocked to see that the Gods were clearly running away from the madwoman with the sword and shield. The final image portrayed the Pantheon huddled around their motif beneath a mountain, while to the side, above ground, the ninth figure looked to be celebrating with sword and shield raised high. Saul's forehead furrowed at the ancient art. It was said the Temple was as old as the first man, older than the Witches, thousands of years old. He wondered if these images had been there since the very beginning. Nobody had told him any such story of the Gods nor told him of such a carving. He did not like to see the Gods he worshipped drawn as weaklings who lost a battle to a mystery woman.

"What is this?" he shouted at the wall in anger, then tilted his head back to roar at the ceiling. "What is this bullshit you show me, Zibeltor? I have hauled my arse all the way up this sodding mountain for you, for your blessing, and this is my reward? To see you and the other Gods as losers, to learn that you are not as strong as I believed? Why would you lose a battle to a random woman, even if she was a God? And why are you not sending me fur? My blood is freezing in my veins, Zibeltor, do you not even care?"

The howl of the wind was the only answer. "To the Nether with you then, you and all the other Gods! Turns out you were never real anyway."

As he turned to leave the Temple, he saw a pure-white snow leopard speckled with dark rings prowling out of the storm toward him between two frost-laced pillars, its teeth bared and its muscular shoulders rearing up out of its back only to slip down again with the rolling rhythm of its gait. It was easily as long as he was tall, dusted with snow along its back, and its head reached up to his chest. Its whiskers twitched as it snarled, revealing large yellow fangs. Its pale blue eyes, bright as chips of ice, locked on to his. It stank faintly of wet fur and rotten meat.

"I take it all back," Saul breathed with a sparkle in his green eyes, slowly tugging his thick, pine-hafted spear free from its position strapped to his back. "You *do* exist! Oh, thank you, great lord Zibeltor, thank you! Baldr, watch over me now; I need this fur."

He crouched into a fighting stance, still moving slowly, but did not have time to level his spear at the great cat before it pounced. Jumping to the side, he lashed out with the spear and whacked the leopard on the side with the haft to gain some space and time. He gained neither; the vexed animal roared and sprang back at him with savage alacrity, raking his shoulder with a claw as he ducked and dodged.

Saul hissed as warm blood ran down his arm, but never took his eyes off the creature and so was able to dart aside again when it jumped, this time sliding far enough away that he could jab his spear at it. He pierced its side and retracted his spear in a flash as the leopard snarled and mewled and circled him.

The leopard ran at him and he tried to sidestep, but the creature was ready this time and followed him, springing at the last minute so that he had no time to slide away again. Saul stabbed at it desperately, but the point of his spear glanced off the leopard's ribs, and the haft snapped under its weight. Then, the creature was on top of him, bearing him to the ground, its hind legs scraping his thighs, its forelegs on his shoulders, and its snapping teeth held back from his face only by his powerful hands on its neck.

Saul thought he might die then, with the beast's fetid breath on his face, and he knew real despair for the first time. At least, he thought morbidly, he would die in battle, and so the Valkyries would come for him and take him to Valhalla.

He understood then in a flash of insight what his father had meant by his words: "you'll war with yourself out there." He recognised in that instant that he was his own greatest enemy at that moment, not the leopard. Those dark thoughts that were seeping into his psyche would overwhelm him if he gave into them, he knew, and would get him killed. He had to do as his father had said: "Be brave." So, he seized despair by the neck and flung it out, slamming and locking the door behind it. I can do this, he told himself.

The snow leopard was a fierce beast, faster and stronger than anything else on the mountain, an apex predator. Yet, clenching his huge muscles, Saul was able to roll the leopard over so that he was on top of it. Leaving one hand on its neck, he used the other to snatch at his belt for his knife. The leopard saw its chance, however, and wriggled and jerked its way free of the Prince's grasp, throwing Saul off and making him lose his grip on the knife, which clattered across the stone floor, out of reach.

Man and leopard clawed their way to their feet in the same instant, and when the leopard charged, so too did the man. Meeting the bounding creature at a run in mid-pounce, Saul wrapped his arms around it in a bear hug, mindless of the clawing he received. He used his strength and momentum to carry the snow leopard across the Temple and – at full pelt – smack its head against the back wall, his shoulder driving the cranium into the rock. The leopard's skull made a crack like a dry log snapping, but it still squirmed, so the bellowing Prince hit it against the wall again and again, spraying blood over the artwork and making the staccato clacking of a rockslide as its broken bones started to grate on one another.

He slammed it into the wall until it stopped moving. Then, Saul threw down the dead animal, grimaced, spat blood and tried to wipe it out of his thick beard, noticing then his ripped, bloody clothes and the plethora of cuts he had attained during the brief fight. Despite all this, a smile crept inexorably over his face as he looked down at his kill.

"I did it," he muttered in wonderment.

Sweat from the exertion began to freeze on his face. The Prince grabbed his knife precipitously and set to skinning the animal, careful not to damage its pelt any more than necessary. This done, he rolled up the fur and strapped it to his back where his spear had been.

"Thank you, Gods," he said in earnest, looking up through a break in the snowstorm to behold Zibeltor's constellation, the Lightning Bolt, shining down on him directly overhead. "I should never have doubted you, and I never will again."

With those few words, the taciturn young man left the Temple and started down the mountain, heading back to Baldr's Safe for his new fur to be cleaned and treated. He ambled cheerfully through the blizzard and howling wind, whistling between winces.

17

The Nomads of Lama Kulul

"Argh, you're a cheat, Majbolji! A dirty cheat!"

"I am no cheat, Stein!"

The Nomad Chieftain held up his hands, unhurt by the good-natured accusations. He had a thick accent and only a limited grasp of Traveller's Tongue, like most Nomads. He was lean and fit, though still old enough to be grey-haired. His hair was tied in complex topknots creating two elevated circles. His face was heavily tattooed with intricate red patterns, and his cheeks were stylistically scarred. A scimitar was belted at his waist, marking him as a warrior. He wore a loincloth, leaving his legs bare, and light leather armour on his torso. "When you ask Gods for wine, they give piss! Ha ha! Why they so mad at you?"

"The Gods aren't mad at me," replied Sir Stein Kreeger, Knight of the Order of *Pacia*, laughing and then frowning and swatting at a tiny translucent scorpion scurrying in the sand nearby. "You two are just the luckiest sods this side of the sea! I swear I've never lost so much money gambling!"

In truth, he had lost far greater amounts trying his hand at dice, cards and other games of risk in the past, but Stein was a calculator and he calculated that it was in his best interests to butter up these Nomads, to have them think him a friend. Only then would they give up more of their intoxicating spirits.

The game they played with marked bones was as simple as any other game of chance Stein had played and had helped to while away the hours while they had waited. The Knight looked out across the midnight-blue desert to where the Great Fissure lurked; a bottomless hole in the earth, down which sang a sad waterfall. He looked up at the clear skies that lit the landscape, where a million stars jostled for space. The storm had dissipated, and the moon's silver smile was high in the sky now, the rays of its silent song like a lullaby. Despite heavy eyelids, though, Stein knew he could not sleep.

The shaman of the tribe, an old leathery man with a shining dome named Kasha'a, chuckled throatily at the Knight's words. "You behave strangely for a Knight," he observed, handing Stein the skin he held, on which he could see the other's eyes lingering. The Knight gulped down a few swigs and then coughed, grimaced and punched himself in the chest.

"That's good stuff!" he wheezed with watery eyes.

It was true. Stein did behave strangely for a Knight, gambling, drinking, whoring and brawling at any given opportunity. He did not look the part of a Knight either; bulky and burly he was, like a black bear. He was tall, wide and muscular with thick, coarse, black hair all over his frame. He had prolific black stubble on his lantern-jawed slab of a face and atop his dome, overshadowing dark, greedy eyes and smashed, crooked features. He looked more like a bar-room brawler or hired thug than a Knight on first impression, and his rough and uncultured speech did little to improve that image. Nevertheless, he fought for the knightly cause just as fiercely, if not more so, than any other in the Order of *Pacia* and so had risen to a position of respectability.

"Kriigi firewater strong," Majbolji agreed, smiling.

Stein nodded and tried in vain to speak through the fire that consumed his throat. It was an aptly named drink, he thought; to say it was strong was an understatement. Sir Kreeger had sampled some of the finest wares from across the world – fermentations so strong that they made his eyes bulge – but this had a particular kick to it, like a mule's hoof to the chest.

It was as he savoured the flavour that he heard it; a dull booming far beneath his feet. It was swiftly followed by a mad shudder underfoot, like the sand rippled outwards from the Fissure. Looking over, Stein saw an eruption of dirt and dust from the vast crevasse, which now rumbled like a lion preparing to roar. Around the Nomads' camp, all was disrupted; tents strewn everywhere, cook fires hissing and throwing up sparks, horses and camels panicking, little lizards fleeing into the night, people running and shouting, and the board on which they had been playing the game of bones had been knocked out of sight. Guess they can't take any more of my money now, Stein thought happily.

"What is going on down there?" he muttered, realising as he tried to stand that he had drunk perhaps a sip too much of the firewater.

He swayed, his face mottled and his mouth punching out gibberish, but he got to his feet. This was not the first time he had gotten drunk on the job, thought Stein with a tipsy smile, and it would not be the last. Within moments the Knight was down again, for the ground continued to buck and heave beneath him as if in the grip of a nightmare, and he was convinced it was not the spirits making the dunes judder either.

He did not let this deter him, though. In chaos and in battle, in pain and in stupor, Stein always remembered his mission, keeping his eyes firmly fixed on the Fissure even if his feet were no longer fixed on the ground. After a short while, amid billowing mists of dust and smoke, something flew up from the hole in the earth at speed; a dark, fluffy-edged silhouette against the stars that rose into the sky, only for the fluffy part to vanish like fog in sunlight, leaving the figures atop it to plummet from their peak.

"I think that's them!" Stein roared out, his words only slightly slurred. "Mount up and let's go get them!"

He and the ninety Nomads thundered across the dunes on horse and camel towards the Great Fissure, where they scattered a clan of hyenas by the lake's edge. Further on, they encountered Stein's fellow Knight, Sir Raphael Fyrstsvard, along with Tar Feng and the other mercenaries who had survived the quest, all splayed out in the sand in the penumbrae of circling falcons and bat hawks, groaning, moaning and poking delicately at bruises.

"My arse! My arse!" Ratnik was exclaiming over the bird caws.

"Old fool!" Izdaju was muttering darkly.

"Bah-hah! Nice landing, Wizard!" Jumal said in good humour.

"Yes, exceptional work getting us out of there, old boy," Fyrstsvard agreed, to Stein's surprise.

Tar Feng just giggled, "Teehee!" and then slumped in the sand, passed out.

"Good to see you all again!" Stein announced his approach jovially, dismounting. He laid eyes on the unfamiliar, tall, white-haired figure. "Is that him?" he asked Fyrstsvard.

The younger Knight nodded, picking himself up and dusting himself off. "That is the Prophet."

"Hello there," the Elf shouted with a wave.

"Good," said Stein shortly. "Let's get back to the campfires then, and you can tell us all that transpired."

"No!" objected Fyrstsvard, his eyes haunted. "We must flee at once, Stein. We have to get the Elf away from here ... We will be followed."

Stein eyed his comrade uneasily. "By who?"

Fyrstsvard thought back to Heldig's dark transformation, and a shadow flitted across his face. "Death," he told his companion. "There is evil magic in that pit, Stein, believe me. We must get away from here."

"Death," barked a voice from behind Stein, high and melodious, "is but another journey; one on which we all embark. It does not give chase. It bides its time, patiently awaiting slumbering souls brought to it along rays of star-light."

An ancient Nomad tremblingly stepped, with the help of a walking stick, into view to Fyrstsvard's left. His skin – like all who lived in the desert – was tanned deep mahogany, and his face looked old beyond defining. It seemed his voice was all that retained the vigour of youth.

"That's wonderful, Kasha'a but we have no time for your philosophy now!" said Fyrstsvard quickly, looking over his shoulder. "You must run with us, or you too will fall victim to the evil in that pit!"

Stein nodded slowly. Fyrstsvard appeared unusually rattled, and so sense dictated listening to his words, for the man was normally ice-cool and controlled.

"Very well, brother," said the older Knight, who had accompanied Fyrstsvard from Justiqua, "but I hope you'll tell me what happened down there as we go."

"Of course," nodded Fyrstsvard, "now get Tar Feng and the Elf on the horses, and let us leave!"

*

Despite Fyrstsvard's hurry to get away from the Great Fissure and the subterranean city of *Dwarhummer,* the Knights, their comrades and the Kriigi tribe did not get far beneath the scorching sun the next day before fatigue from all the underground madness caught up with them and demanded slumber. The desert had other ideas, however, and after they decided to bivouac down in the open that night, it kicked up howling orange clouds of dust hundreds of feet into the purple sky. Having failed to pitch their tents in time, the Nomads and mercenaries were forced to press on to find shelter or else be flayed raw by the stinging sand.

It was not until dusk swallowed the land on the second day that the sandstorm began to relent and the rescuers of the Prophet finally hid from the lingering dust clouds in the midst of a gathering of bone-white stone pinnacles in the desert, after heedlessly galloping their mounts west for leagues unchecked. They had whipped the camels and horses to their limits to put as much distance as they could between their shadows and the evil brewing in the east, as well as to escape the sandstorm, their terrors giving them no sympathy for the beasts of burden that carried them.

By the time true night had drenched the desert in darkness, the storm had died down and the mounts were frothing heavily at maw and nostril, their eyes wild with imagined fear. It took Fyrstsvard, Izdaju and the tribesmen a long time to calm the beasts, while giving them a good brush and feeding them a few oats. The camels, once fed and watered, lay down in unison to sleep as if in protest of their treatment over the course of the day. The people knew how they felt.

The score of strange, ivory rocks among which they made camp ranged from four to forty feet tall and surrounded the travellers like a circle of silent sentries. While they had provided a certain shelter from the sandstorm, they gave Ratnik goosebumps – and not only because of the few giant, hairy tarantulas found burrowing there. The stones looked to the young man like the upraised, time-bleached fingers of a massive, half-buried hand or claw, perhaps belonging to some sunken behemoth. The pinnacles defied the laws of reality by being bigger and heavier at the top than the bottom – thanks to the scouring of the sand-laden wind, Kasha'a explained.

The Kriigi and the mercenaries all sat on red, woven rugs stretched out on the sand. There were cook fires off to one side, which attracted the cawing vultures, whilst on the other side the horses and camels were picketed with a number of their young. More of the white and beige camels could be seen frolicking with young riders around the encampment with a few bay horses. Surrounding and sprawling across the rugs were dozens of conical beige tents created of tanned animal hide with a few robed and turbaned people wandering in between. Beyond those were the bony fingers of rock, and on the far side of those, they could see only sand stretching for leagues beneath the star-studded sky.

Fyrstsvard took a much-needed sip of water and exhaled happily. Just then, that gulp tasted more exquisite to him than the most expensive wines of the vineyards of his homeland. He placed the bowl down beside him and rubbed a calloused hand over his face wearily. His eyelids were heavy, but he could not sleep yet. A snake hissed somewhere in the night. Questions tumbled around the Justiquan's mind, disordered and chaotic; a high-stakes jigsaw puzzle with insufficient pieces.

"Damned savages," Stein muttered to him, lumbering over, throwing himself on the rug beside his fellow Knight and looking around with a low brow and set jaw at the simplicity of the camp. Fyrstsvard could see disappointment in Stein's hairy face. Sir Kreeger had become used to the finer things in life, he thought.

"We must be grateful for their kindness," the younger Knight reminded his friend. "They have guided us, watched over us, and the tribe has offered us their hospitality … such as it is. Rest easy now, brother. Soon, we will be home, celebrated as heroes!"

Kasha'a, the shaman, coming near enough to hear the last part, swept closer. "Rejoicing in victories, friends?" he asked them, beaming to see them in good spirits.

His limbs were stick-thin, making his head appear huge by contrast. He was grinning widely and toothlessly. His face was creased like folded leather, and skin hung loosely from his cheekbones, reminding Fyrstsvard of a bulldog. His dark, beady eyes were deep-set in his leathery, ritually-scarred face, and his hairless head gleamed silver in the ghostly light of the moon. His face was given further strange cast by tattoos plastered across it in purple swirling patterns. The configurations were repeated on a rag around his shoulders; the ceremonial markings of a desert shaman.

"Yes, we were," said Fyrstsvard with a fading smile. "It is so good to be free of that infernal cave and breathe fresh air once more, but perhaps we get ahead of ourselves. It is a long and dangerous journey back to Justiqua."

"Our religion," Kasha'a preached in Traveller's Tongue to the Knights with a little trouble, putting emphasis on the wrong vowels and elongating sounds where he need not, while superfluously shortening others, "teaches us that Celeste, the Goddess of Sun and Sky, the Giver of Life and Bringer of Light, walks the dead along the sun's rays until their souls are … the same … as the eternal light. In such a way are they taken to the next life in the Oasis of Tomorrow, where there is no death, where soulmates are intertwined as one being for the rest of forever. So do not fear the end, *pahr kong,* for your soul is in good hands, Fyrsvard. Celeste shines her light on you."

Fyrstsvard broke into a weary smile as he regarded the chirpy, bandy-legged shaman wearing nought but a loincloth, sandals and the patterned rag about his shoulders like a primitive cloak. He liked the eccentric old shaman, for he was full of odd ideas and exuberance about them. The Knight did not even mind the mispronunciation of his name, for he understood it was a difficult one.

"Pah!" broke in Tar Feng as he sauntered past, having only recently regained consciousness. "Sounds just like any other religion. They're all the same, and they all teach the same lesson; it is not the specifics of the theology that are important, but the belief and faith behind the mythology. Life is nothing without faith, without hope – even hope in the hopeless. For without faith, there is no destiny, and without destiny, there is no reason, only chance and chaos. In Quing Tzu, we are taught to find solace in the knowledge that, when the body passes on, the soul becomes one with the world's energy. One with the magic, one with the *Chi.* No Gods, no afterlife – only eternal peace."

Kasha'a bristled, drawing himself up to his full, short height. "Mythology?" he repeated incredulously. "I speak the truth, not myth!"

"Pah, it is all tosh," tossed in Jumal as he, too, dawdled past. "Dere is no God, no life after det. Dere is only da world we see, da world we know. We only get one sea to sail, so we have to make it a good voyage, yarr!"

Tar Feng only rolled his eyes. The shaman opened his mouth to speak again, but Fyrstsvard beat him to it.

"We too believe in a Mother of All, you know, shaman," the Knight said quickly and loudly while Jumal passed from earshot, "a Creator of us all. But *our* religion teaches us that it is only if we are decent – *good* people all our lives – that our eternal souls may be permitted to enter paradise, *Citta Pacia.* If we are judged unworthy by our Mother or by the Prophet – or by whomever it is that judges us – our souls are doomed forever to fiery torment at the hands of the Lord of the Nether, Gastar the Cruel. That is as it should be, of course. The wicked should be punished, and the beneficent should be rewarded – otherwise what would be the point of good deeds? Morality would be purposeless without such concepts. That is why we Knights try to live righteous lives – to follow in the Prophet's footsteps, to reach *Citta Pacia*."

"The Prophet that you have now rescued?"

"The very same," answered the Knight, glancing over to where the Prophet sat, staring into space. He expected the Elf had a great deal to think about, but so did the others and so far the fabled figure had said naught.

"You succeeded so far, then," stated Kasha'a, stumbling over the long word slightly.

Fyrstsvard nodded. "Yes, we have the Prophet, thank the … Prophet. Or we have an Elf, anyway …"

The Nomad shaman's eyes narrowed. "Yes. Even we here in the desert have heard of the Elf Prophet of the Knights of Justiqua and of the paradise he created, thanks to your people's Crusades. Some of our people have even joined your religion for the promise of life after death it offers. But let me ask you a question, young Knight. How can you be sure this Elf is the Prophet of legend who created *Citta Pacia* and not just some trick of the fiends that dwell below? That cave is, as you say, infernal. Beings of darkness, of despair and of death dwell in the deep … Beware, Knight, of placing too much faith too easily."

Fyrstsvard scanned the old man's eyes carefully. "I will beware, Kasha'a. Thank you. But the beings of despair of which you speak do indeed exist in the deep darkness, and we rescued this Elf from their evil clutches. He *is* the one we seek."

Stein stroked his black stubble thoughtfully at Fyrstsvard's fervour.

Kasha'a nodded, though he looked far from convinced. "As you say, Knight."

The night was cool with a gentle desert wind. The stars shone down on them coldly like a thousand diamond eyes watching them, and the moon gleamed brightly like a razor-sharp sickle. Its meagre light cast the desert in blue. The undulating orange dunes of the day became a seascape with the twilight, where dim waves rose like behemoths from the surface, poised to sweep the tribe away.

A disquieting notion for most, but the reminder of the ocean brought warm feelings to one pirate's heart. Ratnik gazed out over the land longingly and imagined it was his beloved mistress.

The group pitched hide tents on the cold sand. Izdaju set his tent a short distance from the others, hardly enough to be noticed, and yet notice it Fyrstsvard did. There remained a definite tension between the Knight and the nomadic warrior. As they sat down at last to share some hardtack, cheese and tough horse meat, Stein – growing impatient – said to Fyrstsvard, "So? Shall we talk to the Elf?"

Fyrstsvard, feeling much the same, nodded. “I think we should.” Louder, he said, “Everybody! Gather around – it is time for some questions and, hopefully, some answers.”

18

Scribbles in the Sand

Fyrstsvard moved to sit by the silent Elf, making the symbol of *Pacia* with his hands as he did so – a peaked roof, fingers touching and palms apart. The Elf was dressed now in a simple white robe given to him by the Nomads; he looked like a young acolyte back in the churches in Justiqua, thought the Knight. Soon, the rest of the band joined them, surrounded in concentric rings by the rest of the Kriigi tribe. Before long, a hundred heads had turned in to face the fey creature of myth that sat on a rug, facing them all through the orange aurora of the embers reflected in the sand, while all around was blue. A scuffle in the darkness signalled the movements of some nocturnal desert-dweller.

Fyrstsvard saw then that the Elf had folded back the corner of the rug on which he sat so that he could scrawl patterns in the sand with the tip of a feather, and he could hear the Prophet murmuring a repetitive mantra. He wondered if the pale creature was performing magic and felt a thrill. The excitement faded swiftly, though, when the Elf did not look up from his mumblings for several long minutes, even when he plucked out one of his own ghost-white hairs and deposited it in the sand in the midst of his scribbles.

Eventually, feeling like all eyes were on him, Fyrstsvard – afraid to break the spell of silence – breathed, "Excuse me, Prophet? Do you mind if we speak with you?"

Opening his eyes more fully and ceasing his humming, the Elf regarded them all placidly.

"What were you doing?" Tar Feng moseyed over, his bone jewellery jangling like castanets, to see what the Elf had written, but his brow creased in confusion over glazed, blind eyes. "What have you drawn?"

"It is a sigil," answered the Elf, his voice high, soft as velvet and deliberate. "An arcane symbol invented by myself and the All Mother for communication. In times past, I could use such a drawing to commune with Gaia over great distances and between realms, but I cannot make it work now. The sigil is failing, or Gaia will not speak to me. It is strange … she was always easy to contact before."

"Maybe you need your powers to be able to speak to her?" Tar Feng suggested. "You had your energies with you in the past, but – according to that Demon back there – not any more. Maybe that is the missing ingredient."

The Elf looked thoughtful. "I do not think so," he said slowly. "We made the ritual simple enough that it needed only a feather to succeed. Gaia said the birds would tell her I called. One of these tribesmen was kind enough to supply me with a quail feather, so there is no reason for it to fail … but it is possible my powers were intrinsic to the process."

"If you have no powers, how do we know you are really the Prophet?" the Wizard asked, squinting suspiciously and jabbing his crook at the pale figure.

"I suppose you cannot – not for sure," the Elf replied calmly after a moment's thought. "Although if I were not the Prophet, why would Gastar have brought me back?"

"Hmph," the old man grunted, dissatisfied.

"Say, *you* have eldritch energies at your command, do you not, my friend?" the Prophet asked suddenly, looking up hopefully into Tar Feng's creased face. "I know you do, of course, for how else would you have flown us out of that chasm on a cloud? That was an impressive feat, by the way – not a simple spell."

Tar Feng shrugged. "Meh, I am a modest Wizard at best. My people kicked me out of Quing Tzu many years ago, and I could not stop them. But there are a few spells that come easily to me. Luckily, the cloud is one of them."

Amril nodded as though he understood. "Well, you have power, at least – that is for sure. Would you mind attempting to reach the All Mother on my behalf? Perform the incantation and the drawing of the sigil in my place, and we will see if my lack of energy is holding me back."

Tar Feng raised a hand, unable to suppress the question bubbling up inside him any longer. "I would be happy to try, willow wand, but first answer me this. If you are who you say you are, then how did you get to be so powerful without the use of *Kun-Yao-Lin?* As I'm sure you know, we humans cannot perform magic without such crystals – not unless they are Witches – and it has taken my people many many generations, yes yes, to uncover their secrets. Legend has it that Elves and Goblins, being such ancient and adept practitioners of the art, needed no such totems to command the arcane energies … how can that be?"

The Prophet turned moon-round eyes on the old man. "My race was always very advanced in communicating with the life force of the realms without the need for *Kun-Yao-Lin*. For us, it was as simple as learning a new language. I take it, then, that your staff is imbued with crystal shards?"

"It is."

"Very impressive, my friend."

Tar Feng stroked his crook with a gummy grin.

"Here," the Elf continued, patting the rug beside him, "sit by me and we shall see your powers in action while we try to reach out to the All Mother. That's it. Here, take the feather. Now, just follow the symbols I have traced with the point of the feather, over and over, while chanting thusly."

No one stopped them. All were frankly fascinated by the process. Ratnik blinked at the flowing quicksilver language that poured over the Prophet's tongue then, but could not make out a word nor remember any of the strange sounds when they were gone, as though they were not designed for his brain, or his brain was not designed for them. He could better understand the whistle and hiss of the wind through the dunes.

"Then," said the Elf, switching back to comprehensibility, "when you have a good rhythm going and you have pushed some power into the incantation, I will drop a strand of my hair in so that Gaia knows it is I that calls."

"Can I hear the incantation again?"

"Of course."

Ratnik did not understand any more of it the second time around, but he gawked at the Magicians – his food forgotten in his hands – completely absorbed as Tar Feng took the feather from the Prophet and used it to repeatedly retrace the swirls, curves, lines and flourishes that the Elf had already inscribed into the soft grains of sand.

"That's good. Now, the chant."

With the Elf leading him, Tar Feng ventured into verse, his dry voice raised in lilting, singsong melody. He repeated the invocation exactly as the Prophet directed, and the crook of his staff began to glow with a gentle green light. When the Wizard was singing by himself, his teacher plucked another of his long, moon-white hairs from his scalp and placed it gently in the sand atop the pictographs formed by the feather in the Tzunese man's hands.

They all watched for a long while. There was no effect. The Prophet's prayers went unanswered, and he soon relented and allowed Tar Feng to give up.

"Thank you for trying, my friend, but it seems that we will not be speaking with the All Mother tonight."

"Well, at least we know that lack of energy was not the problem, eh?" asked Tar Feng. "You saw my staff shining, did you not?"

"I did," put in Ratnik, impressed by the show of radiance.

"I did," the Elf echoed more grudgingly. "I hope Gaia is alright … we desperately need her aid and counsel. I am worried now that Gastar has somehow become more powerful than I could have imagined. I do not know how he could have toppled Gaia, but equally I see no other reason this spell of communion should fail if she is well and no other way that the Dark Lord could have come to plunder Maradoum … I fear we must accept that, for all intents and purposes, the All Mother has somehow been incapacitated and cannot help us."

He looked pallid, shaken by his own words. "Always, her guidance has proved sage in the past. Without her …" He shook his head. He had been going to say that he did not know what to do, but was loath to admit such ignorance in front of his new companions. After all, he was over nine hundred years old and was supposed to be wise. "We will just have to rely on our own wits, that's all," he finished lamely.

"It's got us this far," Fyrstsvard observed.

The Prophet was silent awhile, downcast. The wind whispered its secrets to the desert. When the Elf looked up to his rescuers and the tribesmen, he did so with sad eyes. "Apologies for keeping you waiting. Blessings," he began softly, "and thank you all for your helping me elude Gastar's foul grasp. We were fortunate to escape with our lives."

"Not all of us did, mate," Jumal reminded him dolefully, stuffing crumbled baui flower into a small brown leaf.

"You are most welcome, Prophet," Fyrstsvard hurriedly interjected, horrified at the lack of deference. He quickly came forward to kneel on the rug before the sitting Elf, head bowed. "We are your servants. We are the Knights of the Order of *Pacia,* and we revere you as the true messenger of the omnipotent All Mother, Gaia, and the saviour of all our souls."

The Elf blinked at the Knight, taken aback. Fyrstsvard looked up at his idol, then glanced back down at the rumpled, stained fabric beneath his dirty fingertips, unsure what to make of the situation. He had imagined this moment a thousand times, but it was not unfolding in any of the ways he had envisioned. In truth, he had pictured the Elf as a ten-foot tall sage whose voice was thunder and who shot lightning from his radiant eyes. The fragile, pallid creature before him was far from what he had expected. The night was eerily still and silent, the moment stretching, immeasurable.

"How long has it been since my passing?" the Elf asked at length, his high voice melodious and calming, like a cool salve on a sore mind.

"I … I regret to respond that we cannot answer that with exact accuracy, Prophet," stammered Fyrstsvard, ashamed to have to give such a half answer, "for much of our history and lore has been lost to us since the rule of the dreaded Witches of Convent."

At this, the Elf's eyes narrowed sharply, but then he mastered himself and his peaceful mien returned.

"The year is 311 AC," Fyrstsvard continued. "311 After Convent. We have counted the years since the fall of the Witches."

The Elf absorbed this silently for a moment. "You call me Prophet," he said softly. "A word I am familiar with and honoured by, I assure you. I do wonder, however, was one of the many pieces of lore you lost in the time of Convent my name? For you do not call me by it."

Fyrstsvard bowed his head, again chagrined at what he had to admit but excited to be the first man in centuries to learn the great Prophet's name.

"I apologise, Prophet, but it was indeed. Would you honour us by introducing yourself?" His voice shook with anticipation.

"Of course, my friend. It would be rude not to, and I hope that after I do, you will return the courtesy." Everyone inched closer to hear the Elf's name. "My name is Amhrahil Serenpitua."

Before anyone else could wrap their heads around the complex name, Tar Feng cackled and pranced over, kicking his heels together en route. "It is indeed a *remarkable* pleasure to meet one so famous worldwide as your good self, Ram-a-hill. A truly *remarkable* pleasure. And how do I know, you may ask? Because I just remarked on it! Teehee! Yes, yes, yes…"

"And who are you, my friend?"

"I go by Tar Feng in these lands! My home, as I said, is Quing Tzu, and my real name is so long I've forgotten how to say it – let alone spell it! Teeheehee!"

"It is a pleasure, Tar Feng."

"It is an honour to make your acquaintance, Amrahil," Fyrstsvard added quickly, having recovered from his embarrassing moment of stupor. "My name is Sir Raphael Fyrstsvard, at your service."

"The honour is mine, Sir Raphael Fyrstsvard," the Elf graced the Knight with a gentle smile and enunciated the man's name carefully and flawlessly. "My name, however, is pronounced *Amhrahil.* I do understand that it is a difficult name to pronounce. You need not fret."

One by one, the others came forward.

"An honour to meet you, Prophet," Stein said gruffly, proffering his hand. "I am Sir Stein Kreeger, also a Knight of the Order of *Pacia*, at your service."

"The honour is mine, Sir Stein Kreeger."

"Celeste shine upon you, Armhill," offered Kamilah, bowing. "My name is Kamilah of the Kriigi."

"And may she shine upon you, Kamilah of the Kriigi."

"Good to meet you, Armil. I am Chief Majbolji, and this my tribe, the Kriigi."

"It is good to meet you, Chief, and I would like to take this opportunity to thank you and your tribe for everything you have done for us. You have my eternal gratitude and blessings in all your endeavours."

"You welcome." Majbolji gave a lopsided grin.

The Prophet returned the smile, then looked from side to side for a moment with eyes lowered as if embarrassed, before continuing, "I know that my name is difficult to speak, and I am not offended by your mispronunciations. So please, to save time and for ease, you may all feel free to call me Amril. Is this agreeable?"

The company nodded and smiled, sighed sighs of relief.

"Thank you, Amril," Fyrstsvard spoke for them. "We are glad we have not offended you."

The Elf's smile waned as he regarded those who had not come forward. "And I recognise you three from that cave. What are your names?" he asked them tentatively.

Izdaju was scarring his cheeks with a bone needle in the Nomad tradition for those who have taken lives. Red dots gleamed brightly on his face in the firelight alongside darker, older marks as he looked up and scowled openly at the Elf. "Izdaju."

Jumal was lighting his roll-up with a smouldering twig from the fire and breathing out smoke through his nostrils. He glanced at the Elf askew, disinterested. "Jumal."

Ratnik took the roll-up from Jumal when it was offered. He looked suspicious as he puffed, his brow furrowed and his eyes narrowed. "I'm Ratnik."

"Is … something wrong?" asked the Elf.

No one spoke for a moment. Fyrstsvard was on the verge of jumping in when Ratnik explained, his young voice surprisingly bitter, smoke billowing from his mouth, "The Knights might love you, Prophet, but our peoples have all suffered at the hands of your religion – your Witches and your Knights. Honestly, we didn't believe you were real. We were only coming along for the gold we were promised. Now that you're here … well, if you really are the Prophet, we're wondering what we should do with you … deliver you to Labogé, or do the world a favour and kill you where you sit."

19

Legacy

The night became very still, and the atmosphere suddenly felt as taut as a bowstring, ready to snap at the slightest provocation.

The tension broke as Fyrstsvard leapt to his feet in fury, glowering at the reticent three, and said in a dangerous voice, "You gave your word when you came on this mission – all of you! And if you go back on it now, I will be obliged to deal with you as we do all oath-breakers."

He thumbed his sword an inch free of its scabbard with a hiss. Stein stood up beside his fellow Knight, dour-faced, his hand also on his sword hilt.

"Just telling the Elf how it is," Ratnik said, eyeing the pale figure and puffing on baui. "We lost a good friend down there rescuing you, *Amril.* You'd better be worth it."

The Prophet was stung by the young man's sneer and general disdain. "Then, why did you come to rescue me at all?"

"We never thought we'd *actually* find a long-dead Elf! The deal was, whether we found you or not, if we made the attempt we got paid either way. Now, I wish we'd never taken this cursed job!"

"Excuse me?" Fyrstsvard snapped sharply. "You thought what?"

"Well, yeah," said Ratnik almost sheepishly. "We thought we'd find a corpse at most – but not *this!"*

"And you all felt this way?" Fyrstsvard asked, astonished, sweeping the group with his gaze.

Izdaju, Kamilah and Jumal were nodding. The Knight was stumped, speechless. He had thought he could rely on these people, but they were as much enemy as friend, it now seemed – a potential threat to his mission.

The pause stretched into an awkward silence before the Elf said quietly, "I did not intend for Convent to be –"

"Save it for your sermons," dismissed Ratnik, waving a hand. "I don't wanna hear it. Don't worry, Fyrstsvard, we'll help you take the Elf to Justiqua – we wanna get paid for all this hassle – but then me and Jumal are out. I don't wanna die for a dead Wizard's dream."

Izdaju nodded. "At Justiqua, me and Kamilah are out, too."

"So be it," snapped Fyrstsvard, "but if any of you harms so much as a hair on his head before we get there, I swear by the Word I will kill them myself."

Such was Izdaju's snarl as the Knight spoke that Fyrstsvard had a flashback to the Nomad's sword sticking in his stomach, and he thought once more he was likely to be gutted. Izdaju did not move, however; only glared. The pirates said nothing, but exchanged the roll-up again.

"So, now that introductions have been made," Amril addressed Fyrstsvard, trying to nullify the awkward atmosphere, "perhaps you could explain to me what has been happening here since I … departed? You speak of Convent as if it is some ancient malice, but I did not found it to be so, and I am intrigued to learn of how you came to rescue me."

"Understandable," Fyrstsvard responded, sitting again, his stern face softening. "Ahem, very well, a history lesson then. It is recorded in our earliest histories that your protégé, a man named Balthazar, betrayed and murdered you in order to become the next leader of the Witches of Convent."

The Elf's eyebrows rose slightly at this. "I called them Sisters of Convent when I founded them," he interjected sadly, gazing into the fire's smouldering remains.

"Right, sorry. Sisters," Fyrstsvard amended, wriggling slightly with discomfort. "Anyway, after … your demise, your protégé was in charge of *Citta Pacia* and of ferrying noble souls to their eternal afterlife therein. That is the duty with which you charged him, is it not?" The Prophet did not answer, only looked on sorrowfully. "But this Balthazar led Convent on a reign of terror that lasted for centuries – how long exactly nobody is sure, thanks to the loss of records from before that time. I am sorry to have to tell you this, Amril, but immediately after your death, Balthazar used some sort of magical weapon to wipe the old, Vayloric Elves from the face of Maradoum. Every single one of them, so it is said. Very little is known about that period of time or about your people, most of it learned from ancient manuscript scraps, story and legend."

The Elf's white face turned a shade more ashen if that were possible. He looked deeply nauseated but said nothing, barely moved.

"The lesser peoples," the Knight continued gently, "those who could not fight back against the dark and powerful magic Balthazar employed, were terrorised into your religion. Prayer times at the temples became mandatory on pain of death. And it was said that death was no release … for the Witches had corrupted your life's mission, and they soon became all powerful by absorbing the souls of the dead instead of caring for them on their way to the City of Peace. Eventually, it is said, Balthazar and the Witches came to treat people like cattle all over the world; kept them alive in subjugation so that they could serve Convent and, upon death, drained the people dry of their energies to add to their own, making them immortal and invincible, like Gods.

"But, in time, the corruption of unlimited power spread, and Balthazar was himself betrayed in turn and killed by the Witches. A short time later, in history's lens, the Witches – whilst experimenting with titanic cosmic forces best left alone – brought about their own destruction. Their greatest city was torn apart from the ground up by primeval forces opposing their evil reign, and all that was left was that enormous Fissure from which we just escaped.

"After that, the subjugated races – men, Goblins, Elves, Dwarves – rose up against their oppressors across the land and threw off the yolk of their tyranny. We men formed the Order of *Pacia* under the rule of the first Lord Protector, Sir Barrett Heron, when he rediscovered your Word," the Knight held up a small, worn blue book, "and learned of your noble original goals behind the establishment of the religion of Convent; a paradise for all sentient kind."

"Let me see that," the Elf said, and the Knight handed him the tome. "This *is* my Word, albeit missing some pages. Remarkable!"

"They're really your ideals?" Fyrstsvard asked, his eyes shining.

"Yes, I … I wrote this long ago, I suppose, though it feels like only yesterday … And you say this book helped you to rediscover the truth about my religion? I am glad you found it then!"

"Indeed it did," the Knight affirmed, beaming. "And now, every Knight carries one. Anyway, after its establishment, the Order set to exterminating every Witch and Magician that had dared to vilify your grand dream, selfless Prophet."

"Exterminating?" exclaimed Amril; his loudest proclamation yet, barely louder than a sea breeze. "But that is atrocious! You said you were an Order of *Pacia*, of Peace!"

Stein cut in pragmatically, his voice thunderous against the Elf's zephyr tone, "We are. And we kept the peace by slaughtering those who would have broken it! Stories passed down through generations told of the Witches' cruelty, of how they enslaved and debased all creatures before them. I understand your shock, for they were perhaps good people once – but they became corrupted by their power, and we did the world a favour by ridding it of them."

Amril could only stare at the big man silently through the curling smoke from the dying fire; his life's works besmirched, ruined. "But … I have never slain anyone!" he murmured eventually. "I am a pacifist …"

"Ask anyone about Convent," the brusque Knight continued, waving an arm at the faces around the fire, "and you will hear only tales of horror and loss. They needed to be dealt with."

"We Nomads were civilised once," Izdaju put in, struggling with the formidable word. "We live in towns, and we farm. The Witches kill most of us, slave the rest. Those that not run away to the desert were kept like pigs in pens – animals for slaughter. When the Witches die, the Knights not let us leave desert – they try to force us to follow their ways," he pointed a finger at the Elf, "*your* ways. When we say no, they kill us. So," he scowled at Fyrstsvard, "desert is home."

"Yeah, Heldig told me the Knights were always trying to convert the Freemen in olden times, too," Ratnik added thoughtfully. "Forcibly convert them with swords and sea raids, that is."

"It was da same for Chilpaea," Jumal agreed, exhaling a plume of blue-white smoke. "I have heard stories of da Witches' atrocities – and dey are no worse dan dose committed by da Knights in more recent years. Out of da frying pan, into da fire, as my people say."

Having looked from speaker to speaker in growing dismay, Amril fixed his gaze once more on Fyrstsvard, his eyes plaintive. "Is this true?"

"There *were* a series of Crusades to … encourage conversion," the Knight admitted quietly, not meeting the Elf's gaze. "But we gave up such tactics a long time ago!"

Jumal snorted. "Because you were failing everywhere!"

Amril looked like someone had defecated in his shoe.

"We *are* of the Order of Peace," Fyrstsvard insisted, downcast. "Our ancestors vanquished the Witches, because they no longer followed *your* ways, because they had smeared your noble act with selfishness and greed. And as for more recent frictions … Our Order sought only to free the people across the world from the indomitable rule of evil under which they had languished and to reconcile the ideals of the nations with the ones *you* had preached so many years before."

"Pfft, dey wanted to control da world, you mean," Jumal snorted, handing back the roll-up.

"Wanted to wipe out all worship of the old Gods," Ratnik added, taking the baui.

"The only freedom your people brought was death!" Izdaju snarled.

Dolefully, the Prophet told the Knight, "An Order of Peace does not exterminate."

"Regardless," Fyrstsvard said, spreading his hands wretchedly, "that is our history." He then lowered his head as if in shame and began to doubt everything he had ever believed.

"And so for three hundred years the Knights have flourished?" the Elf whispered as if aghast at the implications. He rubbed his left temple with two long, white, delicate fingers. "So, how did you know to rescue me from the clutches of the Lord of the Netherworld?"

The companions looked at one another for a long moment amid flickering shadows as gusts tugged at the light and smoke of the embers.

"We do not know *how* we knew when and where to look for you," Fyrstsvard responded slowly. "That is something you will have to ask Lord Protector Labogé when we see him. The Lord Protector is the head of the Order of *Pacia.* On his orders, Sir Stein, Tar Feng and I set out from Justiqua months ago to be here in time for your rebirth. We met with other agents known to the Lord Protector in Jungleside – three sailors from Kauapunki-Meren; Ratnik and Jumal here, plus another, Heldig, whom we lost in that chasm in the desert.

"The Nomad tribe, the Kriigi, were waiting at the desert's rim to lead us to the Great Fissure, where our information dictated you could be found. There, we met with Izdaju and Kamilah, as well as a warrior named Jerrat from the Empire to the north, Shimyahein, who also died in the caves. Egobal was the last to join us, since he came from the opposite direction, from the deep desert. How the Lord Protector contacted him at all, I'll never know. Together, we descended into the Fissure and fought our way through packs of *Rodici,* a city of angry Dwarves, mutated rat-monsters, a giant worm and a Dark God to rescue you and escape." Fyrstsvard looked almost pleased with himself and a little defensive.

"No doubt killing Dwarves, *Rodici,* rat-monsters and worms in your path?" Amril frowned sternly, disapproval rife in his tone.

Stein cut in again dourly, bushy black brows lowered like he was offended by the Elf's judgement of his Order. "What about your story, Prophet? Is it all true? Did you really create a paradise for all? Was it your apprentice who killed you?"

Fyrstsvard felt mortified by his brother's accusatory tone and held his head in his hands, wishing the nightmare would end.

The Prophet's soothing song, however, lifted the Knight from his melancholy. "Yes," he responded simply, and that one syllable was the most glorious Fyrstsvard had ever heard, like a drop of water on a parched tongue. "It is true. Together with my people, the *Vaylorici,* the Life Mother, Gaia, and the black-hearted Balthazar, I created *Citta Pacia* to be a realm for the eternal rest of benevolent souls. I did so because death frightens us all. It is a fact of life, as real to man and Goblin as to Elf and Dwarf.

"We all knew of the Nether, which awaited us should we lead unfit lives. The threat of Gastar's foul depths lurked in the back of every mind, for it is the eternal that forever torments the present. I reasoned with Gaia that if the Nether existed for souls that deserved punishment for their abuse of life, then there should be a haven too for those who had lived a nobler life. She agreed to the principle, but some souls – she told me – had to be remoulded in her Star Forges in what she called the Wheel of Life to make new life from their substance in a grand cycle."

"Pssht – and you believed her?" Ratnik relit his roll-up on the embers and took a drag, then passed it to Jumal.

"What was she like?" Fyrstsvard asked the Elf excitedly, ignoring the buccaneer. "The All Mother. What was she like?"

Amril smiled dreamily. "Gaia is the personification of the matronly instinct. The mother of mothers. The creator of all. She is, of course, powerful beyond belief – the godly energies at her command are truly staggering – but she is also kind, thoughtful, magnanimous, sweet and ethical. She was willing to help the sentient races down the right path with the creation of the Nether and a haven, humble enough to listen to my suggestions. She is … was … beneficence itself, my friend."

"Wow. So, what was it like – creating *Citta Pacia?* Was it difficult?"

Amril nodded. "It was the most challenging undertaking of my life, but it was worth it." His brow wrinkled and he twined his fingers. "It's strange. My memories of the time are … fuzzy. I wonder if it's something to do with my rebirth … I remember creating *Citta Pacia* with Gaia and Balthazar by my sides, but I only vaguely recall stealing the portal away –"

"Stealing it away?" Fyrstsvard interrupted more loudly than he had intended. "Why did you do that?"

Amril remained patient. "Well, a few years after the creation of *Citta Pacia,* I began to hear worrying rumours about Balthazar – that he was using blood magic most vile in order to absorb the souls of others into his own to augment his own energy reserves. Some of my acolytes whispered to me that he wanted *Citta Pacia* for his own, that he wanted to absorb the reservoir of souls within for himself. I did not believe the stories, but I thought it best to be safe with my greatest creation nonetheless.

"I removed the doorway to *Citta Pacia* from its spot and hid it away in a place known only to me for safekeeping. Nobody needed to know where it was to worship it or for the souls to reach the afterlife I promised. I thought it was a smart move."

He shook his head. "The acolytes were right, though. That must have been the last straw for Balthazar, I think. It was not long after he found out I had moved it that he came after me … and we all know how that ended. So, with my death, the secret was lost to the world and Gastar had no choice but to bring me back – for the same original purpose as Balthazar; to absorb all the souls within for his own personal gain."

"Why would a God need such gain?" Ratnik blurted, frowning. "Aren't they already all powerful?"

"I do not know if he wants or needs the power," Amril replied slowly, his brow creasing slightly again, "but I wonder if it is simply his nature to be envious of the beatitude, the joy, of others, or perhaps he felt affronted that I was offering an alternative to his afterlife. Whatever the reason, I am confident he wants the souls for himself. I have suspected for some time that he warps these souls in his sadistic torture chambers and transforms them into the Demons that plague the land."

Fyrstsvard shook his head and scowled at mention of the evil creatures.

"His appetite for damned souls to punish is insatiable," the Elf continued. "That was another reason I moved *Citta Pacia* – because on more than one occasion my acolytes and I had to fend off Demons attacking our temples. We suspected them to be Gastar's servants, searching for the doorway on his behalf."

"Do you remember where you moved the doorway to?" Tar Feng asked slyly.

Amril granted him a soft smile. "Of course. What I do not remember well, however, is what happened after that … I know I went travelling to spread the word of my haven, but my recollections of the time are fragmented and disjointed, dreamlike even – right up until my death, which stands out in my mind as though it happened yesterday. I can still feel Balthazar's dagger in my back. I know I left my apprentice in charge when I left. Evidently, he became power-mad … I will never forget the crazed look in his eyes after he stabbed me …" He shook his head, looking down.

"So, you say souls have been able to reach *Citta Pacia* since your demise?" Fyrstsvard asked worriedly after a long silence broken only by the snap and pop of the dung cinders.

"Oh yes," Amril lifted his eyes with the ghost of a smile. "The Ferrymen, the Soul Guides, take souls where they belong regardless of my state of being, and so those who have prayed to reach *Citta Pacia* and whose conscience is clear will have achieved their wish, rest assured of that, Knight."

Fyrstsvard smiled back in relief. "Thank the All Mother," he said gratefully. He looked pensive for a moment. "Forgive me for asking, Amril, but how do you know souls are being safely ferried? I'm not asking if you trust the Soul Guides; I mean, how do you know souls exist at all? How do you know they are there to be taken to *Citta Pacia?"*

Amril flirted with a smile. "Magic. More specifically, a spell known as the Third Eye, which allows the user to observe the ebb and flow of the energies of life and the energies within us all." This confirmation of the existence of souls, of the invisible in which he had believed all his life, was staggering to the Knight and left him momentarily speechless.

Then, the Elf continued, "In fact … I may sound crazy here, and perhaps I am … It may have been a dream or … wishful thinking … but I think I saw them with my Third Eye. The Ferrymen. The moment I was revived … or the moment before I was revived, maybe. They came to me, appearing as three dark-skinned, beautiful women, and they spoke to me, though I could barely make out their words, as though they were shouting through a waterfall. I think they apologised for failing to safeguard my soul and deliver it to its resting place. They told me that they had tried and that the Dark Lord, Gastar, had thwarted them. They warned me … that I was going down the wrong path. They ... urged me to alter my course."

Silence struck at the camp like a blade to the heart, and then the wind whined and the world seemed almost normal again.

"What did they mean by that?" asked Stein.

"I don't know …"

"So, who are these Ferrymen?" Ratnik asked at last, curiosity outweighing his belligerence. "Is it true then that they take souls to the afterlife?"

"They go by many names," replied Amril thoughtfully. "In Fjelburg they are called Valkyries, the Goblins call them *Ashringari'ke,* you Freemen call them Ferrymen of the Dead. Some call them Norns, others Angels or Messengers of Death. Most just call them Soul Guides, for that is what they do: they guide souls after death. Even those of us powerful enough to recognise their existence, however, know little more than this about them. They are something of a mystery, truth be told, but they were intrinsic to my plans for *Citta Pacia,* for without them, souls would never reach my haven."

"Praise be that these Ferrymen exist then!" remarked Fyrstsvard fervently.

"Indeed," agreed Amril with a smile and a nod of the head. "So, if I may look forward rather than back for a moment: what are we to do now?"

"We will escort you across the sea to Justiqua, where our Order is based," Stein answered shortly. "There, you will be safe. There, we will have thousands of our brothers to fight this menace that hounds us."

The Elf said nothing for a time as the firelight dwindled, then: "And what if I do not wish to-"

"Then, I will hunt you down, knock you out, string you up and drag you all the way there behind my camel – which has a very stinky arse," Stein growled.

Fyrstsvard looked like he might faint. "Please, noble Prophet, understand that we have our orders, and those orders are in your best interests as well as ours. We will be safe in Justiqua. We can raise an army there to fight on your behalf if needs be."

"Who has put you up to this?" Amril was staring at Stein like a peeved cat, narrow-eyed.

Fyrstsvard broke in before the bigger Knight could cause more damage. "It was our Lord Protector, the Grandmaster of the Order of Peace, Sir Claud Labogé."

Amril glared at Stein, who was entirely unperturbed, a while longer and then cast his eyes up to the illustrious stars, whose familiar forms he recognised even after centuries away.

"Tar Feng, Amril," Fyrstsvard eventually dredged the wise men from their celestial reveries, speaking gently as if to horses that might bolt, "was that truly Gastar himself, Lord of the Nether, that we saw down there?"

"Well, I can't say for sure," the old Tzunese man began slowly, dragging out the word 'sure' to emphasise his intent to hypothesise on the subject. He quickly sped up as he continued. "What with me having never met the man or God or monster or whatever the Nether he is before and therefore having no facial comparisons available – present against past viewings, you know what I mean. Comparing faces to see if the man can be recognised. No no, I couldn't do that, not at all, no I couldn't!

"Couldn't compare his voice, smell or feel either, what with me having never met the man, monster or God or whatever the Nether he is, no I couldn't, don't you see? But," again he elongated the word, "from what I have read and heard, heard and read, yes, mostly in the Viper Spire, yes, in my homeland, yes, but little bits elsewhere also! Mustn't forget about the elsewheres of life must we? No, in fact I don't think we should! Anyway, what I have read, heard and seen drawn leads me to deduce that ..." He paused to catch his breath. "I *believe* that yes, yes it was in fact no monster, man or God other than Gastar. It was he. He was it. *I* believe it was Gastar, the Lord of the Nether himself!"

"I too can only conclude it was none other than the ruler of the Nether," Amril agreed evenly, looking at the Wizard askance.

The group exchanged troubled looks with one another, shivering as the heat from the fire faded and darkness closed in all around them. Even if all did not follow the Prophet's path, all had heard tell of the Lord of Torture and Misery, Gastar the Wicked, God of the Nether, where damned souls languished in eternal torment.

Fyrstsvard pinched his nose, squishing his fingertips against his eyes for a moment, while Jumal scratched his beardy cheek, puffed on baui and muttered, "Well, trow me in da swamp and call me a crocodile!"

"And that worm ..." Fyrstsvard murmured slowly after a while, looking up to meet Tar Feng's innocent milky eyes. "You and Labogé never mentioned a giant worm in the debriefing!"

"Well," Tar Feng began slowly, "that is true, but I'm fairly sure I may have expressed a distinct possibility that Demons would guard the Elf's soulless body … And I suspect that the worm was not a worm at all, no, no! But a worm *Demon*, yes, a Demon it was. A warped and twisted, cursed and torn soul moulded into a new shape; a thing of hate and vindictiveness!"

"A servant of Gastar," growled Fyrstsvard with furrowed brow, fingering his sword hilt uneasily.

"I have a question, if you don't mind, Feng?" Ratnik chimed in, taking the roll-up back from Jumal.

"Not at all, my boy, not at all! Anything you want to know!"

"What in the Nether happened back there?" The simple pirate was so confused by what he had seen and heard that he barely knew how to formulate his question. "What happened to Heldig?"

Tar Feng shrugged. "You heard as much as I, dear boy, so expect me to know little more. Gastar said he was to be the first of the *Thakshir,* and evidently that is what he became. What that means, I am not sure." He looked troubled.

Ratnik's lower lip wobbled and he cleared his throat before speaking again. "So, did Amril here come back to life? 'Cos he seemed mighty dead at first, but then that creepy guy, Gastar, chanted that horrible spell – or whatever it was – and I *felt* his darkness in the air around me! Seeping into my very lungs as I breathed – it was so cold!"

"Teehee, that is the mark of powerful magic being wrought, my boy, dark and powerful magic indeed! Soul magic! The Elf was not brought back to life, strictly speaking; more, his *soul* was returned to its rightful place. His body. Like a hermit crab switching shells. His spirit must have been held by Gastar somehow for all this time! Ever since he died, centuries ago, the Dark Lord has kept it, presumably in torment, misery and pain, whilst he healed the body! And now, for reasons on which I must admit even I am not entirely clear, the Prophet's soul has been brought back to this plane by the Lord of the Nether. I can only deduce that Gastar does indeed desire the Prophet's paradise, *Citta Pacia,* along with all of the souls therein!"

At this, the Knights' expressions became grim as the grave.

"Yes," agreed Amril quietly, "and he will stop at nothing to get them. He will hunt me to the furthest corners of Maradoum to find *Citta Pacia.* I'm sure he is on our tail already."

A cold wind blew through the camp at his words, and folk looked around, expecting to see the God of the Nether looming out of the darkness.

Stein muttered something about that being why they needed to get to Justiqua, and the Elf studiously ignored him.

"How *did* we know exactly when the Prophet would be awoken?" Ratnik asked then, exhaling a thick cloud of curling blue-white smoke, stifling a cough and looking out at the rolling dunes contemplatively. "We were there at the exact right time. How did we know?"

Tar Feng grinned and turned his milky eyes on the pirate, their gleam faint in the dimming radiance. "Oh, my master *always* knows, Ratnik. Teeheehee. Believe me, he has his ways."

"If I may ask, Amril," Fyrstsvard began tactfully, "if you are the greatest Magician who has ever lived, capable of creating a realm of your own where souls can abide for eternity, why then did you not cast a spell to help free yourself from Gastar's clutches?"

The Elf bowed his head. When he spoke, every syllable dripped with sorrow. "I cannot cast a single spell anymore. My magic is gone."

"Why?" the Knight whispered. "What happened?"

The Prophet kept his eyes averted and twined his fingers. "I … do not know … I do not remember … But it is gone."

Silence had apparently been creeping up on them again all this time, thought Fyrstsvard, for it pounced on them now with irresistible force. The only one with the strength and sorrow to resist it was the Elf who had lived for almost a millennium.

"If you do not mind," murmured Amril, "I think I will sleep now. We should all get what rest we can before Gastar comes for us."

No one had the heart to object.

20

Titan's Pass

"Wow," breathed Saul Aodhson, craning his neck atop his trusty steed, Faafoor. "I've never seen it before."

The Prince's travelling companion, a temperamental warrior woman named Terra, chuckled and brushed her fiery hair out of her freckly face. "The mighty Prince Saul has never even seen the full extent of his own Kingdom," she teased.

"I've only just come of age!" he objected. "I've not had time to explore every nook and cranny yet – give me time, woman!"

She shook her head. "It is a sight to behold and that's the truth, whether it's your first time or your hundredth."

A black wall named Titan's Pass dominated sight to the south, set between enormous, impassable mountains. It was so vast that it had been in sight for the last few days of their two-month-long journey from Baldr's Safe. The wall – unmarked by dent, seam, or sign of building – stretched from the final mountain that comprised the range known as the Great Divide across three hundred yards of open space to merge, without blemish or sign of handiwork, with the sheer grey side of the tallest mountain in Fjelburg, Sol Top. Titan's Pass provided one of the only entrances into the Highlands; the other two being Jaata Murgen in the north and through the Alfa Wald in the west.

There were hundreds of rumours surrounding the ancient wall; that the enormous barrier had not been created by men, and that it was sorcerous, for there was no gate, door or any other form of entrance that would allow passage through the wall, and yet pass through people did.

"So, who do you think built it, my Prince?" Terra asked.

Saul regarded her quizzically, drawing his white fur mantle tighter around him as the wind nipped him, howling down from overcast skies. Not for the first time, he noticed the goosebumps adorning her smooth, milky skin. She wore only riding moccasins, tartan trews, a woolly green tunic and a thin, sleeveless leather jacket, tied down the front with black thread.

The Prince patted Faafoor's chestnut neck. "Call me Saul. Are you sure you don't want my mantle?" He gestured to the thick, white snow leopard pelt he wore draped over his shoulders, which was marked with dark rings and clasped around his neck with a steel clasp in the shape of a horse.

She shook her head decisively, and her mare, Keyli, snickered. "As I have said, it wouldn't be proper, Prince. Now, answer the question."

He sighed. "Nobody knows who built it," he said slowly, as if explaining to a child. "It has been around since before the Time of Convent, like Baldr's Safe and Northbane – since before records began."

Terra frowned at him, swaying from side to side with the motion of riding. "I *know* that," she said, "but if you had to take a guess, who do you *think* built it?"

Saul thought about this for a moment while the hooves kept clip-clopping. "The Gods," he replied eventually.

"Not the Witches?" Terra asked, dragging her auburn hair out of her face again.

"There are some theories that the old buildings in Fjelburg are too ancient to have been built by Witches," Saul commented.

Terra nodded, a smile playing about her plump lips. "We shall see if you still think it is the work of the Gods when we get there."

When Saul and Terra arrived at the foot of the monumental wall, they dismounted and the latter placed the palm of her right hand against the smooth black rock and encouraged the former to do the same with a small smile. The Prince placed his hand gently against the black rock, expecting a shock or coldness, but to his surprise the alien rock was pleasantly warm to the touch.

His jaw dropped in amazement, and Terra chuckled at the look of wonder on his big, open face.

"You should see your face!" she said, chortling and stroking her palomino mare's nose.

"How is it so warm?" he asked softly, eyes alight with curiosity, moving his hand over the incredibly smooth, almost glass-like, wall.

Terra shrugged dismissively. "Don't rightly know," she replied, gesturing vaguely upwards. "Maybe the black just absorbs the sun's heat."

"Do *you* think it is the Gods?" Saul asked, turning to look his companion in the eyes, brimming with interest. "Or do you think the Wall is magical – and that we pass through a portal to get to the other side?"

"No one knows who built the Wall," Terra echoed the Prince's earlier words. "It could be the Gods, or there could be magic involved ..." Terra's smile seemed more provocative to Saul than usual.

"Fah!" Saul broke in, deciding for himself the truth of the matter and waving an authoritative hand. "Magic is not real. The Gods gave us the Wall. There is a mechanism of some sort that controls the Pass, allowing through only those who are approved by the hands working the mechanism. Whatever and wherever this mechanism is, it is known only to and controlled by the Commander of Titan's Pass and his top officers." He looked up at the cloud-wreathed top of the mighty wall. "I wonder how they know when to open the Pass when we come from the other side, though …"

"A bell alerts officers when the Wall is touched by those seeking passage," Terra explained, her serious face belying the fantastic nature of her words. "The Wall can then be made translucent from this side so that officers can identify who seeks to pass." Together, they turned to study the mysterious wall, but could see nothing but blackness.

"Pass opening!" came a call from a nearby officer, and Saul remembered that he was surrounded by his all-but forgotten countrymen.

With that, the Pass through the Wall – as it was colloquially called – was activated. Saul was alerted to this fact by his stallion rearing and a sudden deep and resonant humming that seemed to vibrate throughout his entire frame. As he spoke calmingly to his horse and stared at the great barricade, the section of wall in front of him shimmered and a ripple seemed to cross over it as if it were suddenly liquid. Radiance burst from it, illuminating a shining, ethereal corridor comprised of light itself. Saul blinked repeatedly, disbelieving his eyes. Surely it was a trick of the light, he thought, but the ghostly passageway did not vanish.

"Touch it again, Prince," Terra encouraged gently, watching the young man's enchanted face.

"Call me Saul." The Prince reached out a tentative hand to the Wall once more.

His fingers passed into the light. He yanked back his hand in surprise with a yelp, and then his ears turned red.

"Warm, isn't it?" Terra asked knowingly and a little smugly, wrapping her mare's reins around her hand.

Saul nodded and smiled.

"The Pass is open," she confirmed, drawing her mount, Keyli, forward. "Follow me."

Terra led the way into the spectral luminescence of Titan's Pass, confident of her ability to survive. With the solid Wall on either side of him and the glowing walkway directly in front, Saul clenched his hands tight on his horse's reins and took several steps forward with tightly clenched eyes.

"It'll be okay, Faafoor," he kept saying, though he knew it was himself he was trying to reassure.

After ten paces, when the tingling warmth faded and he reopened his eyes, the young Prince was on the other side. He turned to look back. In the Wall behind him, the son of Aodh beheld the translucent, gleaming passage of light, and through it he could see – as if in a haze or a dream – the Highland soldiers they had left behind. He patted Faafoor's side and took a deep breath, glad to be out in the open again. The chestnut stallion pawed the ground impatiently, shook its head and whinnied.

Saul grinned at the beast. "Okay, okay, we're going!"

Despite his father's assurances to the contrary, the Prince was not altogether convinced that the Wall was not magical, even though every Highlander knew magic was a myth. Titan's Pass certainly seemed enchanted to him.

On the south side of the Pass, Saul got his first glimpse of the calm and cultivated lands of the Fringe and the calm and cultivated folk that walked them. Anyone of six feet in height was considered a tall man in the Fringe, and so it shocked the Lowlanders' sensibilities to meet a Prince of the Highlands who towered at more than seven feet tall.

The Highlanders – despite being men, with the same anatomy as the Fringe men – were, in fact, a breed apart. The men of the Fringe, the Knights of Justiqua and even the men of the east – the Nomads, the Sandpeople, the mountain mercenaries and those in the Sultanate of Bab – were all of similar stature, peaking at no more than six and a half feet for the most part. To put it simply, the Highlanders were bigger than the rest of mankind, and they lived longer too, averaging at two hundred years.

Height amongst the Highlanders ranged from seven to eight feet tall in men, whilst their women tended to be a more modest six feet in height. The men had enormous barrel-chests and broad shoulders. They had long, thick arms that bulged larger and larger with muscle as adolescent grew to adult, as well as thick, trunk-like legs and hands almost twice the size of an average man's, like shovels on the ends of their ape-like arms. Their fearsome appearance was offset by their wide, open faces that were – more often than not – lit up in general joviality. The most common hair colour was red, but brown, black and blonde were not unheard of.

The general theory of the populace behind the differences between the Highlanders and the Fringers was that those in the Highlands had evolved to deal with a more difficult, dangerous land. There were few threats in the Lowlands besides pirate raids and storms, but there were Elves from the Wald to worry about in the Highlands, as well as sabre-tooth cats, mountain lions, Rock Trolls and giant insects from the north, not to mention the freezing climate, biting winds, endless snow and exhaustingly rugged terrain. All of this difficulty of lifestyle had led to the development of greater stature and strength in the Highlanders, it was believed, for they had needed it over the centuries just to survive in their inhospitable home.

Saul sighed reluctantly, looking out at the slate skies and the flat road running through the grassy landscape stretching endlessly away before him. Even the wind had died down, not wishing to break the monotony. He mounted and nudged his stallion into a slow walk.

"Come on, Faafoor. Let's go see the little people."

"Don't call them that in person," Terra admonished him.

21

A Tangle with the *Thakshir*

The air swam with heat as dawn scorched the desert, its searing rays shining through the gauzy tents of the Kriigi tribe and lighting Fyrstsvard's eyelids red. The Knight groaned and blinked, stretched and sat up. He looked down at his aching body. He was naked apart from undergarments, and small cuts and bruises adorned his frame – nothing to be too concerned with, he decided. As he looked around for his apparel, however, pain reminded him that his neck had been singed by Gastar's power blast in the caves beneath *Dwarhummer* and he winced.

Before he could rise from his horsehair blankets and dress, his tent flap was swept aside and Kamilah stepped boldly through, letting the flap of fabric that served as an entrance fall shut behind her. She assessed his state for a moment: huddled under the blanket for the sake of modesty. He returned her assessment, and his jaw tightened as he laid eyes on her black eye and cut, swollen lip that had not been present the night before.

"I come to thank you, Knight," she began without preamble. "We would have died down in that pit if not for you. We all owe you our gratitude."

"No thanks necessary, milady," Fyrstsvard responded self-consciously. "I was just doing my job, same as you."

Kamilah stepped nearer. "Yes, but you were right down there and Izdaju was wrong. So, I am glad you were there."

"Did your betrothed do that to you?" Fyrstsvard asked her, gesturing to the marks on her face and trying to keep his voice light, though it felt strange, like a tiger waited to pounce from his throat.

Kamilah nodded. "He did. He says I dishonoured him in the pit, that I favoured you over him. That is not how a Kriigi wife should act, he says."

Fyrstsvard's gut tightened at the same time as his fist and his teeth. Rarely had the easy-going Knight felt so angry. Swallowing the fury, he gently reached out a hand and Kamilah took it.

"Where I come from," he said softly, looking up into her dark eyes, "men who treat women in such a way can be punished with imprisonment." Seeing he may have used too advanced a vocabulary, he tried again. "Where I come from, men do not hit women. It is a … bad crime."

"I would like to see this place," she murmured huskily, bending at the knee.

The tent flapped open again, and in stepped Izdaju. Fyrstsvard hastily let go of Kamilah's hand, but the damage was already done.

"What are you doing in here?" Izdaju growled at his betrothed.

"I just –"

"I wake up in our bed, *alone,"* Izdaju spoke over her like climbing thunder, "thinking that you have gone out to make yourself useful to the tribe, to honour yourself, to honour me … And I find you here, alone in the tent of another man, like a brazen whore!"

"Nothing happened," Fyrstsvard tried to help.

"My love, I was merely –" Kamilah tried to speak again, but was cut off by a hefty backhand to the face.

"Do not lie to me!" Izdaju roared in her averted face, while the near-naked Knight scrambled to his feet in protest. "You dirty *funta*! Get out of this tent now, or I will shame you in front of the whole tribe! Go keep lookout on the rock! The Knight and I need to talk!"

Kamilah darted a sad, apologetic look at Fyrstsvard and then silently exited the tent.

Once she was gone, Izdaju turned on Fyrstsvard like a jaguar on a cornered monkey, prowling across the tent towards him as sinuously.

"Who do you think you are, Knight?"

Fyrstsvard held up his hands remonstratively and tried to explain, but Izdaju was in no mood for explanations.

"She is mine!" the Nomad hissed as he drew close, lashing out with an explosive right hand that almost knocked Fyrstsvard through the tent fabric.

The Knight rubbed his jaw and got to his feet purposefully slowly, trembling with suppressed rage. "Izdaju, stop!" he said firmly, though the darker temples in his mind that worshipped violence prayed for the Nomad to attack again, thus allowing the Knight to defend himself with honour. "Nothing happened between us!"

Izdaju would not listen, his wide eyes throbbing with rage. Instead, he attacked the Knight again, bludgeoning his body and then whipping a left hook to his face to knock him to his knees once more. The Knight rose again, slowly at first like a new-born calf, but once his legs were under him, he sprang at the other and tackled him in the midriff. The force of the rush bore them both through the tent flap, and they sprawled on the rugs outside, Fyrstsvard's shoulder still in the Nomad's gut.

"Stop, Izdaju!" Fyrstsvard grunted.

The rest of the Kriigi, the Elf and his rescuers swiftly gathered to see what was causing the ruckus and then stayed to witness who ended it. It was brutal savagery versus practised precision, thought Ratnik as he came to watch.

Izdaju elbowed Fyrstsvard in the back, but the Knight squirmed upright, sat atop the Nomad and began to pummel Izdaju's face with his fists. Izdaju guarded his face as best he could, writhing and dodging from side to side, but still he received a few solid blows. With a wild growl, he managed to toss the Knight off him.

Izdaju scrambled to his feet and launched a new attack even as the other struggled to his knees. Slipping in close, he grabbed a fistful of Fyrstsvard's feathery blonde hair and yanked back his head. He snapped back the bearded head twice more with vicious punches and then kicked his opponent in the ribs. Fyrstsvard groaned and sagged, but Izdaju would not let him. The Nomad dragged the Knight back up again by his hair and punched him repeatedly, like striking a gong, until his face was dripping with blood.

Fyrstsvard had had enough. He smacked Izdaju in the stomach with the back of his left fist, and then – catching the Nomad's swinging fist firmly in his right hand – he quickly wriggled as high as he could to get leverage. He released the Nomad's hand as it tried to pull back, and as it did so, Fyrstsvard moved precipitously. With one hand on the fist that held his hair so cruelly and one hand grabbing the elbow of the Nomad's same arm higher up, the Knight stood and twisted the arm so that it bent the wrong way, pushing the elbow down, twisting and pulling the wrist towards Izdaju's back, palm up.

Despite this reversal of fortune and the painful grip in which his arm was now held, the Nomad's clutch on his opponent's hair did not weaken and he tried in vain to punch the other with his free hand. Tightening the grip meant an awkward bowing movement from Fyrstsvard, due to the hold on his hair, but he tightened it until he thought any more would mean breaking the Nomad's arm.

"Let me go!" the Knight growled through his teeth, whilst Izdaju panted, clearly unwilling to relinquish his hold.

Fyrstsvard bent the arm further to near breaking point. Izdaju inhaled sharply with the pain, and his fist jerked open. The Nomad then tried to spin and elbow the Knight with his free arm, but Fyrstsvard used the hold he had on Izdaju to shove him away.

Eyes glittering like stars of malice, Izdaju slowly drew his scimitars from their leather-covered wooden sheaths at his belt, the wide curved blades whispering of dark things impending. Fyrstsvard, unarmed, cast about for a weapon.

Any imminent swordplay was postponed, however, by a shout from the bandy-legged shaman in the eloquent Nomad tongue, which was only half-comprehensible to the young, concussed Knight, consisting of sucking and clicking noises and ululating bass voices. The shout sounded belligerent, which was highly unusual for the serene, senescent shaman, causing both Fyrstsvard and Izdaju to turn in surprise to seek out the source of the disturbance.

Seeing that the rest of the tribe was looking up at something to the east, the two combatants did the same. Blinking and squinting against the dawning sun, the Knight could just make out what everyone was ogling. The shaman, the Chief and the entire tribe were all staring at a figure silhouetted in black standing atop one of the shorter, ivory pinnacles that surrounded the camp. The figure stood motionless, but it clearly held a curved, naked blade in one hand.

Chief Majbolji demanded an answer from the figure – at least, that is what Fyrstsvard assumed from the tone – his anger and volume rising by the second, presumably regarding the newcomer's identity and purpose in the Kriigi camp. The Chief held his spear threateningly, and the younger warriors had their weapons out too.

The shaman began to walk forward slowly toward the silent stranger, hand held over his eyes as he tried to get a better look. He finally came to stand in the shadow of the great rock, which poked out of a high dune and leaned over the camp, ten feet off the ground at its peak. There, Kasha'a was apparently able to identify the newcomer, because he turned around and waved to the Chief, shouting in Traveller's Tongue so all could understand.

"He is of the Unduru tribe! They have long been our neighbours and allies. Why he should act this way is something of a mystery …"

As the ancient spiritual guide of the Kriigi began to turn back to the man atop the pinnacle of rock, Fyrstsvard screamed out a warning, but it was too late.

The Unduru newcomer leapt from the great rock to come crashing down on Kasha'a, his scimitar spearing gorily through the shaman's astonished mouth and out the back of his neck. The shaman's corpse crumpled like wet parchment beneath the Unduru warrior's weight, and his blood stained the sand.

Fyrstsvard's heart battered his ribs, and he gasped desperately for breath. When the man had leapt, he had eclipsed the sun for a moment, but a moment had been enough and the Knight's blood had run cold as he had realised what it was that faced them. He had seen the man's blood-coloured eyes, grey rotting skin, and the thick red veins that tore through his face.

Before the killer could so much as recover his scimitar from his victim's mouth, the Chief had run him through with his spear. The Unduru, however, was now a creature of the foulest sorcery, and such a trivial obstacle as a spear in the gut would not stop him from his mission of direst purpose. The Unduru roared in the Chief's face and backhanded him viciously with a mangled arm that looked like it had been savaged by wolves, sending him sprawling in the dirt.

"Let us finish this another time, Izdaju!" Fyrstsvard suggested hastily.

"I will not forget, Knight!" shouted back Izdaju, but he nodded and spun away from Fyrstsvard.

Then, he pushed his way past the Kriigi warriors in front of him, headed for the conflict, while the Justiquan made a beeline for his tent and his gear.

"Careful!" shouted Tar Feng from somewhere in the crowd. "It is another *Thakshir,* a monster of evil magic!"

As he finished speaking, two Kriigi warriors approached the *Thakshir* Unduru cautiously. One was short and skinny, holding a scimitar and wearing a blue robe, while the other was particularly dark-skinned and huge, his bald head towering above most every other.

The enormous man swiped a great axe at the intruder, but the Unduru lurched out of the way and swung savagely with its own blade at the robed man, who dodged just in time. Pushing his way towards the fracas, Ratnik was yet too distant to intervene and could do nothing save watch helplessly as the *Thakshir* spun, a lustful moan on its carious lips, to parry the great axe and leap on the towering Nomad wielding it.

The foul magic-begotten creature sank its teeth deep into the flesh of the big man's neck above the collarbone, ripping free a mouthful of gore. The Nomad bellowed wildly in pain, struggling with all his might to disengage from the walking corpse, until the robed swordsman stepped up behind the *Thakshir* and cut a cruel slash across its back. The swordsman's robe was spattered with stinking, congealing blood, and he retched and spewed bile on the sand.

The giant Nomad collapsed to the ground, eyes rolling back, and the Unduru warrior whirled – quick as a flash – to sever the swordsman's off-hand at the elbow with its blade. Droplets of blood looked like tiny rubies in the eye-watering morning rays. The screaming swordsman's own blade came up reflexively at the movement, and though it impaled itself upon the sword's length, the Unduru corpse dropped its own scimitar and pulled itself closer to its victim along the length of the blade with iron-strong hands clawing at robe and flesh. The sword burst from its back, but the carcass did not care. It got a hold of the man's sword arm and bit deep into it with what could only be described as a low moan of pure pleasure.

"Impaling it doesn't seem to do the trick!" Stein shouted, moving forward, watching the *Thakshir* feast gorily on the Kriigi swordsman's throat with the man's blade still stuck in its guts. "Take off its head!"

The armless swordsman soon planted his face in the dirt with the Unduru still atop him, feasting, but as he did so, his huge, muscle-bound companion slowly returned to his feet. The man's deep neck wound no longer gushed blood, but looked black with infection, and his skin was no longer the rich ebony of his people. Now, it was mouldy grey, peeling back from his skull before their very eyes as thick red veins pulsated their way to the surface of his skin to throb and flow malevolently across his face and body. He let out a low drone as he laid beaming red eyes on the rest of his tribe; a moan of hunger.

"By da melons of Merejulanna, dey're infectious!" Jumal cried out, hefting axe and cutlass. "Don't let dem bite you, desert-men!"

Izdaju, Stein, Ratnik, Jumal and thirty Kriigi warriors had, by now, formed a line of defence between the *Thakshir* and the surviving Nomads, with weapons bared. Ratnik darted forwards to swiftly sever the head of the gorging Unduru, but even that did not stop it. The headless horror continued to writhe and reached out its veiny arms to grip Ratnik's leg in a vice.

"It's dead, but it's not dying!" the young pirate roared worriedly.

His cutlass flashed in the sun once more as he gritted his teeth against the pain and chopped off the offending arms with three quick swings. Cold blood spattered uncomfortably against his legs and calico breeches, and his face pinched into a grimace of disgust.

The Unduru corpse, now bereft of head and arms, writhed about on the floor like a giant snake, evidently trying to prop itself up on its legs. Ratnik smashed his booted foot against the wriggling corpse, knocking it flat, and then he hacked off its legs. It took him a few tries, for they flailed wildly. The corpse and the stumps of its arms and legs squirmed on afterwards, as if determined to exact revenge for their mutilation.

Meanwhile, the giant Kriigi who had been transformed had leapt, like a pouncing leopard, on one of his tribesmen. The brute force of the leap made the big man unstoppable, and he sank his teeth into his former fellow's flesh with a satisfied gurgle despite a scimitar through his ribs.

Stein slashed his broadsword through the spine of the evil creature as it feasted, but like the other it turned around and came on for more, even with mortal wounds. Having witnessed from the corner of his eye Ratnik's treatment of the other corpse, Stein lopped off one of the towering *Thakshir's* legs at the knee, and it collapsed in a puff of sand. The Kriigi tribesmen soon finished it off, severing all its limbs until only the thrashing torso remained.

Before anyone could stop him, Izdaju had done the same to the third man who had been bitten; a Kriigi warrior who had stood beside them in the line. The man's decapitated head gaped open-mouthed in astonishment up at Ratnik as the pirate beheld Izdaju in empathic disgust. The man looked like he had bathed in blood – a true symbol of the savagery of the wandering desert Nomads, the buccaneer thought.

With the deed done, nobody said anything against it. All understood the necessity of the gruesome act even as they hated it. It was clear now that if you were bitten, you would transform. If you transformed, you would turn on your own friends in a heartbeat, therefore the bitten could not be allowed to transform.

"A foe that turns your very comrades against you!" Stein gasped, face pale with fear of the supernatural. "One foe turned into three so fast! Imagine if there are more of those things …"

Suddenly, Izdaju was sheathing his scimitars and shouting out in the Nomad tongue, Hashpaji, with arms held aloft in a gesture of pacification.

Ratnik looked around, eventually locking eyes with and nodding to Jumal, his pulse drumming a high-tempo beat, terror drying his throat and moistening his palms. He was relieved to see a similar fear of the preternatural in his crewmate.

"Dat was like a nightmare," Jumal murmured.

Ratnik nodded, feeling weak at the knees. The stench from the bodies was appalling. "Yeah … the thought of becoming one of those things … it makes me –" The Freeman threw up in the sand, dribbling bile and coughing up spittle until he was drained.

Fyrstsvard, clothed and armoured now, saw Izdaju yelling in Hashpaji and guessed the Nomad was assuring his people that the threat was gone. The Knight turned to observe that the rest of the camp had emerged from their tents to see what had transpired. The people were ragged, filthy and skinny, and yet there was about them a palpable sense of concern, of community and of care for one another. They consoled each other and grieved visibly at the sight of the mutilated, squirming bodies of their friends.

The Kriigi warriors rushed past the Knights when they saw that their Chief was alive. They clamoured around him and were evidently relieved to see that he was relatively unharmed. The Chief reassured them wearily that he was not seriously hurt.

"Stein is right." Fyrstsvard turned to his group.

Stein, Ratnik and Jumal all looked at him expectantly, the Chilpaean wiping his whiskery chin. The Knight could see Tar Feng and Amril, huddled out of the way by one of the tents. What he had to do was difficult, because he wanted to help the Kriigi, but Fyrstsvard had been trained to be cool-headed and to command in the best interests of both himself and his men. So, he swallowed his pride and anger and continued after a deep breath. “There could be more of those things out there. We must leave this place at once if we are to complete our mission.”

Izdaju joined them. Fyrstsvard took another long breath. “We must leave immediately if we are to survive and complete our quest, Izdaju. Perhaps our disagreement can wait until the Elf is safely delivered?”

Izdaju nodded once with a face like he had sucked a lemon, his dark eyes never leaving the Knight’s face.

“Excellent. Then let us away. I’ll –” The Knight broke off in mid-sentence, and his head cocked suddenly to the left. After a heartbeat of careful listening, Fyrstsvard said, “Excuse me,” and rushed off, sprinting past the great rock fingers pointing at the sky to the east to get a better view from the top of one of the high dunes behind them. After a moment’s observation, he turned and dashed back, even faster than before.

As he drew nearer to the Kriigi and his companions once more, it became clear that he was hollering a warning.

22

The Sorrowing Horn

"More! More are coming!"

Once this was understood by the Chief, he began barking orders to all and sundry, waving his arms around like he was caught in a tornado.

The women sprinted back past Fyrstsvard with nary a scream to the heart of the camp where the majority of the tents were staked out, and the Knight was impressed by their efficiency, speed and quiet fortitude. They quickly began to get their belongings together, while the men hurried to ready themselves for combat, grabbing spears and bows and arrows. The men of the tribe formed a line facing the great white rocks, bows held at the ready.

All could now hear the pounding of a great many feet approaching at some speed from the east, just beyond the white crags and the nearby tall dunes that stretched to meet the sky, out of sight for the moment still.

Camels and horses were groaning and struggling feverishly against their bonds, thanks to the thump of approaching feet and the scent of blood and death. Fyrstsvard watched the women with children grabbing the beasts to flee, riding bareback in many cases where there was judged not enough time to grab a saddle. Then, he noticed that not all of the women were fleeing; some of the elders grabbed knives or hatchets and walked purposefully to join the men in defending their camp.

The men and women of the tribe flexed fingers on their weapons, licking lips nervously and testing bow strings in the face of the bloodcurdling roars they could hear approaching, growing louder and more terrifying by the second.

Fyrstsvard forced his way through the throng to the Chief to try to convince him to flee, but it was difficult to be heard and despite all of his unsubtle gesturing, the Chief would not be swayed. There was a gasp from the battle line of Nomads as a second invader topped the dune behind the grand bony fingers and became clearly visible to all. It was another *Thakshir* Unduru man with the same grey face, red veins and scant attire as the one already dead. A Kriigi Nomad impaled the Unduru warrior through the eye socket with a well-placed arrow and propelled him back through the air out of sight.

The ambulant corpse was almost immediately replaced by three more, however, who leapt on the smaller rocks and the dune and screamed horrifyingly at those gathered below, all festooned with rough-edged, black, festering wounds. There was no intelligence in the shrieks, only hate and bloodlust. They jumped down and rushed the line of Kriigi tribesmen wildly, whilst others began to appear behind them. More and more appeared – death-grey Dwarves as well as gangrene-black men – stumbling and skidding down the dunes with careless abandon.

They attacked the Kriigi warriors ferociously with no apparent concern for their own wellbeing – as well they might, thought Fyrstsvard, since they had the strength of several men, allowing them to pick up and fling the tribesmen around like playthings once close enough, and they were far from easily killed.

It worried Fyrstsvard most, however, how fast they had spread. Only born two days ago, they now numbered more than a hundred at a quick count – which was hardly surprising if they could forcibly recruit anyone with a bite, the Knight thought darkly. They had had all the Dwarves in *Dwarhummer* and any Nomads they had encountered since to feed on and to swell their ranks. Their numbers would only increase exponentially unless they were stopped soon, Fyrstsvard knew.

Tar Feng, in the midst of the defensive line of warriors, zapped one *Thakshir* missing three fingers with a green glob, and it went down but got back up again, despite the smoking singe in its chest. The old man kept shooting off globs, but the *Thakshir* kept clambering back to their feet and coming on, and eventually the Wizard was forced to watch in dismay and helplessness as the tribesmen on either side of him began being felled one by one.

Stein grabbed Fyrstsvard's arm and jerked him back unceremoniously from the Chief. His grip was painfully tight.

"We have to go now! We have to get out of here before they get overrun!" he shouted in his comrade's face to be heard over the clamour of battle surrounding them. Fyrstsvard tried to rip his arm free of Stein's grip, but it was no good; the older Knight was too powerful.

"Let me go!" Fyrstsvard roared. "We cannot abandon these men to die at the hands of this evil! This evil that *we* unleashed! I will fight with them, now let go of me!"

Stein clung on tenaciously through his comrade's attempts to break free. "If you fight, you will die! They are *all* going to die! We have to escape while we still can, while the Kriigi have the veiny monsters distracted!"

Fyrstsvard looked at his friend with disbelief and contempt. "Let me go, coward! I *will* fight with them against this evil – like a *true* Knight!"

"And what will that accomplish, eh?" Stein bellowed at his friend furiously, his fingers digging into Fyrstsvard's arm like steel. "You will *die* a true Knight, fool! We have a mission, remember? We *must* get the Prophet to safety! He is in no condition to defend himself, and we have orders to safeguard him, dammit! You said so yourself just a moment ago!"

Reason crawled sheepishly back to Fyrstsvard's combat-riddled mind, and he spat on the sand to try to relieve the taste of cowardice that sat so bitter upon his tongue.

"You are right, brother," the younger Knight cried more calmly, unable to meet Stein's eye just yet. "Fetch the Elf. I will gather the others."

Stein beheld him doubtfully for a moment, not releasing his grip, but then he relented. "Very well, I will see to the Prophet, but you had better do as you say!"

As Sir Kreeger hastily departed, Fyrstsvard turned back to the Chief. Majbolji was a formidable figure with arms thick with muscle and a face given a sinister cast by the pointed beard, dotted ritual scars and swirling patterns tattooed across it. Despite his intimidating form, however, as the Knight turned back to him at that moment, he could tell there was something different about the ageing Chief. Gone was his posture of confidence and surety, gone was the pride in his stern face.

The man who stood before Fyrstsvard now was a despairing being as he watched the remorseless *Thakshir* attack. He had witnessed, in the few seconds while the Knights argued, one monstrous corpse with its skull showing through its cheek scrabbling all over a Kriigi warrior who had clearly been disarmed and knocked down. As the Chief watched, the undying Unduru bit into the Kriigi's exposed neck, ripping out a chunk of flesh between bloodstained lips, while stringy lines of tendon stretched and ripped juicily. The unfortunate man beneath the corpse howled in agony. The chewing *Thakshir* was quickly beheaded after that, and the Kriigi warrior slumped on the sand in death beneath him.

Mere moments later, however, the Kriigi warrior who had been bitten on the neck tossed aside the wriggling carcass atop him and slowly rose to his feet. Before the Chief's eyes, the man – a friend of Majbolji's for many years – changed. His wound darkened and dried, and his skin rotted, morphing into a lifeless grey colour with swollen red veins, just like the Unduru. He wasted no time in turning on his friends of minutes before; leaping on the back of one, he wrenched the man's head to one side and savagely bit into his neck as had been done to him. An arrow catapulted the Kriigi *Thakshir* off his screeching victim, but the damage had been done and Majbolji understood that now the newly bitten man too would die and transform into a nightmarish horror that feasted on the flesh of his friends.

As the Chief turned back to the Knight, his doom was clearly written in the lack of lustre in his eyes.

"You, you run now!" the Chief ordered Fyrstsvard roughly in Traveller's, jabbing a finger toward the remaining mounts not taken by the women and children. "Izdaju! Knights go now. You go with!"

Izdaju bowed his head solemnly and shook the Chief's arm, wrist-to-wrist in a gesture of farewell.

"I am proud of you, son," Majbolji shouted over the scuffle and roar of combat in Hashpaji, laying a hand on Izdaju's shoulder. "You must go now and not look back. Live life for all of us, understand?"

"I will, father," swore Izdaju, placing a hand on his father's shoulder, the solemnity of the moment broken by screams. "But I could help you here …"

"No time!" the Chief roared and threw back Izdaju as a *Thakshir* broke free of the defensive line and rushed the heart of the camp.

A group of knife-wielding women, intercepting the limping red-veined Dwarf, could do little but slow him with useless cuts at his bone armour at first, but eventually they used their weight to bear him to the ground. They hacked at his pus-filled flesh, heedless of their blows' killing relevance, squirming over his septic body and smearing themselves in his cold blood.

Majbolji pointed towards the tents. "Food, clothes, Elf, go, go!" he shouted.

Izdaju ran off inside a tent to grab provisions, and the Chief stepped closer to Fyrstsvard, looking him in the eye.

"You good man, Knight. You not bad. That bad," he said, indicating the *Thakshir* who looked dangerously close to overwhelming the poor Kriigi, who were now vastly outnumbered. "They come from east," he said, indicating the way from which the *Thakshir* had come, where the sun still climbed in the sky, having crested the tallest obelisks now. "You go west," he pointed the opposite way. Fyrstsvard nodded understanding. The Chief placed his right hand over his heart and then placed it on the Knight's left shoulder. "You are Kriigi friend, Knight."

Fyrstsvard repeated the gesture and replied, "Thank you, Chief. Your kindness will not be forgotten."

Majbolji nodded quickly and turned away from the Knight to watch the bloody conflict that was nearing a brutal and extensive end.

Fyrstsvard, too, turned his eyes on the conflict and cursed quietly.

The *Thakshir* threw themselves by the dozen against the brave wall of nomadic men mercilessly, scurrying forward to face the cold iron in the Nomads' hands without fear, like carious grey insects. Fyrstsvard's reason for cursing was that the central bulwark of the defence was comprised of Ratnik, Jumal and Tar Feng. How he was going to extricate them from the conflict without allowing the *Thakshir* to overrun them all was beyond him at that moment, but he had a well-trained and logical mind, which he set to struggling with the dilemma.

Having decided on a course of action, Fyrstsvard barged his way through the gathered Kriigi all around him to get to the front line of fighting. Soon, he stood behind his three companions.

"Tar Feng!" he cried, cupping a hand to his mouth, for the din of sword clashes was near deafening. "Tar Feng!"

Fortunately, the Wizard heard him and stepped back from the skirmish to turn and listen. Ratnik and Jumal took up the slack while he was away.

"We cannot beat them!" Fyrstsvard shouted, hoping that the Nomads could not understand him, for he did not wish to destroy their morale. "We must get the Prophet to safety! That is our mission! I need you and Ratnik and Jumal to help me accomplish that! Can you use your magic to create a lull in the conflict in which you can retreat?"

Tar Feng's wrinkled old face bobbed down swiftly in understanding, and he pivoted once more to face the infectious enemy. There were fewer defenders than he had thought, and he knew he had to act now. He waved his arms in occult patterns, slowly at first and then quickening with fervour.

Pointing his crook, he shouted, *"Pa'ptheon!"* and barged Ratnik aside with his shoulder to blast their slavering, putrefying attackers back with an invisible wave of force. Half a dozen of the closest monsters were hurled back through the air to sprawl among their fellows, knocking them down too. The *Thakshir* were not seriously injured, and they immediately started scrabbling to their feet again, but the defenders were given the brief respite they longed for to pant and wipe sweat from their brows.

During this brief intermittence, Tar Feng pulled back Jumal from the defensive line to join Ratnik, who was regaining his feet after having been knocked down by the Wizard. Three Kriigi warriors stepped up to fill the gap they had created, just in time to block and parry the vicious swings of the drooling *Thakshir* warriors' blades.

"What the Nether was that all about, old man?" Ratnik demanded, turning on Tar Feng with the heat of battle reddening his vision.

"My apologies, sea-strider, but I had to get you out of there!" Tar Feng quickly shouted back, raising his hands in supplication.

Fyrstsvard laid a restraining hand on the battle-mad pirate's shoulder as his muscles bunched for action. "Take it easy, young man!" he told him. "Tar Feng was acting under my orders! We have to get the Prophet to safety, as instructed, and I need your help to do so! Come now, hurry!"

"We must go, Ratnik," Jumal nodded agreement, chest heaving. "Det awaits us here."

Ratnik shook his head, and some sense returned to him. He blinked as though awakening from a violent dream and then nodded, before following Fyrstsvard and Tar Feng away from the skirmish with the red-eyed monsters. As they passed the old Kriigi Chief, they saw Izdaju running toward them with bags – hopefully containing clothes and rations, thought the Knight – and Stein close behind with Amril.

The Chief shouted to them, "Go now, go!"

They ran past him gratefully, knowing they would never see him again, never glimpsing the tears in Majbolji's eyes as he watched his only son leave, before turning to meet his doom with a smile on his face and a battle cry on his lips. Of the ninety Nomads that had comprised the Kriigi at dawn that morn, less than half now remained and more were being transformed with every passing second.

The eight of them mounted up; most on camels, but Fyrstsvard and Izdaju grabbed horses. The Elf was yanked across a saddle atop a white camel by Stein, where he bounced along, safeguarded by the veteran Knight. They galloped away from the camp with scant seconds to spare as over a hundred *Thakshir* creatures that had once been Dwarves, Unduru, Kriigi or men and women from other nomadic tribes hurtled at them at a sprint with blood-chilling howls. Their horses whinnied in fright at the overpowering scent of blood and set off as if whipped by Gastar's fiery lash itself.

The group galloped hard and fast across the sandy dunes to outpace the infectious biters. They finally reined in the horses and camels atop a sandy ridge as narrow as the edge of a blade as the day began to darken. Izdaju turned his mount to face east and the sorcery-wrought creatures that could still be seen struggling to follow them, far behind.

Raising a long white horn from his waist to his lips, the Nomad blew two long, doleful notes to the sky, before lowering it slowly and gazing east. After a minute, he placed his right hand over his heart and then held it to the east for a moment. By his side, Kamilah copied his gesture, then reached out a hand and laid it silently on the shoulder of her betrothed.

"What is he doing?" whispered Ratnik, unsure if he would disturb the tribesman by talking louder.

"He blows the horn to check for answering calls from any in the tribe who might have survived," whispered Fyrstsvard from behind him.

The deepening dark smothered the land in silence. There were no answering horns. Izdaju blew a last long, dolorous note.

"He mourns for his family," whispered Ratnik, and it was obvious from the catch in his throat that he too grieved for the loss of the Kriigi. He nudged his mount closer to the last remaining Kriigi tribesman. "Come on, Izdaju," he said hoarsely. "Let's leave this place. It holds nothing for us now, my friend."

They turned their mounts and began to trot across the barren plains towards a small village known to them, where they might be able to get some rest.

Kicking his heels into his camel's sides and pulling ahead of Izdaju, who had sat in his saddle wordlessly with his head hanging low since his horn toots, Ratnik overtook Tar Feng and shouted to the Wizard.

"I don't mean to be rude, old timer," he began, at which the Tzunese man snorted, "but I've been wondering something since we met. How do you see where you are going?"

Tar Feng grinned and tittered, bouncing madly up and down on his groaning camel's hump. He tapped his forehead with a finger, making the bones on his bracelet jangle and almost making him lose his balance.

"Teeheehee! My two eyes are blind," he replied wheezily, "but I see with my Third Eye – with my mind – and a far more reliable sightseer it is, too!"

"How is that possible?"

"All things are possible through magic. I see you more clearly now than I ever did when my eyes worked."

Ratnik was unsure how to respond to that. Then, he remembered something. "Wait, didn't Amril say that's how he saw souls? The Third Eye?"

"Indeed, indeed! It is how I see souls, spirits also, teehee, yes! It is how I have seen that Heldig's soul is long, long gone."

"What?"

"Oh yes, long gone the minute Gastar ate his heart, I'm afraid. All gone, just like the rest of the *Thakshir."*

"They are soulless?"

"Oh my, yes! Not a flicker!"

"What happened to their souls?"

"I have no idea! Taken, I think, by Gastar!"

Ratnik was quiet for a few minutes, wondering with a lump in his throat what had happened to his Captains' spirit; whether the Ferrymen would take him, whether Heldig would ever see *Citta Pacia* or El Vandu's Eyrie, or whether he had been dragged down to the Nether. Perhaps his soul had simply been snuffed out like a candle, Ratnik thought, or – worse – absorbed into Gastar himself somehow, into madness.

He wondered what had happened to all the people's souls then – all the people that had been bitten and transformed. Whatever had truly happened, they seemed to be gone forever from what the Wizard was saying. The thought scared him. He had not even known for sure that he had a soul before, but now that he knew he did, the idea of dying and losing it – or of having it taken from him and potentially plunged into madness or unending nothingness – was terrifying. He reminded himself that Amril could yet be lying, but all of the oddities he had witnessed suggested to him that this Elf knew what he was talking about.

When the lump would allow him to, he shouted, "What in the Nether were those Dwarves and … Unduru things? They looked just like Heldig with the big red veins and red eyes! They're not alive, but … they're not dead, either."

"Dey are da undead," Jumal rumbled ominously like thunder. "My people have foretold such creatures for centuries."

"Don't be ridiculous," scoffed Stein from ahead of them.

"The undead?" the younger pirate repeated, the tremor in his voice having nothing to do with the jolting tan camel beneath him. "You mean like the living dead from old myths? Nah, it can't be!"

"Strange as it is to consider," Tar Feng called thoughtfully, "there may be a crumb of truth to the Chilpaean's words! Every race and religion around the world has a myth about the undead. Whether those we encountered took inspiration from the myths or gave it to them, I think that we must accept that undead is what they are! They do not breathe, they eat flesh, they drink blood, and they do not die. Only the undead do not die."

Above the horizon, Fyrstsvard's sharp eyes could just about make out multiple spires of gold pointed at the sky like lances in a knightly parade.

"Calypra," he murmured, praying he would live to see the golden city again.

23

The Fringe

The sun rose late in the Highlands of Fjelburg, for before it could light that harsh and savage land, it first had to overcome a mighty barrier; a series of jagged-topped mountains that ran more than a hundred leagues from north to south down the centre of the continent. This indomitable expanse of rock was named the Great Divide, or sometimes the Jagged Wall. It separated the Highlands from the Lowlands by the east coast and the Flatlanders, or Fringers, who dwelled there.

Another mountain range – named Skalda's Teeth – ran perpendicular to the Divide at its northern end, and this range segregated the reclusive Highlands from the icy wastes of the north with all of their hidden perils.

At the southernmost extent of the Great Divide, the impenetrable black wall named Titan's Pass blocked access to the Highlands from the Fringe, running between the last of the mountains in the Divide's range and Sol Top, the largest mountain in Fjelburg.

To the west of Sol Top and its smaller sister mountains, to the west of Fjelburg – paralleling the Highlands' entire length from north to south – was an enormous strip of forest named the Alfa Wald, made impassable by the stuff of nightmares lurking in its confines; flapping wings and cawing beaks.

Those few that had essayed circumventing the Alfa Wald to the west over the centuries had either never been seen again or else had returned completely insane, babbling gibberish, and so the terrain there had long been named the Madlands.

Since neither passage into nor exit from the Highlands of Fjelburg was particularly easy – or advisable, most Highlanders would say – the huge men and women of the snow-blown, rugged lands west of the Divide tended to be a reticent folk and did not often venture beyond their own naturally strict borders into the worlds of other men and creatures.

Some, however, had to, and when they did, they grumbled incessantly about it.

"D'you know, Terra, d'you know," rumbled one such young Highlander unhappily, his voice heavy and deeper even than its usual rolling bass tones, "I'd rather fight an entire army of Elves barehanded than be in this shithole a moment longer!"

Terra did not smile. She had heard a hundred such complaints since sunup, two hours ago. She understood his boredom, though. It had been another uneventful morning thus far with a light and constant drizzle from the shrouded skies being the highlight. They were beset on all sides by green fields, beset on all sides by boredom. Normally, Terra could have shut the Prince up by telling him to go climb a chetland pine, which were an easy ascent in the Highlands with massive branches and soft needles. Here, though, there was not a chetland or any other tree bigger than a bush for leagues.

"You go where you must, Prince, not where you please."

A six-foot fiery-haired maiden, Terra was lean and muscular with a delicate chin, wide hips and a buxom bosom. Her eyes were light brown and hard as shields. Her brows were usually low, and her full red lips were perpetually pressed in a pensive frown, giving her attractive, freckled face a severe, judgemental appearance. Her voice was husky and soft for the most part, but it too held a sharp and, at first, unexpected edge. Many were the tongue-lashings Saul had received from that razor voice already for some nonsense about 'improper decorum', 'public exposure' or 'neglecting to use an appropriate privy'.

"For the hundredth time, woman," Saul Aodhson responded exasperatedly, sighing and patting the huge chestnut stallion he rode, Faafoor, on the neck. "Do not call me Prince. My name is Saul. Use it."

"And my name is not woman. Regardless, your name doesn't matter," Terra fired back coolly, gazing absently at the hazy outlines of the southernmost mountains of the Great Divide in the distance ahead of them and imagining their return to the Highlands. As cold and unforgiving as it was, Terra missed their homeland as dearly as did Saul. "A Prince of Fjelburg, son of King Aodh Stonebrow – *that* is who you are."

"Seventeenth son," Saul grumbled quietly, testing how far he could spit to pass the time. More loudly, he said, "It's the tiny doors down here that are the worst, you know, Terra. Not a decent-sized door for leagues around – how can that be? I tell you, I am sick to my stomach of these little men and their tiny doors! Everything about this place is small. They have tiny cups that hold little more than a mouthful of the swill they call ale, tiny plates you could never heap a decent meal onto, beds made for Dwarves and weapons that look like child toys! The only big thing about these Fringers seems to be their grins. I tell you, Terra, if they are grinning so widely because seeing me is the highlight of their lives, then I pity these dull little men!"

"Perhaps they always grin so widely, my Prince," Terra offered absently, swaying slowly with the motion of her palomino mare's walk.

"It cannot be!" Saul exclaimed, turning to her, his verdant green eyes affronted by the very idea. "There is no way they grin so hugely all the time! What do they have to be so damned chuffed about, eh? No wrestling, sparring, watching of blood sports, hunting or fishing! All these damned men do is sit around and talk about utter crap!"

He put on a whiney nasally voice to mimic the aristocrats he had been visiting. "Economic decline and amelioration, travesty of poverty, existentialism, what does it mean to be a *good man?* Philosophy this and poetry that – by Baldr's arse, the boredom never ends! These men claim to rule over vast swathes of land, and yet I wonder if they've ever been beyond the hydrangeas in their own gardens! When I asked if they wanted to take a fishing trip, they told me they would just order up fish from the kitchens! The kitchens! 'We have people for that', they would say ... That is no way to live, Terra. Away from rock and tree, stream and field ... Ugh!" Saul shivered at the thought. "I could not stand it!"

"It is their way, my Prince," the young woman replied, mildly amused, locking her brown eyes on Saul's green ones. She reminded Saul of a wolf whenever he looked into her eyes; fierce and loyal. "You have stained your fur again – with ale, from the looks of it," she chided him. "You really must be more careful. First impressions can be important you know, Prince." Saul looked for the stain on the white snow cat fur draped over his shoulders, but could not see it. "I'll take care of it when we next rest."

Beneath the pelt, Saul wore an elk-hide jerkin over a long-sleeved, red tunic, grey woollen trousers and thick, brown leather boots. Twin bearded axes hung at his belt. Terra braved the elements wearing black trousers trimmed with leather on the inner legs to prevent wear when riding, moccasins, an olive tunic and a muskrat-fur overcoat. A round wooden shield, painted red and yellow, with a metal hub was strapped to her back, and a straight longsword was scabbarded at her belt.

"The wealthy here acquire what they call 'luxury' and 'sophisticated' tastes," she said, "all the while growing further and further distanced from the lands and folk that they should be serving. Your father wanted all of his sons to appreciate that not all people are as the Highlanders are. We in the Highlands are the vanguard of man – the anvil against which the hammer of savagery beats. The brunt of hardship falls upon us, and *we* must hold back the ever-night, for the sake of all men. King Aodh wishes you to understand this."

"*That* is why he sent me down here?" Saul asked incredulously. "To see that these men are weak and small and need protecting? Did he hope I might sympathise with these tiny little creatures with their infuriatingly big smiles and false, fawning voices? Fah! If any of these men were to come to the Highlands, they would be dead within a week! Leave them to their mind-numbing discussions, I say. We will live true men's lives in the mountains and forests beyond the Pass!"

"It is because the Highlanders live their lives of danger and battle that the Fringe men are able to sit around 'talking about crap', as you so eloquently put it, my Prince." Terra sighed, and her mare, Keyli, snickered as if in agreement. "It is the way of things. But you are right about one thing; none of these little men would survive a week in the Highlands."

She paused for a moment and cocked her head to one side, as if listening to the gust of wind that whistled past.

"No one knows who will be crowned King," she went on. "Aodh seeks only to ensure that all of his many sons and potential heirs are educated in their worldly duties and allies. Learn well, Saul Aodhson. You never know what fate may hold in store for you."

Saul ran a thick-fingered, calloused hand through his long, straw-blonde hair. The young Highlander thought about what his companion had said for a moment, able to take his mind off the road, for it was so very straight, flat and dull. Terra was right in that none could truly know who would be crowned King after Aodh. The last brother standing. It was impossible to guess who would be the next King with all of the assassinations, duels, poisonings, illnesses, freak accidents and battle wounds that could occur to any of the twenty six Princes of the Highlands at any given moment.

Saul tossed the thought aside carelessly. He had other questions for the reticent and mysterious Terra; queries that required a certain delicacy in the raising of their subject. Saul, however, was not a delicate man.

"Listen here, Terra," he began in his deep, brooding voice. "I have a question to ask you that might be a little awkward ..."

As he pondered the best phrasing to use, Terra coolly interrupted.

"You are wondering why you have been stuck with a mere woman for a companion when each and every one of your brothers has a man to watch his back. Are you not?"

"Err, well yes, I am. That is – that is what I was wondering. Yes," stammered Saul, taken aback. He was used to the slow wit of his mother and the kitchen maids, and the city girls he had flirted with so freely in Baldr's Safe. Terra was a new breed.

"The simple answer is that I was appointed by the King, your father. You are not alone in wondering why, though, my Prince. I too have questions on that account. However, fear not, for I am as stalwart a companion as any man and as fierce a fighter as a great snow cat. Your back is perfectly safe with me, I assure you."

With that, she kicked her heels into her palomino's flanks and sent it trotting down the road ahead.

"Crag save me!" grumbled Saul, glancing skyward and scratching his beard. "Stuck with a woman in a flat land of tiny little men. How could it get any worse?"

24

Visk

Visk padded briskly down the ostentatious corridor that led to the private chambers of the ruler of the golden city of Calypra and the surrounding lands: Sultan Bab.

The claws on his feet tore at the plush, purple carpet as Visk's mind wrestled with a conundrum. He ignored the masterfully sculpted, and all bearded, busts of Bab's ancestors that adorned the hall on plinths and the intricately wrought tapestries that covered the walls on either side of him, depicting scenes from history; the fall of the evil Witches of Convent over three hundred years ago, the rise of the lineage of Bab to royalty, and scenes from the major battles of expansion and subjugation since then. The tapestries had been woven by expert hands. They were colourful and detailed, innately narrative and eye-catching, but despite their allure, Visk's mind focussed all of its energy on solving his dilemma, as it always did. It was what made him such an effective advisor, in his eyes.

He had needed that focus and skill over the last few decades of his life. Thrown out of his home by his own clan, he had wandered the Lama Kulul for a long time and seen a great many things, before arriving at Calypra and convincing the royal family of Bab to take him in and use him in service so long ago.

He had watched over the family of Bab for two centuries now and had seen the city around them change dramatically in that time; not in terms of the structures or architecture, of course, for those were as golden and proud as ever. No, in Visk's long-lived eyes, the change came in the people and the societies that dwelled in the golden buildings.

The Sultans of old had been far more interesting than the current crowned oaf in Visk's eyes, had reacted far more violently to the Nomads and had put down far more inner-city revolts caused by poor treatment, murders and mayhem than did the current Sultan. Visk had felt he had found home at last when he had found the political intrigue and corruption of Calypra, but he had a mission and he knew it could not be avoided. The day had come at last for which he had waited half his lifetime, and he wondered what would happen next.

He arrived at the end of the corridor where ornate and heavy double doors of gold stood, sculpted beautifully into floral patterns with techniques now known to no one. Two guards barred the way, fully armoured in ceremonial gold battle armour with giant gilded halberds crossed in front of the door.

"I am here to see the Sultan at his request," hissed Visk, his yellow eyes narrowing in contempt, the slit pupils unnerving the guards as they had done everyone else since his first day in that bustling nest of humanity. "As you should well know, given that I have been in his service far longer than the two of you fools!"

The guards, who had recently replaced the Sultan's lifelong bodyguards in order to give them a retirement of sorts, were still relatively young in comparison to the Sultan and most of his associates. They blanched at this reminder of their inexperience, despite their long tenure as warriors of the Sultanate. Such was Visk's power; to bend the minds of the weak-willed and the gullible to his will and his control.

They rapped precipitously on the door with golden gauntlets, shouting through, "Visk requests entry, Your Majesty!"

"Send him in," came the booming reply from within, and the guards disappointedly opened the opulent doors to allow the Sultan's first advisor into his chambers.

Visk walked in to be greeted by a sight that was now as familiar to him as the faces of those who had disgraced him in his homeland. Golden inlay all around the white marble walls continued the storytelling traditions of the tapestries outside, though told far more mysterious and ancient tales of woe and glory, having been there since before any Bab. Beaked men and women danced in etching.

Marbled pillars held up the high, domed, gold ceiling where several chandeliers of gold and diamond hung to cast jewelled refractions of radiance around the Sultan's chambers, like rainbow light. Visk almost felt pity for the many servants who had fallen to a grisly end from their high vantage point while trying to relight the candles up there, and for the servants who not only had to clean up the blood and mess from those that had failed, but then had to attempt the task themselves. He smiled; almost, but not quite. Life was what you made of it, he believed, and he had spent a long time moving up the ranks and becoming important. He felt no care or sympathy for those that did not or could not do as he did.

Sultan Bab's antechamber – the reception chamber leading to more than a dozen other rooms, including privies, baths, bedchambers and chambers for his harem – was completely empty of anything that might interest his first advisor, such as books and knowledge, but was filled with what the Sultan considered to be luxuries. The ostentation was despicable to Visk's mind, but he could never voice such an opinion to the Sultan.

Thick carpets, fur rugs, silk drapes, satin sheets and downy pillows and duvets bedizened the room, making it one big, plush cushion. There was a long table with wooden legs, wobbling so heavily was it laden, constantly stocked with fresh food and water by the numerous servants who attended solely to the Sultan. Not for the first time, Visk wondered that there was not even a desk on which the Sultan could write down important things for his realm; no, such things were left for others, for simple scribes who wore nothing but a simple brown robe and a hood that, in Visk's case, served to cover his scaly cranium.

Sultan Bab entered abruptly through a purple curtain the opposite side of the room, which led back to his bedchambers – like a hippopotamus clambering from the muck, thought Visk amusedly with a carefully blank visage, watching the ruler wriggle free of the clinging gauze.

Two skinny, young women darted from the bedchamber behind the Sultan, giggles tugging up their full, rosy lips. The two made haste for the door with elegance, skipping gaily. Ample glimpses of their ample behinds were to be had as the pink gauzy robes they wore fluttered up and down like a butterfly's wings, but while the Sultan enjoyed such pleasures, his first advisor did not.

Visk waited patiently for them to exit, his eyes iron and the Sultan the lodestone. Bab was a paunchy, if not downright bloated, man with thick, dark curls atop his beardy boulder of a head. His fiery crimson skin spoke of his ancient, otherworldly heritage, but he knew little of it; less than Visk, in fact, his roots lost and abandoned in the mists of time, swept away on a selfish tide by the sea of wealth that had fallen into the laps of his forebears. Gold adornments clung to him like leeches on his wrists, ankles, fingers, ears and neck; enough to support a family for life, Visk calculated idly.

"Ah, snake man!" greeted the Sultan in his booming voice, resonant and full of warmth.

The Sultan, in contrast with his unassuming companion, was dressed gaudily in the latest obnoxiously colourful fashion in the ever-shifting trends of the rich and powerful of Calypra. That day, he wore loose-fitting yellow pantaloons, a blue silk shirt with gold weave in the low-cut collar that displayed his chest hair, and a gauzy gold and crimson robe, whilst a white hat sat atop his hairy head complete with enough feathers to create a false bird if he wished.

All in all, it was a ridiculous getup, Visk considered, especially when the Sultan was bulging with so much lard that his skin was forced up against every seam. His huge belly was visible through his low-cut collar, swinging over his belt cord, dragging the silken shirt down with it.

"Your Majesty," replied Visk, with a small bow. "As you well know by now, my people are far closer to the lizard in anatomy than the snake."

"Yes, yes, snake man. You are all reptiles of some kind, I understand," the Sultan replied with a broad smile. "Ugly enough to shatter eyeballs the way regular ugly shatters mirrors."

Visk hated that smile.

"Indeed, Your Majesty," he hissed. His forked snake-like tongue slithered from his reptilian lips as he spoke.

"How are our plans progressing then, reptile?" asked Bab.

The Sultan's demeanour became more serious as he sat and waved over a servant, who had been waiting patiently in the corner of the room, and had the man pour him a drink of cooled water and citrus fruit juices. He then invited Visk to sit in one of the ghastly chairs.

Visk had to bite back a smile at his words. *Our* plans? No, Sultan, thought Visk, these are not *your* plans.

"Drink?" asked Bab, swigging his own from a crystal goblet and grabbing an orange offhandedly.

Visk shook his head, and the Sultan put down his drink and peeled the orange carelessly, squirting juice over his clothing. He waved a hand for his advisor to answer his question.

Visk turned his snake-like gaze on the Sultan, engaging his vision fully. His eyes swelled to their maximum width, and soon all Bab could see were the great yellow orbs with the barely visible slits of vertical black that served as pupils. Bab slowly rested both orange and drink on his knees, and his mouth gaped open vapidly. His mind was sieved empty until it held not a single thought, other than those implanted by Visk.

"Perhaps we should speak in private, Your Majesty," suggested the serpent man, speaking slowly and clearly.

"Yes," Bab slurred. "That will be all."

He waved away the servant, who left promptly, likely glad for the opportunity to take a break. Who knew how long he had been standing in that corner, thought Visk, waiting until the dark-skinned servant was gone before speaking further.

"Our plans are progressing well, Your Majesty," hissed Visk, baring his needle-sharp teeth. As he spoke, his eyes did not blink nor did Bab's attention waver from them. "It is the height of summer, and you know what that means. It is time for the Prophet's Day festival and for the Purge of the lower town."

Visk's eyes began to glow bright yellow, like lanterns, and then they began to radiate rhythmic orange pulses that served to hypnotise those that could not look away. In this case: Sultan Bab. The monarch was completely mesmerised, staring unblinkingly into the yellow and orange thrumming glow, drooling slightly from the corner of his dumbstruck mouth.

The orange fell from his vacant fingers to roll along the floor. Despite his massive stature – the Sultan stood at about six feet tall, well over a head taller than the small reptile that faced him and with a girth at least four times that of the skinny advisor – his terrifying tattoos and his intimidating, bushy black beard, the once great warrior was helpless before Visk. He no more had his own will than did a slave.

"Good, good," said Bab blandly. "I love Prophet's Day."

"Your breakfast will be served in the jasmine lounge after your announcements."

"Most important meal of the day."

"Indeed." Visk's upper lip curled in disgust at the man's gluttony. He knew the Sultan wanted to hear about food before all else, so he lulled him into a false sense of comfort, swaddling the big man in his velvety voice.

"After the announcements will be the Prophet's Day sacrifice – I believe you know the woman already, Majesty? Beyond the announcements, you have no further duties today until attendance of the celebration itself, Sultan. A mid-morning snack will be available in the rose gardens, lunch will be available at noon in the cypress grove pavilion, the kitchens will ready sweets and pastries throughout the afternoon in the third art gallery, the evening meal will be held in the royal dining room at six, and supper, too, will be served there at nine and eleven. The entertainment for the celebration will be held in the Audience Chamber after the evening meal, Your Majesty – jugglers, singers and acrobats."

Visk eased the Sultan's feeble mind into vacancy with words the man wanted to hear. The serpent knew Bab did not want to be informed about the logistics of acquiring the gallons of wine and ale, the performers, the tons of food and all the servants, cutlery, cups and china for the festival. No; Bab left the details to others, and the Gods forbid anything should not be perfect, or the true organiser would get it in the neck. The Sultan wanted only to partake and to enjoy the festival.

"Mmm," Bab hummed happily.

"After the morning announcements," Visk's voice annealed as he neared his point, "all the entry gates to the lower town will be left open throughout the day for the Purgers, will they not, Your Majesty?" asked Visk, staring loathingly into the Sultan's glassy eyes, projecting his hypnotism with all of his might.

"Yes, they will," replied Bab obligingly.

"Good, good," Visk permitted himself a small smile at his handiwork. The Sultan had been under his spell for years now, and his power over the man had grown almost complete. "You will tell any who argue that it is for the greater good of the city and that we will, of course, be perfectly safe up here. The gates to the upper city will remain sealed to protect the elite, do you understand?"

"Yes. I will tell them," the big, red-skinned man murmured.

"Good. I have contacted the Purgers, and they promise to be here on time, as always. One final thing, Your Majesty; you must send your children down into the lower town this morning, *before* sealing the gates to the upper city. They *must* witness the necessity for the Purge. They must see the filthy criminals in their homes and know that, if they do not continue this noble tradition, then this beautiful city could be overrun and they would be killed by the ungrateful mob outside our gates. They will better understand their people when they come to the throne and be better rulers for it. Do you understand?" asked Visk, focussing all his energy to convince the Sultan to send his offspring to their deaths.

"My children?" asked Bab confusedly, his eyes narrowing. "My children?"

Visk realised he was losing him. "They will be completely safe, Your Majesty, but they *must* witness the Purge if they are to continue your noble traditions," he hissed quickly and persuasively, eyes still drilling into the Sultan's.

"My children?" Bab asked again.

He seemed to be becoming more cognitive. Visk leapt on top of him in an instant, pinned down the Sultan's arms with his clawed hands and forced back his head with a long and powerful, scaly tail, so that Bab looked up into the reptile's eyes as they bored into his brain, commanding his obedience. The Sultan's white hat fell off unnoticed.

"*You will send your children down to the lower town, and they will be perfectly safe!*" Visk rasped into Bab's face frantically, a migraine threatening his control as he bent all his will to subverting that of the Sultan. Failure now would mean certain death.

After a long moment of staring into the reptilian creature's enormous orbs, basking in their orange and yellow glow, the Sultan said calmly, "I will send my children down into the lower town this morning. They will be safe enough with Karth, Riton and the Ogre to protect them. They must witness the Purge to know it is needed, you are quite right."

Visk breathed a silent sigh of relief and got off the Sultan slowly, holding his gaze the entire time.

"Good, Your Majesty. Excellent. And you will give the order to seal the gates to the upper city behind them?"

Bab nodded obediently. "I will."

"That is excellent, Your Majesty. Then, I believe everything is in order. Go now and give your orders as we have discussed."

"I will."

Visk closed his eyes, and the hypnotic glow came to an end. Bab blinked many times all of a sudden, hugging his head.

"Urgh, I have a horrible headache, lizard," he said, clearly back in his own mind once more, looking up to see Visk sat calmly opposite him. "Leave me now. I must go and give the orders for the day – and you know how uncomfortable the courtiers are in your presence. You are so ugly, you make an alligator look appealing," he added with a chuckle.

"Yes, Your Majesty," hissed Visk, rising smoothly to his feet and bowing once more before leaving, satisfied that his problem had been solved.

His master had wanted all of Calypra brought to its knees – even the royal heirs – and now it would be, Visk thought.

He smiled evilly as he walked away along the purple carpet.

25

Prophet's Day

Sultan Bab drank some fruit-infused iced water to seek to soothe his headache and left his chambers, wondering at the orange on the floor as he did so. He did not pick it up. After all, what else were servants for? He grabbed a handful of baui from a dainty bowl painted with blue birds in flight and stuffed some messily into a polished cherry wood pipe until the bowl was overflowing, before lighting it with a lavender-scented taper and chuffing until smoke wreathed him like an aegis. Rumbling contentedly, he took his pipe for a walk.

"Come on, boys. Let's see what of interest occurs in my realm today," he said jovially to the young guards outside his chambers as he passed them. They dutifully fell in behind him.

Bab strode purposefully through the tapestried hallway, though with the short steps to which his stubby legs were accustomed. His predecessors' quarters had been housed in the heights of the residential tower in the Palace complex for safety reasons, but the current Sultan had felt that convenience far outweighed safety during his reign. Plus, the first time he had climbed the stairs to his new quarters, he had been out of breath and covered in sweat and had been forced to rest for a few hours before attempting the journey back downstairs. Now, Bab lived alongside the Audience Chamber, so that his commute was infinitely less stressful.

After traversing a few red-carpeted hallways, Bab and his guards arrived outside a side door to the Audience Chamber, located beneath the great golden dome in the centre of the enormous labyrinthine Palace, which was home to five huge golden towers, including that in which his forefathers had laid their heads. Aside from the dome and the towers, there were dozens more buildings conglomerated together into one vast complex.

Entire wings of the Palace were dedicated to housing residents, guests and servants. The Prophet's Temple – dedicated to the All Mother and Prophet – amassed to a monolithic structure beside the dome. There were numerous smaller temples and shrines dotted around the complex, too, for those who did not wish to have to travel far to pray, as well as reception chambers, games rooms, luxury pools, baths, massage parlours, sports areas, art galleries, incense rooms, saunas, courtyards, verandas, gardens and mazes.

There were, of course, also areas where the servants worked and stored their equipment, and areas for dishwashing, clothes-washing, food preparation, and the slaughter of livestock. Although he ate more than anyone else in Calypra, however, the Sultan knew little of these places.

Despite the shortness of the journey, Bab nevertheless had to stop outside the door to the Audience Chamber to regain his breath so as not to appear flustered once inside. He tried to cover his lack of stamina with bravado in front of his guards.

"Mmm, it's so nice to take a moment of peace in the morning, before the hyenas begin to worry at me!" he remarked, trying to breathe evenly.

"Indeed, Your Majesty," replied one of the guards.

"Your duties must be a burden at times," said the other. Both had faces as serious as stone, but the Sultan's paranoia told him they were amused by his weakness.

"Nonsense!" Bab drawled with a wide smile. "I am the Sultan, and monarchical duties are no burden – they are my birth right!"

He pushed open the door – smile plastered on, ready for the morning – and entered the Audience Chamber of his Palace, where he received his subjects every day. The majesty of the room never failed to disappoint him, and he knew it projected the right combination of opulence and intimidation to any guest.

Grand, golden double doors led the way in from the front, large enough that only a battering ram the size of one of the adjacent towers could knock them from their solid metal hinges. The great chamber always reminded Bab of the enormous splendour of the city that his people had discovered. None now living knew who had built Calypra nor how long ago, but it was an immense work of craftsmanship and expenditure. The gold throughout would equivocate to more than ten times the entire population's wealth by Bab's estimation.

Gold and marble comprised the entirety of the upper city of Calypra; marble walls and flooring, golden adornments, doorways, ceilings and roofs. Where all the material had come from to build such a marvel, no one knew. The great city had been rediscovered soon after the fall of the Witches, whose foul shadow had once dominated the land, and had again become inhabited as people returned to love and live in the safety of its indomitable solid gold walls.

The pillars propping up the roof and mezzanine in the Audience Chamber were cylinders of solid, glittering emerald, and the polished floor was striped blue and white with marble and lapis lazuli. Inscribed golden statues ringed the room, displaying ancient and unknowable figures mid-act, in front of which the more modern stone busts of the Bab Sultans of times past sat atop marble pedestals, looking shoddy in comparison.

The Sultan looked up, as he did every time he entered the chamber, to the golden-railed mezzanine that circled the room high above them, linking it to an external ring of marble balcony. He craned his neck back further to behold the great domed ceiling of pure gold two hundred feet above and wondered, not for the first time, what kind of race had possessed the architectural ingenuity to erect such a city in such ancient times. What had been before the Witches?

He looked around at the brilliant, stainless marble walls, the fine tapestries, the portraits of Sultans long since deceased, the stone busts, the golden statues and the huge, famous weapons that hung on hooks. He was the latest link in a long chain of history and continuation, and he was determined to leave his own personal mark on the pages of posterity.

The wide open doorways on the upper level that led to the balcony allowed in more than sufficient light to brighten the room, especially reflected from the white marble. For this reason, all who came to see the Sultan were often blinded during their encounter, whilst Bab was comfortable on his throne in the shade of a small, silken awning. Bowls of perfumed oil were scattered around the chamber, set upon golden pedestals, waiting to be lit but already filling the air with the sweet scents of jasmine and honeysuckle.

Bab sat down on his throne with a content sigh. Plump maroon cushions supported his back and backside to ease the otherwise unpleasant experience of sitting on the cold, hard, glinting throne. Like the city itself, the creator of the throne was a mystery, but a throne it surely was, for there was only one of its magnificence in all of Calypra. Its frame was simple, consisting of four legs like lion paws, wide golden armrests in the shapes of wings, a straight seat, and a perpendicular straight back that lifted high above Bab's tall body, topped by the stylized head of a fantastical beast that none now recognised; a beast reminiscent of a mountain lion, but with huge fangs, drooping ears and tusks poking out either side of a short snout.

Now, the beast's head aided in supporting the silken awning over the Sultan's head along with two golden poles complete with disc-like bases in front of the throne. Crafted of solid gold and displaying beautiful animalistic patterns, still clearly this had not been enough flamboyance for the builder race, for almost every inch of the throne was encrusted with a staggering number of gems of every conceivable hue, shape and size. Two rubies comprised the alien beast's eyes. So, despite his aversion to its hard seat and superfluous ostentation, nevertheless Bab – like all of his predecessors – had decided to use the throne the first moment he had laid eyes upon it, for the mastery behind its craftsmanship and the symbol of wealth and power that it brandished were unmistakeable.

The Sultan waved cordially to his sycophantic, ubiquitous, dark-skinned courtiers, noblemen, officers, jesters, courtesans and servants who already occupied the spacious chamber, having been awaiting his arrival for quite some time in some cases. All bowed as he passed.

The courtiers always reminded him of a flock of tropical birds with extravagant and colourful displays of plumage, or clothing in this case, to attract the eye, tweeting away to one another and perpetually twittering at the Sultan's mildest jokes. They fawned over him irritatingly, but were necessary for the Sultanate. They represented wealthy families whose support of Bab was vital to maintaining his authority over the people.

The jesters were chequered fools, and the servants were drab mice in brown, hardly noticed as they scurried this way and that with their heads down, bearing platters and trays. The courtesans, on the other hand, wore varying colours and lengths of translucent gauze to tease the eyes, their dark skin and gracefully curvy bodies easily distinguished. Their skimpy, silken garments fluttered around at their expert touch as if lifted by a breeze, like delicate wings or petals. Bab grinned at the beautiful women as they curtsied and danced and sought his eye.

There, too, stood his eldest child; his only son, Eli, of whom the Sultan was very proud. Prince Eli was a fine warrior and had a cunning mind that tended mostly to self-serving. He was moderately tall, and his lean figure and dark crimson skin had ladies from all over swooning in his presence. At twenty five years of age, Eli was progressing well as the heir to the throne in Bab's eyes.

Waving him forward, the Sultan greeted his son with a handshake. Eli's face was stern and drawn into a perpetual frown, in contrast with his jovial and rotund father. Both, however, had the same thickly curled black hair, trimmed and oiled daily. Where the father had a magnificent oily, black beard, however, the son showed only shadow.

"Good morning, son," said Bab with a warm smile.

Eli, standing rigidly with his hand resting on his sword pommel, did not return the smile. "Good morning, father. I trust you slept well."

"Like a baby!"

At that, Eli's lips twitched. "It is good you are well-rested. Today is important."

"I know," Bab replied, amused by his son's ever-serious nature.

"You understand then the necessity of this day?"

"I do."

"That is good, my son. When it is your time to rule, follow our traditions and all will be well, as the Prophet wills it. Trust me. Now, stand back and I shall make the announcements."

"As he wills it," Eli agreed, stepping back.

At last, the room settled from hubbub to silence with the Sultan's bodyguards at their stations by his sides, his son standing behind him, the servants crowded in a corner awaiting a command, and the courtiers taking their places on long benches that the Sultan had ordered brought in for them. The benches had no cushions and were exceedingly uncomfortable; it was a small victory, perhaps, but it made Bab smile churlishly inside. The courtesans fluttered about the room, elegant predators. The servants, some of whom doubled as trumpeters, formally announced the Sultan's readiness to begin his morning audience.

"The year is 311 AC in the Sultanate of Bab, praise be to the Prophet for the continuation of his ideals," announced the Sultan ritualistically in Babese, his voice booming around the chamber. "Today is a special day, as I'm sure you all know. Today signifies midsummer, which we have celebrated for as long as memory recalls as Prophet's Day, a day so named to commemorate the ancient Prophet who died at the hands of his own brother in order to protect paradise for us all. All hail the Prophet! All hail *Citta Pacia!"*

"All hail the Prophet! All hail *Citta Pacia!"* men and women cheered until Bab waved his arms for silence.

"Let us not forget, however," the Sultan boomed, "that while it is Prophet's Day – a time of celebration for us here in the upper city – it is also the day of the Purge for the lower town. Let us remind ourselves of the necessity for this, our duty to the Sultanate. The tradition began, according to our histories, in the year 76 AC, during the reign of the third of my ancestors to sit atop the throne of Calypra. At this time, the people of his Sultanate had become relatively wide-spread, despite being poor folk for the most part. A great deal of the land was uninhabitable and, of course, still is; thick rainforest to the south, unwelcoming mountains and ravines to the north, and impassable desert to the east.

"When the few towns dotted around the Sultanate became full of people and could expand no further without losing valuable growing ground for crops, some began to move to Calypra. So many men, women and children flocked here, in fact, that the space of the original city was insufficient, and – of course – they could not be allowed to mingle with those of us who lived in a higher caste of society; we, the elite, whose job it is to protect them and rule over them wisely. And so, the lower town was created and the great golden gates given further purpose.

"The lower city as we know it now was built over many years by and for the new residents, but before long our advisors informed my family that the city could not continue to expand as it had done. A great deal of land is needed to sustain such a vast population as ours had become, land for grazing and growing. At the same time, the Bab of the period was forced to put down his seventh or eighth internal uprising, in which the commoners who lived down below sought to overwhelm the city proper with their selfish and greedy ways, not knowing that if they killed us – the elite – they would have only anarchy as a reward with no one left of any sensibilities or learning to govern them. Therefore, the ritual of the Purge was begun.

"Originally, this unenviable task was carried out by guards and militia of our own people, who were forced to turn on others just like themselves, forcibly taking them out to the desert to find a new life. That unpleasant task has since been assigned to a nomadic mercenary group with whom we have enjoyed good relations for generations now.

"The Purge is and has been a necessity for centuries, in order to keep our population at a reasonable level and to maintain subjugation of the commoners, whose impatience and violence would inevitably lead to their own destruction," Bab finished solemnly, looking around the room from face to face. Murmurs of agreement met his announcement. "Time now for me to lead the morning prayers."

Bab led the congregation through the thirty six hymns detailing the Prophet's life – in which the Prophet, an unnamed man, siphoned power from his disciples in order to grow wings and ascend to a city in the clouds to speak to the ruler of the world, the All Mother, where he became a God and was taken from Maradoum so that he could build an eternal paradise for his people – and mandatory twenty one stanzas, asking permission to enter the paradise, *Citta Pacia,* praising the All Mother and giving thanks to the Prophet, who died so that all could live on after death.

With this done, Bab stood and stretched and yawned. "That completes the morning prayers. Now, as has been tradition since the third Bab rediscovered the Prophet's holy Word, on Prophet's Day we memorialise the sacrifice of the Prophet and his disciples with one of our own. Follow me to the balcony."

So saying, Bab left his throne in a sweep of silk and began the arduous process of climbing the elegant marble slab stairs – which were crafted with metal wiring so that the steps appeared to be floating in the air – to the mezzanine above. By the time he neared the top, he was huffing and puffing like an elephant trudging through clay, for it was a long staircase. His retinue followed at a respectful distance.

Reaching the wide, red-carpeted mezzanine, Bab paused. Leaning a hand on the golden railing ringing the level on the inside, he took a deep breath to try to even his breathing before proceeding through the nearest gilded threshold; one of many that led to the wide marble balcony outside, where the views of the glimmering city and crystal blue morning sky were enough to give the Sultan goosebumps even at a glance.

Bab turned to face his flock and spread his arms wide, his silken robe splaying between his arms and body like red and gold wings, glowing as the sun's light shone through.

"Here we are, at the appointed place at the appointed hour," he intoned solemnly.

In truth, he had risen late and missed the true appointed hour, and traditionally the ritual took place at the Prophet's Temple not the Audience Chamber, but he cared little for the extra walk. He did not think anyone would notice.

"Bring forth the sacrifice."

Two guards, fully garbed in the richest and most ceremonial of ancient Calyprian armour, clanked their way through the amassed crowd. Light from the rising sun glittered on the guards' gold and silver shells, granting their entire frames the gift of luminescence. They shone like Gods, and all who saw them marvelled. In reality, however, the two men beneath the armour were wheezing with the effort of moving around in so much heavy metal, blinking dirt mixed with sweat from their eyes and licking it from their lips, trying to ignore the rank smell and taste of their helmets.

Between them, they dragged a young, dark-skinned woman along the smooth red carpet. She struggled with all her might against their relentless grasps on her arms, spitting, shouting, cursing and wriggling her entire body in the panicked fervour that can only be brought about by knowledge of one's impending doom.

Bab addressed the hoarsely hollering young woman, who was not yet as old as his son and who begged and pleaded for mercy while tears streamed down her pretty young face.

"Srenda Haam, you have the privilege of being the Prophet's Day sacrifice," he told her in a kind, deep voice, speaking loudly to be heard over her yowling, "an honour commemorating those disciples whose sacrifice the Prophet accepted to bring us peace in life and in death. May you find that peace, Srenda."

Bab nodded to the guards. They hefted the young woman high and tossed her off the balcony. Srenda wailed as she sailed through the air, until her voyage came to a grisly end.

"We thank you for your sacrifice, Srenda Haam, just as we thank the Prophet who came before," Bab completed the ritual, head bowed and hands forming a peaked roof in front of him, fingers touching and palms apart, "and we commend your soul to the land of eternal happiness, *Citta Pacia*." He raised his head to face the gathering. "This completes the morning ceremonies. Have another wonderful day, my people. Spread the Prophet's love. Eli, General Ghan, wait a moment."

The Sultan's charming smile faded as he turned away and walked over to the golden pattern-wrought balcony rail, scattering a few perched colourful parakeets and ignoring the gathered flock of courtiers now as some departed and some fluttered around, hoping to catch his eye.

Prince Eli and Ghan – a senescent, gold-armour-clad, dark-skinned man with silvering black hair and a grizzled beard trimmed to fork below the chin – stood on the balcony with hands clasped, waiting patiently. Bab looked down to where Srenda Haam's remains blemished with red the immaculate white of the courtyard a long way beneath. Already, servants were cleaning her up.

The golden upper city glittered and sparkled in the sun, its lustrous shine almost blindingly beautiful, like a jewel in the desert.

The lower city sprawled around the golden marvel untidily; an impassable labyrinth consisting of far simpler buildings of sandstone taken from a quarry to the east in the Lama Kulul. The whole of the slums was riddled with plague and vermin of both the human and rodent varieties. The houses were tightly packed, the streets narrow and thick with people, with little gutters that carried away the foulness of human waste only when it rained – and it did not rain often. It was mainly for this reason that Bab did not often visit the lower town, only passing through when necessity or duty demanded it. Beyond the city, the land was pancake-flat to the horizon, ochre and barren to the east and north, dotted with life and green to the south and west.

Raids had been less frequent in recent years as relations improved with the Nomads, Bab pondered as he gazed out at the serene azure skies to the east, but not all tribes were cordial and sometimes they decided that the potential gain outweighed the risk of attacking. Occasionally, a starving tribe of reptile men like Visk would emerge from the desert and mount a desperate raid in search of nourishment, be it flesh or food. Bab had known great cats that had wandered down from the mountains to the north in search of difficult-to-find food in winter. He had known wild armies of men who had come for conquest from the north and even savage apes from the southern jungles tearing through his realm. It was a ferocious region and he had to be strong to protect the men and women of his Sultanate, but it seemed to the Sultan as though they were finally nearing peace, other than the constant furore in the slums.

Bab had been to the lower town, and he knew what the streets were like; disgusting, rancid, stinking of rot and mould, with criminals around every corner. Bab knew that the Purge was necessary, but he now felt that – as he understood this – so his heirs needed to comprehend the need for the cleansing of the town in order to maintain its wellbeing. The Sultan turned from the stunning view of his realm to face his son.

"Eli, fetch your sister and Riton and Karth. This is something you must experience." Eli bowed and left briskly. "Ghan, I must speak with you."

"Anything you need, Your Majesty, I am here," replied the sombre-toned General of Calypra's military.

"Good. The gates and checkpoints that allow entry and exit to the lower city are to be left open from now until sundown for the Purge. The gates to the upper city will remain sealed shut – just in case these Nomad savages decide to rob us blind," he said with a small chuckle, while the lingering courtiers cheeped and chirped their approval loudly.

"Yes, Your Majesty," answered Ghan, bowing and summoning a servant to his side.

"One more thing, Ghan. My children are going down into the lower city to see the Purge this year. It is time they saw the necessity for it. They will take Karth, Riton, the Ogre and a few of your men as protection, but I feel they must witness it. Therefore, you will allow them to enter the lower city through the south gate, before sealing the gate once more until the Purge is complete."

Everyone within earshot gasped audibly. What Bab proposed was a terrifying notion to them, for they lived in absolute luxury with only contempt for those in the slums and indifferent indignation at the barbarity of the cleansing. It was not an event they would wish their enemies to witness, much less their children.

"Yes, Your Majesty," Ghan finally said again, bemused; the Sultan adored his children. "You there," he turned to the waiting servant, "take word to the guards at the Palace gate that the Prince and Princess will be permitted to pass through and given an escort of four men." He looked to the ever-jovial Sultan hesitantly before continuing. "After this, the gates are to be closed until the end of the Purge. Remember that, and I will be there before they leave to reiterate." The servant dashed off. "With your leave, your Majesty, I shall set your wishes in motion."

"Of course. Thank you, Ghan."

Ghan bowed again before departing more slowly.

The old General passed the Prince and Princess and their two bodyguards, Karth and Riton, in the entrance hall to the Audience Chamber. They had evidently been on their way to the morning ceremonies, and from the look on the Princess' face, Ghan knew the messenger had already told them the news.

"Prince Eli, Princess Palasia, it is so good to see you," he greeted the royal heirs with a bow and a smile and nodded to the warriors by their sides.

Ghan looked upon the Sultan's children with great affection, although he reminded himself that they were children no longer. Palasia had just turned twenty years old and Eli was twenty five. The General had known them since their birth, had played with them and even watched his own son grow alongside them until he had been killed in a vicious Nomad incursion years ago. Ghan's wife had passed away shortly thereafter; death from grief, it seemed. The General had never been the same since and doted on Eli and Palasia as if they were his own.

"It is good to see you too, Uncle," replied Palasia with a beautiful, albeit strained, smile.

There was no word but beautiful that Ghan could conceive of for Palasia – other than perfect, perhaps. She was gentle but fiercely loyal, brave, smart and compassionate. She was the object of every man's desire now that she had matured, with flowing black hair, warm red skin, stark golden eyes and a stunning, curvaceous body. This morning, she wore thin wooden clogs and a gauzy green dress laced with golden floral patterns. Ghan sometimes wished that she were a man; then, perhaps, she could become the next ruler of the city as opposed to Eli.

The Prince was a good lad, in Ghan's eyes, but no more than that. Eli was the image of the perfect warrior; tall, lean, well-proportioned and even handsome with his incarnadine complexion, cropped curly, black hair and ever-stern face. He was not a great man, however, nor was he especially intelligent or compassionate. He was headstrong and arrogant, in fact, and while he was a fine warrior, the General worried he had not the skills to be Sultan.

"Uncle," Eli nodded to him sombrely – his brown eyes as uninterested in his breath-taking surroundings as ever, thought Ghan. The Prince liked to wear dark clothing, unlike his father. That day, he sported a dark green shirt, a maroon jacket and ochre trousers and sandals.

"What *is* father thinking sending us to the lower city?" Palasia demanded of the General, her hands on her hips.

Meekly, he replied, "I don't know what has come over him, Princess, but I assure you that all measures will be taken to procure your safe return. I cannot presume to speak for the Sultan. You will have to ask him his reasons yourself."

"Hmph," the Princess huffed, crossing her arms angrily. "Don't think I won't!"

"Hello, Ghan," said Karth into the silence.

"Karth, Riton!" said Ghan, turning to the old warriors with relief.

They were big men, both of whom had seen more than forty

summers. Both were over six feet tall, dark-skinned and more muscular than a pair of bison. They had battered, broken faces and scars aplenty from their years of service to the Sultan. Karth was slightly shorter with a round, open face, a moustache and short-cropped, tan-brown hair. Riton was the epitome of the surly, tall man with a thunderous shaved face and dark stubble all over his large dome. Both wore minimal armour – gilded cuirasses, pauldrons and greaves over simple trousers, padded jackets and tunics – and both were sweating in the heat.

"General, it is good to see you. I hope you're holding up well enough without us," said Karth, his refined speech belying his fierce appearance.

"Ah well, these young upstarts will never be as good as us veterans, eh? Hehe," replied Ghan, wiping away a bead of perspiration on his forehead. "Not much of a retirement the Sultan has given you now, is it?" He chuckled again.

Karth laughed. "No, I suppose not, but I wouldn't know what to do with free time at my age anyway. I have been doing what I do for far too long now. And besides, I can't complain. The company is significantly better now." They laughed, whilst Eli raised his eyebrows.

"You take good care of these two now, you hear?" Ghan said mock-sternly, though his concern was real.

"We will, General. You have our word. We have never yet let Bab down, and today will not be the day that we fail," said Riton, his voice deep and rough.

"Good lads. Come see me later. I'll likely be in the royal dining room, getting stinking drunk with the Sultan," said Ghan, shaking their hands. "Eli, Palasia, please be careful in the lower town. Remember what I have taught you, and you will be safe."

They assured him that they would, and Ghan departed to ready the Ogre, content that the Sultan's children at least had the finest warriors in the Sultanate to protect them.

26

The Prince and Princess Prepare

Palasia watched Ghan's departing back for a moment, worried by the fear she had seen in his eyes. She understood it well enough, however; her father had been going insane for years now.

She was sure he listened to the evil serpent, Visk, far too much. He was out of his mind to send his children down into the Purge, she thought. The Nomads were notorious savages, barely able to comprehend even the concept of language, she had been told. She forgot all about her intent to apologise for missing the morning prayers then – a meaningless pleasantry anyway, since neither she nor her father wished her to witness the sacrifice – as her mind set off on a voyage of outrage, fuelled by righteous indignation, stuck unerringly on a path to confrontation.

The Princess turned from the grizzled, old General and marched purposefully into the Audience Chamber, her brother hurrying to keep up with her angry pace. She stormed into the room, sweeping across the blue-and-white striped floor – past the sheepish-looking courtiers who tried not to look in her direction – and made a beeline for her father, who had managed to once again traverse the stairs and now stood, red-faced, in front of his throne.

"My children," Bab greeted them jovially, spreading his arms and his smile.

"Father," responded Palasia tersely, her tawny eyes flashing with anger. "I hear that you would have us venture into the lower city to observe the Purge. Is that correct?"

"Ah, Palasia, do not frown so! The worry lines crease your beautiful face. Yes, that is correct, my dear," responded the Sultan, sitting on his throne with a contented sigh.

"Take it easy, sister," Eli advised quietly. Louder, he said, "If that is your wish, father, we will, of course, comply. I am sure that it will be of great benefit to both of us to observe the necessities of life in our great city."

Palasia scowled at her brother's placation. She tried to raise further objection, but was cut off by her father.

"Good, good. Thank you, my children. You do me much honour and make me as proud as a father can be. You will be perfectly safe, and as you say, it will be beneficial. Go now, the ritual begins soon. Karth, Riton, take good care of my children as you have done me all these years. I trust you implicitly. I know you will not let me down."

Riton bowed, but Karth stepped forwards. "Your Majesty, the best care of your children can be taken from here in the upper city. Perhaps they could be permitted to observe the ritual from yonder great balcony?"

"Can you not protect my children in the lower city? Is that what you are saying?" demanded Bab, eyes narrowing in anger. He was far from used to having his will thwarted or questioned.

Karth sighed resignedly. "No, Your Majesty, that is not what I am saying. We will protect your children with our lives, as we have done you; have no fear."

Bab nodded, placated once more.

"Well, *I* do not think it is a good idea either, father," said Palasia, crossing her arms.

"You will see that I am right, little one, trust me. No harm will come to you. The All Mother protects you."

"You have let that snake talk you into this, haven't you?" she said, fists clenched tightly.

"No, Palasia. I am the Sultan. I make the decisions." They looked one another in the eye.

"I can see there is no talking to you, so goodbye. I hope that we survive – for your sake," she said with jutting chin, before twirling quickly and stalking away.

The courtiers did not know where to look after such an unseemly display, most taking to a study of the domed ceiling with remarkable swiftness. Riton and Karth quickly bowed and followed the Princess.

"We will not let you down, Father," swore Eli, bowing deeply and respectfully before leaving. The courtiers loved the display of fealty, and Bab beamed brighter than ever.

Eli hurried to catch up with his sister, overtaking her in the anteroom to the Audience Chamber, grabbing her arm and spinning her to face him.

"Why must you embarrass father and I like that, *phutan*?" he demanded in a low growl, locking his dark eyes on her golden ones.

"I embarrass you?" she replied incredulously, wrenching her arm free, her blood boiling at the disrespectful term. "*You* embarrass *me* with your constant fawning over our father! It is permissible for us to have our *own* opinions, brother! And what is father thinking sending us into the lower city with only a few men to observe such a dangerous ritual?

"We have only been there a few instances in the whole of our lifetimes and always with plenty of guards and on far safer days. I know why he is doing this. That snake has hypnotised him, I swear! You know I am right, brother. You know how much time he spends alone with that reptile," she continued, lips curling toward a snarl. "He would never send us down there of his own volition. You know that, as well as I do! Have you ever heard a good story about the Nomads, Eli? Have you?"

Eli shook his head, his stern face beginning to relax in the face of her barrage of logic. "No, I have not, sister. You are right. By all accounts, they are little more than animals in human form."

"Exactly. So why, all of a sudden, is he putting us in danger?"

"There will be no danger, Princess," Karth interrupted with a smile. "Have no fear. Riton and I have never yet found a foe we could not vanquish nor a member of the royal family we could not protect. These are not just for show, you know," he added, gesturing to the fearsome weapons the two of them carried; Karth's radically curved scimitar and Riton's gigantic war hammer, as well as a more discreet assortment of knives. Eli, too, carried a sickle blade, though it was thinner and flashier than Karth's with a large ruby for a pommel, flaring golden quillions like wings and gold wiring encircling the white horn hilt.

"I must go and change my clothes," Palasia announced, tossing her hair back from her shoulder, "if I am to be subjected to the reek and grime of the lower town. I had not expected such drudgery when I arose this morning."

"Of course, Your Highness," agreed Karth, bowing. "We shall escort you back to Nuova Bela Tower now and wait for you at its base, if that is agreeable?"

"It is," the Princess decreed haughtily, her head tilted back. "Perhaps you bodyguards will prove to be useful after all."

Karth had to hide a smile at that.

"I will help Ghan with Gug and meet you by the gates, Your Highnesses," Riton told them, before loping off down the corridor with a long stride.

"Or perhaps one of you will anyway," amended Palasia, watching Riton depart with furrowed brow.

"He means no disrespect, Your Highness," Karth apologised for his friend. "He only wants to protect you as best he can."

"And so he should! Now come, let us get this over with."

"Lead on, Your Highness," Karth gestured.

Palasia swept around with upturned face, sauntered out of the Palace into the bright morning and followed the marble path leading to the left; the opposite direction from where Srenda Haam's remnants were still being cleaned.

Bees buzzed and butterflies fluttered around fragrant flowers of a hundred different colours flanking the path. Light flashed intermittently over the Princess' face as sparse canopies of fruiting and flowering trees in rows either side provided scant shade overhead, and palm and fern fronds tickled her legs as she swept past them, but Palasia had no mind for flowers, fragrance or beauty at that moment. Head high, she ploughed on toward her many chambers, thinking about the great injustices fate had committed against her.

"Do you need to change your clothes, Your Highness?" Karth asked the Prince. "Or do you wish for some armour?"

"No, thank you. I am sure you and Riton will perform adequately," responded Eli tersely. "I see little need to be weighed down by such apparel at the height of summer."

Great, thought Karth sarcastically – now I must endure your company while we wait half the year for the Princess to get ready. He wished he could convince the Prince to wear some armour, but knew from past experience that trying to change the young man's mind was both pointless and thankless. He looked at the Prince's clothing – studded leather sandals, tight, ochre trousers, gold rings and necklaces and a baggy, maroon, linen jacket with a wildcat pattern on the back highlighted in gold – and sighed. Eli's apparel could feed a thief in the slums for half a year, and every slums thief was hungry.

The two men followed Palasia to the smallest of the golden towers; a pyramidal affair festooned with engravings, busts, effigies and balconies. There, the Princess moseyed inside and Karth invited the Prince to sit by him on a liana-draped marble bench outside. The bench looked out over a wide marble courtyard – one of many in the city, surrounding the Palace – and beyond that was a relatively small landscaped area in which grew more flowers, ferns, pencil cypresses and fruiting trees. He saw that the ericoso trees, which looked like coconut trees but were head and shoulders taller than their brethren, were dangling their furry brown fruits on green vines. The nuts were still much too high for a man to reach, but parakeets had been trained to snip the vines with their beaks, thus freeing the fruits.

"The gardens here really are beautiful," Karth said in earnest, watching the colourful birds in action. He had lived in Calypra all his life, and still he was impressed.

"Yes. They are," agreed Eli tightly.

Karth sighed. There were not many topics of conversation that interested the young man, but the middle-aged bodyguard knew of one.

"So," he began, regretting it already, "is there any news on the war to the north, Prince?"

"Oh yes," replied Eli more animatedly. "The war in Shimyahein is coming to a close, as you know. General Theodore writes that it remains only to deal with the irksome rebel guerrilla warriors in the forests. And General Abkar writes to father weekly to describe his northward route. Last we heard, he had long since crossed into Al Kutz, laid waste to its southernmost cities – Harrukah and Vuum – and was laying siege to one of their larger settlements, Qabdara, which he estimates holds half a million people inside its thick stone walls. The city refused to capitulate, Abkar says, so the General has already begun the assault, battering the walls and those inside with catapults and mangonels. Qabdara's gates are prodigious, he writes, and they are finding that they have to reinforce their battering ram …"

Eli blathered on contentedly about the strategies, techniques and equipment used in warfare in the north, and Karth slowly tuned the young Prince out until his voice was just a dull drone in the back of his mind. When the Prince had to leave to void his bladder, the bodyguard thanked the Gods for the moment's peace. Eli enjoyed flapping his lips about that which he did not yet understand, thought Karth.

The young man had not yet been in war nor even in battle and so did not understand the gruesome realities that the soldiers faced. War was still all poetry, glory and honour to the young man; the older knew better. With just a few prods and nods, however, Karth was easily able to keep Eli talking until Palasia returned, though the bodyguard feared rheumatism had set in while he waited. The door to their side squeaked open to emit her, interrupting the Prince's monologue, and Karth got to his feet with a groan and a creak of the knees at the sight of the Princess.

"I am ready," she said sullenly.

Indeed, she looked far more ready, thought Karth – not that he wished to be taking her to the lower town at all. Now, instead of the dress, she wore soft leather sandals, green silk pantaloons, a golden snakeskin sash and a frilly, turquoise blouse. Her black hair was tightly braided behind her head, held with red ribbon and gold wire.

"Are you ready, Prince Eli?"

"I am."

"Then follow me, please, Your Highnesses," replied Karth, bowing and moving off toward the gardens. "Rest assured that we shall deliver you safely home again in no time."

Palasia looked around, not entirely reassured. She looked back up at the Nuova Bela Tower, the place she had called home for as long as she could remember; a magnificent golden giant glittering in the morning sunlight. She had barely ever left the upper city, in fact, she realised, truly seeing and savouring the sights, scents and sounds of the wonderful gardens for the first time.

She wondered how she had never before noticed the healthy glow of the oranges and lemons on the trees and the grapes, melons and guavas on the vines, the magnificent height of the cypresses, the brightness of the flowering acacias, the glossiness of the leaves, the lushness of the lawns, the chirpiness of the crickets, the warm hum of the bees, the sugar-sweet fragrance of the flowers and the melodiousness of the hornbills, barbets, finches, thrushes and parakeets.

It struck her then that her life was idyllic, and she did not relish change in the form of a trip to the lower city. Something was definitely amiss with her father, and it had been growing worse of late. She hoped they could find some way to uncover Visk's treachery after the Purge, so that she could get her life back on track.

Palasia, Karth and Eli walked downhill through the immaculate city proper toward the south gate to the lower city. The upper city was a wonderful place, Palasia thought as she swept along the bright marble path between gold and white buildings. Tall palms lined the main path where they walked now, overshadowing them with wide fronds. In between the palms were sprawling ferns, spiky aloes, aromatic herbs and spice plants, such as cumin, coriander, and cinnamon.

The people they passed were all dark-skinned and waved and greeted them in a friendly manner; noblemen and women for the most part, dressed in rich vibrant fabrics interwoven with enough jewellery to sustain a miser for years, out for a walk or on errands, often with a raggedly-garbed servant trailing along behind. Other serfs could be seen here and there, sweeping the streets, removing garbage and generally maintaining cleanliness. A zephyr arose, rippling the greenery like every separate leaf moved in tandem, coordinated by one encompassing mind. The streets shone glorious white under the baking midsummer sun and the gold gleamed blindingly, making the eyes water with the sheer splendour of it all.

They left the upper city, passing the high golden wall through a shiny, barred gate that was discreetly shut and locked behind them. Palasia did not begin to fret yet, however. Glancing around brought more beauty to the eye as she sauntered downhill.

Surrounding the path now was a great swathe of sloping, well-maintained gardens and pools, with benches, verandas and pergolas scattered around in which to appreciate the seasonal attractions of the beautiful grounds. White paths crisscrossed – like the web of a gigantic, marble-weaving arachnid – throughout the gardens that circumvented the entire perimeter of the small hill, on top of which wallowed the self-absorbed spider itself, Calypra.

The gardens created a moat of lush greenery, artistic topiary, hedges, mazes, ivy-draped statues, colourful fruit trees, flower beds, liana-drowned gazebos, reflecting pools and marble water fountains between the golden city above and the sandy city below, which lay sprawled at the base of the hill. The main marble paths – wider than the others and lined by palm trees – led like the spokes of a wheel straight down to the few great gates that broke the monotony of the ringing golden wall, through which access to the lower city was achieved, but never recommended, by those living above.

The flowerbeds to her left were particularly profuse, she noticed as she passed by. They were brimming with spiky pineapple plants, orchids, alliums, crocuses, daffodils, chrysanthemums and irises, all vying for supremacy in a riot of colour. On the other side of the blooms basked orchards filled with all manner of gaudy fruit trees from plums, peaches and cherries to dates, figs and pomegranates. Scattered around the groves were a plethora of big-leaved banana plants, as well as reed-ringed pools and marble fountains, reflecting the sky and the charming gardens in their rippling waters, obscured by lackadaisically pretty waterlilies and overhanging weepers.

As the trio walked slowly along the path – observing the bountiful gardens to either side and the gleaming golden wall rearing up ahead, smelling the flora, staring at the immaculacy of the blue sky, watching the sun slowly soar toward its zenith, soaking in the heat and listening to the drone of the bees and the calls of the birds – they were silent. Palasia snagged a succulent, round orange absently as she passed a fruiting tree. Peeling it partially, she lazily sucked the juices from it and then discarded it carelessly for the orioles, tanagers and bluebirds to fight over.

They reached the end of the path, where twin marble towers were set into the wall on either side of the exit, and she looked through the thick golden bars of the gate to the beginnings of the slums. Filthy brown streets ran afoul of one another between dull and decrepit buildings of sandy orange that decayed before her eyes. The blazing sunlight failed to light those tight, little alleys and they looked cold and unwelcoming, carpeted with brown sludge. From the cesspool of streets and the dingy doorways, emaciated folk wandered aimlessly across the sunlit square the other side of the gates or else eyed the folk from the upper city with a look that reminded Palasia of her hounds when she forgot to feed them. The royal heirs' escort of four golden-armoured guards was awaiting them at the gate, hands resting on swords, eyes alert and ears perked.

"What a mess," said Eli as they came under the penumbra of the golden arch above the gate, his nose wrinkling in disgust at the vile aroma that wafted up from the lower city. "Stinky *jac skra!* Oh, no offense intended to you, Karth," he added as an afterthought.

Karth was offended, far off in the back of his mind in a region never given voice for fear of the death penalty, because like everyone on both sides of the golden gates whose last name was not Bab, he was a *jac skra* or *dark skin*. However, he knew at the forefront of his mind that the young Prince used the word solely in a derogatory fashion – careless of the concepts of solidarity it could invoke – and therefore he truly had not meant offence to Karth, for his outburst had been intended solely for those in the lower city. As usual, the bodyguard forgave the oversight.

"None taken, Your Highness," he said smoothly.

They could see skeletal children beating one another mercilessly in the dirty square and men milling around, clearly jobless, carrying crude weapons like bats.

"Thugs," said Karth, face darkening like a storm cloud.

Women, too, wandered around, scantily clad, clearly offering their bodies as their wares without shame.

"Not all bad, though," amended Karth, seeing them with a grim smile.

Palasia shook her head at the sight of her people penned in, enduring these conditions.

"It's deplorable," she murmured to herself, eyes watering again – though she was not sure if that was a result of the sadness she felt or the vileness she smelled. Probably the smell, she thought, resisting the urge to plug her nose.

"Here come Ghan, Riton and Gug," Karth told them, and they were glad for the distraction.

Turning, the Prince and Princess beheld the grizzled General and the tall, surly bodyguard coming down the sunny white path. By their side was Gug – one of a few Ogres to have been brought up from birth and trained by the Babs of Calypra to serve as bodyguard to the royal persons. There had once been multiple Ogres for protection in the city, but the creatures were so territorial and aggressive that they had killed one another off. Now only Gug remained, the last and biggest, assigned to the Prince and Princess.

The sight of the Ogre's raw, visceral power never ceased to amaze Palasia. The creature had skin the colour of weathered granite and was completely hairless. His limbs and torso were huge, his inhumanly broad shoulders reaching eight feet even though he was constantly hunched over, walking on feet and large knuckles like an ape. His body was bunched with rings and lumps of muscle everywhere the eye could see – and the eye could see a great deal, for Gug the Ogre wore only a ragged hide loincloth.

Above this mountainous frame, there towered not the rock of a head that one might expect; more a pebble, fit only to contain the most cardinal notions of intelligence, survival instinct and coordination. The Ogre's single eye was miniscule in comparison to his size; one tiny, black dot in the vast, craggy landscape of his gnarled, twisted knot of a face. Two enormous, round ears stuck out from his small head like wings, giving the impression of a bird nested atop a rugged mountain. His lipless slash of a mouth gaped open vapidly, and his huge purple tongue lolled out like a sunning hound's over large, flat teeth that could grind bones to dust in seconds. Gug waved one great hand at the Prince and Princess, smiled crookedly and grunted with pleasure and recognition. Palasia felt safer already.

"Well, are we ready, Highnesses?" asked Karth, indicating the great gates.

"Yes," answered Eli readily.

"Yes," said Palasia after a breath.

Ghan hugged both of the royal offspring, saying, "Take care, you two, and I will see you when you return."

The Princess wished the old man was coming with them and felt butterflies in her stomach at his expression; round eyes and a brow creased in concern.

The guards opened the gates just enough to allow them to slip through in single file beneath a great golden arch. The four men who had been chosen to accompany them walked through first, hands on their weapons to warn the gathering crowd of lower city residents in the square not to come any closer. Palasia went last, taking another deep breath before passing through.

The staring eyes of a skinny, young street boy made her nervous.

27

The Slums Orphan

The street boy's name was Bala. He stared unabashed at the young Princess, unaware of the discomfort he caused her, stunned that such beauty could exist in the world, for it did not exist in his.

"They're all so clean," he muttered, looking down at his ragged, dirty brown tunic, which had once been red, and equally filthy brown shorts. His bare feet were plastered with the slime of the streets.

He had never been in the city proper, as most people had not, and it was quite a rarity to glimpse a member of the royal family venturing past the golden bars of the great gates, through which the residents of the lower town were permitted to observe the unattainable glory beyond. It was cruel to tempt the poor folk so, in Bala's eyes.

It was unheard of to see both the Prince and Princess along with the famous bodyguards, Karth and Riton, who were said to have torn apart armies with their bare hands. Bala could almost believe the hyperbole looking at their enormous muscles and fearsome weapons. They wore magnificent ceremonial armour; golden breastplates and greaves inlaid with patterns mimicking the muscles beneath. They looked like Gods of War basking in the late morning sun to the young boy.

The four accompanying guards held long pikes – which the young boy had always thought looked to be unwieldy weapons – but they had swords belted at their waists. Their armour was far less ornate, simpler and without the intricate patterns. They wore metal helmets with conical tops that looked comical to many an eye in the lower city. The Ogre attracted a deal of attention, but after he growled threateningly at any that came near for a few minutes, the novelty quickly wore off and people skirted around him more carefully.

Seeing that the Prince and Princess were not going anywhere anytime soon as they loitered by the gate, chatting among themselves,

Bala's companion, Arak, drawled, "C'mon, Bala, let's go get some food before the Purge, man. I'm starving."

Arak turned and began to walk away. Bala stared for a moment longer, hoping to catch the beautiful Princess' eye, but to no avail. He turned and followed his companion from the square into the alleys.

Arak was older than Bala; taller, too, and he had more hair. Bala looked up to Arak a great deal; he was ruthless, quick and cunning, which made him an excellent thief. He was just as dirty as the younger boy, however. It was difficult not to be perpetually mucky in the slums. Here, there were no servants to sweep the streets nor were the streets safe enough to dawdle in to sweep, and so the trash and ordure mounted every day.

Flies and mosquitos raced to the excretion to lay their eggs, and soon swarms of them – thousands strong – feasted unquenchably on a daily basis, along with the hordes of rats who had long since taken up residence. The insects and vermin spread plagues throughout the lower city like rumours; nobody knew their source, but everybody knew of them. There was barely a soul in the lower city who did not have a cyst, rash, infection or boils oozing pus from every pore.

Bala and Arak were among the lucky few who were not visibly plagued. Being young and strong, they were able to fight off the rampant infections, for a time. Both already knew the day would come when they would wake to find their bodies ravaged by disease or dagger; there was no other way for them to live out their days in the slums. Both were orphans, taken in by a funded orphanage when they were children – though where the money from the local funding went, Bala never worked out. The place was disgusting, riddled with bugs, rats and callous caretakers.

Neither boy knew who their parents were or what had happened to them. For all they knew, they lived in Calypra alongside their sons and simply did not want the responsibility of paying to feed and clothe them. The dozens of orphans had therefore learned to become thieves to survive from the earliest age; more than this, they were encouraged to do so by the men who ran the orphanage. They stole food to eat and were encouraged to steal whatever they could that looked valuable enough for the men to sell.

Growing up in the orphanage had been tough. Bala had taken many a beating over the fifteen or sixteen years of his life; he wasn't exactly sure how old he was, as no one seemed to have bothered to note down the day of his birth. He had learned his hard lessons well, though; he was tough, fast and as agile as he could possibly make himself. He was a good thief. He had no respect in the orphanage, however – among the Pinchers, as the young thieves had come to call themselves – because he had never yet stolen anything other than food to help the men who oversaw the youths.

While perfectly happy to steal food to survive, he did not steal excessively and never too much from any one merchant. His unique code of ethics told him this was the best way to do things. Stealing valuable items, which could potentially be treasured by their owners and which he did not need, just to sell to others to make money was far more dishonest than stealing food to eat to survive, in Bala's opinion. More than that, stealing valued objects required complete secrecy and no witnesses, since being caught would result in a far more stringent punishment than stealing a few bits of fruit and bread.

In contrast, Bala stole food in the open in broad daylight from market stalls, and his escape was only assured by his speed and nimbleness. It created a game of sorts to pass the day, and as a result all of the merchants knew a great many of the boys. Bala had even stopped to chat to some of the vendors from whom he stole, before pinching their wares. Of course they chased him, but because of his novel morals, he felt a certain bond had grown between them. Some had to hide a smile when they saw him coming nowadays. Not all youths had such scruples, and so whilst his fellows did not respect him, the merchants did.

Bala traipsed along behind Arak, not relishing the prospect of the day's events. The annual Purge was a scene of violence and bloodshed every year. While some, such as Arak and the more violent Pinchers – usually those who stole more than they needed, Bala had noticed – seemed to look forward to this day as some sort of vent for their inner furies, Bala did not. Every year, hundreds of men all over the lower city grabbed makeshift weapons and headed out the door to fight the Nomads who came to 'escort' them to the desert to die.

Rumour all over the city – rumour passed down for generations – was that all the wrongdoings in the entire Sultanate, and particularly the Purge, were the fault of the slithering serpent who had dwelled in the golden heights of Calypra for centuries: Visk. The name instigated hatred at every corner, and – while there was obviously no proof, as few were permitted to enter the golden walls and no one in the slums had ever even seen the serpent – every single soul in the dark streets blamed the word Visk for all their troubles. It was said that the annual bloodletting had been Visk's idea, generations before – though exactly where this intimate knowledge of the Sultan's first advisor's decisions had come from, Bala had always wondered.

It must have been started by the sweepers, thought the boy. Sweepers were those who were permitted to enter the golden city above to sweep and clean it; it was even considered a good profession, for they were paid and got to experience the glories of the upper world for a time. They were much sought after in the lower city – to give them a good beating and rob them blind, Bala thought grimly as he padded through a tenebrous alley with slop underfoot and rearing sandy walls either side that always incurred a feeling of oppression in the boy.

After a short run through the filthy alleyways, Arak and Bala emerged into a brightly lit scene of chaos: the great bazaar. Bala squinted against the sudden sunlight after emerging from the streets, where the buildings were tall and ran into one another, creating solid walls and shade throughout the alleys. Very little sunlight saw the streets of the slums of Calypra, save at noon when it was too blazingly hot to venture out into direct sunlight at any rate. That time was fast approaching. When Bala's watering eyes had gotten used to the adjusted level of light, he was shocked by what he saw.

While the wide expanse of space – virtually the only wide expanse of space in the slums – that constituted the bazaar was thronged with so many people that some were sure to be trampled over the day, as usual, there was something off about the scene. The garish colours all over affirmed that the city was thriving, and the roar of noise – over which even shouting could not be heard – was at the same volume he had expected, but still something was missing. To remedy the noise concern, the Pinchers used their own sign language; an extremely useful adaptation for communicating and stealing in concert with one another without alerting their targets.

Targets! That was it, thought Bala – the loud and varied sales calls from all the merchants that should have been there were missing. He wondered where in the world else would they be on such a day.

Normally, every vendor known to the thieves would be thronging with the rest of the population, taking advantage of the enormous gathering to sell their wares throughout the entire day. Merchants thought of it as one of the best money-making days of the year – as Bala understood it – and well they should; everyone knew that fighting against kidnapping Nomads worked up quite a hunger for a bargain.

Today, however, Bala could see only a few stalls set up around the edges of the crowd, which was becoming more and more aggressive as the day wore on, knowing what was coming. As he stared at the few stalls around, he realised that they were all resident merchants; they all lived in the city. More than that, he thought, looking again, they were the few merchants whose warehouses were in the city itself. Many hawkers had warehouses a short way out on a farm or in a barn, and while they lived in the city as the others did, they had to go and retrieve their wares from outside of the rising wall around the slums of Calypra.

That was always a dangerous thing to do, in Bala's experience; every story he had heard and every person who never came back after leaving the slums told him that it was a very dangerous business indeed venturing out into the wide world beyond the stinking alleys and general cesspit that was his home.

Those whom he knew had to fetch their wares from storehouses outside the city every morning before setting up their stalls were missing, Bala mused, disconcerted, as were those who lived outside the city growing crops, who came in to sell their produce from time to time – especially on Prophet's Day, he would have thought. Usually on the day of midsummer, the farmers should have had plenty of food to sell; fruits, herbs, vegetables, wines and berries especially. Bala normally looked out for the latter in particular; he loved berries.

He had almost a friendship of sorts with one farmer, who had the juiciest and most delicious blueberries Bala had ever tasted. He had told him so one day, before stealing from him, and had enjoyed the merchant's smiling roar as he waved his arms mock-angrily at the escaping thief. The next time the seller, Asiliff, had come into the city, he had placed his finest berries off to one side where few others were likely to look. Bala smiled; he had enjoyed a lot of delicious berries that day while the trader was busy with his back turned, vending his other wares.

"Dammit, Asiliff, where are you? I'm hungry," he muttered.

Furthermore, there should have been a sizeable influx of nomadic tradesmen; they normally mobbed into the city to sell to the mob already in it, and as Nomads themselves, they were ignored by the invaders who came to kidnap folk and take them away. Equally, it was an opportune time for them to meet, greet and sell to their fellows from other tribes, Bala had noticed in the past whilst fleeing.

All of these merchants were missing, as though everything outside of the festering slums was dead, thought Bala morbidly, his mind darker than the dingy alleys, despite the fierce sunlight that beamed down on him. There were few explanations for the absence of every merchant who either lived outside the walls or had to venture outside of them.

Bala glimpsed a fellow Pincher, Yashi, along the edge of the turbulent, noisy crowd and, using their sign language, quickly asked him if he knew the location of the vendors or the cause for their absence.

Yashi waggled his fingers equally fast; no, he did not know. He, too, looked anxious, however. Both understood that the dangers of today meant that survival until tomorrow was not guaranteed, and it seemed as though the chances were lowering further still.

Bala looked up, avoiding staring directly at the sun, but getting a decent idea of its location from the blinding rays. The Purge should have started already, he thought. It would not be long now. He decided he had to risk getting to the merchants on the other side of the great square, where they had set up their stalls by the sides of the main gate, to get both food and information, before fleeing back into the relative shelter of the darkness of the streets. He needed to be quick.

He signed Yashi again, and the young Pincher came running over to join Bala and Arak. The three of them rapidly concocted a plan over the roar of the masses with their waggling fingers, and Yashi sprinted off to the left around the edge of the crowd.

Arak ran straight into the mob, barrelling a couple of people over with his shoulders, before stopping to crouch on his hands and one knee. Bala ran up to his prone figure, leapt onto Arak's shoulder and launched himself high up into the air. His grasping fingers found what they sought as they clasped tightly around a thick wooden pole – one of many that ran horizontally across and above the bazaar.

The great wooden framework that loomed over the plaza had been there for as long as anyone could remember; an addition to the slums by one of the ancient Babs. It served a purpose beyond aiding an acrobatic, young thief, however. When the monsoons came, the torrential downpour barraged the city for days. The merchants had struggled in the past to keep their goods dry to sell to the starving people of the city, but with little success. Every year, hundreds had starved. The simple solution to the problem had been an enormous canvas that stretched over the wooden framework, keeping it and the bazaar beneath dry so that the hawkers could happily sell their wares.

Bala swung agilely from pole to pole like a monkey. No one else could do what he did, as far as he knew, and he had seen plenty of Pinchers try and fail. The poles were spaced wide apart, and it required a tremendous swing to get enough momentum to traverse the gap between them. He swung high enough that the mob beneath was perfectly safe from his flailing legs. Many people looked up, in fact, and marvelled aloud at the feat they witnessed above their heads.

Bala stopped about halfway across the bazaar, his breathing beginning to grow heavier, and shimmied to the left along the pole to which he clung. He reached the far side of the bazaar, where the wooden pole came remarkably close to a wall. There, the frame had a cleverly fashioned joint that connected the pole on which he swung to another that leant diagonally upwards from the first to join with other beams that sloped similarly upwards from other points in the latticework to create a slight dome at the top, in the centre, on which the canvas would sit when rolled out so as to allow for rain drainage.

Where the two poles met, they were close enough together that the young thief could reach up from the first to grab a hold of the second. Putting all his weight on one arm for a moment, Bala reached up swift as a striking snake to snag a grip on the upper pole. He let out a relieved breath as he grabbed it; hovering mid-air with only one hand clinging to life was daunting, and he loved it. That moment alone was worth living for in his mind. It was – as always – a perfect grab, because it needed to be. One slip would result in a Bala-sized puddle on the bazaar floor below. He might not die from such a landing, but he could easily be crippled.

Trying not to think about this, Bala swung up the diagonal beam until he reached the top, where he used his momentum to leap through the air once more to grab on to the beam that led toward the merchants, at a right angle from the first. During the leap, time slowed for the urchin as he savoured the moment, life and death both within reaching distance. After another flawless execution, he swung quickly downwards towards the far side of the bazaar. It had taken him moments to cross the plaza; a method often faster than trying to barrel through the thick press on the ground.

The scene he swung towards was a riot of colour and activity. Hundreds of people swarmed the narrow stinking confines of the alleyways surrounding the bazaar, pushing and jostling to get to the plaza itself, where Bala could see there was no salvation. People were packed in like dates in a crate, pressed up tight against one another in the throng with hardly enough space to breathe, much less walk around.

The traders, the few that were there, were yelling themselves hoarse trying to be heard over the roar of the mob, and – while continuing to call out to potential customers with every breath – they were, to a man, rushed off their feet. They literally could not move fast enough to please everyone who crowded and shoved at the front of their luridly painted stalls below the enormous garish signs, for they had thrice the number of customers that would have been the norm for the day of celebration as a result of the monopoly on business they held that day, thanks to the missing merchants.

Then, Bala spied his companions. Yashi was approaching the merchants – who were arranged in a convenient straight line on the northernmost side of the plaza against one of many sandy walls that represented the dull, cracked housing which overran the city – from the left. Arak was advancing from the right.

Having absorbed all of this while clambering rapidly down the beam, Bala halted his swing at the edge of the lattice by the wall. Wriggling up onto the beam awkwardly, he climbed and rolled onto the thick green canvas there, which was rolled up expediently along this side of the great wooden framework, ready to be pulled out by attached ropes when it was needed. The sun-warmed tarp bowed slightly under his weight, but there were numerous supporting beams on this side built into the woodwork, designed to hold the canvas' thick folds of material, and the young boy was far from heavy.

Bala grinned once in place, his dark skin creasing with joy, his ragged, brown, curly hair whipped around messily from his antics. There, on the canvas directly above the merchants' stalls, the young thief sat happily for a moment, until suddenly a woven reed basket flew up from below to land in front of him on the folds of the enormous tarpaulin, and he remembered why he was there.

He scurried over to the basket, picked it up and stood, wobbling on the shifting folds of canvas. Below, Bala saw apples, pineapples, guava, bananas, grapefruit, melons, grapes and all manner of fruit distributed over the sandy ground in front of the middle stall. Dozens of people clamoured over the fallen goods, grabbing as many as they could and jostling one another violently for their share. The merchant, meanwhile, had grabbed a wooden switch and – leaning over his stall – begun to lay about at the mob with all his might in a vain attempt to reclaim his goods. Such was the way of poverty, Bala guessed.

With such a commotion beckoning attention toward the middle kiosk, there was a momentary lull at the other stalls as people inevitably craned their necks to see the source of the hubbub. This was the perfect opportunity for Yashi and Arak to infiltrate the mobs in front of the other stalls.

Peeking over the edge of the canvas at the turmoil below, Bala saw that his fellows had both snuck their way to the fronts of two different kiosks. He put the basket down for a moment and swung his head over the edge of the canvas to shout merrily at the merchants.

"Gooood morning, fellas!" he roared down at them, grinning, his voice cracking through lack of moisture. "I tell you what, boys, you really are the most sorry-looking bunch of ugly, motherless goat-molesters on which I have ever laid eyes, and that's solid gold truth, right there!"

The merchants looked up and began to shout belligerent insults back at the cheeky young street boy, but his head disappeared a moment later and while they continued to look up at where the young thief had been, they noticed fruit and bread flying up past their faces.

Looking down at their displayed goods once more, they saw the cause; young hands grabbing whatever they could lay their thieving fingers on and throwing it all up into the air over the top of the canvas. The merchants smacked and swatted at the grasping hands precipitously with their switches, lashing hands and faces and anything else within range. Arak and Yashi yelped, backed off and ran away, angry red welts their reward.

One merchant risked taking a pace away from his stall in order to get a look over the tarp. There, he saw Bala, holding the basket which had originally held the fruit that had been upturned over the ground. Only now, the hamper was full of the stolen fruit and bread that had been thrown up by his two accomplices.

The young boy grabbed and ate a handful of berries from the basket, relishing them with his eyes closed, listening to the outraged cries of the merchants below. He savoured the moment by himself with a hamper-full of food, for he would have to depart and share it with his accomplices before long. They would feel they deserved a share for receiving a good thwacking, Bala thought with a smile, swaying to dodge an apple thrown accurately at his face by one of the merchants.

While he savoured the berries he heard a ripple of inquisition pass through the mob, coming from the south where lay the entrance to the slums, as dozens and then hundreds of men and women began to question the entrance of a *pal skra,* a *pale skin*, into their city.

Bala looked to the south, toward the entrance to the lower town, down the long passage created by the two parallel sandy walls being thrown up; an inlet from the wall moat that was being built around the slums. The Sultan would not have hired the infamous *pal skra* from across the water to perpetrate the Purge, thought Bala, would he? From what the urchin had heard, they practised cannibalism – preferring infants to adults – as well as being no strangers to black magic, incest and bigotry.

After a few minutes of careful listening to the rumours abounding throughout the bazaar of what was occurring, he got only one overall impression; that there was more than one *pal skra* entering the city, among other men. Bala stretched his neck to try to get a glimpse of such an oddity. Occasionally, *pal skra* would come into the upper city and stay at the Palace with the Sultan – so the word went from the sweepers. Bala had not been fortunate enough to catch a glimpse in the past and was determined not to miss another opportunity. Besides, he thought, the Purge was overdue and he was awaiting the mass panic that would indicate the arrival of the perpetrating Nomads.

After watching the throbbing, pulsing crowd – so massive and tightly packed that it seemed to gyrate like one great beast – for a few minutes more, Bala caught a glimpse of paleness; easy to spot in the bright sunlight against the riotous bright colours and dark skin surrounding it. Concentrating hard on the spot where he glimpsed it, Bala caught his first glimpse of a *pal skra*; a man of about thirty, armoured in shining steel like a legendary Knight of the old Crusades, bearing shield and scabbarded sword. The street boy gasped as a second hove into view; taller and older than the straw-haired Knight, this one had dark hair and just as much armour. A third *pal skra* appeared then, younger and dressed differently from the first two. He wore no armour, just a red bandana, a loose white shirt, particoloured breeches, and wide-brimmed boots like those corsairs were said to wear whilst on land.

Beside the rare piratic *pal skra* were two Nomads, even darker-skinned than the Calyprians; a man and woman in their twenties, whom the residents of the city gave a wide berth. The street boy deduced, however, that these Nomads were not here to Purge the city's residents and drag them off to the desert; they threatened no one, did not grab or net anyone or drag them off behind a horse. They were not even riding horses. Bala could not believe his good fortune; the *pal skra* and Nomads were forcing their way through the aggressive multitude towards the great bazaar and the young boy perched in safety high above the crowd.

Then, he heard the sound for which he had been listening so hard all morning, a sound he had dreaded, for it meant the arrival of death and destruction to the city and its people; the shrill ringing of a scream of fear. It sounded like a woman, but he couldn't be sure; terror unmanned men as well as women.

As Bala stared to the south, he saw that the spectacle taking shape under the sun's hammer was vastly different to what he had expected from previous years' experience. There were no terrifying horsemen thundering through the crowd, throwing nets upon defiant folk; no horsemen at all, in fact, as far as Bala could see, and he could see it well, unfolding unstoppably before his eyes like a bad dream.

28

The Purge

In place of the horse-riding Nomads young Bala had expected to witness at the end of the wide tunnel between the sandy walls, a veritable swarm of men was slaughtering the hapless population; not dragging them away to the desert to die, but massacring them where they stood.

Bala watched in horror, food and companions completely forgotten. His ears were assaulted by shrieks from all over as the crowd's mood changed in a heartbeat from aggressive to panicked. Bala was sure that dozens of people were trampled by the terrified herd beneath him in the first few seconds after the initial scream, as people sought the safety of shelter with no thought to the cost of those around them.

The young boy tore his astounded eyes away from the scene of carnage at the end of the ill-lit passage, his heart racing. He watched breathlessly as the *pal skra* and the near-naked Nomads fled through the wailing mob, bowling people over in their haste, for the murdering men were not far behind them. The pale skins and desert-dwellers were armed to the teeth, too, from the looks of it, but they did not attack the fleeing citizens, only knocked them out of the way.

As Bala covered his mouth with a trembling hand, he noticed that there were more people with the group; an old, golden-skinned Tzunese man who sprang along with surprising nimbleness, leaning not at all on his crooked walking staff, a dark-skinned man with dreadlocks sporting black and yellow, and behind them, another *pal skra* that the boy had not spotted before. This last was a strange-looking, tall fellow with stark white hair, garbed in a sand-stained white robe.

He saw this tall figure more closely a moment later, as it bobbed about, becoming variably more and less visible with each passing second amid the jostling of the crowd. The figure had a long, slender face and bright blue eyes. Something about the fellow, however, made Bala wonder if he was even a man at all, for he looked somehow older than time, like a fossil rather than a man.

The ancient being looked up and locked eyes with the young boy for a moment, and Bala felt his gaze as well as saw it; almost basked in its glow as though the sun were directing all of its glory towards his face. The figure's eyes were like a portal; such a vivacious sky-blue that they seemed a window to a new world totally unlike Bala's own, a world that promised lush new life. It was a strange feeling, but definitely enjoyable. Then, the ivory-haired figure looked away and continued to flee toward Bala with the others.

The street boy could not stop himself from looking again to the Purgers behind the unusual group. Now that they were closer, he could see them far better and what he saw almost made him retch with horror and fear. The attackers were not men at all; they did not even look human. They wore the shapes of men, but their skin was grey – or coal-black in some cases – and looked to be rotting, as though they were walking corpses. Thick red veins had swollen all over their faces, standing out like demonic brands, and their eyes shone with a feral crimson eagerness. Most wore Nomad-style loincloths, but some wore the garish gear of Calypra and some were stumpy, beardy fellows with odd white armour. Weapons stuck out from the flesh of some, whilst in others mortal wounds openly festered, attracting the flies. The carcasses walked on heedless, moaning like a mad chorus.

Everywhere Bala looked, blood and mouldy flesh assaulted his eyes, juxtaposed bizarrely against the peaceful blue of the sky. Hundreds of attackers swarmed over the tightly-packed people in the bazaar like a locust plague, leaving most little hope of escape, and carved up the masses with crude weapons or leapt on them and beat them with flaky fists and tore at their flesh with black teeth. The corpses moved like animals, lust for flesh seemingly their only motive, Bala thought, as he witnessed Yashi trying to fight back and then having his throat torn out by the teeth of the monsters.

"Enough of this shit! I'm outta here!" Bala said – an attempt to steel his nerve that came out as a whimper. "But where can I go?" he whispered, pulling at his hair frantically.

Then, he remembered the Prince and Princess. Above all others, they would surely be kept safe and alive, he thought. There was no way their father had sent them down here to die, and they had the Ogre for protection. Perhaps there was a mistake of some sort, he pondered, for this was not an ordinary Purge. Bala knew it was irrelevant why it was happening, however; only important that it was and that he had to survive it, just like he had the others.

"I have to get back to the Princess," he told himself, working up the nerve to move.

Before he could, though, he saw the *pal skra* group overtaken by the foremost grey skins. He was sure they would be overwhelmed within seconds, but he was wrong. The male Nomad, the *pal skra* pirate and his dreadlocked companion hastened to the rear when they realised the group was in danger. They quickly beheaded the monsters who rushed them, the Nomad with scimitars and the other two with cutlasses, while the Knights forged on ahead, dragging the tall, white-haired fellow with them.

The three warriors at the rear fought a bloody retreat, for those they beheaded did not die, Bala saw, but continued to attack with as much – if not more – vitriol than before until their limbs too were hacked off and they could harry the warriors no longer. This was a painstaking method, however – even the street boy could see that – and so soon the warriors began to chop off arms wherever they could and kick back the rest.

Bala realised he needed their help, his brain racing. The group was now running in full retreat, passing under the canvas on which the boy stood. Without further thought, Bala made himself turn away from the massacre and the gore-strewn tunnel – now slick with red all over the walls and floor – and sprint along the tarp, wobbling a great deal as he sought balance.

When he reached the end of the canvas he bent down, throwing his hands before him as though to plummet from the edge. His hands wrapped around the final supporting beam for the tarpaulin however, and his feet flipped over his head, pivoting about his hold on the beam. The result was that he ended up hanging from the beam, feet dangling a distance from the floor. He had no time to shimmy down the pole, however; he dropped and bent his knees as he landed. His legs and feet were subjected to not unfamiliar agony for this mistreatment, but his aim was achieved.

He turned around from his painful crouch and stood carefully to face the astonished motley group of Knights, Nomads, Freemen, a golden man, and the white-haired enigma – to whom Bala's gaze was instinctively drawn – who had witnessed him flip down through the air to land agilely before them.

"Tai woon!" exclaimed the old golden man, who was so hunched over he was almost the boy's height.

"Follow me if you want to live!" was Bala's only reply – fortunately in Traveller's – before he ran away, down an alleyway to his left, where there were fewer folk and movement was possible. It was a circuitous route to the gate by which he hoped the Prince and Princess were still waiting, but potentially the quickest under current circumstances, he thought.

The Elf, Amril, took off after him without a thought, his robe billowing. The others followed behind, running through the slime of the narrow streets between the towering sandy walls, splashing one another with the waste in the gutters in their haste. They put some distance between themselves and the main force of the pack of nightmares that pursued them, but some trailed them, and bloodthirsty groans raked the group's ears as they fled.

Bala wove rapidly through the labyrinth of dark streets, dodging this way and that to lose the monsters, but continuing in roughly the same direction. The others struggled to keep up with him, the old man even shouting, "Slow down, young'un! I have only short legs!"

"Oh no," muttered Bala as he skidded around another corner.

From three of the four adjoining alleyways, the veiny walking corpses slavered, droned and staggered towards the group like drunkards, for most were injured in some way. They walked on broken legs, entrails gushed from open stomachs, and some had clear weapon wounds through their skulls where their shattered brains could be seen, like grotesque burrowing parasites behind their faces that slithered, shook and bled. Bala almost vomited as the wind whipped up the alley from behind the creatures and the boy was subjected to an overpowering stench of mould and maggots.

"Move, boy!" roared the bigger of the two Knights from behind.

He gave the boy a shove as he came running past, his face red from the exertion of running at full pelt in steel plate armour. His breath was beginning to grow ragged, and his arms pumped furiously. Smashing the first of the corpses to the ground with his armoured momentum, the big man clove the next in half at the waist and lopped off the third's leg with his broadsword. Bala was astonished.

"Lead on!" growled the Knight to the urchin.

They sprinted on. Bala cut to and fro across the streets, attempting to maintain his course towards the safety of the royalty lurking by the great golden gates, whilst also trying to dodge the grasping hands of the grey skins, who came disturbingly near to snatching him a few times. On the last of these, he had to swerve his torso athletically to dodge a grasping leprous hand, before the big Knight sent the assailant flying back through the air with a fist to the face. As the grey skin was jolted backwards with a wounded cry, Bala caught a glimpse of its mangled visage.

"Asiliff!" he gasped, stumbling to a halt, eyes wide with wonder.

The urchin was torn away from the figure by the large Knight, who hoisted him by his collar and dragged him along a few feet until the boy began to run on his own again.

Bala looked up. They were near the gate now, the boy saw. It was just at the end of the oppressive tunnel down which they sprinted, horrors chasing them with bloodcurdling roars every step of the way. A figure darted out of a side street in front of Bala; the boy's back was to the urchin, but Bala could recognise Arak from any angle.

Without thinking, Bala cried out for joy at seeing his friend still alive, "Arak!"

He winced an instant later, realising it was dangerous to distract his friend at such a time. It made no difference, though; Arak did not look back, just kept sprinting with his head down, leading the way in front of Bala. The young thief watched as his friend reached the end of the shadow of the long alleyway and stepped into the glaring sunlight that beat down over the whole city.

The boy's black silhouette ran forward into the light just as Bala came in view of the sun, and it flashed blindingly bright for an instant, forcing him to cover his eyes and look away. He looked forward again just in time to see Arak take a second sunlit step, only for a blade to dart out from behind the wall and sever his head from his body.

Bala did not even cry out. He froze in his tracks, mouth agape as he watched the boy's head topple from his shoulders in a geyser of blood to land bouncingly in the sand, the movements seeming too slow and surreal for reality. He had known Arak for as long as he could remember; he had been like a big brother to Bala, a safe island in an ever-shifting, treacherous sea.

"No! Arak!" he heard someone roar distantly, not realising immediately that it was him. It sounded like waves were crashing in his ears.

Reality flashed back to its normal speed for the young boy as danger reared its omnipresent head. Grey skins clamoured over Arak's body instantaneously, thrusting one another aside in their haste to rip into the corpse with teeth and nails. It was clear all of a sudden why one of them had a blade; one of the monsters writhing on top of the boy was a royal guardsman whose nose had been bitten off, complete with full golden armour, weapons, thick red veins and rotting skin. He had known Arak as long as he could remember, and now suddenly there was no time left even to mourn.

Bala sprinted forward on tottery legs, his pulse drumming in his ears, and while the bloodthirsty creatures were snacking on his beheaded friend's insides with their heads down, he stepped on one of their backs and replicated his earlier leap from Arak's back to clear the group of hungry monsters. In mid-air, he prayed for his friend's soul to reach *Citta Pacia*, not believing for an instant his prayer would be heard, and then he resolved not to look back.

He skidded to a halt in the dirt-paved square beyond the hungry carcasses, where he had first spotted the royal heirs earlier that day, the scene before him as grim as any he had seen in the past few minutes.

"Prophet's balls!"

Dozens of the grey skins had beaten him to the gate. Bala could see the flash of the golden entryway fifty feet away, on the other side of the square. Through the moaning crowd of carious flesh ahead of him, he also caught fleeting glimpses of the Prince, Princess and their retinue defending the golden bars, pressed back into the narrowest point where the jutting, adjacent houses stymied too many cadavers from accessing the gate at once. The golden wall – which towered above the houses and adjoined the great gate, arching over it and blocking entrance into the upper city – was too smooth to be scaled, Bala knew from experience. The twin minarets overshadowing the gate were no help either; on the wrong side of the wall, inaccessible from the slums.

The Prince and the guards fought ruthlessly in a red haze kicked up by their antics, brutally chopping down anything that came too close, but it was clear they were close to being overwhelmed by the nightmares' unceasing numbers and fearless savagery.

"Come on, I see the gate!" the urchin hollered.

29

Ban-Hodre

"There it is."

"There what is?"

"The town we were just talking about – Ban-Hodre!"

"Oh, right yeah, I see it now. Let's hope it's better than Tchaipolis. I cannot stand another day of boredom like that."

"I would not hold your breath for any excitement," Terra advised practically.

Saul sighed in disappointment. "Bollocks."

Ban-Hodre waited, straight in front of them, at the end of the long, flat road. Saul had never been so bored in his life. Travelling anywhere in the Highlands was a challenge and an adventure even before one reached a destination, but here in the Lowlands voyaging was uneventful, and the constant monotonous clopping of his normally-beloved Faafoor's hooves was driving him insane.

Looking up at the listless, cloudy sky that showed neither sun nor rain and then looking left and right at the rolling, hedge-lined fields of grass without so much as a tree to break their uniformity, he wondered if the tedium would ever end. He was certain it was not yet noon, and at the same time it felt like he had been trekking for eternity since dawn.

Ban-Hodre was a sprawling mass of stone houses without any defensive perimeters, unprotected by walls, a moat or even lookout towers. Saul was appalled by the settlement's lax security, while Terra laughed at the Prince's expression of mixed shock and contempt, well knowing that the town had little to fear. Pirates and Goblins rarely raided far inland, and the Flatlands had been at peace for more than fifty years now since the last Justiquan Crusade.

Nobody challenged the duo or their purpose as they abandoned the road and started up the central street through town, and Saul looked around in perplexity, wishing someone would accost him for the town's safety's sake. No one did, and any Flatlanders that they did meet – walking, loitering or manning the stalls lining the street – regarded them with wide, unblinking eyes and gave them wide berth, pointing and whispering.

The Highlanders ignored them and continued along the straight, paved avenue until they were so deep in the town that Saul could no longer see green fields anywhere – only small allotments and gardens – and his joints began to twitch in discomfort. He told himself it was no different to being at the top of Baldr's Safe, surrounded by rock, but it felt different. Baldr's Safe was home. This place was foreign to him, and although he would never admit it, he was unnerved by the strange ways of the Fringers.

The squat, grey buildings became larger and more crammed as the duo neared the town's centre, where the Thane's slate-roofed manor was easily distinguishable as the largest of them all, separated from the others by a ring of bountiful, neat gardens, which were in turn encapsulated by a spiked, iron fence. Saul nodded; here, at last, was some common sense.

Dismounting outside the spiked gate and looking in on the flowery gardens dotted with firs, oaks, cedars, birches and spruces and the grey stone manor they half-hid, Terra said to Saul, "This is Thane Umbrich's manor. From all I have heard of the man, you will like him well."

"From all I have seen of Flatlanders, I will not," the Prince disagreed.

"Well, me must pay our respects now we are here, regardless," said Terra pragmatically. "Knock."

Saul raised his hand towards a round knocker, but before he could touch it, a Flatlander in neat, black and white attire rushed out from the manor and ran along a lawn-bordered path across the gardens towards them, waving his hands. Two boys in drab brown that smelled of dung stumbled along in his wake.

"Prince Saul Aodhson, I presume!" the man shouted, drawing up on the other side of the gate, tugging a large keyring free of his belt and sorting through the many keys, one by one. "We were not expecting you so soon – you mustn't have slept to have made such good time!"

"I slept," said Saul, stroking his stallion's nose, "but Faafoor here is fast."

"He must be," said the out-of-breath, friendly little man, finally finding the key he required, sliding it into place with a click, turning it with a crunch and swinging open the gates with a whining creak. "Welcome, Prince, to Thane Umbrich's manor. I am the head butler here. My name is Farquhar. May I know the name of your companion for the sake of introductions?"

"This is Terra," complied the Prince shortly. "What is a butler?"

Farquhar's balding, grey-haired head bobbed. "A servant."

"And a servant is a slave you pay, right?"

"Mmm, not quite …"

Saul shook his head and rubbed his beard. "You people are strange," he said, unable to understand such luxuries and laziness. "Where is Umbrich?"

"If you will pass your mounts to the stable boys there and follow me, I will lead you to him."

They entered the manor and found it to be quite spartan. It was filled with essentials like furniture, but little ornamentation, wood-panelled for the most part with varicoloured rugs warming the floor. Saul was warming to the Thane already.

Following the butler, they found the man in his armoury; a circular room with a large round open space in the centre, surrounded by a ringing stone bench broken only twice, on opposite sides, to allow entrance. The floor was polished pine, and the walls – covered in the same wood – were covered with weaponry, hung on brass hooks.

Saul warmed further to Umbrich as he looked upon the range of rare arms. From golden-hilted swords to jewelled daggers to flamboyant halberds to massive tridents to fancy, multi-headed flails to spiky maces to two-headed battle axes to giant claymores, the Thane had almost every type of melee weapon imaginable.

Umbrich himself was walking around the room with his hands clasped behind his straight back when they entered. He was a short, senescent man with frizzy black hair and a patchy beard, dressed in a black shirt and doublet and black trousers and boots.

When he spotted them, an excited smile wrung his puffy, pocked face. He shuffled around the stone bench hurriedly to meet them, leaning on an oaken cane and extending his hand to be shaken long in advance of reaching them. He had about him a nervous energy, Saul thought, like he was always on edge, ready to run away at the slightest fright. Such a strange collection for such a man, thought the Prince, regarding the walls. He doubted Umbrich could lift half the weapons on display.

"Prince Saul Aodhson, I presume!" the Thane hailed them heartily in his natural falsetto, and when he finally shook the Highlander's hand, it felt to Saul like greeting a child. "It is so good to meet you. I have been looking forward to this for a long time! Your father does me great honour by sending his sons to meet me on their quest for maturity, and I like to think that I can be of help to you young warriors."

Saul doubted that, but he liked the man's optimism.

"How was your journey?" the Thane enquired.

"Long and flat," responded the Prince in a low monotone.

"Haha, yes, your brothers never much cared for the terrain, either.

You will tell Aodh and his sons that I wish them all hale health and bonny sons when you return, won't you, my boy?"

"I will pass on the message," the Highlander assured him, while Farquhar the butler snuck away to stand by the entrance, out of the way but nearby should he be needed. "And he asked me to wish you and your sons the heartiest of health in return." A bald-faced lie, but Saul was starting to get used to diplomacy.

"Thank you, thank you. Now, pray tell, who is this divine beauty by your side?"

Saul chuckled. "This wench is my travelling companion, Terra Dax."

Terra struck him on the arm when he called her wench and then shook the Thane's hand with a perfunctory smile. "It is a pleasure to meet you, Thane Umbrich. Thank you for your hospitality."

"What an enchanting creature!" Umbrich marvelled, kissing her hand once he had hold of it. "Forgive my curious nature, Prince, but your brothers have all come to Ban-Hodre with a large, warrior bodyguard. Why do you travel with a woman?"

"My brothers were appointed their companions by the King, as was I," Saul answered, not offended, because he too had wondered the same. "You would have to ask him why he chose as he did."

"I am as competent a warrior as any man," Terra put in heatedly.

The Thane hurried to agree with her and put up his hands in surrender. "As you say, as you say, I have no doubt. Speaking of a warrior's competence, Prince, I am sure that you – like your brothers – are bored by this point in your trip, are you not?"

Saul was taken aback. "Err …"

Umbrich chuckled at his transparency. "It is okay, my boy, it's quite alright. I know that you young Highlanders crave action, and I know that by the time you have visited a few of the other Thanes, you are ready to drop from the tedium! Well, my boy, I am here to tell you that the Flatlands are not all talk and no play. I am here to redeem your trip. We're going to have some fun today!

"I have been preparing for your visit for a while, and I know just the thing to put some spring back in your step. That is why I have organised a tournament." Saul's eyes lit up at the word, and Umbrich smiled. "You will test your mettle against my guardsmen – and anyone else brave enough to step into the ring. How does that sound?"

"Sounds perfect!" the Highlander enthused, baring his teeth in a broad smile. "Thanks, Umbrich, you really know how to welcome a guest."

"Pish tosh, it's my pleasure, it really is," said the beaming Thane. "I love watching the finest warriors in Fjelburg battle it out for pride and glory.

Now, we will need a short time – say a couple of hours – to set up the area and ready the combatants," he continued, waving at Farquhar, who turned and hurried out of the room to make preparations. "In the meantime, you would do me great honour if you would accept one of these weapons as a gift from me, in honour of your maturity, Prince." He swung his arms to encompass the walls.

"Oh, no thank you," said the Prince immediately, patting the weapons at his belt. "I have these axes that I forged myself and a claymore waiting for me back at Baldr's Safe, so I have everything I need."

Terra obviously thought he was being rude, because she stamped on his toes, making him huff and stare daggers at her.

"Surely," Umbrich was saying meanwhile, "a warrior can always benefit from another weapon?"

"Not if it just weighs him down," Saul began, but Terra stamped on him again, cutting him off.

"He would be honoured," she said.

"I couldn't possibly accept such a treasure," Saul contradicted tactfully, waving his hands.

"Please, I insist," Umbrich wheedled.

"I would not want to break up such a wonderful collection," the Prince tried.

"Please," begged Umbrich, "it would warm my heart to know that a Prince of Fjelburg is out there in the world, using my weapon not only to survive, but to protect our country and to make it a better place for us all to live."

"Really?" asked Saul sceptically. "Any weapon?"

"Any one you like!"

"Ugh, very well." Stamp. "Ow! Stop that! I'm taking a bloody weapon, woman! Now then, let me see what we've got here …"

As Umbrich had been doing when they entered, the Prince began to slowly amble around the edge of the room, favouring one foot. He longed for a large, fearsome weapon like a glaive, but practically he knew he did not want to lug such a heavy weapon around the entirety of the Flatlands, hence why he had left his claymore at home. He decided he needed something smaller, and he already had axes, so there was no need for more of the same.

Swords, daggers, maces, flails … The multi-headed flail caught his interest; a short, thick, black handle linked to a short chain, which linked to three more chains which all ended in a morningstar-style mace head covered in spikes. He grabbed it off the wall and hefted it; it was not too heavy. He turned away from the wall and swung it a few times experimentally, enjoying the humming whistle the weapon made with each attack and imagining the havoc the spiky heads could wreak. He looked up from the weapon to the Thane, who was watching him in awe. "I will take this one, if that's okay."

"Of course, of course," exclaimed Umbrich, clapping his hands together. "A handsome weapon for a handsome Prince. Now, I have a feast awaiting us in the dining hall, but perhaps you would like to train with your new flail before the tournament? You would do me great honour by using my armoury as your training ground and allowing me to watch."

Saul looked at the central, circular space. It would suffice, he supposed. "Very well," he concurred. "I *would* like to practise with this thing, anyway. Terra, up for some sparring?"

"Any time," she said, drawing her longsword and hefting her shield with a trace of a smile.

Saul moved into the central circle in the room and she followed, crouching to mimic his fighting stance. They circled one another, their lips tweaked up in good humour.

Saul charged in, waving his flail in a quick arc to come down at Terra's head, but she blocked overhead with her shield, and the mace-heads thudded down on the wood loudly. Even as they did, she stabbed out with her sword, and Saul had to sidestep to avoid taking a hit, wrenching his flail up and around as he did so to swipe at his companion from the side.

With her shield on the wrong side, Terra had to spin to use it to block the attack and, from there, she kept spinning to lash out with her sword at head height. She hit nothing when Saul ducked. She had to leap back when he tugged his weapon back to him and then lashed out and up at her. He followed the flail and used its momentum to swing it back around as he moved to launch a diagonal overhead assault, which Terra blocked as he had expected.

Having not used too much effort in the swing, however, he was able to whip the flail around quickly over his own head to attack from the opposite side. Spinning away from the attack, Terra cut at the flail with her blade in the hopes of parrying it away from her, but instead she severed a link. A spiked ball and chain clattered loudly to the floor and rolled with a noise like a growl under the bench.

Saul, however, was in battle mode now, and a minor loss was not enough to distract him. He did not falter in his attack, but swept the two-headed flail wide and low to attack Terra's legs on her shield side. She blocked with the shield and slashed down at the flail again, cutting its main chain, so that its two remaining heads thudded down and rolled away with chains clinking. The Prince was left standing forlornly, holding a black handle at the end of which dangled a short length of broken chain.

Terra put her blade to his throat, unable to keep a straight face. "Do you yield, Prince?" she asked, her lips flickering and her cheeks bunching.

He sighed, dropped the handle and looked at Umbrich with a disapproving frown, before turning back to his companion. "Yes, Terra," he said, "I yield – but only because I was poorly armed! Don't let this victory go to your head."

"I wouldn't dream of it," she murmured as her grin fully bloomed, lowering her sword.

"Your weapons are no good, Thane," Saul called to Umbrich, waving at the fragmented remains of the flail on the floor.

Blushing, Umbrich, on the other side of the bench, said quickly, "Oh, I am so sorry about that, Prince! I have tried to build an admirable collection here, but evidently the flail was valued higher than its worth. Please, choose another – with my blessing."

"No, thank you," refused Saul flatly. "They all look more ceremonial than practical. I will use my axes and show you how I fight."

He tugged the twin axes out of his belt and hefted them. Each was blade-heavy, but felt perfectly balanced in his practised hands. On each of the bearded axes, a short wooden haft held a curved blade on one side counterbalanced by a small but deadly spike on the other. Terra gripped her sword and shield tighter in anticipation of the whirlwind to come.

"Ready, Terra?"

"Ready."

Saul initiated combat again, leaping in with axes swinging to chop one after another into Terra's upraised shield. She lashed out low with her blade, but Saul was slippery as an eel and had danced away already to her right to chop low at her unshielded side.

She spun fast, parrying one axe with her sword and barely deflecting the other with her shield in time. She was left no time for a counterattack, because Saul's first axe was already swinging again. She leapt back from a body swipe, leaned back from a head swipe, ducked under another and pivoted around the Prince in time to block an axe on her shield.

The other axe was swinging slightly wide, so she did the unexpected and pushed forward on her shield against the first axe, barging into the Prince, putting the danger of the swinging axe behind her and making him stumble back. Taking advantage of his temporary lack of balance, Terra began her own attack, swinging her sword in tight arcs on either side of her body, bashing with her shield relentlessly to force the desperately parrying Prince back until his legs hit the stone bench and he almost fell over backwards. Throwing himself into a sideways roll, the Prince saved himself but had no time to take the offensive when he came up to his feet, because Terra was already in striking distance again, hammering at him with sword and shield.

She was fierce, he had to admit, but not infallible. He dropped down suddenly on his haunches, his loose straw hair flying up in his wake to be cut by Terra's whistling blade. From there, he leaned back and shot out a foot to kick her in the lead shin. Had they been in real combat, the Prince knew he would have gone for her knee and likely broken it. As it was, she yelped and toppled over forwards, but his plan backfired when she landed on top of him and almost clove his skull in two with her blade. She stopped herself from doing so by punching him in the chest with her pommel and hilt instead, the blade halting an inch from his creased forehead.

Wheezing, red-faced and sore, Saul let go of his axes, threw Terra off him and rolled over, clutching his chest and coughing weakly. He looked up through watering eyes to see Terra and Umbrich regarding him in apprehension, and he could well understand why.

The Stonebrow temper was infamous. If any of his brothers had lost a public bout, their fury would have risen on wings of vengeance to a bloody sky. Often called berserkers, some of the brothers could not have tolerated such a dent in their honour – even from a sparring match – and would have demanded that the matter be settled in a duel to the death.

Though Saul's blood boiled, his stomach clenched deathly tight, his vision hazed in red, and his heart hammered his ribs like a war drum demanding retribution, he did not want to be like his brothers. His father had the same infamous streak of temper, and when Saul had been young, the King had frightened him with such displays on numerous occasions. He had seen how people feared his father and how such fear interfered with camaraderie, and he had decided at a young age that he would be different.

Part of his brain roared at him that Terra had almost killed him – that she needed to be dealt with – but another part of his brain said calmly that he had to expect such mishaps when sparring, that her fall had been his fault, and that – other than a bruise – there was nothing to be angry about, because he was alive. He chose to listen to this latter voice, though it was a struggle, he had to admit. He reminded himself – to salve his pride – that he always held back; that he was never as fast or as strong in sparring as in real combat, especially when fighting Terra, for he had no wish to hurt her.

Forcing a smile, he croaked, "Thought I had you for a second there, Terra. You had some nice moves."

Terra and Umbrich visibly relaxed, and the former said, "Thank you, Prince. You did, too. Sorry about hitting you."

Saul sat up and stopped rubbing his aching chest. "It's okay. I don't think you meant to, and the alternative would have been to kill me. Besides, it was partly my fault. I think my move needs some work."

"Maybe," agreed Terra with the ghost of a smile, offering a hand.

"Well, that was just incredible," applauded Umbrich. "You were so fast! Thank you so much for letting me watch – and again, I am sorry about the flail – but now I just cannot wait for the tournament! I haven't been this excited in months! What a display of skill!"

"Where exactly will the tournament take place?" Saul asked, climbing slowly to his feet with Terra's help, scooping up his axes and tucking them into his belt, haft-first.

"In the marketplace in the centre of the town," responded Umbrich happily, "where all can see and any can participate – one at a time, of course. Shall we go see how preparations are coming along?"

"Yeah, and let's get some food," Saul agreed.

30

The Tournament

Chicken bone in hand, Saul followed Thane Umbrich to Ban-Hodre's humble marketplace; a grand open space normally filled with people, livestock and stalls that had, this day, been cleared out for the special event.

Houses ringed the open space, as did an avid crowd patrolled by a ring of leather-garbed guards. Past the mob of people hollering for the entertainment to begin and the soldiers trying to keep the peace, they glimpsed Farquhar the butler overseeing the simple preparations. A red circle five yards wide was being painted on the pavement over the faint outline of an old crimson ring. A large, decoratively carved, wooden chair awaited the Thane's rump, and there were smaller chairs for the cronies that followed him around like so many shadows. A regiment of men – unarmoured soldiers from their bearing and tight ranks, Saul guessed – stood still and silent nearby, lit by one of a few dots of light that peeked through the cloud veil.

"It's almost ready!" Umbrich, who stood beside them, had to yell to be heard over the rising hubbub of the masses.

It looked to Saul like half the town was in attendance. At least two hundred people were packed into the marketplace, he guessed. He smiled grimly.

"Then, who is first?" he shouted back, biting into the chicken leg and savouring the warm meat on his tongue.

Not long later, the chicken was eaten, the ring was painted, the crowds were heaving, the clouds were pouring, and Saul stood alone in the scarlet ring in only his grey trousers, leather boots and red tunic rolled up to the sleeves, the fabric becoming darker and darker as it was splotched with increasingly heavy rain. His face was as flat, hard and expressionless as stone. His long, straw hair was tied tightly back in a ponytail, his jaw was set beneath his thatch of beard, and in his mighty, calloused hands were his axes.

He went through some gentle exercises, sweeping his feet around and looping his weapons about him in glittering arcs to loosen his shoulders. His opponent stepped into the ring, carrying a sword and shield. He was the first of the ranked men; all the largest Saul had seen in the Flatlands. Not one was as tall as the Prince, however, who towered over everyone present at more than seven feet tall, his bulk immediately recognisable as that of the only Highlander man there.

"Hello," Saul greeted his opponent amicably, holding both axes in one hand in order to extend the other. "What is your name, my friend?"

"My name is Peter Borgen, and it is my honour to fight you today, Prince Aodhson," the man said, shaking the proffered hand in as tight a grip as he could manage, and yet still squeaking in pain at the tightness of the Stonebrow's grip.

"Nice to meet you, Peter, and it will be my honour to fight you as well."

As they separated, Umbrich – now sat in his grand wooden chair, segregated from the peasantry by the ring of guards – shouted out in his high, warbling voice, "Quiet! Quiet! I will have quiet! You – quiet there!" The palaver lessened.

"Ahem," the Thane cleared his throat, before continuing, "today, good townspeople, we are graced by the presence of a rare guest. Prince Saul Aodhson, seventeenth son of King Aodh Stonebrow, like his brothers, has come to visit our quaint town at the time of his maturity. In his honour, we will hold a martial tournament in which he will take centre-stage, pitting the legendary talents of the Stonebrow sons against Ban-Hodre's finest. The winner of each bout will fight on in the next, until all combatants have participated. Prepare, my good people, for a display of skill so dazzling you will rue the moment you blinked! The first from the Flatlands to challenge the Prince is Peter Borgen. Peter, are you ready and willing to begin?"

"Yes, Thane!"

"Prince Saul, are you ready and willing to begin?"

"Aye, Thane!"

"Excellent!" Umbrich clapped his hands together. "The fight will be to yield, to knock out, or to first blood. We do not want any fatalities today, but accidents can happen and you are both aware of this, yes, combatants?"

"Yes, Thane!" they answered in unison.

"Grand! Then, I hereby announce the tournament of the year 311 AC begun." The crowd was silent, holding their breath in excitement. "Combatants – fight!"

Peter Borgen was a young man in his prime with light blonde hair, strong and fast and experienced in combat, but he dared not charge the younger Prince. He circled the bigger man warily, watching how he moved and watching the twin axes rise and fall with each prowling step.

Saul was not a patient man, however, and he quickly took the offensive, swinging one axe down on the right – which Peter blocked with his shield – and then the other down on the left. Peter swung away from the second blow and then pivoted back to jab his sword at the Prince's chest, but Saul parried the blade away with his right-hand axe held head-down and then whipped the blade back past the other's throat, aiming for his shoulder so as not to kill him.

Peter swayed away again, barely avoiding a cut, and then threw his weight forwards behind his shield. Since Terra had tried a similar tactic earlier, however, Saul was on lookout for it and as soon as he saw the other's shoulder bunch, he swivelled, spinning around the barging shield to the right and elbowing Peter in the back of the head as he rushed past. The Flatlander went down with a splash, and Saul placed a heavy boot on his back.

"Do you yield, Peter?" asked Aodhson.

"I yield," Peter rasped, coughing in the wet grime that covered the paving.

"Prince Saul is the winner!" Umbrich declared loudly, throwing his arms up in the air in jubilation.

The volume of the crowd's cheers was boggling to the Prince; he could not hear himself think and was grateful that the people had been quiet during the fight itself. Nevertheless, he forced himself to smile and wave at the overwhelming mass of small folk surrounding him, all standing in the rain, bellowing at the top of their lungs and waving until their arms cramped. Meanwhile, Peter's comrades helped their friend to his feet and out of the ring.

"Who will be next to step into the ring?" the Thane asked, yelling over the multitude.

The next man entered in Peter's wake; a bullish man with a shaved head and bushy beard wielding a spear.

"Hello friend," said Saul, panting only slightly. "What is your name?"

"Hello, Prince. I am Astelvart, and it is my honour to participate in this tournament today."

"Nice to meet you, Astelvart, and an honour to fight you."

They shook hands and looked to the Thane.

"Combatants, begin!" cried Umbrich.

Astelvart was more headstrong than Peter. He bulled at Saul, water spraying from his heels, seeking to skewer the Prince on his spear, but Saul batted the spear away and twirled to the side, before sweeping in close for an attack. The Flatlander retracted his spear in time to use the haft to parry an axe, but then a second axe jabbed at his stomach and he leapt back to avoid being hit.

Not giving him time to bring his spear to bear, Saul charged in, swinging low only to spin and hit high, then dart to the side, swipe a blow at the man's middle and then cleave low and high again. Saul continued this fast attack pattern, switching lead foot and axe, noting after its first usage that Astelvart barely kept up, and – sure enough – when he repeated the strategy, the spearman faltered. Saul's axe slipped past his upper defences, careening towards his unprotected skull. Seeing this, the Prince managed to twist his weapon at the last instant, so that he struck the man on the head with the flat of the blade with a clunk like planks knocking together, laying him low and rendering him immediately unconscious.

"Saul is the winner!" Umbrich announced joyfully, and the crowd went wild, celebrating the Stonebrow Prince.

Saul grinned and raised his axes victoriously, hearing the patter of the rain again over the patter of his heart in his ears. Though the opponents were far from difficult, this was the most fun he had encountered in the Flatlands.

"Who dares to be next?" piped the Thane.

An older man with long, grizzled hair and a short beard stepped forward from the ranks into the ring, holding a ridge-headed mace and a dagger. "I am Yatzpah," he declared in a strong voice, "and I will gladly take up this challenge!"

"Hello, Yatzpah," said Saul with a haggard smile. "Let's see what you've got."

"Combatants, begin!"

Yatzpah hurled the dagger at Saul's arm, seeking to nick his flesh and so win the bout in a quick and underhanded manner, but the Stonebrow son had fast reflexes. Saul swayed and the dagger flew past him, luckily falling short of the crowd and skidding with a loud, scraping noise – easily heard in the sudden hush – to a stop at their feet.

Saul looked from the dagger to the man with grizzled hair. "Oh, Yatzpah," he said ominously, crouching into a fighting stance once more, "that was foolish – to endanger lives over a bit of sport. I will be happy to show you the error of your ways."

Yatzpah gulped and brandished his mace. Saul leapt at him with axes hammering down hard, and though the older man blocked the twin blows with his mace held horizontal, he staggered back under their force. He just managed to block an axe swinging at his side, but then the Prince's lashing foot caught him in the back of the leg and he fell to his back with a thud and a grunt.

Saul stamped on his mace arm, pinning it and making the man cry out in pain. Then, he crouched down low and held his axe blade to the man's throat, which silenced his moans as quick as a cut.

Saul looked into the man's eyes and growled, "Be careful in future. Some things are not worth the risk, understand?"

"Yes, yes, Prince," Yatzpah breathed. "Sorry, Prince."

"That's okay," said Saul in a gentler tone, but then he used the axe blade at the man's throat to cut a shallow line in his chest, which welled with blood while Yatzpah hissed. The Prince stood up and took his foot off the Flatlander's arm, showing the crowd and the Thane the blood on his axe.

"Saul is the winner!"

The audience's cheers shook the ground the Prince stood on, he was sure of it, and he could not help but join in their merriment. It felt good to make so many people cheer, he thought. Meanwhile, Yatzpah – clutching his arm and moaning in pain – was half-lifted, half-dragged from the ring by his comrades, leaving a trail of smeared blood that was soon pocked with clear spots as the rain slowly washed it away.

"Who will stand in the ring next?"

A dark-haired man with hair no longer than his stubble advanced into the ring confidently, performing for the crowd as he did so, throwing his muscular arms in the air and brandishing his broadsword ferociously.

After the start of the fight was signalled, Saul battered the man to his knees in seconds and then kneed him in the face, making his nose crack audibly and squirt blood. The man sprawled on the flagstones, squealing and then shouting angrily about cheating and unfairness. The Prince thought he was going to have to put the man down again, but his opponent saw the look in his eye and stalked away, clutching his nose and muttering curses under his breath.

Saul was panting now, and sweat patches were beginning to show under his armpits. The breaks between bouts had become dreamlike, joyous respites from the labour of swinging his axes, but he would not give up. He had defeated four already, and only six more stood waiting.

The next man to step into the painted ring with the Prince was Harold Marvill; a big man with red hair, a protruding gut and a single-bladed axe not unlike Saul's. Saul was surprised to find that, despite his size, Harold was a fierce fighter and faster than expected. The bat and clatter of axe haft on axe haft resonated throughout the marketplace like the clopping of a horse's hooves as Harold held his own against Saul's initial assault, and the young Prince realised he was fighting a wily warrior.

Harold never moved far, but he would spin around the Prince when attacked and bump him with his bulk as he did so to knock him off-balance, before retaliating in a flash like lightning. More than once, Saul barely avoided the nick of the other's axe by twisting his body uncomfortably and cracking his spine, only to throw a savage attack back and find it blocked or dodged.

A smile slowly and inexorably contorted Saul's face, and he felt like a madman grinning in the face of death, but he could not stop. He could spare no thought for his appearance when all his efforts were focussed on the fight and so he fought on, exhilaration flushing his senses, his mind and muscles working in euphoric tandem, his skin tingling and his eyes wide. As the Prince's excitement rose, so did his power and speed.

While Harold was tiring with every passing second, he could swear that the young Stonebrow was getting stronger. Each blow was heavier and faster than the last, harder to block or even see coming. After only a couple of minutes, the senior man's advantage had faded, his stamina spent, his reserves depleted.

Saul, on the other hand, radiated energy like the sun, bounding around the other man on his tiptoes with his axes flashing out as fast as striking snakes. Their axe hafts made a staccato rapping at first, but as Harold tired, the sound of his huffing became more telling. Having given up on a finishing blow for the time being, the Prince had decided to wear the man down with a relentless battering from all angles. It worked and soon, as Harold slowed, Saul started to notice openings where a finishing attack could be attempted. He let the first few of these slide in case the sly soldier was trying to trick him, but when Harold almost slipped over in the wet, Saul knew victory was within his grasp.

Feinting and springing around his opponent, the Prince attacked from the side and – when he was blocked – spun in close around the block, using his body as Harold had done to him. He elbowed the Flatlander soundly on his forehead, seeing as he did so that the older man's swinging fist had been mere inches away from his face. Even in defeat, Harold had almost won. Standing over him, Saul pointed his right-hand axe at his foe.

"Do you yield?" he asked.

Harold smiled weakly as he sat up and rubbed his forehead. "Yes, I yield. Do you have rocks under your skin, Prince? You hit like a hammer!"

Saul's stern face relaxed into a wide grin, and his eyes lit up as he offered his hand. "Haha, thank you, Harold. That was a lot of fun. You are a very talented fighter. I almost lost a few times there."

As Harold took the Prince's hand and was pulled up, he said, chuckling, "Maybe, but you did well, Prince. Congratulations on your victory. The better man won. I hope that we can share a horn of ale when this is all over."

"Well, fetch the horns and the ale and let us not leave it to hope, my friend!"

"Haha!"

Umbrich's reedy voice reached them, announcing, "The mighty Saul Aodhson is the winner once again, bringing his total count to an amazing five victories! Have you ever seen such a powerful young man? Have you ever seen such a display of strength and skill?"

The crowd cheered wildly, and Umbrich smiled. "We are going to take a brief break from the festivities now to recoup. Empty your bladders and fill your cups and bellies! The tournament resumes in one hour!"

Saul used half the time to sit and stuff as much food down his throat as his body could handle – enough to put a dent in Ban-Hodre's reserves and a clink in her pocket – and half the time to excrete. He had a few minutes to spare and shouldered through the army of well-wishers back to the central space kept clear by the guards, where he found Terra, who had eaten a little with him and then returned to the ring to wait patiently like a statue for the tournament to begin again. The downpour had only grown heavier in the intermittence, Saul noticed.

"Hey, Terra, what did you think of the tournament so far?" he asked, drawing to a stop by her side.

"You have fought well, Prince," she stated, still looking at the red circle, "especially when you overcompensated for the overconfidence of the man with the broadsword."

"When I over-what?" Saul asked, confused, looking at her profile.

She sighed, but her lips flicked up slightly. "When you fought twice as hard against the arrogant man, because you worried his arrogance was well-founded," she explained.

"Yeah, well," he rumbled, reaching up to scratch the back of his neck in an awkward voluntary motion, "better safe than sorry, eh?"

"Indeed, like I said, you did well. Harold Marvill was a worthy foe."

"He was, wasn't he?" agreed Saul, pleased by the memory. "It is a little comforting to know there are men of valour wherever I go."

"Not everywhere," Terra murmured lowly.

"What?" Saul asked.

"Nothing. You have food stains on your shirt. Looks like you found another spicy chicken, am I right?"

"I like chicken – ain't nothing wrong with that."

Terra sighed and shook her head at the Prince's grammatical skills. While she was trying and failing to impart to him valuable information about verbose double-negatives and their redundancies, Thane Umbrich found them and approached with timid step.

"Excuse me, excuse me, Prince, err – my lady," he interrupted them. "I was wondering if you are ready to continue the tournament?"

"Ready when you are, Umbrich," replied Saul vigorously, clapping the Thane on the shoulder and almost knocking him to his knees.

"Excellent, excellent. Very well then, I will get things underway." Umbrich hurried off to his cushioned chair. Once sat, slaked and comfortable, he called, "Gather round, good people, gather round!" He turned his head slightly to mutter to the guard Captain by his side to maintain strict control of the masses. "It is time for the tournament to resume!"

"Be careful out there," Terra said as Saul turned to leave.

He turned back and looked into her eyes, grinning cheekily. "Aren't I always?" She rolled her eyes at that.

Saul's first opponent when the tournament continued was a rangy man named Deren with short brown hair and a scar on his cheek. He walked into the ring with mace and shield, batting the two together to get pumped up.

"Combatants, fight!" Umbrich yelled.

The rangy man was cautious and had a solid defence, using the shield to good effect and constantly moving so as never to be pinned down by the Highlander, lashing out with his spiky mace only if he saw an opportunity. Saul hated Deren's patient tactics, but he could not help but admire their results. He had hit nothing but shield and mace so far. He could hear Terra calling for him to be patient and wait for the perfect opportunity, but although he hated to expend too much effort when he still had several bouts remaining, he decided against patience.

Charging like a bull, he swung his right axe in a vicious arc at the man's head, which was blocked by a shield. Though Deren tried to counterattack, his mace was smacked aside as soon as it was in view, the Highlander's axe biting into the thick haft and embedding there. Both men were thrown off-balance by this turn of events, but neither released their grip. Axe pushed against mace, and shield pushed against axe in a heave for supremacy for a moment, until the Prince heard Terra again over his drumming pulse and the swish of the rain.

"You're fighting like a buffoon, Prince!" she was shouting. "Use your brain, not just your muscles!"

Smiling ruefully, Saul realised that she was right. He released the pressure on his left axe and swung around so that the mace, with the axe attached, swung aimlessly to his left. Determined to keep hold of his weapon, Deren fell prey to Saul's clubbing fist when it let go of the axe entirely. Poleaxed and bleeding, Deren blinked up at the drizzling sky in bafflement.

"Prince Saul is the winner!" Umbrich declared, and the crowd verbalised their joy in a raucous roar.

Saul nodded weary thanks to Terra, who shook her head, glowering.

The Prince's following opponent was a thickset man with sword and shield. Saul was getting tired of fighting against shielded men and would have loved to batter them into submission with a simple show of strength, but he could not have Terra scowl at him all the way home. So, he endeavoured to perform better, more strategically, this bout.

Springing up and down on his tiptoes and ignoring the burn in his legs, Saul readied himself. The thickset man stepped into the ring, and a similar dance began to those that had gone before, the other testing Saul cautiously with feints and jabs from behind his shield, while the Highlander grew testy dodging half-hearted stabs and slamming his axes against wood.

Saul danced around the man nimbly, weaving away from the sword and lashing out from all angles to keep the man spinning. He was still striking the shield, but now the other was tiring and growing dizzy. The Prince's opponent tried to sidestep away and put himself against the edge of the ring so that Saul could not encircle him. The Highlander did not let up, springing from left to right and back again to overpower the man with the speed of his axes, which left gleaming arcs in the air for a brief moment before splintering the defending shield a little more with each bite of their blades.

The thickset man slipped up, misplacing his sword for a block in tiredness, and the Prince's axe sailed past it towards the man's leg. Saul tried to retract the axe to lessen the devastation of the blow, but he still shuddered as he felt the tip of the blade scrape against the man's shin bone. While his opponent collapsed, screaming and clutching his bloody leg, and was subsequently dragged out of the ring, Saul raised his arms tiredly to the whoops of the saturated masses ringing the marketplace. Terra nodded to him expressionlessly.

After a brief moment to catch his breath, Saul was pitted against a thin, bald spear-wielder, whose jab was fast, but whose weapon was weak. The Prince trapped the spear under his arm precipitously and cut through the haft with a single chop, at which time his opponent backed away and shouted loudly, "Yield! I yield!"

"Are you ready to continue, Prince?" Umbrich shouted to him over the noise of the rain.

There were only two foes remaining and the afternoon was waning, so Saul nodded wearily. "Send in the next, Umbrich!"

His next opponent was a swarthy, hairy man who looked like he had wolf fur growing out of his face and who carried a heavy wooden club.

"I am Yurgen," the club-wielder growled, "and it will be my pleasure to show you how the Flatlanders fight, Prince."

"Let's do this," Saul rumbled.

Yurgen was a muscular behemoth amongst Flatlanders, but he could not intimidate or overshadow a Highland Prince. His club swings were slow, but weighty and sweeping enough that Saul had to leap back out of the weapon's range often, unable to block or dodge closer. Darting around the ring like a caged panther, Saul evaded the hefty club swings and watched for his chance, his axes flicking out now and again when he spied a brief gap in the other's defences, but never landing a blow.

His opponent was surprisingly flexible in bending his body around the Highlander's attacks, but he was not infallible. When Yurgen was too slow in lifting his weapon overhead for a downwards blow across the body, Saul lunged under the swing and rolled smoothly to his feet, gratefully hearing the hum of the club behind him as he flicked a wrist and nicked the Fringer's calf with an axe.

"Saul is the winner!" Umbrich cried quickly, excited by the speed of it all.

Yurgen either forgot the rules in his eagerness for battle or else did not care, because he swung his club at Saul again. The Highlander – not expecting the blow – tried to dodge, but was too late and took a glancing blow to the shoulder that staggered him. The crowd booed and hissed, but neither combatant heard them.

Saul thought Yurgen was going to bash out his brains for a moment when the man came at him with club raised high, but then fiery-haired Terra appeared in front of him. She parried Yurgen's club to the side with her shield and had the tip of her sword at his throat before he could blink. Once in that situation, however, all he could do was blink and gulp, which was unfortunate, because every time he gulped his throat pressed sorely on the tip of her blade.

"The fight is over," Terra told him forcefully. "Go home before I do something I regret."

Yurgen came to his senses and slowly backed away with the tip of his club dragging on the ground. "I am sorry, Prince," he called ashamedly. "I lost my head. I hope I did not hurt you."

He turned to walk away, his cheeks burning, but the Prince halted him with a call that cut easily through the tense silence strung across the marketplace.

"Yurgen!" said Saul, and the man turned around nervously to watch the Highlander approach. The Prince offered his hand, and Yurgen shook it, looking into the younger man's eyes wonderingly. "That was a good fight, thank you, my friend."

"You are not mad?" asked the Flatlander, blinking rain from his eyes.

Saul smiled. "We all make mistakes, Yurgen. No, I am not mad. No one is seriously hurt and the rain has stopped. All is well. Do not beat yourself up. Go with the Gods."

"You too, Prince," said the man earnestly. "May they watch over you."

"As they do us all."

They parted ways while the crowd noisily celebrated the amicable ending, freed from the web of awkwardness that had ensnared them all. Terra offered Saul a cup of water, which he guzzled in a heartbeat.

"Are you ready, Prince Saul?" asked Umbrich, shouting from a short distance.

"Born ready," the Prince assured him with a wave.

"Excellent!" the Thane exclaimed, clapping his hands and turning his attention to the crowd. "Then, good people, may I present you with the last of the planned bouts of the tournament. Today, Prince Saul Aodhson will do battle with the Champion of Ban-Hodre – Garric the Bludgeoner!"

31

Tar Feng's Tricks

Bala looked back; he could not help it. The Knights, Nomads, pirates and the rest were at the edge of the alleyway he had just left behind, hacking mercilessly at the corpses that were eating his erstwhile friend, Arak.

Tearing his gaze away once more before the tears could well, Bala saw that the monsters scrabbling and clawing their way across the square towards the Babese Prince and Princess had not yet noticed the newly arrived group behind them fortunately, but he was sure they did not have long before they would be spotted.

Bala almost screamed in fright as the old Tzunese man materialised next to him in a cloud of purple smoke with a small *poof* noise, but remembered at the last moment that he was surrounded by bloodsucking corpses and decided against it.

"How in the Nether did you do that?" Bala whispered, astonished.

The emaciated elder winked and grinned toothlessly. "Magic, my boy!"

Bala's breath caught in his throat; there was such a thing as magic, then? "Can't you just magic us all away from here then?"

Tar Feng shook his head, a gleam in his eye like madness. "No, no, I would never get far enough. I will need my energy for fighting back rather than running today, I think, my dirty little friend."

"What are these things?" the street boy demanded quickly and quietly, gesturing to the *Thakshir* and shaking his head to clear it of a dream of being a great Wizard.

"They are the undead. We call them *Thakshir*," replied the Wizard, glancing around for danger. "Magic monsters that infect everyone they kill with a bite. Chop off their limbs," he added with a knowing nod toward his companions.

Bala watched with the old man as the *pal skra* and the others made short work of the knot of *Thakshir* over his friend's body, severing each and every limb in bloody sprays before turning to fend off the grey skins who threw themselves at the living from the narrow alleyway, baring their teeth like animals and trying to sink them into exposed flesh.

"We have to get through that gate!" Bala swung away and pointed across the square at the great golden bars on the other side of the dozens of roaring, blackened undead. "I don't know why they haven't fled through it already," he muttered, brain racing wildly like a frightened stallion.

"Is it possible they are just stupid?" the hunched man asked brightly.

Bala ignored him, fingers pressed hard against his temples.

The smaller Knight, Fyrstsvard, stood in the alley mouth, the others of his group just behind him. He looked up from finishing off one *Thakshir* to witness dozens more appear at the end of his tunnel-like view down the backstreet.

"By me, brother!" he roared out.

Fyrstsvard held his ground in the alleyway, facing the cataleptic mass that swarmed at him like cockroaches skittering for cover, stiff-legged and jerky.

"I'm here, Svard!" Stein replied, before spinning from the swarm to bark out, "Izdaju, pirates – brace us!"

The Nomad and pirates set their shoulders against the Knights' backs, ready to take their weight. Stein turned back to the hungry undead, and he and Fyrstsvard stood shoulder to shoulder to block the alleyway, sweating beneath a peaking sun like a bronze shield.

"Shields up!" Stein bellowed just before the staggering, running corpses were upon them.

He and Fyrstsvard raised their shields and, together, created a small wall of sorts comprised of steel armour and shields to block the alley mouth, against which the furious wave of slobbering, moaning *Thakshir* smashed forcefully. Stein and Fyrstsvard were knocked back a step before the weight of the men behind gave them the strength to stand fast against the onslaught. They hacked as best they could over their shields with their blades, but could achieve little damage doing so, for even multiple wounds were a mere trifling concern to the desiccated undead. The best they could hope for was to buy time, but even as Fyrstsvard thought about it, his heart plummeted. There were *Thakshir* behind and ahead. They were not buying time to escape. They were buying their last breaths.

Amril stood in the relative calm between the *Thakshir* in front – who had not yet noticed them – and the Knights' position behind, surveying the scene surreally as if sure it must be a nightmare from which he would awaken. His white robe was speckled with dirt and blood. There was so much horror being perpetrated and so many dying for his sake, he thought sorrowfully with a kindling of self-hatred. The undead were following him to capture and kill him, and now hundreds of innocent bystanders were suffering because of where the Elf and his companions had chosen to run. The peace-loving Prophet was numbed to the core by the feeling that he had single-handedly doomed an entire city.

Meanwhile, Bala cowered to the side of the alley with Tar Feng, unmolested, looking more like a bloody corpse than a breathing boy as he twitched and jittered nervously, breathing through his mouth but unable to escape the blistering heat and abounding stench of decomposing flesh it augmented. There must be a reason the Prince and Princess had not yet fled, he thought frantically. Why had they not opened the gate? They must not have the key, he realised with a burst of inspiration – but if they did not have it, where could it be?

Then, it hit him. He scrambled over the corpse-strewn ground on all fours to avoid the attention of the monsters by the gate. The young thief reached the many dead bodies that surrounded Arak's decapitated carcass, gagging as he came near. The boy's body stank and wriggled slightly, even though it was split open like a rotten melon and eaten for the most part. Flies buzzed around the myriad wounds, settling and dispersing like a little black cloud. Bala barely controlled his recurrent urge to vomit, but searched through the strewn, writhing bodies until he found the headless royal guardsman who had killed his fellow Pincher moments before. The guard wore the same ceremonial armour as those that stood with the Prince, hacking down the undead who never stopped coming for their flesh.

Bala fumbled with the armour, his nostrils clogged with the stench, aware that time was a factor yet unable to undo the simple clasps with slick fingers and a mind frozen with terror. The corpse's incessant wobbling around, like an upturned turtle, did not help. Eventually, he got the clasps undone and yanked off the embossed breastplate. He then searched through the man's tunic and trousers as quickly as he could until he found what he was looking for.

He held it up in the air for all to see, shouting delightedly, "The key! The key! I've found the key for the gate!" It was a large, heavy golden key that perfectly matched the thick golden bars of the gate.

Fyrstsvard's heart began to hammer hard with hope, and he yelled with a slight tremor in his voice, "Very well, let us take our leave!"

He and Stein shoved back the remaining *Thakshir* on their shields with a concerted heave, spitting with the effort. The clumsy undead tripped over the mound of headless corpses that had piled up, blocking the alleyway and knocking over more of their fellows as they rolled backwards. In this small respite, the group made its move.

Since the Knights were forced to hold a running retreat against the

Thakshir regaining their feet behind them, Fyrstsvard yelled out orders as loud as he could to the air and prayed that they were followed, "Ratnik, Jumal, Izdaju, Kamilah, create a spearhead, move toward the gates! Tar Feng, help them clear the way! Make a path to the gates! Amril, stay in the middle! Stein and I will run rearguard!"

From behind them, Bala could not help but admire the warriors' brutal efficiency in dealing death. Charging in seemingly recklessly, the *pal skra* in the red bandana, Ratnik, rapidly sliced off the leprous pair of hands that sought to ensnare him with his cutlass and cut off the ratty-haired head of one of the monsters on his backslash, before ramming another to the ground with his shoulder to trip any who attacked from the right.

To his left, the Chilpaean, Jumal, swept his dwarvic axe in a vicious two-handed arc up and away from the *pal skra* to carve clean through the bare rotting torso of one corpse, the arc of momentum sweeping the weapon up to slam to a finish in the black-toothed skull of a second. Yanking free the axe required a moment and left him vulnerable, though. Ratnik finished decapitating his opponent, kicked him back and – whilst his cocoa-skinned companion crouched as low as he could, his weapon retrieved – spun to behead a gore-faced, limping corpse who sought to sink his teeth into the exposed Jumal. Then, Ratnik crouched and lashed out at a new adversary's rotten legs, while the older pirate sprang into action, rearing up once more, swinging his axe in a great high arc to smash through rotten flesh once again.

Whenever one became exposed, the other was always at hand to protect them and deal death to the danger quick as lightning. It looked to the young boy like they must have been fighting together for years, for they fought with seamless teamwork.

The Nomad, Izdaju, fought to Jumal's left. His near-naked frame was draped in blood like a mantle, though none of it seemed to be his. His swords whirled and spun and stabbed with such a furious speed and frenzied surety that Bala felt sure he must be the greatest swordsman alive.

Just as it looked like the brave little group might be overcome by sheer numbers, arrows from the bow of the Nomad woman, Kamilah, sang through the air to catapult the undead from their feet and bright bolts of green flashed from the crooked staff in the hands of the little Wizard, Tar Feng, to launch the *Thakshir* through the air.

Since he had fallen behind, Bala ran to catch up with the unstoppable heroes, ducking a swinging rotten hand on the way. He caught up with the Magicians and archer, but realised that without a weapon he was defenceless against the groping arms. So, he dropped to all fours to scurry along the ground like a crab, moving forward, darting agilely between legs and avoiding notice and ensnarement easily.

Bala could tell, though, that the three warriors were hard-pressed to push forwards, even with the magical aid from behind, as they fought back seeking limbs from every angle. The young thief darted to the side and then overtook the Nomad and pirates, still on his hands and feet, continuing forward through the thick press of rotting, stamping legs that confronted his vision, some of which bore black bite marks. Moving speedily, dodging most limbs he encountered and knocking over the few he could not avoid, he managed to squeeze out on the other side of the swarm, through the legs of an unknowing tall, skinny *Thakshir*. He emerged underneath one of the enormous, gold-armoured bodyguards, who deftly sliced the arms off the reaching horror above the boy, dappling Bala in cold blood, and kicked it back into the crowd.

The scimitar-wielding bodyguard, Karth, spotted the urchin sprawled in the blood and dirt with his hand reaching up for help. Through the rage and din of battle, he dimly heard the boy shout something about a key. Without further thought, the muscly bodyguard took advantage of the chaos caused by his kick to reach down, grab the young thief and pull him joltingly up to his feet, before thrusting him behind his own body with a sweep of his spare hand to protect him from the next wave of unrelenting ferocity that threatened to purge his royal charges.

He mercilessly sliced a cracked-open skull from its grey shoulders with a growl of defiance, shoved back the corpse, clove low into a leg, toppled that peeling carcass, stomped on it, then came up swinging his scimitar high, whipping it through throats and making death-grin-ridden heads dangle, all the while never losing track of how his companions fared. Eli stood to his right with Riton on the Prince's right and Gug furthest away. The three surviving guards covered the bodyguard's left. Karth kicked the half-headless *Thakshir* back into the crowd and swiftly cut off a grey arm as it reached for him.

He heard the young boy again through his blood-rich vision. "That's it! Chop off their limbs to stop them! If you want to escape, you must help my friends over there get through to us! They have the key! They have the key!" Bala hollered hoarsely as loud as his small lungs would permit.

He turned to see if there were any others who could help. It seemed the Princess could not; she watched with an unhealthy pallor and terrified eyes and seemed frozen to the spot.

The bodyguard, Karth, heard Bala's cries and roared as loudly as he could in relay to his friend, Riton. "Go for the limbs, Rite! Those guys there have the key! They have the key! We have to help them get through!"

Riton nodded understanding. "Forward, Gug!" he bellowed.

He and the Ogre moved forward as one, smashing and shattering anything in their path with hammer and Ogre hand alike.

Karth cut through a bulbous, vein-streaked face, roaring, "Let's kill these sick dogs!"

Riton responded with a grunt and then pulverised a peeled skull with his immense hammer, so that it spouted shards of bone, brain and blood in all directions.

Karth smiled grimly. "Cover me," he roared, after chopping the legs off another as it tried to run by. Riton and the guards moved quickly to position themselves in front of Karth. Riton waved his huge hammer threateningly, powdering bone whenever anything came within range.

Karth took the opportunity to look up from the fight. Through the black, carious masses that consumed his vision, the bodyguard spotted a dreadlocked man with an axe, a cutlass and skin like mahogany. The man had companions, too, and they were struggling to get through to where Karth and Riton now fought; an unenviable task as dribs and drabs joined the fray from the rear, meaning that they faced danger on every side. The boy must have been telling the truth, Karth thought. These strangers must have grabbed the key from the guard, and if they had not, they would all be dead within minutes anyway. He turned quickly and beckoned the young thief who stood gaping beside the beautiful Princess to come help them. The boy had no weapon; that much was obvious.

"What's your name, boy?" Karth said rapidly but with an even tone, while squatting to speak face to face with the street urchin.

"Bala."

"Bala, you're going to help me save the Princess," said Karth with a slight smile.

He looked down at his belt. Which weapon could he afford to lose, and which would be best for the boy? He took from his belt a razor-sharp, wickedly curved hand scythe and handed it to the filthy orphan from the slums.

"You're too short to aim for the heads, but cut down their legs and you can be of help. Come now, don't be afraid," Karth said, patting Bala's shoulder and rising to his feet once more. "Time to be a hero."

Karth leapt back into the fray beside Riton, high-kicking a bearded, moulting monster back so that it knocked over some of the others. The bodyguard advanced, ducking clawing hands and slicing through the wound-pocked offender's grey neck, while Bala joined the line between Karth and the guards, quivering like a strummed string.

The thief hacked viciously at every leg that came near for the first few moments before he was particularly noticed by the *Thakshir,* making it easier for the others to kill them. The guard beside the boy was overwhelmed by several of the undead suddenly, but the remaining two guards closed together and quickly dealt with the sprawled monsters on their companion, barely holding their side. Meanwhile, Bala was abruptly swarmed with flaking faces leering at him.

The thief gripped the scythe tight and swung at the nearest clawing fingers, half-severing an arm at the wrist with the razor-sharp blade. Cold, rotten blood sprayed the young boy's face, but he blinked it away desperately, never losing sight of the horrors in front of him. The handless monster reared back with howls of pain, while its stump gushed gore.

Bala, now slightly more familiar with the weight and efficacy of his new weapon, swung again hard. He chopped halfway through the leg of one of the creatures, its sick flesh ripping noisily, wetly, and the bone giving way with a flinch-worthy crack. The semi-limbless *Thakshir* roared at the young thief, who gripped the scythe with tight white hands.

It snaked out its neck to take a bite, and Bala sidestepped, raising the scythe up and then bringing it down to slice deep into the back of the undead's neck, severing its spine and soaking him in more icy, abysmal-smelling fluids. He yanked his weapon free with a grimace of effort and a red spray. The *Thakshir* around were now well aware of the street boy's presence, and many turned their attention to the smaller target, coming at him with alarmingly hungry red eyes.

"On me!" Karth bellowed, seeing the boy's plight.

He and Riton pushed forward with renewed vigour, cutting into and shoving back most of the *Thakshir* who had sought Bala's blood – much to the boy's relief – and they continued to push forwards, their mighty muscles straining with every step and every swing as they sought the key that would unlock their freedom.

Riton followed Karth's lead without question, staying by his side and smashing anything that threatened the two. The hammer was a slow weapon, but Riton was an extremely strong man. He wielded it quicker than any other he had met, and with Karth's swifter style by his side, he had never yet been conquered. He loved the efficiency of the war hammer; slicing and dicing enemies was unnecessary in his eyes. Brute force and a heavy object was all that was required, Riton had always thought, and he relished the tremor through his body as he caved in another fiery-eyed skull with a well-placed blow.

Eli struggled to keep up, battling hard with his thin, ornate scimitar but lacking the weight behind the blows that the bodyguards had. Almost overwhelmed time and again while flailing his thin sickle at too many foes, he was saved at every turn by the Ogre by his side. Roaring like a half-tongued lion, Gug would spin toward the Prince now and again and smash his enemies to bloody kindling. Then, the Prince would attempt some fancy swordplay, get into trouble and the whole rigmarole would start over again.

The two bodyguards, meanwhile, hacked, smashed, kicked and

elbowed their way through the decaying crowd as best they could, but it was tough going, like slogging through thick mud, for the press of bodies seemed never-ending and harassed them every step of the way. Both were saved from bite and blade more than once by their golden armour. The pauldrons – in particular – were well placed, they realised, for the *Thakshir* infected people by bites, and some of the easiest regions to bite were people's necks and shoulders. Many were the corpses that smashed in their teeth trying to bite through the golden pauldrons.

Ratnik, Jumal and Izdaju were struggling, too, each dripping with gore. Despite all their efforts, a great swathe of walking, drooling corpses still obstructed their passage through to the other side. Behind them, Stein and Fyrstsvard were almost overrun again and again, only their knightly armour and shields saving them from the flesh-hungry jaws of the undead. Each time they almost buckled, they would retreat as far as they could and then lay about them in a frenzy with their blades to lessen the pressure.

"Tar Feng! We must get to those gates *now!"* Fyrstsvard roared desperately, smashing lunging yellowed teeth away with his shield at every angle, hoping the Wizard had a trick up his sleeve.

"Understood, your Knightliness!" responded Tar Feng cheerily, his light voice somehow loud enough to be heard amid the clanging, cursing and clamour of the skirmish. "But I will be weakened for a time afterwards, so you may need to protect me, agreed?"

"Agreed!"

"Protect me while I incant," Tar Feng ordered, shutting his sightless eyes and spreading out his arms like a morning stretch before any response to the affirmative could be made. *"Jangala bronzaquika!"*

The little Wizard's arms slowly reached up towards the sky. Gusts whipped past him in all directions in response to his crescendo of arcane chanting. He seemed unaffected by the buffeting, though; his feet were solid on the ground. The sand by his feet, however, began to hover, floating in the air.

"What in the name of the Prophet is happening?" Karth roared.

The gale had become so strong that it held the majority of the *Thakshir's* attention and even knocked some from their shuffling feet. Bala had given up fighting and simply held on tight to the gate, lest he be swept away like a feather in a hurricane. The Princess grovelled in the dirt against the wall, a ball of sobs.

The mysterious whipping winds halted abruptly as the Wizard's chanting came to a close. There was a moment of dead silence as even the *Thakshir* ceased their bloodthirsty roaring for a heartbeat.

Tar Feng spoke without moving, "Stand still."

He did not say it loudly, but they all heard him – Prince and

Princess, bodyguards and guards, street thief and Elf, Ogre and Knights, Freemen and Nomads – clear as day like he spoke in each of their ears. They all froze.

The *Thakshir* lunged at them all greedily once the winds stopped howling, but not one of them managed to lay a grey, rotting finger on the uninfected warriors who slogged through their midst. They were interrupted by the aftershock of the Wizard's spell.

The sandy ground bucked and heaved suddenly beneath the feet of the undead, sending them sprawling, while leaving the ground beneath the bemused living unaffected. A growl began deep in the throat of the earth, growing until it became a roar to rival a Dragon's, and with it the whole square began to vibrate, juddering bones. The roar grew and so too did the earth's gyration until the floor heaved, ebbed and flowed as smoothly as water, and then the waves of the little dirt ocean began to grown in stature.

The localised earthquake rocked the ground beneath the *Thakshir* until it fragmented, sending great chunks of earth up to tower above the warriors and at the same time creating great gaping holes in the ground down which a great many of the grabbing, biting horrors fell while bellowing their wrath. Others were entombed in rubble. Not one was left standing, and the entire square was in ruins.

The warriors watched, astounded, as feats of magic beyond their knowledge or even suspicions were enacted. Yet all had heard the chanting, and all saw the little golden man standing amid the thick smoke and dust beneath the roasting noon sun, as calmly as if gazing out over his favourite spot in the garden.

"Follow the path," Tar Feng said softly, again heard by everyone who needed to hear.

He then set off, one slow pace at a time, leaning on his crook, toward the grand golden gates.

32

The Golden Gates of Calypra

A slender path wended its way through the carnage, fissures, cracks and holes between the Prince and his bodyguards, and the Wizard and his companions from the desert.

The Prophet's rescuers hurried across the crumbling road, whilst all around them the *Thakshir* had been thrown into death and disarray. When they reached the end of the meandering, narrow lane through the earth's fragmentation, they were confronted silently by the sweaty, sullen band of warriors at the far side, who stared at them blankly for a long moment, stunned at what they had witnessed. They gawked at the Tzunese man in awe as he stood before them, grinning urbanely. Once his companions from the desert were clear of the treacherous path through the quake, Tar Feng snapped his fingers and the slim road too collapsed and fell in a cloud of dust. Only chasms and sundered earth remained.

"Most impressive, Tar Feng," Amril complimented the Wizard with a nod.

Tar Feng beamed like a child given a treat. "I thought it best to use my powers to hurt and slow them, rather than just run away."

After a short time of gauging one another in the scorching heat, Eli spoke, switching from his native Babese to Traveller's. His tone was, as usual, commanding. "Well?" he demanded of them. "Where is the blasted key we damn near just died for?"

The companions looked at one another, bemused.

"I tought da boy had it …" Jumal muttered, scratching his head.

Then, from behind the Prince, Princess and the bodyguards, a loud click was heard, followed by a louder grating noise. Everyone spun to see Bala, the young street thief, standing by the now partially open golden gates with the golden key securely in the lock.

"Well, are you lot coming or not? I don't know about you, but I don't much fancy dancing another number with that bunch," he said suavely with a wide grin.

He gestured to where an increasing number of the undead stared at them malevolently from the smooth ground behind the damage inflicted on the earth by Tar Feng's enchanting. Then, as one, the *Thakshir* began to climb across the uneven ruptured dirt to seek the flesh they so lusted after. With that, Bala stepped through the gate, leaving it open, and began to saunter happily uphill along the crystalline marble path that led up to the golden inner city of Calypra, the first from the lower city ever to do so without permission.

"That little boy had the key the whole time," said Karth, his mouth agape.

"He could have opened it for us to flee at any time?" asked Eli quickly, his face clouding over with a storm of anger. "Why did he make us -?" he continued angrily, but was interrupted by his sister.

"They are coming, brother! Enough talk, let's go!"

Palasia pointed to where the grey-skinned monsters were slowly but surely coming after them, before sweeping past her angry brother to slip through the gate and set off after the urchin. The guards followed her swiftly.

Eli glared at the newcomers, but held his tongue and stalked after his sister. Karth and Riton sized up the bloody figures before them.

"Excuse me, but are you an Elf?" asked Karth politely, he too switching to Traveller's Tongue to communicate with the outsiders.

"Yes, that is the prevailing opinion," responded Amril with a small smile. "My name is Amril."

"I see," responded Karth, thunderstruck. "Well, it is an honour to meet you, Elf, and thank you and your companions for your aid back there! It was most welcome. Allow me to introduce us, since we appear to be fleeing together. My name is Karth, this is Riton, and that is Gug the Ogre over there. We are the royal bodyguards," he said proudly, shaking Amril's hand. Riton bobbed his head in greeting. "The young man and woman ahead of us are the Prince and Princess, Eli and Palasia." Karth stared hard at the two Knights for a long moment. "I'm sure I recognise you two. You were here a short while ago, weren't you?"

"We were, Karth," responded Fyrstsvard quickly, looking over his shoulder anxiously to behold the *Thakshir* slowly crawling nearer over the debris. "My name is Sir Raphael Fyrstsvard, and this is Sir Stein Kreeger. We were hosted here by your Sultan on our journey east, but now we have what we came for and are returning to the west."

"You are Knights, yes?" asked Karth, matter-of-factly.

"Yes, my friend, we are Knights of the Order of *Pacia*," responded

Fyrstsvard with a thin smile. "Perhaps we could make with the introductions at a later time, however? Seeing as an army of evil undead warriors is slowly creeping nearer with each passing breath, I would rather like to not be here when they reach this point."

The bodyguard nodded with a rueful smile on his broad, open face. "Of course. Riton, lead on. I will lock the gate."

The motley group hurried through the gate, which Karth locked behind them, taking with him the key that had been the cause of so much strife. The gates clanged and rang as the undead pressed up against them only moments later, howling through the gold bars with frustration at being thwarted, sticking their arms through and grabbing at the air.

The warriors began to hike up the marble path through the sunbathing gardens, and suddenly the world seemed perversely light and care-free despite the horrors lurking and groaning just behind them, for the skies were blue and beauty and fragrance abounded at every step in the form of herb gardens, flowerbeds, orchards, topiary, pools, fountains and climber-laced gazebos. Palms and ericosos with wide fronds cast transient dancing shadows on the path as their heads flickered in the breeze. Massive, dense cypresses overlooked them all like callous giants, their penumbrae striping the path in places.

The group could almost forget that they were drenched in blood and stank of rot and guts.

Catching up with the Prophet, Karth said, "Amril, would you like a weapon to protect yourself?"

"No, thank you. I am a pacifist. I do not believe in harming any creature of this world, and certainly not in killing any – not even to save my own life."

"What about my life? What about the Prince and Princess?" Karth asked, dumbstruck. The Prophet just looked at him. "You won't even take up a sword against these … things? But you've seen what they are – they're monsters! They're not human – they're not even intelligent beings. They don't feel pain, and they don't fear death. Killing them is not taking life. It is an act of mercy that finally allows the rotted person to rest."

The Elf shook his head firmly. "Justifications are a slippery slope. Justify one type of killing, and it becomes easier to justify the next. I will take no life, no matter what form in which it may appear."

"You would let people die just to let those villains live?"

"Everybody dies. It is not my responsibility to save anybody, not even myself. Death is but the natural end to our journey – not to be feared, but to be accepted. No matter when they die, all those with beneficent souls will end up in the same place."

Karth made a noise of disgust in the back of his throat and sped up to overtake the Elf. Both were left with strange thoughts from the short interaction, though.

"So, Riton," Fyrstsvard said, hurrying to keep up with the tall man's long strides, leaving red footprints in his wake, "are there defensive measures in place for an event such as this?"

"None," grunted Riton. "We have armies. For the most part, they wage war with Al Kutz and Shimyahein, sometimes the Nomads. We have a small contingency force here, of course, but we are little prepared. Nothing like this has ever happened here. We were not expecting it. We don't even know what they are! Evil monsters that don't die! But smashing them to pieces with my hammer still takes them down."

For the taciturn Riton, this was quite a rant. He smiled darkly as he thought of pulverizing that rotten flesh with his giant hammer.

"They are *Thakshir,*" supplied Fyrstsvard. "Abominable creatures moulded of dark magic, forged in the Nether."

Riton glanced at him sharply, but said nothing more.

"Is there an escape route from the city?" asked Fyrstsvard of Karth when he caught up.

The bodyguard rubbed his chin and gazed carefully at the Knight and his companions for a moment. "Yes, I'm sure there are escape tunnels – or there were. They have never been used as far as I remember, though. In fact, I don't even know where they are. You must understand, we will try to aid your escape if we can, but the two of us," he gestured to Riton and himself, "must protect the Sultan and his children above all else. It is our duty."

Fyrstsvard nodded his understanding. "Of course, of course."

"Who is the Elf?" Riton asked brusquely.

Fyrstsvard hesitated for just a moment. "He is the Prophet."

Again, Fyrstsvard was subjected to Riton's dark, forbidding glare. He thought for a moment the big man might attack him so angry did he look. Then, the bodyguard turned his head further to look behind them. His dark eyes widened slightly, and he pointed.

"Rider!"

They all turned to witness a single horseman galloping toward them down one of the wider, corpse-thronged avenues leading through the slums to the golden gate; a route they had bypassed with Bala's know-how. As the rider reached the sunlit square on the far side of the gates, they could see that the mount was an unusual one.

The snorting horse was skinless, and like a gaunt shell its bones protruded sickeningly. Its flanks were dark red with coagulated blood, and its eyes burned with evil flames. The rider carried a longsword and wore full black battle armour – cuirass, gauntlets, pauldrons, greaves and boots – with crimson patterns and edgings. As the noisome horse came yet nearer, the company that had rescued the Prophet from the fell pit to the east were able to recognise the rider's face, even through the cruelly distorted, putrefying skin and huge red veins.

"Heldig!" Ratnik whispered, the blood fleeing his face as if afraid to see what the eyes beheld. "Heldig!" he roared at the lone rider. His voice cracked with anguish. Jumal grasped his friend's shoulder in sympathy.

The company had all stopped and turned to view their erstwhile companion. They watched him ride nearer, and when he reached the obstructing carnage in the earth caused by Tar Feng's handiwork, the demonic mount that held him reared, whinnying violently. He, too, was halted by the ruptured land, the group thought with relief. The accursed Heldig sat for a moment astride his ghastly beast, staring at them through the wreckage.

Then, with a swipe of his hand, he swept aside all the messy rubble, the piled devastation, and sundered the earth as though a giant hand mimicked the motions of his own. In place of the earthquake debris, all that was left where the square had once been was a smooth, scooped out crater in the ground.

The company gaped, wordless. The demonic mount charged forward, bounding into the crater and, after a few lengthy strides, bounding out of the other side to pursue them.

"Someone has taught him something of the arcane arts … The gate will not hold them," realised Amril aloud, for he knew even as he looked at the strong metal bars and the cloud-high golden wall that it was not enough to stop this terror. "Run, you fools!"

He turned and began to run up the marble path, the surrounding beauty and tranquillity now a mocking testimony to dashed hope. The others followed swiftly.

After only a few moments of ragged running, they heard a mighty banging and looked back to see the enormous, ornate barred golden gates – which had stood for more than three hundred years since before the first Bab – launched across the gardens as though the battering ram of the Gods had bent its will to the task. One twisted, bent half of the gate smashed into a fountain, shattering the decorative white stone, before bouncing to a rest in a flowerbed of fragrant orchids. The other mangled half flew at the group on the path above.

Seeing it, they gasped and could do little more to prevent whatever fate had in store for them. At the last moment, the gate careened into the path before reaching them, shattering the marble, and bounced with tremendous force over their suddenly crouching figures to skid, screeching, to a halt across the path ahead, as though seeking to reclaim its former duties. Heldig, the demonic rider, charged through the gap where the now-ruined gates had once protected the upper city, as did hundreds of shuffling, droning corpses, each after its share of the blood of the living.

"You cannot escape, Prophet!" the undead pirate's words bounded, booming, up the path after them.

The group did not hesitate – apart from Ratnik, who had to be yanked forward by Jumal – but continued to flee with as much haste as they could muster over the broken gate and on toward the second ring of golden walls that represented the inner sanctum of the great jewel, Calypra.

The barred gate ahead was mercifully open. As the group drew nearer to it, Fyrstsvard shouted joyfully from the vanguard, "It's the Prince! And he's not alone!"

Eli awaited them at the gate, now carrying a bronze shield as well as his curved sword. Beside him stood a fully-armoured General Ghan. Behind him, a force of a thousand soldiers awaited his command, arrayed in bronze lamellar armour, with crescent swords. Their hauberks were made of hundreds of little bronze scales laced into rows. Each scale glittered separately from the others, making the warriors shine and shimmer like the sunlight was dancing over them.

As the company sprinted up the pristine white path through the lush, vivifying gardens toward the haven of gold that waited, they heard Ghan bellowing orders in Babese and then the small army was sprinting toward them, the General at its head. Prince Eli and Princess Palasia awaited the company and their bodyguards under the aegis of the golden wall's shadow.

For a moment, seeing hundreds of soldiers running at him with weapons bared, Fyrstsvard was concerned that he and his company might be under attack along with the *Thakshir*, but he strangled the thought. He could not turn; he could only run forward and hope. The army broke to pass around the fleeing company like a river around a rock, shouting out war cries and brandishing bronze weapons as they tore down the path toward the slavering menace that staggered nearer beneath the peaking sun.

As the Calyprian soldiers clashed voluminously with the forerunners of the *Thakshir* – bashing with round, bronze shields and burying their sickle-like blades into blackened flesh – they were able to slow the undead down and hold them at bay for a time even, but they could not do the same against Heldig. The skinless, malefic mount he rode charged clean through the ranks of soldiers like a hot knife through butter, trampling a red path through those that dared stand before him. He did not stop to taste any flesh. He had gleaming red eyes only for the company that had once been his friends, drawn to them like a moth out of the darkness.

The fleeing band did not notice at first, but Ratnik could not stop himself from twisting for one last glance back. His eyes widened in fear when he saw Heldig – his transmogrified face pinched in a malicious snarl – smash through the last ranks of the Calyprian army and gallop on after them with demonic speed.

"Look out! Behind us!" he yelled to no one in particular, knowing only that if he stood in his old Captain's way, he would be cut down and trampled just like the others that had tried.

Most of the company turned, yelled in garbled fear and continued to run, pumping arms and tiring legs furiously for their last remnants of speed. Tar Feng, however, did not. Despite his fatigue from his recent spell-casting, the emaciated Wizard turned and, seeing the problem, fired off three rapid bolts of sizzling emerald energy at the mounted Demon. His crooked staff bucked violently with the release of power; the old man grasped it firmly, though it writhed like a snake.

Two bolts seared off into the air – dodged by the wily, meandering mount – but one smote the creature that had once called itself Heldig in the chest and knocked him flying from the saddle of his Nether-steed to land in a crumpled heap on the white path. His sword went spinning off into the gardens. The skinless, fuming horse galloped straight on at the little Tzunese man. The Wizard fired off more magical blobs of energy at the beast, but it dodged them all, weaving this way and that, whinnying furiously and exhaling incarnadine smoke from its nostrils angrily.

When the horse reached Tar Feng – who now stood alone behind the engaged Calyprian army, blocking the ivory road to the gleaming city – the twisted creature reared high above him and lashed out with its lethal hooves. The withered Wizard ducked beneath the attack, missing being brained by the narrowest of margins, jabbed his staff at the beast's belly and let loose a blast of power. The green energy glob lifted the horse high into the air and threw it back to plummet to a gruesome end, splattered with the force of impact across the previously pristine white path.

A river of blood ran down the avenue back toward the slums from whence they had come. The beauty of the luscious gardens was tarnished, the flowers' exquisite fragrances lost amid the reek of death. The ancient Wizard hurried to catch up with the others, bones clanking and feet slapping. Heldig and his *Thakshir* would not be held for long by the Calyprian army, the old man knew, and the numbers of the undead would only be strengthened by their inevitable victory.

The company that had rescued the Elf – as well as the Prince, Princess, their bodyguards and the street boy, Bala – awaited Tar Feng as he hurried up the path, leaning on his trusty shepherd's crook. The Bab heirs were again left breathless by feats of magic beyond their wildest trite dreams.

"Come!" the Prince, Eli Bab, ordered sternly as the Wizard finally flapped to a halt before him. "We must reach my father. He will know what to do."

He turned and stalked off with his innately angry gait. With no better ideas and little to no knowledge of the layout of the city, the company followed, Tar Feng inhaling and exhaling hard before doing so.

"What were you thinking?" Ratnik asked him as they went, amazed by his bravery.

"I know this must be a touchy subject for you, sea urchin – yes, I do – but I have seen a … link of some kind between your old Captain and the rest of the undead, and I was thinking that maybe if we killed Heldig, he being the First of the *Thakshir,* that the rest might stop or … be directionless."

"That sounds unlikely."

"Hmm, maybe, probably, I agree, but I think it worth a try, I am sorry to say. But know this; he is not the man you once knew anymore."

The young pirate nodded, his blue eyes hard as sapphires, but his voice cracking. "I know. And you are right; regardless of whether it stops the rest, he must be slain."

"You do not tink he is dead den?" asked Jumal.

"No," Tar Feng answered softly, "I am confident he is not."

Karth hung back with the two Palace guards who were stationed by the gate into the city of Calypra proper. While the army was gone, the Palace Guard had remained at their stations. The royal bodyguard felt reassured that there were still a hundred blades throughout the city ready to defend the Prince and Princess.

As he looked out of the gate at the gory mess that had once been the beautiful gardens of Calypra, however, his heart failed him. Blood speckled the lawns and coated the path, and the undead were blotting out the entirety of the grounds, trampling the herb gardens and flowerbeds. The bodyguard's eyebrows twisted in sympathy for the life and vision that had been sullied there. Thousands of carcasses clogged the estates, and more kept coming through the gap in the golden wall below. It was a colossal force, all seemingly single-minded. A lump clogged the bodyguard's throat at the sight of the army's demise; men he had known and trained for years snuffed out like so many candles in the blink of an eye.

He took a half-step forward when he saw General Ghan bravely battle to defend a downed comrade, but went no further, knowing there was nothing he could do. So, he watched with gritted teeth as the comrade was torn from under the General's nose, and then when Ghan leapt into the fray to seek to reclaim the man, the General got his sword stuck and had his shield wrenched away. Decaying teeth and heads smashed in vain against his golden armour for a moment, but then the corpses covered Ghan's face, thankfully hiding it from Karth's sight, though he could well imagine their yellowed teeth tearing into the old man's nose and cheeks.

Blades skirled and shields banged, but neither halted the corpses' advance. Bronze armour, gleaming in the afternoon sun, was quickly stained black and brown with cold viscera. Men shouted and screamed, but to no avail. The veiny monsters moaned and snuffled as they stumbled inexorably on. The undead rolled over the small army like a wave, biting and tearing and pouncing and gouging, groaning with pleasure when they snagged a victim and then sucking loudly on his blood.

Though the soldiers fought back as best they could, slashing with swords and smashing with shields, it only took one bite to not only bring a man down but also to add him to the enemy's repertoire. With such an advantage, the fearless *Thakshir* were unstoppable, for even when mortally wounded they could still bite. It was barely a battle, the bodyguard thought sadly; more a massacre. In a matter of minutes – with the sun barely past its zenith, though it had felt to Karth like an age – the undead had surrounded and wiped out the Calyprian contingent and were hollering hollowly as they set to devouring portions of the army.

Karth watched in fascinated revulsion. When the *Thakshir* rose and started shuffling toward the gates to the upper city once more, he wondered what compelled them; why they had not eaten every last scrap of meat on the soldiers if they were so hungry – which he could tell they were from the burning in their eyes. They left a trail of black blood on the once-white path as they came, groaning with greed.

The bodyguard guessed the undead had to be under the sway of another. If they were but wild, voracious animals, then surely, he reasoned, they would have eaten their fill after the slaughter rather than abandoned their meal to seek out another. That meant they were not mindless beasts, he thought worriedly; they were evil soldiers in a dark army.

Karth watched as the last soldier alive, a young beardless man, fled for his life up the path towards the gates. Before the man could get near, he was swarmed while screeching and pleading by the red-eyed horde at his back and bitten countless times by faces wearing sadistic masks that cruelly resembled people, friends, he had once known.

"Lock the gate," Karth ordered the Palace Guard, his voice thick and his eyes wet.

The barred golden gates closed with a reverberating boom, and moments later the *Thakshir* slammed up against it in force, sticking arms, legs and faces through the bars with such ferocity – shoved with such vehemence by those behind – that their squeezed appendages were torn off in places in gory sprays. The stench was gut-wrenching, and the severed limbs flopped around on the sullied marble floor like eels. The gates squealed ominously, audible even over the corpses' howling. Ordering the guards to accompany him, Karth turned and marched after his charges, for like the Elf had said, the gate would not hold the undead.

The company hurried through the shining city, past golden towers and domes, crystal colonnades and marble statues and houses, ignorant of the opulence in their fear. They heard the banging clatter of the heavy golden gates as they too were blasted from their sizeable hinges by a revived Heldig, and the shuffle and stomp of hundreds of rotting feet as the undead infiltrated the upper city, pouring this way and that like water into a maze.

The Bab heirs knew exactly where they were going and the quickest way there, however, and so they were able to outpace the *Thakshir*, keeping ahead of them until they reached their destination. The Palace – the greatest of buildings in mighty Calypra with its marbled walls, golden domes and elegant spires – was the radiant heart of the jewelled city. As the company came in sight of its entrance, it sang out to them like a beacon of hope and safety, for the majority of the Palace Guard had rooted there, blocking the twin inscribed solid gold slabs that served as doors; a hundred blades ready to protect their Sultan.

"Who goes there?" a soldier shouted out nervously as the company approached.

"Prince Eli Bab and Princess Palasia approach!" Eli snapped, pushing his way to the front. "So make way and let us in before those cursed monsters get here!"

The soldiers quickly acquiesced; the Prince's temper was well-attested. The company passed through ranks of dark-skinned, bronze-clad soldiers once again. The flutter of the butterflies and the innocent chirping of the birds as they passed the sun-drenched gardens outside the Palace seemed incongruous amid the fear and bloodletting.

They walked past the Calyprians swiftly with heads down, averting their eyes from the glittering armour, not looking at the soldiers' faces, for they knew they might see them again one day, rotting, grey, peeling and wrought with huge, red veins. It was an odd feeling for the group; to walk past men whom they knew were going to die so that they might have a better chance at life, at escape. It made them feel unworthy, insignificant and callous, but their sense of self-preservation put one foot in front of the other, time and again.

Even Amril, who would have loved nothing more than for no one to die for him, knew he could do nothing. With his wasted muscles, he could barely run and had been supported during their fleeing by Stein since they had passed the gardens. He needed to preserve his strength in order to survive. The thought made him hang his head in shame, but he told himself he could still do good in the world, make it a better place.

He could stop more deaths if he lived, he thought, but the ache in his heart told him he was wrong. He would never fix this. The deaths of these people were on his hands, and there was nothing he could do to save them. The only thing he could think to do was to ensure that they reached the paradise in which they believed, and that was what he intended to do. He had been amazed when Fyrstsvard had told him of the Calyprians' faith in *Citta Pacia* after all these years, and he felt now like he had let them down.

Karth, at the rear of the company as they traipsed dirt and blood into the Palace along the expensive purple rugs, halted once more to regard the scenes carved into the golden doors; tableaus of grand battles that seemed ominous to the bodyguard now. As soon as he caught his breath, he spoke to the Palace Guard.

"Who's in charge here?" he asked, looking around.

A man stepped forward, garbed in bronze like the rest but with a plumed helmet. "I, Yemet, have the honour," he responded.

"Ah, Yemet! Good man," Karth responded, pleased, clasping the man's wrist in greeting. "Get your men inside and lock the doors behind you. Send men to lock all the Palace doors, in fact! Split your men between each of the entrances, but keep them away from the doors themselves, for there is an enemy coming that can smash down gates like Gaia does a heretic! Await them inside in confined quarters, where you can best hold them off, and be ready to fall back if I give the word."

"Where is Ghan – and the army?"

The bodyguard placed a hand on the man's shoulder. "All gone. You are the last hope for the Sultan, the Prince and the Princess." He looked around at them all. "You are all responsible for the continuation of the Bab bloodline! Honour your vows today, men! Hold the fiends back! I will do my best to get the Sultan and the heirs to safety. You will be remembered, my brothers! And your glory will ring true, told in tale and sung in song until the end of days!"

The soldiers cheered. Karth winced and wished his speech had been a modicum less rousing. The *Thakshir* nearby heard and began to swarm from every alley and street, every hole and gutter, every nook, cranny and shadow, gurgling, moaning, shouting incomprehensibly and drooling at the sight of their meal.

"Everybody, inside now!" Karth shouted, ushering the men with swift hand gestures.

The soldiers fled inside, and Yemet shut the grand golden doors behind them with a bang, sealing out the sunlight.

"For glory, brothers! Hold them out!" Karth shouted again.

As the men cheered and shouted war cries, the veteran bodyguard swiftly slipped through the frenzy, leaving the men to their fate in search of his own. His duty demanded that he remain with the Prince and Princess.

Bodies could be heard slamming against the locked doors as he left.

33

The Champion

The man who stepped into the ring looked deserving of his title, thought Saul with an inward grimace, flexing his aching muscles and glancing up at the grey skies and ever-worsening downpour.

Garric the Bludgeoner was redolent of a bear; huge, wide and hairy, the man ambled with a stomping tread. He wore heavy, dark boots, grey trousers, and a leather vest over a sleeveless shirt. His arms, neck, shoulders and face were covered in dark, curly hair, and a thicker mass grew atop his large head. Saul regarded the man's weapons with narrowed eyes; twin rods, each lined on every side and angle with as many metal spikes as would fit. They looked thin enough to be fast, he thought, and sharp enough to be deadly. He would have to be careful.

"This should be a match for the ages," Umbrich declared, "for Garric here ended Saul's older brother Rork's winning streak only two years ago!" Saul's eyebrows shot up at this, and he made a mental note to tease Rork at the next opportunity. The roar of the crowd mounted in a surge of excitement to a sonic upheaval at the Thane's words. "Can Garric replicate his amazing feat? Can the younger Stonebrow conquer where the elder could not? Let us find out! Combatants, fight!"

Garric let fly with his spiked clubs in an upward swing across the body. Saul stepped back to avoid it, and combat was commenced. Seeing the other retreat, Garric pressed forwards, swinging his clubs in tandem in quick, vicious swipes across the body. Like the club-wielder Saul had fought earlier, Garric's swings left little room for riposte, but Saul felt that the man was wasting his weapons.

Upon seeing the dual rods, he had feared attacks from more than one angle, but so far the clubs had been used only in unison, effectively making one redundant in his opinion. Nevertheless, an alarm bell in the back of his head told him to proceed with caution. If this man had defeated Rork, then he must be holding back because it was early in the fight yet, trying to lull the Prince into a specious sense of security, so that he could attack from multiple angles later to take him by surprise.

Saul was determined not to fall for any such trickery, and so he continued his pattern of evasion, weaving and whirling, watching the man closely for any change in tactics.

The man continued to attack in fast but predictable patterns, whirling his rods in tandem, and Saul ducked, dodged and sidestepped every one of the blows, concentrating hard. He was watching the clubs too much, he realised too late, remembering that there are always other weapons. Agony blossomed in his crotch as the Flatlander's foot lodged there, and Saul collapsed to his knees in the wet with a high-pitched gasp and dropped one axe in order to cup his hand protectively over his privates.

He never stopped watching his opponent though, even when his slit eyes swam with tears. When Garric raised his clubs overhead with a triumphant smirk, Saul forced his pained body to move. He collapsed onto his side, but it was enough to dodge the rods, which thudded down on the ground next to him. He was slowly regaining feeling in his numbed parts, so he flailed his remaining axe, forcing Garric to back away. Fuming, dripping and glaring, Saul clambered shakily to his feet, scooping up his fallen axe as he did so.

"I know that Umbrich did not declare low blows out of bounds," the Prince panted, while the crowd cheered and roared, hissed and booed, "but you dishonour yourself with such dirty fighting, Garric. Fight me like a man!"

The Bludgeoner growled at the smear on his name and rampaged forward, twirling his clubs separately at last in continuous overhand strokes. The attack looked intimidating and complicated, but Saul recognised it for what it was: one of the basic patterns for dual weapons. The alarm bell still tolled, telling him to be wary, but he was beginning to suspect that this man had made his name through brute force alone, as opposed to skill.

When the Prince stepped forwards and batted aside a swinging rod with an axe – a simple interruption to the pattern – his suspicions were confirmed. Having batted the club in the direction it was already travelling, Saul added to its momentum and overbalanced the Champion of Ban-Hodre, making him stagger to stay upright. Seeing such poor balance and a complete lack of readiness for such a rudimentary interruption to such a basic attack pattern, Saul was now sure that Garric was not as skilled as he had, at first, believed. He must have gotten lucky to defeat Rork, the Prince thought.

Taking control of the fight, Saul went on the offensive and kept

Garric on the back foot, flailing his axes in the tightly controlled arcs of a more complex pattern, which differentiated between attack heights, unlike Garric's.

The Bludgeoner was at a loss; parrying, blocking, backtracking, ducking and dodging as fast as he could, still he could barely keep up with the Highlander's incredible speed. He blocked a blow to the head in the nick of time only for the blocking club to be smashed out of his fist, wrenching and spraining his thumb. He cried out and, on instinct, stabbed out with his remaining weapon. Too late, he saw that the Prince had been waiting for just such a response. One axe struck the club down while the other whistled up to slice the underneath of Garric's forearm, making him spasm and drop his weapon.

Saul desperately wanted to kick Garric in the crotch in vengeance for what had been done to him, but he forced himself to refrain. He had already won, after all, and he did not wish to be petty. So, instead he took both axes in one hand and extended the other to his opponent, who took and shook it with a rueful smile.

"Prince Saul Aodhson is the winner!" Umbrich roared, delighted.

"Congratulations, Prince Saul," the Champion said, wincing at the Highlander's grip on his cut arm. "You are a magnificent warrior."

A spiteful barb about Garric's lack of ability died on Saul's lips. "As are you, Garric, but remember that honour is more important than victory."

Garric shook his head. "You Highlanders really are a strange breed," he said wonderingly. He patted Saul's hand. "Enjoy the festivities – Champion." The Prince smiled at that.

"Prince Saul has defeated all ten challengers!" Umbrich shouted over the easing shower, and the crowd bellowed their approval. "Before we end the tournament, I want to take this opportunity to extend an invitation to any and all – no matter who you are – to step into the ring and test your mettle." The crowd quietened to a cough and a mutter. "The prize money is five hundred Fjolins if you defeat the Prince."

Still, the crowd was silent as the grave, each contemplating the impossible task the Thane proposed. The rain hissed, and the wind whispered, but no sentient soul under those grey clouds made a sound.

Then, one man spoke up, "I will fight him for five hundred Fjolins."

"Who is that?" Umbrich called, craning his neck to look into the crowd.

A man shorter than six feet tall stepped to the front of the mob to be halted by the line of guards. "It is I."

"I should've known," Umbrich muttered with a dark look. "Prince Saul, a word, please."

Saul strolled over to the Thane, appraising the small man who wished to fight him. The man – who looked to be about thirty years of age – wore a dirty ermine fur coat, had black hair plastered to his head in the wet, a greasy moustache and a sallow, pocked complexion. Strangely, he did not seem to be carrying any weapons.

"Saul," the Thane whispered conspiratorially when the Prince reached him, "I wished to speak with you before I began this bout. You have done yourself proud, young man, and you do not have to take on this challenger if you do not want to. I will understand and end the tournament now, if you wish."

Except he did have to now, thought Saul, because the Thane had already made the offer to the people; if Umbrich rescinded it now, they would know it was not his wish but the Prince's, and Saul would be called a coward.

"I will fight one more bout," said Saul, rubbing his clubbed shoulder with a wince, "and then no more."

"Are you sure?" The Thane seemed concerned. "You do not have to, you know."

"Why are you so worried?" asked Saul bluntly. "Do you know the man who is volunteering?"

"I am sad to say that I do – or I know of him. He is Silquave Molassus. The guards suspect him of being the head of a criminal gang here in town. We can never prove anything – else he'd be behind bars right now – but it is believed that he has personally murdered half a dozen men and ordered the deaths of dozens more, not to mention the charges of theft, pimping, extortion, blackmail, rape and arson that have been levelled at him over the years. If you fight him, you must be careful, Prince. He is slippery."

Saul found it hard to believe that the man at the front of the crowd – a man almost two full feet shorter than him – could be a threat. The sun was getting low, though, and he knew a flickering shadow could be the difference between life and death in a fight. "I will fight one more bout," he repeated wearily, "and *only* one more."

The Thane smiled. "Marvellous. The people will be pleased. Take your position, my boy." Turning to the gangster and the crowd, Umbrich yelled, "Very well, Silquave, on your head be it. Let him pass."

A murmur ran through the crowd at the name Silquave. The guards parted and waved the man through, and he strolled into the empty centre, approaching the ring with a graceful swagger. Like Saul and everyone else in the marketplace, he was drenched.

"I'm Silquave Molassus. It is a pleasure to make your acquaintance, Prince Saul," the oily man drawled, his voice croaky and languid, "and don't worry – I'll take it easy on you."

Saul grinned wolfishly. This sort of banter was his brothers' bread and butter. "Thank the Gods for that – I was quaking in my boots," he retorted.

Silquave's dark eyes gleamed, and his lips flickered in humour, but then he twitched, and two long, straight daggers seemed to appear in his hands like magic. Saul was sure he had retrieved them from inside his coat, and the Prince's smile dimmed; he had not even seen the man's hands move, much less the daggers. Umbrich was right, he thought with a hint of worry; this man *was* slippery. The Prince twirled his axes and cricked his neck.

"Combatants," Umbrich called, "begin!"

Saul thought to overpower the little man and rushed him, tucking an axe under the opposite armpit as he did so. His right-hand axe lashed out, and – a mere moment behind it – the left-hand axe swung from the right, too, but lower, at body height, so as to catch the man out should he duck the first swing. Both axes hit air, and the Prince had to leap to his left to avoid rapidly jabbing daggers to his right, where the gangster had dodged.

Saul ducked a high swing and had to jerk his head aside to avoid impalement by the second dagger; doing so, he leapt backwards to gain some space. Silquave was fast and relentless, however, and he did not let up. His daggers flashed in fatal arcs around Saul's face, coming from all sides, whistling in his ears and missing his flesh by inches. The Prince was forced to keep backing away from the whirlwind of steel the man had become. Though Silquave's blades were far shorter, Saul's blades were too heavy to block, parry or counterattack against the light, speedy daggers.

So, leaping from side to side, moving back all the while with knees bent, Saul retreated. He ducked a high swing and yanked his head to the side to avoid a stabbing point, almost overbalancing, but staggering upright in time to spin away from an ankle cut. Again, he did not have a second to breathe before Silquave was on top of him. The gangster reminded Saul of a snow cat with his speed, and he felt like he was fighting several opponents on all fronts at once, for the man flashed out of sight like lightning whenever Saul turned to face him.

Dodging a slice aimed for his throat more by chance than skill as he turned to see what was coming, Saul recognised that Silquave had leaned too close, and – without a second thought – he punched the gangster in the chest with the haft of the axe he held clutched to his abdomen. It was a good hit, and the air whooshed out of the littler man as he went flying and landed on his back with a thud and a skid. As much as he wanted to take a breather, Saul knew he had to end the bout now if he stood any chance of winning. He rushed the man again while he was down, and – remembering late that this was not a fight to the death – Saul swiped at his legs, but again the axe hit nothing.

Wily Silquave tucked his legs to dodge the axe and then shot them both out, one to kick Saul square in the face and the other to flip the gangster into a backwards roll, from which he sprung at the rattled Prince and almost died as Saul angrily swiped an axe to keep his foe at bay whilst his blurry vision returned to normal. Pulling up short of the whipping blade, Silquave waited for the weapon to reverse and swipe back before he ducked under it and cut low at the Prince's ankles.

Vaguely able to see again, Saul stepped back to avoid the attack and spun to face the gangster who had already swivelled around to his left. Though his axes were slow in comparison, Saul was better able to track the other's movements now that they had been fighting for a while. He chopped down at his foe in his new position, and – when Silquave sidestepped as Saul had guessed he would – the Prince's other axe whistled across in a blow too low to duck and too high to jump. Silquave had to leap backwards, and the axe nicked his trousers as he did so.

Saul went on the offensive, flailing his axes in an intricate pattern, twirling, leaping and ducking to attack from all sides in a persistent barrage of blows from which the other could not escape. The Prince's breath was ragged now, sweat poured down his face, his arms and shoulders burned like they were afire, and his legs felt like they wore leaden trousers. He used his most complicated and energetic attacks, but Silquave was as slippery as an eel and could not be pinned down. As fast as Saul moved, the gangster was always a step ahead, a twitch away.

Finishing the same sequence for a second time, running out of ideas, Saul watched as Silquave leapt away with a slight smile playing on his haggard face. The gangster was an expert fighter, Saul now knew – and worse, he could tell that Silquave knew he was exhausted and running short on inspiration. He stood with sweat dripping from his nose and chin, panting heavily, his mighty chest heaving up and down, staring at the man who was two feet shorter than him in wonderment. He did not understand how this could be happening – he was a Highland Prince, after all – but he had to admire his opponent's skill.

He sought to attack again, but had to stop a swing and duck a dagger as soon as he tried, and he realised ruefully that he was moving a mite slower than he had at the first bout now. He remembered the gangster's tactics in a flash; high swing, then stab. It was too late. A searing burn on his cheek confirmed it, and he checked a long and thorough curse on its way out. He straightened to see Silquave backing away with a tired smile, his daggers having already vanished to whence they had come.

Saul reached up a hand to his face, felt warm blood on his cheek and saw it on his fingers. He checked another curse, wiped his hand on his maroon tunic and forced a rueful smile onto his face as he beheld the man who had defeated him.

"Congratulations on the win," Saul said into the stunned silence that followed the end of the match, the pitter-patter of the rain being the only other noise. He walked forward and, taking both axes into one hand, offered Silquave the other. "You are an incredible fighter, Silquave Molassus. I don't think I have ever fought someone as fast as you."

"And I don't think I have ever fought anyone as strong as you, Prince," the gangster drawled, breathing heavily, smiling wryly. "When you hit me, I thought my sternum had caved in!"

"You're lucky it didn't!" said Saul, at which they both laughed.

Umbrich came to his senses at last and, standing from his chair, cried out, "Prince Aodhson is defeated. Silquave Molassus is the winner! Guards, arrest him!"

To the shock of the Prince and the crowd, the two guards that had stood sentry by the Thane throughout the tournament hurried forward, along with half a dozen others from the periphery of the centre clearing. Silquave tensed and crouched, his fingers twitching in readiness to seize his hidden daggers. When he saw that he was completely surrounded, however, he relaxed, stood straight and held his arms by his sides, where they were swiftly seized and pinned by the guards, who then dragged him away from the flabbergasted Prince to stand in the downpour before the seated Thane.

"Good evening, Silquave," the Thane greeted him with mock-civility. "I am sorry to tell you that you will not be receiving one single Fjolin from me today or any other day. You must be a fool to think you could parade around in the middle of my town without being arrested."

"I won fairly," Silquave said loudly and clearly. "You owe me my prize money. Besides, what do you plan to charge me with?" He snorted and looked down his nose at the seated Thane. "I have never committed a single crime, and – until you can prove otherwise, Thane – this is injustice of the highest order. Now, release me and give me my money."

"Everybody knows," sneered Umbrich, "that you are a high-ranking member, if not the boss, of the Mute Ox Gang. You are Silquave Molassus, are you not?"

"I am, but -"

"For too many years," Umbrich interrupted loudly in his piping voice, standing again with fists clenched at his side in rage, "have we known what you are and done nothing. For too many years have innocent people suffered. For too many years has your gang terrorised my town, and for too many years have you escaped the hangman's noose, Silquave – well, no longer!"

"You have no evidence!" the gangster roared back, sending spittle flying as he began to become alarmed, struggling futilely against the guards' grips. "I demand a trial! This is not justice!"

"My word is law," Umbrich sneered at the man, "and I condemn you here and now to death, gang lord!" He turned to the guards. "Put him in the dungeons. We'll erect a gallows and hang him tomorrow."

As the guards tried to haul the energetically writhing gangster away, a booming voice stopped them in their tracks, and all heads turned towards the speaker.

"Hold there!" Saul Aodhson commanded authoritatively, striding up to Umbrich and casting his penumbra over the Thane. "What is the meaning of this?"

"Like I told you, this man is a gangster, Prince Saul," Umbrich said with an air of righteous indignation, pointing at Silquave. "He is a well-known felon, and I will not stand for his presence in Ban-Hodre any longer!"

"Does he speak the truth?" Saul demanded, glowering at Silquave and then frowning at Umbrich. "Can you prove that your accusations are true?"

Umbrich flapped his lips for a moment, his brain whirring like a rat in a maze, seeking an exit. "He – Everybody has heard of Silquave Molassus!" he stammered. "If you lived in Ban-Hodre, you'd understand –"

"Do you have any proof?" Saul demanded again in a clear voice, drowning out the Thane's ongoing protestations. "Any witnesses or testimonies to confirm his crimes?"

"Well, no," Umbrich admitted, turning his head and rubbing his temple, but then looking back up at the Prince defiantly. "However, as a Thane of Fjelburg, I have the authority to condemn criminals to death on the spot! It is my right, as laid out by *your* forefathers!"

"That is true," Saul agreed readily, "but what does the Charter say of the authority of a Prince of Fjelburg?"

Umbrich glowered and took a deep breath before replying in a mumble, "The Charter decrees that a Fjellian Prince's command outranks the command of any Thane."

The Prince stooped to look the Thane in the face. "Your word may be law," he said quietly with gleaming eyes, "but so is mine. Therefore," he continued more loudly for all to hear, puffing out his chest, "I *command* that you release this man into my custody at once. I will take him away from Ban-Hodre with me, as you wish, but he will meet his fate fighting against the many foes in the Highlands. We could use more men of his calibre up north."

The Thane's expression gradually changed from that of a child that has lost its toy to that of a child who has found its toy again as Saul finished speaking.

Almost laughing out loud at the gangster's twist of fate, Umbrich nodded, "Very well, Prince, very well. Your wish is my command. Take him away, and let him rot in the pass of death – but, until then, I do suggest that we imprison him in the dungeons, to be safe. He is, after all, a dangerous criminal."

"Yes," agreed Saul, eyeing the gangster, "and that's why he's coming with me."

"Death or the Highlands," Silquave drawled. "There are so many perks to each that it's hard to decide …"

The next morning, a messenger awaited them in the Thane's sparse foyer.

"Saul Aodhson!" the man – a Highlander – hailed them, punching his own chest. "I bring urgent word from your father. You are to return to the Highlands at once."

Saul whooped and said happily, "At long last!"

Terra snatched the letter from the man's hand. After perusing it briefly, she looked to Saul solemnly.

"Be careful what you wish for, Prince. We are ordered to Jaata Murgen."

34

Trial at Crossroads

Bartholomew Peakes studied the man sat on the other side of his lavish, mahogany desk with interest, and the young man opposite him returned the silent scrutiny with odd eyes; one purple, the other blue.

Peakes was Governor of one of three regions of the Isle of Justiqua; the region most often referred to as Westshield, named so for it took up the north-western third of the heater-shield-shaped island. Eastshield made up the north-eastern third of the shield shape and the oddly proportioned three prongs that comprised the top of the shield made up the tertiary and final segment of the island. This southern section was called Knightsholme, although it was popularly called Cavalier Ville by its residents, for it was the home of the island's namesake capital; the city of Justiqua, which housed the headquarters of both the Knights of the Order of *Pacia* and the Church of *Citta Pacia.* Knightsholme was governed by the Lord Protector, the leader of the Knights.

Governor Peakes' headquarters in Westshield, on the other hand, was centred in a town known as Crossroads, for it was located where many roads crossed one another near the centre of the island.

Justiqua was a small, temperate island that shared in the good fortune of the Archipelago – also known as the Goblin Isles – to the south in that it suffered no winter. The weather, though cooling at certain times of the year and heating up at others, was always clement and warm, and so life flourished with a vivacity to rival the wild Archipelago's. In the less inhabited parts of the island, thick jungle thrived; lush green plants of all manner entangling and strangling one another in their climb to reach the top where a thick green canopy towered above the earth, ancient giants supporting a leafy awning to shade the lives of the myriad beneath.

Animals of all size, shape and manner lived side by side in the raucous jungle; whistling birds of splendid multicoloured raiment wheeled in the skies, howling orange monkeys swung through the treetops along with their smaller furry mammalian comrades such as lemurs and squirrels, whilst their lazier cousins, the sloths, hung resolute and unmoving on their chosen trunks or branches. Flies, mosquitos and flying beetles filled the air with buzzing, while on the ground, spotted leopards prowled, black panthers growled, and a variety of rodents scattered in fear before them wherever they went.

In the more inhabited parts of the island, conditions were a little more contained and restrained; the thick press of the jungle had been hacked back to create way for wide open spaces for fields for crops and for tall limestone housing with red tiled roofs. Upon this unnatural stone forest infringed the true jungle, its thick grass ever seeking to creep up between the paving of the streets, its wild plants growing vigorous and large wherever they could grasp the scantest of footholds in shallow soil, its tall palms and fruit trees leaning in to cast shade over the town's edges and scattering their seeds throughout its midst that their children could reclaim their homeland.

Without constant work and trimming, it was well known that the jungle would reclaim the island in a matter of weeks. Therefore, Crossroads was a picturesque place full of hardworking, tanned people, its tall, thin, white buildings elegant counterparts to the brown and green spires of coconut palms, dates, teaks, kapoks, figs and cocoa trees, its white streets festooned with greenery where vines, lianas, fungi, lichen, ferns, moss and grass desperately pushed back against civilisation.

The Governor, picturing his home town and resolving to serve it as best he could, was a well-proportioned man past his physical prime. While his copper hair and stubble were greying and his skin starting to crease and sag, he was ageing with a definite dignity. His stony jawline was still as striking, his sharp, brown eyes as piercing, and his aquiline nose as angular as ever.

He wore a ceremonial breastplate with the crest of his station that delineated him as a Governor of Justiqua and also told those who did not know that he had once been a Knight and had retired honourably. He wore no armour beyond that, however. His days of fighting were over; he left such rigours to the younger folk now. Beneath the breastplate, he wore a rich, woollen, green shirt and dark trousers.

He cared for expensive material, for he did not care to itch, though he generally preferred functional clothes to fashionable ones as do most men who have fought most of their young lives. Over the breastplate, however, Peakes favoured a robe – the one luxury that he allowed himself, other than the fine fabrics of his clothes. It was an eastern style that had worked its way west over the years. His robe was green and highly ornamental with gold lacing depicting the symbol of his family as well as decorating the hems. The whole get-up was fancy and garish for a Knight, yet none dared mock a Governor for dressing like an eastern fop, at least not to his face.

Peakes had surrounded himself with others of his like. Behind and to the side of his grand seat of authority were lower brown, leather chairs. On these chairs sat those who accompanied the Governor in trying criminals; his court, who were ex-soldiers and Knights, now aristocrats like the Governor for the most part, though there were, of course, some snivelling merchants, who had managed to weasel their way up the hierarchy into positions of power through bribery and flattery.

The merchants tended to be fulsome sycophants who agreed with anything said by those of higher social status in the hopes that they would gain that person's favour. Peakes kept a suspicious eye on the brightly-coloured traders, who were undergoing a calico fashion trend. He was, on the whole, well-liked by both court and populace, he believed.

Despite the high maintenance he believed in to keep his body healthy, Governor Peakes retained a vigorous mind, too, and believed that his Lord Protector's laws and edicts were – for the most part – fairly obeyed and enforced under his governance. He believed that he and his guards maintained a strict discipline over his people and that they respected his rule as a result.

He did not have to worry about the Goblins of the southern isles or the pirates of Swash Isle, apart from the occasional coastal raid, because the Knights banded across the southernmost pinnacles of Justiqua and their fleet kept the marauders at bay. The fire-breathing Dragons and their masters – the mighty Elves of old that legends claimed had once plagued the Archipelago – were dead, if they had ever truly existed, and so all that Bartholomew Peakes had to concern himself with in his daily duties was maintaining the peace, enforcing the laws, improving his town, dealing with domestic disputes between landowners, and raking in the taxes and paying them on to the capital. His duties had been going well so far in his role as Governor, he had believed. He thought he had been successful in maintaining the equilibrium in his term of office.

Now, however, this one insolent youth across his beloved desk seemed set on single-handedly dismantling the fragile tranquillity that the Governor had worked so hard to perfect.

Bartholomew Peakes scrutinised the young man chained wrist and ankle to the iron chair opposite him.

Nighan Witchson's dirty countenance was partially thrown into shadow, thanks to the high windows above him through which light streamed to bathe the hall. He had a wild mane of umber hair that straggled messily down past his shoulders, caked with dirt and leaves with twigs protruding from every grubby lock.

His mud-stained face was sullen, sallow and pockmarked, and his eyes, disturbingly, were different colours as though proof that he worked in concert with evil powers; one a wild, bright violet and the other – with a lazy eyelid – the brooding teal of the deep sea. He was not a tall man – was, in fact, shorter than most – and was skinny and gaunt as though he were perpetually underfed or suffering from a wasting sickness. His garments – a once-white shirt, dark green trousers and brown moccasins – were filthy and torn, and his skin underneath was pale and white.

As the Governor took stock of the rebellious youth of only seventeen summers who threatened the stability of the system he had built, however, and looked into his demonic eyes, he knew that Nighan Witchson was a dangerous man. His eyes seemed old, thought Peakes, as though they had witnessed too much already, and their depths seemed to dance like debris in a whirlwind.

"So, did you bring me here for a staring contest across this desk that you love so much, old man, or were you planning to ask me some questions?" asked Nighan mockingly.

His face was half-bathed in the light from the high windows, eyes looking deep into the Governor's own, and his voice was rough and unpleasantly grating to the ear. The members of court gasped their outrage at the young man's insolence, looking at one another, aghast.

"Silence, cur! Speak when you're spoken to!" one of Peakes' guardsmen ordered gruffly, stepping forward from behind the boy and punching down viciously with his plated gauntlet on Witchson's hand, which rested on the armrest of his metal chair.

The heavy blow left the boy's hand crumpled, torn up and bleeding, but he made no sound, no gasp of pain or exclamation of shock. Instead, he slowly turned his head to lock eyes with the man who had struck him and who now towered over him frightfully, garbed head to toe in spike-ridden steel plate armour.

Looking the guard in the eyes through his full-faced helmet, Nighan Witchson murmured cryptically, "*So it will be you!*"

The guard – an enormous, barrel-chested man of six feet in height, a hardened veteran whose courage had been demonstrated time and time again on the battlefield – blanched visibly at the words, despite his lack of comprehension of their meaning, and stepped back nervously to resume his position in the ring of guards that surrounded both the Governor and the prisoner.

Governor Peakes had ordered twenty of his best warriors, as well as the four bodyguards who escorted him always, into the High Hall of Crossroads – an imposing limestone structure that dominated the town centre – with the dirty young man before he himself would step foot on the rug-laid stone floor inside with his court.

"Thank you, Ewan," said the Governor, waving back the guard who had struck, his voice still strong and authoritative despite his age. He then turned to his prisoner.

"Nighan Witchson," he began, his voice rising and falling with the practised ease that came from years of public rhetoric and passing judgement on his fellow man. Nighan watched him impassively with his odd eyes. "You have been arrested by the town guard of Crossroads and brought to me, Bartholomew Peakes – overseer and protector of Westshield, appointed a Governor of Justiqua by Lord Protector Labogé – for judgement and sentence. The charges laid against you are as follows; firstly, murder – of the foulest kind."

Peakes looked up from his document to regard the prisoner. His eyes glared his disapproval from beneath thick eyebrows. "Murder of your own father, Sir Nestor Skallgrim, as well as of more than a dozen other Justiquan citizens, including the Mayor of Port-Hav'n, the Captain of the guard, the smith, an innocent young woman and numerous guards. I have two long letters from Port-Hav'n here."

He waved casually to documents before him on the desk. "The first, from Mayor Roberts, tells me of his and his council's intentions to arrest and execute you forthwith for being a Sorcerer and the son of a Witch."

He picked up a letter then and scrutinised it for a long moment, before reading parts from it.

"This second letter is from the new Mayor of Port-Hav'n, Bruce Frank, who writes to tell me of the deaths of the previous Mayor and all of the others whom you caused to perish. Frank writes that you called down air Demons to suck people up into the skies to be shredded by lightning, that you can control people's minds and make them kill one another, and that the ground outside your manor opened up its monstrous jaws to swallow the Mayor and the others whole at your behest. Now, I don't know how much of that is to be believed, to tell the truth, but I find it far too coincidental that I should receive *two* letters about the sorcery of the son of a known Witch. Frank goes on to say that you were spotted that same night leaving the town, heading in the direction of the White Woods.

"This brings us to your illegal foray into the forbidden White Woods," Peakes continued, his voice deep with displeasure, his shaking jowls showing his sense of regret at the young man's dark path. "I find it hard to believe that you braved the shadows of that particular copse, for no other has come out of there in one piece with their sanity intact – and yet here you now sit."

He stared hard at the prisoner. When no comment was forthcoming, he continued.

"Next on the list of criminal activities is illegal entry into the private library of the Governor of Westshield – namely, me. I do not know how you snuck past my household guards to gain access, but what I really wonder about is your stupidity." He sounded almost kindly as he said this, leaning forwards and regarding the youth with pitying scornfulness.

"If theft had been your intention, then why did you not flee once you were in? The guards tell me that, when they found you yesterday, you were sat on the floor in the back of the library with a veritable mountain of books surrounding you and one in your hands which they had to pry away from you! I guess all that knowledge just wasn't enough to help you, since you spent the night in gaol." The Governor spread his hands mock-apologetically with a bemused smile. Witchson stared at him silently.

"Ahem, which brings us to the final and perhaps most serious charge of all – that you, Nighan Witchson, are a Sorcerer in league with dark powers. Moreover, that you used these dark powers to commit a string of murders and to gain entrance where you ought to be disbarred. Now that the charges have been read," Peakes intoned ritualistically, laying aside his parchments, "and since you are being so civil, I will allow you to plead and even tell your story before I arrive at my judgement."

The prisoner smirked, his twisted lips clear in the beam of light that lit them. In the darkness above, however, only his violet eye could be seen, shining like a star in a void.

"And then you will burn me at the stake – as you did my mother?" Witchson asked slowly, venomously, his upper lip curling into a snarl of disgust and his odd eyes alight with hate.

Again, the members of court gasped as one, horrified at the lack of deference shown by the criminal. He resembled an enraged animal with his wild hair, thought Peakes, unnerved. The Governor shifted in his comfortable, hand-stitched, green leather chair for a moment.

"*You* gave the order to execute my mother, Samantha," accused the man in chains, now leaning forwards menacingly, his voice gravelly and full of menace, "for the sole reason that my mother healed *your* wife of a terrible disease of the brain. But even that wasn't enough for you, was it?" His voice grated more loudly as his anger swelled. "No – you had to kill an innocent child, too, didn't you? *My* baby sister! Mia was only 6 months old, and you had her murdered! For what? For the crime of being born of my mother?"

"Your mother used magic," replied Peakes pointedly, though he was shaken by Witchson's fury. "Such is the fate of all of those that do. As for your sister, we cannot risk the return of the Witches of Convent. As long as one Witch lives, we can never sleep safe for fear that those tyrannical women will enslave us all once more! You must know the lore, boy. The

Age of the Witches was a time of horror and hardship for all mankind."

"My mother was innocent in the first place!" Witchson snarled, baring his teeth.

By now, the court had given up with audible intakes of breath as their sole means of conveying disapproval and had begun to tut in earnest, though each and every one of them listened closely to the young man's words, on the edges of their seats.

"She used her magic under *your* orders – and for good means!" Witchson's blue eye seemed to grow ever darker behind his low eyelid with his deepening emotions, while its violet counterpart blazed with a zestful fury. "*You* ordered my mother to heal *your* wife, the Lady Selessa, and my mother did as you bid. As for Mia, you do not even know if she was capable of using magic – and now she'll never know anything ever again!" He was biting off each word sharply by the end.

"As I have said, the risk was too great to ignore," replied Peakes as calmly as he could, looking from side to side for a brief moment to acknowledge nods of agreement and encouragement from his compromised court. "Besides, I am inclined to think now that it is very likely that Mia *would* have been a dangerous Witch. It evidently runs in the family," he said with an indicative wave toward his prisoner. "You all carry the curse it seems."

Witchson snorted.

"I did command your mother," Peakes continued carefully, "but I did not command her to use sorcery, because I did not know she was a Witch! I thought her simply a healer. The reality of the situation, my dear boy, is," said the Governor finally, resting a hand on his desk and trying to remain civil with the arrogant young man across from him, "by law, sorcery and witchcraft are illegal! Thought to have died out long ago with the Witches! Such practises are dangerous. All the legends tell that they corrupt the mind. There will never be a sane Witch or Sorcerer!"

Peakes smacked the desk with his hand. He implored the young renegade before him to turn from his path, but he knew it was futile even as he spoke. He sighed and brushed a hand through his silvering hair, while the odd-eyed Sorcerer in front of him continued to glare.

"Your mother condemned herself *and* her child the moment she admitted her use of witchcraft to your father. The great Sir Skallgrim was a Knight and a good man. She should have known he could never abide living with a filthy, infant-eating Witch!"

Witchson laughed loudly, gratingly, at that. Bartholomew Peakes sat back in his chair, surprised, while the guards and members of court – who had been expecting a more violent outburst – glanced at one another warily, shocked and confused by the enigma they surrounded. As the prisoner's laughter diminished, he wiped a tear of mock-laughter from his eyes.

"Ah, a fine jest, *sir*. But I think we all know that not every part of the legends is accurate. My mother did not eat babes, lost in the woods.

"As for my father, *the great Sir Skallgrim,* he was the worst piece of lowlife shit on this God-forsaken earth," spat Witchson, his face pinching with leftover hate, "and it is beyond me, why – for any reason, for Gods or vows or bad sense – why my mother married that man. She was a great woman, and no one will remember her small acts of kindness – no one will pray for her soul to reach *Citta Pacia*!

"But my father – because he was a *Knight*," the young man sneered, voice growing rougher with anger. "He will be remembered – as one of many arsehole Knights who rode around the realm, cutting, fucking, burning and pillaging whatever they could lay their grubby, greedy hands on. And hundreds will pray for the souls of those Knights, because they will be told that the Knights were doing *the Prophet's* work – doing a little bad for the greater good of the many. What a load of bullshit! The souls of those *murderers* will be prayed for, but my mother's will be lost and forgotten amid the irrelevancies of time!" He swiped a manacled hand angrily in front of him as if to brush away her memory. "A side story that none will wish to recall."

Witchson had built up passion during his tirade and, after his final word, spat a sizeable ball of contemptible phlegm on the wood of the Governor's desk before breaking down into a fit of heavy coughing.

The guard, Ewan, raised his fist to strike the young Sorcerer once more for his disrespect toward the Governor, but hesitated upon seeing the young man's frail-looking body wracked with painful-sounding coughs. Ewan looked to Peakes for instruction. The Governor shooed him back and waved a servant behind him forwards with a silver pitcher of water.

The court members murmured among themselves of the Governor's endless generosity and noble behaviour. The servant, a young stooped man with blonde hair, filled a silver cup with trembling hands, wiped the spittle from the desk with a rag and, terrified of being in the same room as a Sorcerer, departed hastily to stand behind the safety of the ring of heavy-set, well-armoured guards.

Peakes then waited, fingertips pressed together, while his prisoner finished his coughing fit. He did not have to wait long with the help of the cooling water.

Witchson smacked his lips after draining the cup. "Ah, mighty fine of you, boy." His voice grated against the ear harsher than ever as he nodded to the cowering servant behind the guards.

"The price you pay for the pact you made with dark powers, is it?" asked Peakes, looking down his curved nose at the man sat opposite him.

Witchson cleared his throat again. "Yes, yes it is. But you know what, it's a fair price. What I get in return is beyond any of your comprehension," he said darkly, looking from the Governor to the guards behind him and back. "And you are right about another thing, too. My mother did condemn herself when she admitted her powers to my father, but she did not know that. He betrayed her trust and turned her over to you without a second thought – their fifteen years of loving marriage gone overnight!"

Witchson's eyes were red, and he looked like he might cry, but Peakes could tell it was not sorrow in his eyes and in his slow, scraping voice. It was barely controlled fury towards a man he had already killed.

"Ahem, do you admit your guilt then in slaying your own father, Sir Nestor Skallgrim, as well as Mayor Roberts and all the others who perished in Port-Hav'n?" the Governor asked briskly, hoping to move the conversation quickly in the direction he wanted, picking up a quill and dipping it into the inkpot before holding it ready over the parchment.

The young, dark-haired prisoner leant back in his hard, iron chair and sighed. He spoke softly but clearly, "Yes, I used my magic to cause the ground to open up and swallow them like a behemoth." His left eye was a darkened socket, but his right glowed as it stared at the Governor of Westshield, daring him to believe or to call him a fraud.

"Grand!" exclaimed the Governor, scribbling happily. "You admit both to your guilt and to using sorcery. Grand."

Witchson smirked.

The Governor laid aside his quill for a moment, his curiosity getting the better of him. He leaned forward to speak softly to the prisoner, as if confiding in a friend.

"Do you truly believe, young man, that you have supernatural or unholy powers? Do you honestly believe that you have some ungodly pact with the Lord of the Nether, Gastar? I do not understand why, if you genuinely believe this nonsense, you sit here right now – why you don't use your nefarious abilities on us all? Perhaps, it is because you exaggerate," said Peakes with a coercing smile and a wave as if to say *we have all lied at one time or another*, "because you are taking credit for the work of nature. You have no magic, little boy. You're just caught up in your own imagination!

"And I understand. Mayor Roberts' letter outlines the general populace's hostile feelings towards you. You were mocked and insulted from an early age as I understand it, and after your mother died … You were bound to be the subject of their hatred and of your father's too, apparently. *That* is why you conjured up these little dreams of your own where you are the magical hero and you get what you want! To escape reality. Don't you think that seems more likely, boy?"

His tone was not unkind. He was far less superstitious than the Mayor and the small-town folk Witchson had left behind. "You're no Sorcerer, Nighan. You're just an abused youth, whose mind cannot accept reality and so invents its own façade of grandeur that tempts more than the real world ever can."

He paused, still smiling. He was sure the boy was innocent of all except being a madman now. Who else but a madman would claim to be a Sorcerer? "What do you say to that?"

Witchson did not respond immediately, but remained leant back in the iron chair that had seated so many prisoners before him. His pale face was smothered by shadow. There was no discernible movement – his hands did not even twitch – for such a long time that the Governor began to worry the boy might be dead.

Then, Witchson's voice – like a sharp rock scraping a cliff – chafed against eardrums again. "*Perhaps* you would like a demonstration of my *dark* powers, Governor Peakes?"

"Oh, demonstrate away, boy, if you truly must see your lies fail before your own eyes," laughed the ageing Governor, leaning back and waving a granting hand, feeling secure behind his grand desk. "But know this; if you harm me in any way, your death will be neither swift nor painless. Do I make myself clear?"

"Fear not, old man," growled Witchson, leaning forwards, his purple eye agleam with the light of lunacy. "I would not demonstrate my powers on your withered, dithery old mind, for what would that prove? No, I was thinking of the guard stood just behind you," he pointed innocently at one man and then another, "who hates his friend – who is stood two men down on the right there – because he suspects him of committing adultery with his wife while he was away recently, visiting his father on his deathbed in Ecco Bay.

"He's not sure, mind, and he finds it difficult to believe, because they are good friends and have known each other many years now," the boy said mock-pleasantly, before his tone dropped to a baritone growl. "But there is a part of his mind that longs for nothing more than to thrust his sword down his friend's gullet and watch him vomit red. Is that not so, Daric Engel?" Witchson turned his blazing eye on the guard in question.

The Governor and all the court turned to regard the man, whose name was indeed Daric Engel.

"Speak up," Peakes ordered the guard with an obliging wave.

Daric shifted from foot to foot for a second before replying gruffly, looking at the prisoner, "Yes, sometimes I do. But I've no proof, and I shouldn't want to wrongly accuse a man."

"But, in your *darker* moments, in your more violent inner fantasies, you *do* have enough proof, don't you? You have enough to tear that man apart limb from limb with your bare hands in your imagination, don't you, Daric?" said Witchson slowly, his scraping voice seeming to cut through the air to reach the wincing listeners.

"Yes, sometimes in my head I do, but it's just thoughts," replied the guard defensively.

"Yes, you do," the prisoner growled precipitously, pouncing on the first word like a predator on prey. "And, in your thoughts, all the justified outrage, the hurt of betrayal and the desperate urge to avenge your honour pound at you every day, don't they, Daric?"

"I don't see what you hope to achieve here, Witchson," stated Governor Peakes, half-amused by the lengthening proceedings. The members of court watched silently, mildly bemused.

"Don't they, Daric?" repeated Witchson softly, his eyes never leaving the guard's more and more troubled face.

"Yes," replied Daric, his eyes narrowing.

"That the two people you love most in the world betrayed you, and you have not been able to do a thing about it. That seems unjust, doesn't it, Daric? Don't you think you should have *some* justice or, at the very least, some good old fashioned revenge?" growled Witchson, nodding as he spoke as though his words were an irrefutable truth.

"That would seem just." Daric bit off each word, his anger clearly mounting by the moment.

"Stop it now, Daric!" ordered the Governor sharply, realising too late the danger and trying to take control of the interrogation once more.

"And that supreme injustice, that unforgivable betrayal of *your* trust by *your* loved ones hurts, doesn't it, Daric?" asked Witchson of the guard more loudly, drowning out the Governor's orders. "And the hurt chips away at your heart – like a woodpecker at a tree – every moment of every day with every breath that you take, in fact, *doesn't it, Daric*?"

"Yes!" growled Daric, hands clenching tightly into white fists of fury.

"Daric, ignore him, I order you!" commanded Governor Peakes more forcefully, standing to face the guard. The court members began to fidget in their seats with fright, their eyes wide and their faces breaking out in nervous sweat.

"It chips away at you every waking moment, because *that* man," Witchson cried and pointed at the accused man, who looked petrified, "that man, Tholl Burak, betrayed your trust, and you know it to be true!"

Daric looked fit to explode with rage, fists clenched so tightly that his arms shook, jaw clamped so hard that it throbbed, sweat pouring down his forehead, his torso muscles so taut in rage that he thought he'd never be able to relax again. Not until …

"That man, Tholl Burak, ploughed your wife like an animal in heat while you were away, and then they both greeted you with a false smile and a friendly wave when you returned home," Witchson yelled coarsely from his chair, while the Governor shouted to Daric to ignore him and held the guard's arms at his sides.

It was not enough, though; Peakes could not tear the man's gaze from the prisoner. "Shut up, Witchson!" he shouted over his shoulder. The guards watched silently like immobilised statues.

"It is only *justified,*" roared Witchson at full volume in return, "that you should take your retribution upon those who have besmirched your honour and send them screaming to the pits of the Nether where their souls can forever lament the day that *they betrayed you*, Daric Engel!"

With the Witchson's last word, Daric bellowed like a wounded ox and bodily threw aside the restraining Governor, snatched his dagger from its sheath at his belt and threw himself with a feral scream at the man two figures away on the right, Tholl Burak. The guards in between were too slow to stop him, and those behind were occupied with holding up the ageing Governor. The court members were still seated and had no weapons, were powerless to intervene.

Tholl yelped and turned to run, but it was too late. The maddened guard's dagger plunged through his comrade's back where his amour parted, skewering the heart like a delicacy. Daric hollered at the ceiling like a triumphant predator, while Tholl slumped to the ground and rolled over limply, his eyes lifelessly staring up at his killer, who had been his friend only moments before.

"Kill him!" screamed Bartholomew Peakes as he regained his feet. "Kill Daric! He is under Witchson's spell!"

Two guards drove their swords into Daric Engel's body as he stood laughing maniacally at his victory. He didn't stop giggling when his body hit the stone floor. Only when they beheaded him did his peals of maddened mirth cease to echo around the bloody Hall of Crossroads.

An eerie silence suddenly fell over the great space like a cerement, the sound of it broken only by wracking coughs that shook the young Sorcerer's whole body violently. When at last he regained composure, all stared at him in prolonged silence.

When the coughing ended, Witchson looked around and spoke softly, "It is interesting what a person can be pushed to do when they already want to do it."

35

Secrets of the White Woods

The guards closed in tight around the manacled prisoner, Nighan Witchson. The members of the Governor's court at Crossroads were petrified and aghast, their faces ashen at the sight of the two dead bodies and the lake of blood on the rugs lining the stone floor. One old man vomited. A neatly-dressed skinny man followed suit a moment later, looking thoroughly dishevelled as he sat up with flecks of regurgitated food in his beard.

Governor Bartholomew Peakes looked exhausted, as though having just finished a marathon. He sharply retouched his green robe and clothing to optimise comfort and then collapsed slowly back into his luxurious seat with a sigh, feeling older than ever.

"Boy!" The Governor wearily signalled the servant who stood to the side still, looking nauseous. "Clean this mess up." He pointed vaguely towards the two blood-slick corpses that littered the expensive, once-blue rugs. "You and you, help him," he ordered two of the guards.

He then adjusted his position in his green leather seat, wishing he had never stood up from it. Peakes rubbed tired eyes with his forefinger and thumb and sighed again wearily, while the guards helped the boy haul away the fresh carcasses, whose pungent aroma had already begun to fill the Hall. No Governor had needed to worry about witchcraft or sorcery in centuries to his knowledge – this could prove troublesome, Peakes thought worriedly.

"Guards, swords out and pointed at the prisoner! Next time he attempts any tricks, you will cut off a finger – or any other protrusion you can find. Witchson, if you try anything like that again, you *will* feel the wrath of the torturers, and you *will* confess to your crimes – albeit under duress. So save yourself the time and pain and just confess to me here and now!" the Governor said vehemently, pounding his desk, while Witchson leant back comfortably in his chair with a sly smile playing about his lips. "I would know what foul Sorceries you concocted in the White Woods and the reason behind your breaking into my personal library. First, the Woods – why run there after murdering Sir Skallgrim?"

"I don't know," replied Nighan – unexpectedly cooperative – sitting forward and clasping his manacled hands with a clank, a pensive expression replacing his crafty smile. "I guess I was drawn there – for it was where I needed to be. Also, I knew that no one would dare to venture after me – and finally, because it is between Port-Hav'n and Crossroads. I think I knew that I would come here." His gaze burned into the Governor's eyes. "From the moment I left, I think I knew that I would come here next."

It was all Governor Peakes could do not to visibly shudder at the depths of this young man's determination to seek his retribution against this ageing lord who ruled over a few towns of a third of an island.

"Or maybe I subconsciously contemplated suicide," Witchson added, his voice slow and rough, his face clouded by shadow and, perhaps, regret. "I'm not sure. Perhaps there was a part of me that wanted to give up and curl up like a baby beneath those unholy boughs to die. But such was not my destiny – and I am glad for that."

"You are perhaps the only known man to have ever walked out of the White Woods unharmed," the Governor said at last, adjusting his robe fastidiously until his skin had ceased crawling. "What did you see in there?"

The guards and even the nauseated court members about the room all subtly leaned forwards and even held their breath. Everyone longed to know the secrets of the forbidden forest.

Witchson leant back in his chair, aware that he now had their complete attention. He spoke slowly, his voice a grating susurrus like he was telling a ghost story on the Day of the Dead.

"At first, just trees. Tall trees with smooth white-barked trunks like birches, all leant at an angle pointing towards the coast, leafless – as everybody knows. Just before I stepped foot across the treeline, I could have sworn I heard the strangest music; hauntingly doleful music, as if an assembly of saints wept. It was beautiful to hear, so perfect were its notes and melodies, but it clouded the mind with melancholia. I could see no source for the eerie music, but it seemed to beckon.

"As I passed under the shadow of the white boughs from the morning sun, I felt a far deeper cold seep into my soul than any shade could ever bring, and an instinctive terror welled up in my bones, causing every fibre in my body to scream at me to take it away from this fear. But there was no locus, reason, cause or explanation for the panic. I was simply petrified. And I knew then, that had I not been who I am, I would have died that instant, just as every other man has died who has stepped under the boughs of those silent malignant trees.

"As I puffed out visible breath past chattering teeth, I could not hear a single sound. No tree swayed or swished in the wind, no animal or insect rustled in the undergrowth, and no bird or bee tweeted or buzzed in the air. The silence became suddenly overwhelming beneath the leafless, skeletal branches of the white trees. The sharp twigs on the ends of branches seemed to come alive and rake my skin like claws.

"I wanted to turn around, to run back to the sunshine beyond the treeline and never return to that cursed place, but my feet would not obey me. Instead, they forged onwards, ever deeper into the accursed Woods, while the unnatural cold seeped deeper and deeper into my soul with every footfall, stomping a path through the strangely thick, sharp and brutal black foliage that clogged the way beneath the silvery branches overhead.

"My feet ploughed numbly onwards without volition through the darkness. The trees surrounded me like silent sentient sentinels, slashing at me whenever I walked beneath their sorcerous branches. The barbed foliage underfoot had grown to more than my own height in some areas, and it was a struggle to keep moving in the direction in which I was obviously being drawn – and yet keep moving I did, obtaining a plethora of scars in the process.

"My gaze was fixed ahead – through some dark magic or my own fear I know not – but I glimpsed in my peripheral vision pale, ethereal forms by my sides. They were silent and mist-like, but ever-present in the corner of my eye. They marched with me like a ghostly escort – dozens, hundreds, I know not … It is true what men say."

Witchson looked deep into the Governor's eyes, weighing his soul. "Spirits walk the White Woods. Some say they are dread beings that cause ill and strife throughout the world from the haven of their little forest, where they are safe from all harm. Others say that some, if not all, are actually the spirits of those who died beneath the disturbing silvery boughs of those cursed Woods, trapped by the barked watchmen for eternity."

More than one court member fearfully made reverent prayer hands – fingers pressed together, palms apart, to indicate a shelter for all – and mumbled supplications to the Prophet to keep them safe. Witchson sneered derisively at this, before shifting to get comfortable. He looked around at the rapt faces before continuing.

"I plunged through the sharp, thicketed blackness of the inner forest – surrounded by an army of wraiths – between the silent skeletons of trees, who resembled wrathful clawed fiends more than ever in the increasing gloom. The terror which had plagued me since my first footstep under the warped fingers and grasping talons of the White Woods grew until my heart was beating so quickly I thought it was sure to burst out of my chest with fear before long. My fingers and toes felt so cold I was sure they must be frostbitten.

"But, just when I thought I could take no more – when I had given up all hope, had resigned myself to death and awaited its embrace with open arms," continued Witchson dramatically, his voice deep and chilling, "just then was the moment that I reached the heart of the grim woodland. I found myself in a wide, open, grassy glade with a clear, tinkling stream to my right that I had not noticed before.

"In the middle of the clearing, stones of titanic proportion were embedded in the ground beneath a beam of dazzling sunlight, which lit up the glade and, at the same time, warmed both my skin and my soul after the torturous shade of the white trees. The stones jutted out of the ground well over thirty feet in the air, some of them I am sure, for they vied with some of the smaller leaning white trees in altitude.

"The gigantic rocks were covered in ancient symbols and runes. I could feel magic pulsing from every stone like a beacon of power. The symbols were meaningless to me – which I must say was frustrating given that I read Traveller's Tongue, Runic, Fjellian, Tzunese, Chilpaean patois, a smattering of Babese and Kutzpah – oh, and I was admiring some works of dwarvic in your library, too, the other day, but we'll get to that," the young Sorcerer added gratingly with a taunting half-smile.

"The giant stones were placed in a rough circle, and in the midst of that circle, there was a small mound on which no grass would grow," he continued, swiping a hand which clanked his chains loudly. "Instead, a thick moss covered the ground beneath the unshaded sun. The circle within the stones seemed suffused with some sort of magic, for the very air between the stones glittered, swam and twinkled like the reflection of a rainbow on clear waters.

"I drank and washed my face in the stream, a profound sense of peace upon me. As I drew nearer to the magical circle, I could feel the power within. It washed over me like a wave, and I felt almost drowned within it …" Witchson smiled as his eyes glazed in remembrance.

"That's when they appeared behind me … or slunk out of hiding in the foliage, perhaps. Women – the most pretty-faced, full-bodied and beautiful women that any man has ever laid eyes on, I assure you they were, and naked as the day they were born. They stared at me with beckoning, unafraid eyes, shamelessly rubbing their breasts and the downy pubes between their legs as they beheld me."

The Governor smiled slightly – the fantasy of any seventeen year old.

"I do not know how many such beauties there were, but they swarmed about me, slowly, sensually, like a cloud of butterflies, rubbing my body and whispering in my ear of their need to make me happy – and I was happy, you may believe that. For the first time, perhaps, I was happy." Witchson's abrasive voice softened with sadness.

"They took me and laid me down in the moss in the rainbow-filled stone circle … And I took them!" he said abruptly in his rough voice, leaning forwards to glare about the room, violet eye saucer-round. "One by one, I *thrust* into them," he lunged at the uncomfortable court members lewdly with his pelvis, "and we writhed together for what seemed like hours in an orgiastic flesh pile atop that sunny moss! And it was perfect; perfect harmony. A sense of dreamy euphoria gripped me in those beauties' arms, and all I could think was that I never wanted that feeling to end. The sensuous women whispered huskily in my ears that it never would, that I could stay forever.

"After what could have been hours or even days of this unadulterated bliss, however, I felt something sharp digging into my backside during our passions. I pulled from beneath my rump a dusty, moss-ridden upturned skull whose upper teeth had been serving as a seat for my left buttock! I looked around, still euphoric but confused now.

"The mound of sunlit moss to which the naked beauties had pulled me down was made of hundreds of ancient, mossy bones – whose bones, I was not sure … It is said that most men die at the rim of the forest, but perhaps some got as far as I. Anyway, that was when I truly grasped the danger of the stone circle and the sensuous, grasping women.

"If I stayed, I would die as the hundreds before me had, for these beautiful women were not women at all, but Naiads. Succubae! They had sucked me into the Woods with their siren song and now leached my life force with their sensuous touch and their persistent kisses! I tried to move – to get up from under that mound of sweaty, heaving flesh – but I could not. I had already drunk too deep of their waters, had already given too much to their whim. I was completely drained of strength, such that I could hardly lift a finger, and as the beauteous Naiads continued to writhe – oblivious in rhapsody – atop me, I knew I was dying."

Witchson suddenly leant back in his chair and coughed once, then harder and more violently as a fit overtook the young Sorcerer. His eyes watered, and his whole body was soon again wracked with uncontrollable spasms. After a time – during which his attentive audience waited patiently and silently, their eyes round from tall tales of the forbidden – Witchson's fit abated, and he gasped for air for a moment.

"Peakes, be a good soul and send young Errig over with some more water, would you?" Witchson croaked once he was breathing more normally.

The servant, Errig, started at his name and moved to hurry forwards with the silver jug. The Governor said nothing, but held out a restricting hand, and the young servant halted instantly, sloshing a few drops of liquid onto the rug-laden floor of the Hall in his haste.

"Come now, Governor!" rasped Witchson irritably. "I can barely talk."

"Very well, *Sorcerer*," replied Governor Peakes after studying the youth's sallow face for a moment, unsure what to believe. He would have said Sorcerers were a myth the day before, but now he was not so sure. "You shall have your water, but then you *will* talk. You swear that this tale of Nymphs and Naiads is true? It is not simply an allegory constructed of your frustrated sexual drives?"

Errig the servant stepped forward with the water, careful not to spill any more of it, and refilled the prisoner's silver cup.

"Thank you, Errig," said Witchson politely, locking his odd eyes on the young man's and smiling. Errig bowed his head and swiftly backed away once more. Witchson calmly drank the water and placed the cup back down on the armrest with a satisfied, "Ah!"

He regarded the Governor, who was leant forwards, staring at him silently over locked fingers, and then the ring of guards around them, who all silently awaited his next words with eager faces, and then the members of court, who watched him with frightened yet fascinated eyes, and finally looked back to the Governor.

"Do you have any chicken, Peakes? I am famish-" Witchson said eventually with a half-smile, before he was interrupted by Governor Peakes.

"Tell us what happened in the glade, boy!" the Governor demanded tetchily, his eyes curious, but his brow furrowed. "What happened in the White Woods? Clearly you did not die!"

The young Sorcerer leant back calmly in his manacled chair as though it were a throne, shadow his cloak and cowl.

His voice rumbled ominously forth from the darkness like thunder. "On the contrary, dear Governor; I did die." Nobody knew what to say to fill the pause the prisoner left. "And my soul was torn from this place, this realm … ripped free and dragged down to the Nether."

At this, Bartholomew Peakes leant back with a scoff and a smile of growing impatience. "Ugh, are we expected to believe this, Witchson? Dragged to the Nether by Naiads in the middle of the White Woods? It's a tall tale," he said, disbelief even plainer in his face than in his voice.

Witchson quickly shushed him, saying, "Quiet, Peakes; you wanted to hear my tale, and I am telling it." The Governor stared at the boy suspiciously, but held his tongue.

"Good," growled Witchson deeply, his violet eye dancing with what seemed to be humour. "Now, where was I? Ah yes, the Nether. Gastar's realm. The plane of existence in which the Dark Lord dwells and tortures evil souls after their death is basically a prison. A prison of the mind, perhaps, I'm not sure – for all I know, my body never left the forest and the Nether was an entirely spiritual experience – but it is essentially a prison nonetheless." Witchson shuddered slightly, staring unseeing at the mahogany desk. "The most horrifying, doom-ridden, death-filled, sadistic prison since the dawn of time, that even the sickest man in the world could not imagine.

"When I awoke in the underworld, all I could see was red smoke, and I coughed and wheezed and retched until I had no more bile left to spew, for the crimson miasma that surrounded me corroded my airways. It was poisonous. I felt as though my lungs would burst from my chest, or perhaps simply melt away from the intense heat – as though I were the opposite of a bellows, inhaling all the heat of a blacksmith's furnace.

"The floor on which I vomited was a smooth rock that shone darkly like a black pearl. It was unlike any rock in our realm. The egg-shaped pod-like plants that grew on the rock itself were a malevolent dark red, and they oozed the crimson smoke from the hideous pores at their summits. I forced myself to stagger around until I realised my entire situation. I was trapped on a small circular island of alien black rock, on which grew alien plants that spewed toxic fumes, surrounded by a ring of unnaturally swift-moving lava."

His audience was once again encapsulated, though the Governor wondered what the boy could gain by lying to them so. Perhaps he loved crafting falsehoods, Peakes ruminated.

"Although I could see the lava," Witchson continued, his voice smoothing out a touch as his eyes filmed over. He flinched occasionally as he spoke, as if some of the terrors still frightened him. "I could see no further than about a yard of it. Beyond that, the otherworldly crimson vapours coalesced so thickly that they blocked any sight of what, if anything, lay beyond the lava moat.

"The choice I faced was immediately clear to me; stay on the small island – wretched and alone forever – suffocating, or risk jumping into the unknown and hope to clear the lava. It was clear, too, that this was by Gastar's design. The weak-willed or cowardly would never risk the potential escape of jumping the moat, and they would curl up and die on the smooth, black rock. But Nighan Witchson is neither weak-willed nor cowardly, and I would not wait around to die of suffocation and madness," stated the dishevelled prisoner, sitting straighter and more regally in his manacled chair.

"I leapt into those toxic mists, over the lethal moat," he told them, straining against his restraints with the memory of the leap, before finishing abruptly, "and I landed in the lava."

One of the court members gasped, and Witchson smirked.

"The molten rock gushed into my mouth, nose, ears and eyes – all my orifices," the Sorcerer continued. "It melted my skin and turned my eyeballs to mush, but I did not die. That is the true torture of the Nether, you know, the not-dying. I sank to the bottom of the lava and lay there, praying for elusive release.

"In the end, when it did not come, I swam through the fiery liquid to the surface, where I bumped my hand blindly against something solid. I pulled myself up out of the lava – a mere skeleton – onto a smooth rock shore just like the one I had left. I crawled forwards, not knowing what else to do, praying for death and an end to the pain, and I fell into a gloopy pool, which healed me miraculously, but not pleasantly. The healing of the blood pools was perhaps the most painful experience of my time in captivity. There are no reprieves in the Nether, even when you are being readied for the next torture.

"After I was healed and I had stopped screaming, I climbed out of the pool of blood and fell to my knees at an earthquake. A black mountain as big as the world with a face of lava reared up out of the ground in front of me. Gastar, the Lord of the Nether, offered me a choice then, in a thunderous voice; continue to suffer, or promise to serve him forever and be returned to the world of the living. My will was strong. I refused him, and he vanished underground once more, a leviathan in waiting.

"Again, as I looked around, I had only a circle of safety on the black rock. Beyond that circle, in every direction, lay what looked to be leagues – as far as I could see to the red horizon – of red-hot coals. And, of course, the crimson mists that poisoned every breath were present too, for the noxious plants that spewed them grew on the rock nearby.

"I understood the game, then; the Game of Death, the Dark Lord's sadistic creation. This prison offered the same choice as the last; give up and lie alone in the depths of the Nether for eternity, or continue on through horrendous pain just for the offer of temporary release – that tantalising bait of reprieve, knowing full well that your soul is damned, that there is no ultimate escape from Gastar's playhouse. No end to the Game."

Nighan Witchson's eyes were glazed and haunted, his jaw set and his words slow and rough.

36

Sloughing the Snake

Having been the Sultan's bodyguard for years before being appointed to the heirs, Karth knew his way around the Palace perfectly.

He hurried through its ornate, tapestry-lined corridors until he reached the sun-soaked Audience Chamber, where – as he had guessed – Sultan Bab was to be found up on the mezzanine. Crammed in with him was every terrified courtier, courtesan, servant, law-maker and distant Bab relative in the Palace, the majority of whom had been relegated to ground level.

Karth smirked upon entering. The Sultan of Calypra was being thoroughly berated by his daughter.

"What in the Nether were you thinking, sending us down there to that filthy cesspool?" Palasia demanded furiously, finger jabbing, chin up, shoulders back. "What could we have possibly hoped to gain from such an experience? And today of all days! You have never once suggested that we go down to the lower city, even on the safest of days! But today, when there is the most danger, on the day of the Purge – today is the day you decide we need to go down there?"

Bab tried to stammer a reply, but Palasia spoke over him. "And it isn't even a normal Purge! Those monsters out there aren't Nomads coming to take the excess people to the desert to die, you dimwit! Those freaks out there are butchering our people in the streets by the hundred! I have seen it! Because you forced me to see it, you uncaring brute! And now we are all going to die for your stupidity!"

Palasia stood, fists clenched, face flushed, trembling, before her father. Bab gaped back at her wordlessly. Worse than wordless, he had no look of intelligence in his eyes. The Sultan's face was as blank as a slate. Eli stood supportively behind his father with a mottled face, enraged by his sister's tone.

Palasia spun about, found a new focus for her rage. "*You!*" she hissed hatefully, pointing at a nearby figure up on the mezzanine.

From the floor level, the Elf and his rescuers saw only a manlike figure in a brown cloak and hood, but Karth and Riton knew well what lurked beneath.

"This is *your* doing, *Visk!*" She spat the name as if even the sound left a bad taste. "What have you done to my father? What have you done to him, you scaly wretch?"

The figure unfolded scaled and clawed hands from deep sleeves and carefully pried back his hood. His green, scaled tail whipped to and fro behind him hypnotically.

The attention of every person in the room focussed on Visk. All faces turned to his wide, snake-like face, his forked tongue and fangs, his slit-nostrils and – most of all – his eyes, which sucked them in like a maelstrom does ships. Plumbing the indecipherable depths of his vortex eyes, all were held under his spell; unable to look away, but not realising it, because they never tried. All were still as statues, only their respiration giving any signs of life. The serpent's slit-pupil gaze held them like a lifeline does castaways, his large orange orbs pulsating with energy, filling the room with eldritch light.

Visk looked around slowly, ensuring all were under his spell. "Good," he purred, licking his reptilian lips with a flickering tongue.

Then, he suddenly stepped forward and smacked Palasia across the face with the back of his scaly hand. She hit the floor without a murmur, eyes open, but dead inside, just like her father's.

"Ahh, I have wanted to do that for a very long time! I hypnotised your father, you little whore," Visk hissed at her prone form, "just like I have you. You shouldn't even be here, you whelps!" He glanced between Prince and Princess. "You should have died by now – down in the lower city! You were never supposed to get this far! Now, you might have wrecked *my* life because of *your* stinking cowardice! You should have accepted your fates. He'll never let you live."

He cackled at that, before turning away. When he spoke again, it seemed more musing than provocative. "Once he has decided someone dies, they have no hope. I will give you to the *Thakshir* and hope they spare my life. After all, I was only following orders …"

"Whose orders?" a voice rang out, pure, light and fresh as a spring morn, gentle as dew and yet carrying a mysterious weight of authority that was as indefinable as it was distinct.

"Who goes there?" Visk cried out in sibilant tones, suddenly worried. Someone had resisted his allure.

"My name is Amhrahil Serenpitua. I am the Creator of *Citta Pacia,* and I may not have my magic any more, but my will is as iron as ever." Amril stepped forwards from behind Gug the Ogre on the blue-and-white striped floor, the only figure that moved. He resembled an icicle with his pale skin and white robe, and he had his hands clasped calmly behind his back.

"One of the Vaylorics?" Visk hissed, looking down at the white figure, shock in his bright eyes, the pulsations of which wavered unsurely. "*You* are the dead Prophet?"

"Dead no longer," Amril responded with a hint of a smile, "but I am the Prophet, and I am a pacifist, more importantly, which means that I refuse to take the life of any living thing – even one so disturbed and twisted as yourself." At this, Visk grinned evilly. "Fortunately, all I need to do is distract you long enough that the others can break free of your spell …"

Visk's eyes widened. He ducked and spun, dodging Eli's decapitating swing. Quick as a striking cobra, the snake twisted his slithery body behind the young Prince, clamped his claws into the man's hand and took from it his sword. In the blink of an eye, the reptilian creature was back in control; his mind worked fast. He held the blade to the struggling Prince's throat, and Eli stilled, his red face paling several shades.

"Put down your weapons! Put them down, or I swear I will gut this little fish from chin to prick!" Visk rasped, digging the blade into Eli's throat a little. A thin line of red trickled down to ruin the Prince's flamboyant maroon and gold shirt.

Before the advisor could do any real damage, however, a huge, crimson-skinned hand engulfed Visk's own. With brute strength, it forced the arm and sword away from Eli's throat.

Visk found himself looking up – petrified – into the wrathful, unforgiving eyes of Sultan Bab. From under heavy and furious brows, those dark eyes pierced and transfixed the reptile.

"Hypnotised me, you say?" the Sultan rumbled slowly, dangerously. "Time for you to die, snake!"

He crushed the snake man's hand like a walnut in his mighty grip, forcing Visk to release his son, and then wrapped his great hands around the scaly creature's scrawny throat. The serpent began to writhe and buck under the grip, and his eyes were wide with fear. He used his remaining good claw to rake the Sultan's hands and arms at first, trying to break the hold, but it was impossible. Bab's hands were like steel, his muscles clenched like rigor mortis.

Visk scratched and gouged at the Sultan's nose and eyes then, until his face was nothing but a bloody wreck bereft of feature, but Bab only silently choked tighter, his hands finding strength in pain and fury. Visk's tail swung back and forth, lashing the Sultan until, eventually, it looped around behind Bab to stab him in his broad back repeatedly. The reptile's tail was sharp and pointed, and it sank deep into the layers of blubber and flesh, finally sticking between the Sultan's ribs.

Letting out a mangled roar from his ruined visage, Bab lifted Visk from his clawed feet and ran with the snake man in his grip to the great balcony, which overlooked his glorious, golden city. He did not stop running at the balcony or the rail. The Sultan launched himself and his first advisor over the edge before anyone could stop them.

It was a long fall down, but Bab was happier than he had been in a long while. This time, he thought with a smile, he had not let his children down.

"I'm sorry," he said to the wind rushing past and the broad blue sky.

Palasia ran to the balcony edge after them and, leaning out, watched her father and Visk plummet. She looked away at the last second, not wishing to see her father paint the streets below. Her throat constricted until she could not breathe, could not sob, could not see through tears.

She collapsed to her knees and then fell flat when her legs gave out, oblivious to her falling, oblivious to her brother vomiting violently mere feet from her, oblivious to those around her trying to comfort her, to get her back to her feet. Her ignorance afforded her a certain safety, a shield from reality, but it was not enough. All she could see was her father falling, falling, falling, again and again, behind her eyes. She shut her eyes, but the picture of her father's last seconds was imprinted on the inside of her eyelids, and she moaned.

Behind her, on the ground level of the Audience Chamber, Ratnik and Jumal watched her collapse, heartbroken for her loss, but filled with admiration for the Sultan's end. The Princess began to cry softly after a few moments.

"Dat treacherous snake!" murmured Jumal.

"That poor girl," muttered Ratnik.

She was soon surrounded with jabbering relatives, bodyguards and courtiers trying to help her. The pirates looked over to her brother. Eli stood, swaying slightly like a drunk, his lips, chin and clothes vomit-stained, staring vacantly at a stone bust of his father's likeness up on the mezzanine.

The Sultan's young bodyguards were up on the mezzanine, leaning against the wall, half-concealed by heavy maroon curtains, looking sheepish. The pirates did not blame them for the Sultan's end, though, nor did anyone else. It had all happened so fast, and the unspoken consensus was that there was little they could have done against sorcery.

Karth looked as forlorn as a lost child as Fyrstsvard approached him and said gently, "Excuse me, Karth? I know you must have a lot on your mind right now, but we really must get out of here immediately. Where are the exits?"

Karth shook himself from his stupor and answered dully. "There are a dozen entrances to the Palace complex … I say we spirit the Prince and Princess away to the north, up into the mountains if we have to."

"You will not make it," Kamilah protested, having accompanied the Knight. "Dead men are everywhere. They ring us!"

"She's right," Fyrstsvard added, "they will have surrounded us by now – just think of how many there were!"

"We're trapped!" started the calls of the courtiers.

"There's no escape!"

"Those things are everywhere!"

"We're all gonna die!"

"You're not helping!" Karth snapped at Fyrstsvard, turning away from the Knight, who sighed and prepared to try again, but was preceded.

"There is another way," came a broken, cracking voice from the mezzanine above them.

37

A Clash in the Palace

The company turned and looked up to observe that Palasia had regained her feet. She looked dishevelled; her clothes were crumpled, and her hair was wind-blown and tangled. Her face was streaked with tears, which distorted her eye shadow, making it run and spread, like darkness was overcoming her natural crimson hue.

"I have played throughout this Palace since I was a child. I know it better than any other," she said hoarsely, "and there are secret ways for those who know how to use them; passages built under the city by the old Babs."

An eruption, like the boom of thunder mixed with the clatter of a thousand blades, sounded from the way by which the companions had entered. It was a similar noise to that which had announced the destruction of the golden gates by the lower city.

"They're inside!" Tar Feng shrieked, hopping up and down as if to convey urgency through action.

"Where do these passages lead?" Fyrstsvard shouted up quickly.

Palasia sniffed. "There is one in this very room that leads out of the city into the southern slums."

"A stroke of fortune, at last! Let us use it at once. Please, Princess, lead the way. Karth, you must summon those soldiers back to this room at once if we are all to escape through this passage!"

"Yes, of course!" the bodyguard replied, spurred into action, his grieving mind whirring again.

Rushing to the bell placed discreetly to one side of the hall, Karth rang it violently for a few seconds. While the bell clanged deafeningly, Palasia wiped a sleeve across her nose and stumbled as quickly as she could in her vapid state down the floating marble stairs back into the room, nearly tripping over her own foot on the penultimate step and landing on her feet with an ungainly thud and a wobble.

Unconcerned by the minor indignity, the Princess hurried toward the ostentatious throne toward the back of the vast hall. Going straight past it, Palasia went unerringly to the wall behind the throne where sat a golden pedestal topped by a stone bust of one of the ancient Sultan Babs. Behind the bust was an alcove housing one of many golden, larger than life-sized statues. These statue-filled alcoves encircled the entire room. Palasia moved to the right, to the statue next to the one directly behind the throne.

Slapping the golden face atop the statue frenziedly, she croaked huskily, "Move this! Someone, come and move this statue!"

Riton and Gug were stood nearby, as ever. The muscular bodyguard gestured to the bust and said to the Ogre, "You heard the Princess, Gug."

The Ogre grunted his acquiescence before hefting the heavy statue from its niche, grunting and staggering with the weight. Once it was out of the alcove, he dropped it carelessly to the floor, where it bounced on its end and then toppled over to land lengthways and a few folk had to leap out of the way to avoid having their feet crushed. The marble and lapis lazuli comprising the floor were not so fortunate and were marred with cracks from the impact.

The doors slammed open then, making everyone in the chamber leap out of their skin and swivel to behold bronze- and gold-armoured soldiers of the Palace Guard running into the hall from all three great, engraved golden doors providing ingress, equipped and ready to do battle. They slammed the doors behind them with reverberating bangs.

Around eighty bloodstained men grouped together around Karth then, babbling about their losses, demanding to know where Bab was and then, upon hearing the answer, clearly looking to the bodyguard for orders, since their Sultan was deceased and their Prince mewling softly like a cat on the maroon-carpeted floor above their heads.

"Get ready, men!" Karth was shouting, his voice strained with grief. "Those monsters will be here any second, and I'll be damned if I will let any more Babs die today! Form up and make a line across this chamber facing the door. We will show these creatures the mettle of Calypra!"

The Palace Guard swiftly acquiesced, covering the entire breadth of the hall in a line alongside Karth and Gug. One gave the bodyguard a round, bronze shield. They faced the sealed doors to the chamber – one to the left, one to the right and one in the centre – with sweaty palms and quick breath, like a humming, clattering wall of defiance.

"For Bab!" they chanted as one.

Meanwhile, Palasia turned her attention back to the recently vacated alcove, entered the statue's erstwhile space and reached up with her fingertips to behind the arched, decorative lintel where she knew a trigger was to be found. She clamped down hard with her fingertips on a thin piece of metal she had felt often, but never seen. It gave in with a sharp click, and – at the same time – the alcove's back wall shuddered and gaped open with a loud crunching noise, sliding from right to left to leave a small gap on the right-hand side. It was a gap that had been big enough for playing children to sidle through, but was by no means big enough to facilitate the assembled warriors' escape.

"Quickly, open the door!" she gestured frantically, aware of the irony of her desperation to depart the place she had never before wanted to leave. She understood the way her tropical birds felt now; caught in a gilded cage.

Riton recovered precipitously from his shock at the revelation of the secret tunnel entrance in the Audience Chamber and rushed forward around the pedestal to respond to the Princess' wishes, for – though Gug would fit in the small alcove – there was insufficient room for the Ogre to use his brute strength on such a small crack and delicate job. Riton propped his back against the right wall of the niche, in the gap that had appeared, and propelled the stone door with both hands to the left. He strained and grunted, and slowly the door began to slide open with loud, protesting grumbles, but its progress was devastatingly sluggish, and all could hear the clatter and roar of the approaching horde of flesh-hungry corpses.

"Gug, help Karth protect us!" Riton grunted, his face turning red.

Gug ambled over to join Karth in silently facing the oncoming undead orchestra, whose howls careened through the vast corridors and around the grand hall like inchoate, malefic ghosts.

"Palace Guard!" the ageing bodyguard roared without turning from his vigil. "Now is the day of your glory and remembrance! Hold the line with me now, and let us protect the Prince and Princess until they can escape! For Bab!"

"For Bab!"

"Servants of Bab!" Karth cried out, his voice full of authority. "Fulfil your duties today! Go with the heirs to the throne! Go with them through the passage and protect them from harm! For Bab!"

"For Bab!" the cooks, maids, servants and sweepers shouted back dutifully.

Ratnik and Jumal took out their weapons and moved to stand behind the wall of soldiers, ready to fill any gaps in the line as they might appear. Izdaju, Stein and Fyrstsvard joined them a heartbeat later, while Tar Feng hung back to watch for the time being, knowing that the time would soon come that Heldig would seek him out once more. Kamilah waited at the rear of the forces, too, an arrow nocked to her bow. Amril stood by the escape route, hands clasped but thumbs still fidgeting, fretting but helpless.

"Come on, come on," Izdaju kept snarling at the doors.

"The Prophet watches over us," murmured Fyrstsvard. "The All Mother protects us. It is by his will that we know her grace. It is by her grace that we know life everlasting. It –"

"Really?" put in Stein, regarding his fellow Knight askew. "You think this is the time for the Word?"

"This is precisely the time for the Word," Fyrstsvard hissed back without looking.

Stein shook his head. "Prayers won't save us now."

"I hate da waiting," grumbled Jumal, flexing his fingers on his weapons.

"Really?" replied Ratnik, twirling his cutlass, his voice high with surprise. "I thought you'd dislike the part that came after."

The Chilpaean stared off into the distance. "Nah, dat part is easy … It is da waiting dat kills you."

All could hear the *Thakshir* scrabbling at the solid gold Audience Chamber doors now like raving, ravenous hounds. The sound of it tore not only at the gold, however, but also at the minds of those hidden inside, like an itch in their brain they could not scratch. The scraping increased in volume until it seemed there must be hundreds of them piled atop one another, raking the golden doors with their bare fingers and nails. All present could imagine with little further prompting the scrabbling of so many hands at their flesh, ripping and rending. After a few minutes even the hardiest soldiers were trembling, on edge.

Then, a voice as deep as the grave could be heard through the doors – even above the clawing din – and the scratching sounds ceased at once.

"Heldig," Tar Feng murmured.

The giant golden doors to the Audience Chamber were rent asunder with a boom. Flying from their great hinges, they careened into the ceiling and walls, crashing down on the striped marble and lapis lazuli floor and cracking it further, one of them smashing a chunk out of an emerald pillar before landing and the other crushing several soldiers in the middle of the line. When the echoing clanging halted, long after the gold came to rest, the only testimony to the men who had stood their ground so bravely was a spreading pool of blood from beneath the twisted and mangled, solid gold door.

Izdaju, Fyrstsvard and Stein filled the gap in the line, standing with bared steel in their hands behind the fallen door, not treading on it or the wet flesh or bones protruding from beneath it out of respect.

The *Thakshir* swarmed through the door like cockroaches. In seconds they had filled the entirety of their side of the hall, leaving only a slender gap between themselves and the armoured warriors facing them. The Palace Guard found themselves looking into a sea of familiar faces; familiar and yet horridly perverted with rotting flesh, gangrenous wounds, bulging supernatural veins and inhuman red eyes that held no semblance of the people they had once been. One of the soldiers retched and bent double, looking into the undead eyes of his best friend. The slaughtered army had returned, it seemed; half the vanguard were clad in sullied bronze. The *Thakshir,* however, did not attack yet.

Heldig appeared from their midst, towering above them all in full battle armour with a hairless, rotten face crisscrossed by ugly, red veins, and wicked eyes that conveyed only contempt and murderous inclination. When he stood before his horde of heaving, putrefying flesh on legs, he began to laugh lowly, darkly.

"What piteous opposition you present me, oh great Prophet!" mocked Heldig when his abrasive mirth ended.

His voice carried with it a weight that had not been present before his transformation –a hollow callousness that convinced even Ratnik that his father was lost to him forever. Heldig's derisive smile morphed his rotten features gruesomely, like opening up a mouldered fish belly.

"A handful of soldiers and a ragged band of mercenaries are all that you can now muster to defend yourself? Hahaha, such a shame your revival could not have been longer lasting, but … orders are orders, Elf. You are coming with me! As for the rest of you … it is time for the over-privileged, mewling Babs and any who stand by them to die!"

Heldig turned his vindictive glare on the Prince and Princess, who gaped back, afraid and amazed that such evil existed in the world. With the death of their father and the influx of the undead, they felt the advantaged bubble in which they had lived all their lives being popped.

As Heldig looked to the Princess, however, he was smitten in the face by a sizzling globule of jade energy and was knocked staggering back into the *Thakshir* behind, growling like a caged bear.

"Teeheehee!" chortled Tar Feng over his smoking shepherd's crook, jigging for a second on the spot alongside the line of soldiers. "Quit your yapping, Nether-spawn! These children are not yours and neither is the Elf! No, no, no, they are not – not as long as there's life left in *this* old body, no sir! *Woon*!" the Wizard finished with a shriek, bending like a willow shoot to dodge a searing red bolt of energy.

"That's right!" Heldig boomed. "I have a few tricks up my own sleeves now, little Wizard!"

Seeing that he was unharmed, though, the old man just jigged again. "Missed me!"

He stuck out his tongue at the increasingly apoplectic Lord of the

Thakshir. The pirate-turned-monster swiftly sent another scarlet blast after the first with bared teeth, but this too Tar Feng dodged, ducking under it. As Heldig summoned a third bolt from the depths of his dark powers, however, his magics were undone by a thrown knife that snapped his head back with enough force to snap his spine. His head dangled on his back, and the front of his neck gaped open horribly like a wet, red mouth with a spine for a tongue.

"Teeheeheehee!" The wizened Wizard danced with glee and backed out of the row of warriors, applauding Jumal's throw.

For a long moment, there was silence other than the Wizard's mad mirth; even the *Thakshir* seemed to be holding their breath.

Then, Heldig's head slowly began to rise from between his shoulder blades to reassert itself – without aid – atop his shoulders, atop his snapped spine. Reaching up with his hands, Heldig gruesomely pulled his head back into position on top of the open neck wound with sickening cracks and gouts of black blood. The *Thakshir* horde howled their approval like ravening coyotes, while a few men threw up. The pirate-turned-*Thakshir* Lord ripped out the knife stuck deep in his forehead uncaringly and examined it closely, twisting his bloody neck this way and that as if testing it. A thin trail of dark blood slowly dribbled from the hole in his head down his grey, craterous nose and over his bluish lips.

"You still think you can stop me, mortals?" he asked them disdainfully, spitting black blood from his lips towards them with the force of his words.

Quick as a flash of lightning, he threw the knife back at the Chilpaean who had drawn the blade from his boot. Jumal's reflexes were fast, and he moved to dodge, but the blade still glanced from his forearm, leaving an angry line that welled with blood.

"Kah!" the pirate gasped in pain.

Heldig muttered throatily beneath his breath and cast out his leprous hands incriminatingly at the emaciated, little Tzunese man, crying loathingly, "Kill!"

From the *Thakshir* Lord's own form emerged dark mirror images; shadows that held no substance, yet retained Heldig's own vague adumbrate. They flowed from him like he was a malign spring and they his dark, lethal waters. Four of them undulated above the stupefied soldiers' heads as though they were swimming through the air. Now that he had shed them, the pirate monster cast no shadow at all on the walls and floor despite the bright light of day streaming in through the openings on the mezzanine.

"Tai woon!" the old man muttered irritably – which meant *Yak shit* in Tzunese – and tried to shoot them down with green globs from his staff, but they moved too fast, too sinuously and too unpredictably in the air.

The wraiths slowly sank down to encircle Tar Feng, planting their shadowy feet on the marble and lapis lazuli floor and beginning to circle him predatorily like wolves.

While the soldiers were still awed and distracted by the magical shadows and splotches of power flying this way and that, Heldig said to his throng quietly, "Get them."

Only Fyrstsvard, Stein and Izdaju were fully focussed on the oncoming masses of infectious carcasses, for they knew there was nothing they could do to help Tar Feng. They could only hope he was up to the challenge.

"Shields!" thundered Stein, bracing as the undead pounced bodily on the line of fighters.

The men got their shields up in time and held back the rush, but their arms trembled at the weight of suppurating flesh heaving against them, and they knew they could not keep the undead at bay for long.

One man knocked over a golden pedestal, and a second later, a spark from skirling blades dropped into the spilled oil. With a great whoosh, a fire came to life on the striped floor and engulfed several of the *Thakshir*. Men cheered until they saw that the undead were not falling, but were coming at them still, ablaze, their flesh slowly melting off their bones. Men began to scream and back away, and the line was in immediate danger.

Seeing this, Palasia implored, "Hurry, Riton, hurry!"

38

Shadows, Lost Friends and Shattered Domes

The door's rumbling progress was, despite Riton's ox-like strength, infuriatingly slow.

"Just a little more time!" the bodyguard panted, straining as hard as he could against the rock, his muscles bulging and his face contorted in a rictus of stress.

While the men of the Palace Guard, along with the Knights and Nomads, held off the *Thakshir*, Tar Feng was beset by the four shadows sent by Heldig. They danced around him acrobatically – flipping and leaping so that he could never foresee their movements – but when they closed in on him, he was better able to predict them, for he knew what they wanted: his life.

The old man stood his ground and whipped his crooked staff about him with startling speed. Before it even understood that it had underestimated its opponent, one shadow was whacked soundly around the head by the crook and devoured by green gouts of power where it stood, leaving only the echo of a shrill and a burn mark on the blue-and-white striped floor.

The remaining three shadows circled more warily for a moment, but then they leapt to attack once more together. Tar Feng whirled his crook around his head and then ducked a thrusting black hand, whose touch he suspected could only be harmful, to spin the crook around him just above the floor. The nearest shadow did not leap in time, thrusting as it had been, and was engulfed in the Wizard's lethal lime power, screaming piercingly. The remaining two shadow foes pounced, but one was instantly thwacked mid-air as the wily old man whipped his light staff about as easily as a twig;

it too was devoured in an emerald flare before it could re-land.

The final shadow rushed the Wizard silently, getting too close for him to effectively swing his staff and chopping with its lightless outlines of hands at the little man. Tar Feng dodged the first strikes as fast as he could, but he was no match for the shadow's preternatural speed. Just as the old man thought himself overwhelmed, however, the shadow gave out a keening shriek and spun from the Wizard to witness the street boy, Bala –who had been forgotten by all – drop the scythe with which he had struck at the formless terror, stumble back and gasp at the pain in his wielding hand. Before the shadow could do the injured boy any harm, however, it was afflicted with a violent jade garb from Tar Feng's crook, which consumed it.

"Thank you, boy, much appreciated! Now, watch out – get out of the way!" The victorious Wizard spun from Bala to face his nemesis, grinning toothlessly and prancing madly on the spot for a moment, before shouting mockingly, "Is that all you've got, Nether-spawn?"

Heldig only smiled evilly in return. Tar Feng quickly realised why when a magical crimson mesh appeared all around him, on every side and above, and began closing in on him. The shadows had been a distraction; while the old man had fought, Heldig had been readying his cage.

"*Tai woon!*" He blasted it with emerald power from his staff, but it was too well-formed and too strong now to be stopped. Bala snatched up his scythe and scurried away from the glowing red net with frightened eyes.

Meanwhile, Izdaju, in the middle of the fighting line – in the thickest of the tumult alongside Fyrstsvard and Stein to the right and Ratnik and Jumal to the left – was caught up in chaos, swinging his scimitars in a whirlwind. Intelligent and rational thoughts ran from the death and killing like cowards, as they always do, and thoughts of morality and ethics hid from the deeds done in self-preservation like burrowing reptiles in the desert.

Izdaju had given in to his primeval side and become the beast that lurks inside every man. Every rage he had ever had and suppressed now boiled to the surface at once and exploded out of him in barbarism. Survival was foremost in his mind as he clove and chopped the flesh in front of him as fast as he could like a butcher at work. Past and future were alien concepts; now was the only reality. His already tattooed and scarred body was smeared with a fresh layer of ink within the first few moments of fighting; cold, dark, reeking, coagulated ink. He and the others were all hard-pressed, but – without shields like those with which the Knights and Calyprian guards were equipped – the Nomad and Freemen were especially sorely tested.

Izdaju, armed with only his twin scimitars, moved like greased lightning to avoid the plethora of teeth and nails seeking his flesh and to strike them back. Jumal, to the left, fended off the undead with his dwarvic axe – its strong metal frame proving a trustworthy aide – while slicing and dicing them like a delicacy fish dish with his cutlass. Like Izdaju, Ratnik had to work wonders with his cutlass to save his hide at first, whipping it to and fro, desperately cutting off any appendage that came uncomfortably near to him, never pressed for choice. Rotten hands grabbed at them by the dozen, for the *Thakshir* climbed over each other in their haste and dire blood lust.

To Ratnik's left, a guard armed with a sickle sword and bronze shield fought between the pirate and the Prince, Eli. Ratnik suspected the man had positioned himself there in case the buccaneer had any ill intent towards his Prince – which Ratnik could understand, for the Prince seemed vain and foolish and worthy of ill intent – but what he could not understand was anyone thinking that way in a circumstance such as now. The undead were the enemy now, not the living, no matter how insufferable they might be.

So it was that the corsair was sorry to see the guard bitten on the arm. The guard chopped off the offending half-crushed head and shoved the biter back with his shield, looking around furtively to see if anyone had witnessed his plight. As Ratnik booted a perpetually grinning, lipless *Thakshir* in the crotch, he locked eyes with the guard.

"I'm sorry," said the buccaneer quietly, but the guard read his lips and, in them, his fate.

Ratnik's cutlass looped around behind the man and his shield and, with one fell blow, he severed the guard's neck from his shoulders, thinking as he did so that maybe the man had had good reason to be suspicious of him after all, for it had turned out the pirate would be his executioner, no matter his intentions towards the man before he had been bitten.

The guard's body crumpled in on itself like a scarecrow whose stuffing is pulled out, while to Ratnik's right, Jumal relentlessly smote down the *Thakshir* his friend had kicked in the groin and any others that sought the corsairs out.

The decapitated guard's head bounced from Eli's shoulder to the left, making the Prince turn in worry. As Eli spotted the guard's head roll to the ground and Ratnik's killing stance, his face pinched into a stormy scowl, but twisting had left him exposed, and an opportune armless *Thakshir* sought to take advantage, biting at the Prince's elbow from out of sight.

Ratnik saw both the look of loathing and the biting *Thakshir,* however, and hastily lashed out before any damage could be done, swinging his blade up to slice the attacker's face clean off its skull, so that the Prince felt only the cold wet of the undead's brain on his elbow rather than its teeth. Still, it was enough to make Eli flinch back. He gawked then at his decapitated guard, the faceless but still squirming *Thakshir,* and the Freeman who had turned back to the enemy and was now ignoring the young Prince.

"What in the Nether, stranger?" Eli demanded, turning back to the conflict lest he be caught unawares – and he almost was.

He swiftly parried a thrust aimed for his chest and looped his own blade around to chop low, severing his foe's leg entirely. This done, Eli trod on the unbalanced *Thakshir*'s sword, and – with a couple of hacks, for his crescent sword was sharp but not weighty – the Prince lopped off his enemy's head. Ratnik, too, was caught up in swordplay and made no reply.

Fyrstsvard heard Eli cry out. Since he had an enemy's sword safely trapped in a parry against his own, he glanced to his left to see the problem whilst at the same time pushing back his foe's blade with a grunt of effort.

"Tar Feng, now!" Fyrstsvard began to cry out, seeing the line break and looking to the mesh-trapped Wizard for aid in vain.

By then, however, Eli had put the pieces together and understood that Ratnik had done what was necessary. Stamping on the undead guard, who had begun to turn grey and wriggle, Eli inched closer to Ratnik to fill the gap in the line. Then, he glimpsed the buccaneer stoop, scoop up the guard's round, bronze shield and, with it, bash back the numerous *Thakshir* seeking his flesh, making survival that little bit easier.

Eli, crouched behind his own little wall of metal, wondered what he would have done had he no shield. Perhaps he would have killed the guard too, he thought, regardless of whether the man was bitten. The Prince saw Izdaju, in that second of lapse, whirling his scimitars about him like a hurricane, whipping gouts of black blood into the air where it fell on those gathered below like rain. How he kept his foes at bay without a shield, Eli worried he would never know; it seemed impossible, and yet still the Nomad stood.

Fyrstsvard blocked another sword blow from an ugly *Thakshir,* whose poor looks had only been enhanced by his recent scalping, which left blood and black hair trickling down his face, fleeing his gruesome mockery of a tonsure. While the swords were crossed, Fyrstsvard took a moment to observe the plights of his comrades around the room. Peril chose that moment to plague him in the form of one of the undead dragging its legless body to the front of the line. There, unnoticed beneath eye level, the corpse yanked a hatchet from between its own ribs and, with it, struck at the Knight. Fortunately, the hatchet was aimed too high for flesh and clanged disconcertingly off his tarnished breastplate, knocking Fyrstsvard back a pace.

Before he could cut down the truncated *Thakshir,* however, Fyrstsvard had to evade another fierce swipe from his initial scalped foe or else have his skull split open like a cantaloupe. He parried the sword to his right with his own blade and blocked a second chop from the hatchet with his shield. Pushing back the swordsman again, Fyrstsvard lashed a kick into the legless *Thakshir*'s face, squashing it satisfyingly.

Unfortunately, not even a hefty boot to the face could discourage a *Thakshir* from devouring flesh. The crippled monster screamed in frustrated lust and set to trying to smash apart the Knight's steel shield with blow after feral blow, until Fyrstsvard could not risk chancing a return strike lest he lose whatever appendage he stuck out beyond the shield. Equally, he realised, if he moved the shield, the hatchet would quickly find his legs beneath. He looked to Stein on his right as he blocked the same clumsily-wielded sword with increasingly fatigued arms, but his comrade could be no help, for he was frantically bashing left and right with both shield and sword in a frenzy to keep the undead at bay.

As he crossed blades to his right, Fyrstsvard felt a niggling problem to his left; he could no longer feel the bash of the hatchet against his shield. Now, he could feel his shield being pried from him with a grip like death's own. He clung to it fiercely, but his muscles burned from the fighting, and gradually his arm was pulled lower and lower until he was contorted into such an uncomfortable crouch that he could hardly use his sword arm at all.

"Tar Feng! Help us!" he cried out, flailing his blade at the scalped swordsman uselessly.

It was Izdaju who came to the Knight's aid, however. Spotting Fyrstsvard's predicament, the desert-dweller dropped to his haunches, extended a leg and spun as fast as he could. His leg lashed out like a whip, narrowly missing Jumal's heel and neatly tripping the two *Thakshir* confronting the Nomad.

This done, Izdaju reared back up and slashed through the nearest arm of the crippled *Thakshir* that was terrorising Fyrstsvard. The severed hand fell to the floor, and the legless corpse shrieked in ire and raised its newest stump toward the golden dome overhead. The Knight snapped upright just in time to desperately skid the sword that would have ended his life down his own blade, where it could still have slid off to do some damage, had he not also broken his foe's skull with a bash of his freed shield.

"Thanks!" gasped Fyrstsvard, shocked to still be in the land of the living.

Breathing heavily, he glanced towards Izdaju gratefully from the corner of his eye and then turned to be sure his peripheral vision did not fool him. A bald Calyprian warrior-turned-*Thakshir* with a chunk missing from its neck – enterprising and surprisingly balanced – had clambered atop the heads and shoulders of its fellows and crawled over them to the front of the line, unnoticed up until now by any of the living fighters.

Fyrstsvard looked just in time to witness this Calyprian *Thakshir* arrive at the front of the line, and – before he could shout or react, before Izdaju could recover enough from his latest swipe to bring his scimitars to bear – the clambering corpse leapt bodily onto the Nomad, sinking its teeth into the ebony flesh at his collar and noisily sucking in the bubbling blood.

Izdaju got a sword under his aggressor's golden armour and impaled him upon its length, even ripping him open like a gutted pig so that his festering innards splattered Izdaju's bare skin. The carcass, however, kept biting.

"No! Izdaju!" Kamilah, out of shafts, screamed at the sight.

"Tar Feng! Do something!" Fyrstsvard cried out, stamping ferociously on the legless *Thakshir* that had caused all the trouble as it tried to seize him again.

Izdaju pushed desperately to stave off the undead warrior, but the corpse's hold was as tenacious as a mastiff's. Fyrstsvard, stopping only to shove back the nearest undead threatening him, quickly slashed his blade across the spine of the Calyprian *Thakshir* atop Izdaju, severing the backbone and making the jaw unclamp.

Rage incarnate, Izdaju sprang out from under the *Thakshir* like it burnt him, and – smashing back the nearest two slavering shambles with powerful, savage blows of his scimitars – he set to cutting up the corpse that had bitten him.

With the Nomad a step back from the rest of the line, cadavers queued up to face Fyrstsvard on all sides, but this time the Knight was determined not to be caught unawares. Whirling, he careened his outstretched shield into multiple carious faces, mashing them back with a spray of cold blood. Then, on principle, he cut off the legs of the scalped *Thakshir* who had so nearly gotten the better of him moments ago. When the stumpy carcass fell to the ground, he severed one of its outstretched arms.

Turning back to the rest with wrathful swipes to keep them at bay, he stamped hard on the scalped cadaver's skull with his boot. Having already been dealt a beating, it cracked, and Fyrstsvard's heel felt pulp. Pushing off from the skull, the Knight barged forward with his shield to answer the charge of an opposing, near-fleshless warrior with a dagger sticking from his head. They met with a resonant thud of flesh against metal, and despite the sorcerous creature's superior strength, its weak flesh was no match for tempered Justiquan steel and Fyrstsvard threw it back into the crowd with a defiant bellow.

Before that shout ceased resounding around the great chamber in which they did battle, Fyrstsvard had decapitated two more *Thakshir* and set to freeing their limbs from the prisons of their torsos. The Knight was dripping with gore. Izdaju stepped back into line, and together he and

Fyrstsvard carved up the wall of black flesh confronting them.

"Thank you," grunted Fyrstsvard again, ducking beneath an axe, "for saving my life."

"Do not mention it," responded Izdaju tersely, dodging a grabby hand. "I almost wish I could take it back now …"

Fyrstsvard did not know what to say; fortunately, Izdaju said it.

"It is too late for that now. Keep Kamilah safe, do you hear, Knight?" Fyrstsvard could not spare the time to check, since he was busy windmilling his blade, but Izdaju sounded emotional.

"I hear you, Izdaju, and I will, I promise. I regret what happened between us."

The Nomad caved in a shrivelled, raisin-like skull as his eyes welled up. "I regret what I did to Kamilah." Ducking, he cut off the feet of a man who had once been fat in life, but was saggy in death. "Do you think she will forgive me?"

Fyrstsvard could not stop his own eyes from heating up, but he did not know what to say.

"Do you think we will be together in the next life?" asked Izdaju, ignoring another bite to the arm.

Fyrstsvard chopped into the nape of the naked, skeletal *Thakshir* biting the Nomad's arm. "I do, Izdaju, I really do."

Turning grey, Izdaju whispered, "That's good. Thank you, Knight. Oh, and Knight? Do not let me become one of those *things!* Promise! You know what you have to do. Better I die while I remember being a man."

"I promise … I won't let you become one of those things, Izdaju. I promise," Fyrstsvard croaked over a lump in his throat, shoving back the encroaching carcasses with his shield while he spoke.

"I wish … I'd never taken this job."

Another of the undead leapt onto the Nomad then, and Fyrstsvard was too busy with his own foes to assist any further. From the corner of his eye, he saw Izdaju embrace the corpse, reaching around its neck and then beheading it with a wrench of both scimitars. Fyrstsvard risked a sidelong glance then and wished he had not. He knew the vision would haunt him till his dying day.

His face trickling with blood, almost unrecognisable, Izdaju turned to the Knight as if in a dream and spoke in a thick, slurred voice, "We will be reborn – Kamilah and I – as birds to fly together in the Goddess' sky …"

Izdaju sank to his knees then, as if in prayer, and more of the undead piled on top of him until Fyrstsvard finally lost sight of him amid the writhing carcasses. The last the Knight saw of him was his eyes, staring out at Fyrstsvard from within a shifting cage of cataleptic flesh, and then they too were smothered.

Meanwhile, behind the ever-decreasing number of warriors holding back the walking corpses, the glowing red mesh had been contracting closer by the second until Tar Feng could feel the heat emanating from the sorcerous interlaced structure.

Palasia, free from the fighting, witnessed Tar Feng's plight and ran from Riton and the alcove dangerously close to the dam of golden warriors and the tide of dark flesh they obstructed.

"Karth! Karth!" she cried out, but the bodyguard was beset on all sides and deafened by the clang of steel and the tearing of flesh.

Very well, thought Palasia, if he could not issue the orders, she would issue them herself. She was – after all – the Princess, and the Ogre was trained to respond to her command. She only hoped her plan would work.

"Gug! Gug!" she shrieked above the din of death-dealing.

The Ogre, knocking back half a dozen *Thakshir* with one sweep of his huge arm, turned to locate the Princess before his foes could recover.

Once he made eye contact with her, Palasia shouted carefully, "Kill the man in the black armour! Kill the man in the *black* armour!"

Gug looked around, confused for a second. He beheld a great deal of armour on every side of him. He almost tore into the closest man wearing armour, a bronze-clad Calyprian, but the Princess saw and screamed, "No! The *black* armour, Gug!"

The Ogre sighed. She seemed adamant that the armour had to be black, so he took another second to look around, absently swatting away an irksome *Thakshir* like a mosquito. Then, he saw it; the big man who kept making noises and who had the fieriest of eyes. He wore black armour. With a satisfied growl, Gug set his eye on his target. He would make the Princess proud.

Gug beat his chest with a fist, bellowing, "Shak shak shak shak shak!"

He lowered his head and, like a bull, charged the thick press of putrefied people in front of him, relishing the freedom of combat. Most of his life had been spent in a cage, being fed and being taken out for training. Only after many years had he been allowed out to fight, and – when he did not do well – they did not let him out again any time soon. This time, he thought, he would not let them down; then, maybe, he could be free to fight for them all the time.

"Now, Tar Feng, now! For the love of every God of land and sea, help us!" Fyrstsvard yelled desperately.

A note of fear entered Fyrstsvard's demands as Izdaju's killers turned their greedy eyes on him. Fortunately, Jumal – on the other side of the fallen Nomad – recognised the Knight's dire situation and, in a red spray, turned his cutlass on the carcasses between them.

Without the Ogre's brute strength, the line of warriors around the Knight was fragmenting like a cracked vase; with each new crack, the vase came closer to destruction. Fyrstsvard, Ratnik, Jumal, Eli, Karth and the soldiers scrapped like cornered animals, but it took all of their energy to match the relentless, unbridled ferocity of the *Thakshir.*

The red-hot net constricted still further until it was clenched tightly around the Wizard's entire body, and he could not move. It inched closer to his bare flesh until it was burning into him, branding him with a searing net pattern atop his head and on his bare arms at his sides. He screamed out spells amid gibberish, but to no avail; he could not escape.

Scattering *Thakshir* like roaches, Gug bulled into Heldig, who spotted the massive Ogre coming too late to dodge or stop him, so focussed was he on trapping Tar Feng. Heldig was knocked back like a galloping horse had hit him. His bones splintered and black blood oozed out of several new wounds. His head reeled, and he could not find the energy to stand up, much less continue to enforce his enchantment on the Tzunese Wizard. The scorching magical mesh vanished, leaving Tar Feng with interlaced singe marks all over his frame, but having escaped serious damage.

"Tar Feng!" Fyrstsvard screamed, trying to block three *Thakshir* with one shield as Stein, by his side, turned away from him to help the soldier opposite. "Do it now!"

Heldig, recovering from stupefaction, heard the Knight's pleas over the surrounding cacophony and saw that Tar Feng was free and unharmed. The old Wizard looked exhausted, but his lips were moving feverishly.

"Curse you, little man," Heldig growled. It was too late, and he knew it. Worse, the Ogre was barrelling down on him once more, throwing swathes of undead out of his way as he went. Gug walloped the *Thakshir* Lord again, and he crumpled against an emerald pillar with a wheeze.

"The tunnel is open! The tunnel is open!" Riton cupped his hands to his mouth to yell above the clash and roar of battle, his deep voice booming around the chamber, impossible to miss.

Hearing him, Karth yelled his own orders to Gug, who was at that moment pounding Heldig like a pestle does a mortar, like he wanted to turn the undead corsair to powder. "Gug! Gug! Get back here, Gug! We need you! Come here now!"

Palasia, seeing that Karth had everything in order once again, led the way into the open tunnel. Amril, knowing that the warriors fought for his escape, stepped into the cobwebbed gloom behind her after a final lingering look back.

Gug halted, one fist raised, and looked back curiously at the bodyguard's call. He saw Karth's deadly serious expression and sighed.

Like a sullen child, he moped back to his master, clearing a path through the thronging undead with swinging arms like an ape shouldering through the brush of a jungle. He pulverised the *Thakshir* harassing Karth like ants and awaited command silently, his tongue lolling.

Karth peeped out from behind his shield to witness corpses all around him, broken and mashed to paste, moaning piteously. He beamed up at Gug, though his lips flickered.

"Good boy, Gug! Now, listen carefully. Riton and I must get the Babs out of here! We will retreat through that small passage, and you will remain here to cover our exit! Do you understand?"

Gug regarded his pedagogue with a confused eye, calmly flicking away a *Thakshir* warrior trying to climb him like it was a pesky bug.

"You will protect that tunnel! And Gug," Karth stepped up to stab a gutted *Thakshir* in its grey face, before snarling, "kill them all!"

Gug's face lit up like a bonfire. Since his birth, he had always been restrained. Now, he was being given free leash to wreak his natural havoc on the grey men that sought to hurt his masters. He grinned in his own mangled way, roared like a lion and began his slaughter in earnest.

Droves of the *Thakshir* toppled beneath his mighty fists, and then he got his hands on a sword – never before had he been allowed a weapon – and brandished it with rupturing hollers of freedom and joy. Swinging the weapon like a madman cleaving through brush, the grinning Ogre was soon coated in thick, black slime and surrounded by ever-growing mounds of smashed and ineffectual, but still growling and moaning, undead.

In awe of the Ogre's brute strength and savagery, freed suddenly from the burden of combat, the other warriors did not need to be told to flee twice. They turned tail and ran as fast as they could through the cramped tunnel in the alcove.

Although most warriors saw their opponents torn apart before their eyes by the Ogre, Ratnik and Jumal were not so lucky. Gug rammed through the black masses to their left, and – as soon as Eli's foes were knocked down in the chaos – the Prince hightailed it to the hidden passage, leaving Ratnik's flank wide open.

Fyrstsvard fought by Jumal's side – where Izdaju had once stood – but could be of little aid to the Chilpaean, locked in constant combat as he was. Both Knight and Freeman surreptitiously stomped down on the corpses underfoot as they whirred their weapons, hoping against hope that they would trample the undead Izdaju to a second death and not be forced to face him in his necrotic state.

Skirling swords with one bronze-clad Calyprian *Thakshir* – who had half his face hacked away so that he looked like a small Ogre – Ratnik witnessed another with a deep neck wound that left his head lolling step out from behind the first. Knowing a moment's fear, Ratnik managed to swivel his body enough that he whacked the one-eyed undead man into the path of the other, making both stumble, though neither fell. Distracted, stumbling past the pirate, the second Calyprian *Thakshir* with the dangling skull turned his blood-red eyes on those behind; those fleeing through the tunnel.

Bashing back the foe with half a face with his newly acquired shield, Ratnik risked a glance back and saw the throng of drably clad servants squeezing into the darkness in the alcove, all of them oblivious to and defenceless against the undead staggering toward them. It crossed the buccaneer's mind that it was not his problem; that another would resolve it, another would slay the *Thakshir* with the wobbly cranium. His one glance, however, had told him that would not happen. All the soldiers were either fleeing or still crossing swords with the enemy. No one but him had even noticed the grey-skinned Calyprian converging on the stragglers, he was sure.

He cursed, "Ferrymen take me!"

He knew that – if he did not do something – no one would, and then whatever deaths the bronze-clad undead caused would be on his conscience. So, he ducked, looped his cutlass around behind the armoured opponent he faced and cut deep into the back of the corpse's legs, where its greaves did not protect it. As the one-eyed cadaver fell, it landed sword first on the corsair, but Ratnik managed to raise his shield in time and deflected the blade with a clang.

Then, he shouted to Jumal, "Look out, mate!" before spinning away from the fray and taking off after the *Thakshir* that had bypassed him. He caught the shuffling husk after only a few swift, long paces, leapt on its back and bore it to the ground, where he smashed its brains out against the marble and lapis lazuli with repeated blows of the cupped handguard of his cutlass.

As he did so, though, the catatonic Calyprian flailed wildly. Ratnik screeched like a vulture as the point of the scimitar in its hand raked his face from forehead to right cheek, across his right eye. Blood sprayed out from his face, but he carved off the undead's arms with manic strikes even as he wailed.

Jumal – managing to escape the fracas a moment later with a few savage strikes and a quick pivot and sprint – found his friend there, atop the writhing headless *Thakshir*. He grabbed a rough hold of Ratnik's bloody shirt, hoisted him up and then gasped and flinched at the sight of the younger man's face. Blood still ran down Ratnik's visage, covering up much of the ghastliness, but an angry red line adorned him, and his right eye was cloven in two and jellied, dribbling out of its socket like porridge.

Half-blind, Ratnik yowled as he was yanked up and raised his cutlass to confront his grabber, but Jumal seized his sword arm and shouted quickly, "It's me, Jumal! It's me, I've got you! I've got you, come on, matey."

Half-carrying Ratnik, Jumal shuffled toward the tunnel as fast as he could, his arms soon wet with his friend's blood. They moved so slowly that they would have been caught and killed in seconds had not Gug altered route and finally torn apart the carcasses they had faced.

Although he could see that the Ogre was slowing now with myriad wounds riddling his body, Fyrstsvard could not resist stopping to do one last thing before he fled lest waking nightmares of the man plague him in days to come. Before he followed the others, he found Izdaju. The Nomad's guts were spilling out from a gaping, festering wound – black with gangrene around the edges, where he had been chewed until he transformed – and his body was mangled, trodden and crushed.

He looked up at the Knight with unholy red eyes, gnashing his jaws, rasping and spitting with primeval hunger, all vestiges of his former self gone. His putrefying grey arms reached up, wanting to grab the Knight and pull him close enough to bite, but the undead Nomad could not move thanks to the mound of mauled, moaning corpses pinning and crushing his legs.

"I will look after her, Izdaju, and I will keep my promise. *Reccé em Pacia.*" With that, Fyrstsvard cut off Izdaju's head and arms, feeling bad that he wished the man were easier to chop up; slashing through his thick tendons, sinews and layers of muscle with a blunted blade that kept clanging off the variegated floor was exhausting.

His hands trembled as he did it, but he had felt like he owed the man that much at least – though whether it was an honour or an indignity to be mutilated was debatable, he thought. He had fulfilled the man's last wishes, regardless, and that was all he could do, he told himself.

Thinking about it, he realised the fate of the *Thakshir* was one he would not wish on his worst enemy; eternal, brainless half-life, riddled with hunger, mouldy as old bread and flaky as a leper. Better to die, surely, he thought sombrely, than come back as a nightmare to haunt and murder your own friends and fellows. Better to die, perhaps, than to live in a nightmare where you had to murder your own friends.

With a dozen mangled undead crawling closer, he shook off such morbid contemplations, turned tail and headed for the secret passage.

After all had fled into the tunnel's musty darkness, Tar Feng paused at the entrance, still murmuring. Gazing past Gug and the conclave of carcasses that the Ogre was tossing through the air in all directions, the Wizard locked eyes with Heldig for a moment, but the *Thakshir* Lord, still slumped bloodily against the pillar, was too broken to cast another spell so soon and could do nothing but watch in impotent rage.

The moment the Tzunese man's lips stopped moving, the pillars fell away and the domed golden ceiling shattered like glass and collapsed, burying the hungry undead in a rich tomb.

39

Demon Eye

"Trial after trial I faced in the Nether," Witchson rasped, "and prison after prison I endured and escaped. Never was I given time to rest or recuperate. If I tried, Netherhounds as tall as me would appear to harry me on.

"And always, at the end of every trial, Gastar would appear and offer me a chance to live again as his champion … And every time, it became more tempting. I tried to ignore the temptation, tried to ignore everything and do nothing. If I did not do anything, did not do the trial, then Gastar did not appear to offer me a chance at life. No one appeared, and nothing happened … forever … I tried to curl up and lie, wretched and alone, coughing and suffocating for eternity, but I just couldn't … In the end, no matter how many times I tried, I would always get up and face the agony of the trial just for the bittersweet reward of talking to the God of the Nether at the end of the day, as would we all I guess …

"I don't know how long I was down there, but it felt like years … decades … I suffered more than anyone could ever know – or even dream – in my exile down there, for all those long, lonely years. The prisons did not become easier as time wove on. If anything, the trials grew more and more brutal. There was a wall of razor-sharp ice over which I had to climb, suffering hundreds of cuts to the flesh as I did so. It seemed like everywhere I went I left the same red trail of progress.

"There were leagues of thick bushes, growing from the insidious black rock as plants would grow from soil in our realm, each covered every inch in sharp, barbed thorns that tore into my skin and could only be yanked out painfully. And, at the end of the bushes, when I discovered an escape route leading underground, the tunnel collapsed, and I was left buried alive, to wait to die," he said, voice barely more than a whisper.

He cleared his throat and continued more loudly, "That was unpleasant, but I dug my way free eventually. Always the pools of blood would heal me. Always Gastar would appear to offer me freedom in the form of slavery, and then the Netherhounds would harry me if I dallied. I fought the cursed dogs on the black rock, in water, lava, fire and ice, and in barred cages where an exit would only present itself after the hounds had been slain with their own bones …"

Governor Peakes raised his eyebrows at this and opened his mouth silently like a fish. He then snapped it shut and gestured one of the guards to come forward. The guard did so, carrying a box, and knelt next to the Governor, allowing him to look inside it. Peakes pulled from the box a long, curved spike – which looked like some kind of alien bone – and used it to wave away the guard. It was grey at the base where it looked to have been jaggedly snapped from something larger, and it was stained red towards the sharp tip. The Governor examined it for a moment while the guards and members of court waited and watched, their curiosity almost palpable as every neck craned to garner a glimpse.

"Is this what you are talking about? My guards say they found this on you in my library. You say *this* is the bone of a Netherhound that you brought back from the Nether?" the Governor asked at last sceptically, spinning it in his hands.

"Yes, old man," answered the young Sorcerer, his voice grating like a rusty gate hinge. He sat forwards so that his demonic eyes showed in the light. "That is a bone pulled from the back of a Netherhound and used to kill that same hound – and many more."

"Hmm," responded Peakes ambivalently, "continue." He waved the spike encouragingly.

All eyes turned back to the Sorcerer. Witchson glared at the Governor for a moment for the interruption.

"It seemed like a lifetime – or several lifetimes – spent down there." The Sorcerer's words came out slowly, and his eyes remained troubled and horror-stricken. "Yet here I am," he continued more precipitously, coughing to hide a slight warble in his voice, "in the same young body that I had before my nightmare. Time mocks my mind, now." His eyes unglazed and focused keenly on the Governor. "I feel like an old man myself, given a fresh start."

Peakes' eyes were narrow. "How then did you escape Gastar's racks, Witchson?" he asked, his soft voice sounding sibilant in the looming silence of the prisoner's pause.

"I did not. I took his offer."

Stunned silence followed the two statements. Witchson leant back in his chair again, his face ambiguously dark once more as he stared from beneath low brows at the open-mouthed Governor, as though daring him to call it all a fallacy once more. The obsequious court's gaze slowly transferred back to the Governor to witness his verdict on the tale.

Peakes looked shocked. He had a strange expression on his face as though he wanted to disbelieve every word – for it sounded like the ramblings of a madman – and yet it was clear he was beginning to sense truth in the prisoner's words. He knew that the Sorcerer had passed through the White Woods, and the haunted look in Witchson's eyes told Peakes that he had indeed been through the Nether, figuratively if not literally. The guards ringing the prisoner were silent, their faces smooth for the most part with a few doubtful smirks here and there.

Finally, Peakes reminded himself that it was irrelevant whether the boy's story was true. Clearly he was dangerous, even if he only believed it to be true. The Governor absently put the supposed Netherhound bone down on his dark, glossy desk and spoke over pensively entwined hands.

"If I were to accept that you suffered *all* of that in the White Woods and that you were then let go after making some sinister pact with the Dark Lord of the underworld, why then did you travel to my fair city and break into my private archive? Does Gastar have qualms with my library?

"Or, if you wanted vengeance against me, why did you not seek me out as I slept or as I wandered the city? Why break into a grand, guarded building and hide in plain sight among the bookshelves, where you must have known you would be caught eventually? You were caught by my guards in broad daylight in the middle of the restricted section, reading a mountain of books, for the Prophet's sake! What did you hope to achieve? What did you hope to gain by such ridiculous behaviour?"

"Why, knowledge, of course, old man – knowledge!" Witchson sat forwards and stared back at him, desire clear in his bright violet eye. "Yet I found *no* tomes of magic in your *grand library*, Governor. Why might that be, hmm?" he asked rhetorically, leaning back and swishing a hand. "Even in your" – he spoke mockingly deeply and theatrically – "secret, forbidden restricted section, where you house relics from ages past. Ages of sorcery, I might add. But you don't have any relics, do you, Peakes?"

The Governor's mouth opened and closed stupidly.

"No," Witchson cut him off with a wave of his hand, "no, I know you don't, and I bet I know why, too. It's because the Lord Protector is hoarding them all in a fortress somewhere in Knightsholme, isn't it? He doesn't trust you or anyone else with such knowledge – so disappointing," the young man teased, his voice throbbing with irony.

The court members did not know where to look. They were flabbergasted by his accusations and most tried to seem nonchalant by inspecting either the rugs or ceiling beams.

"I had so hoped you would have gained a small iota of his trust by your age," the young Sorcerer finished, leaning back.

"Watch yourself, boy!" snapped the Governor, pointing a wrinkled finger at the young magic-user. "You have no right to accuse the Lord Protector of anything, and he has no need to defend his honour from the likes of you!"

"Knew it – I was right," muttered Witchson with a half-smile.

"I, for one," Peakes spoke over him loudly, "am glad you found nothing, *Sorcerer*, for I am sure you planned to use any such knowledge to murder me, did you not? That was the grand master plan after all, wasn't it?" he demanded, trying to turn the tables of accusation on the prisoner, who sat silently, the smirk still tugging up one side of his mouth.

"Very well," continued the Governor, slapping a hand down on his desk, "but you do admit to trespassing in both my city and my private archives, yes?"

"I do," replied Witchson, looking up from beneath his ragged hair, though his mocking half-smile belied his solemnity.

"Excellent!" announced Governor Peakes, quill scratching at parchment. He was at last satisfied that the prisoner had confessed to everything and could now be executed. "Well, it's been fun, little Sorcerer," he continued, looking up with an amicable smile, "but I think I have everything I need for now."

Witchson regarded him indifferently.

Peakes looked up to the guard behind the chained prisoner. "Ewan, I think we'll skip any sort of ceremony. Cut his throat, please," he ordered, his smile fattening his cheeks until he looked like a smug hamster.

Nighan Witchson smiled his sardonic half-smile back. Ewan did not move. The guard's eyes were clearly open through his helm, but he did not move a muscle, not even to blink.

"Ah yes, Ewan, the man who so rudely smashed my hand," said Witchson patronisingly.

His smile was still fixed, while the Governor's wilted like a flower faced with an avalanche. The other guards looked at Ewan, confused.

"He is unfit for further duty, I am afraid, *Governor*," the young man practically snarled the last word, hate twisting his face and burning bright in his eye once more, lit by the endless fires of fury inside built up against those who had ruined his life: his father and the man now sitting before him.

"Ewan, the bone, if you please?" asked the prisoner in a more casual tone, turning his head to the right slightly.

Ewan, the guard behind Witchson, stepped forward with blank eyes like a mindless thrall. With one swift, sure grab, he seized the curved bone of the Netherhound from the mahogany desk and placed it in the Sorcerer's outstretched, manacled hand before anyone could stop him. Ewan then unsheathed his sword, turned to the nearest guard on his right and wordlessly ran the man through, ramming his blade through his fellow's belly up to the hilt.

The man squealed like a stuck pig. The tableau was frozen by shock and horror.

Peakes cowered back into his lavish chair, eyes suddenly wide with fear at the bloody display of betrayal by his right-hand guard.

"Guards, kill them! Kill Ewan! Kill the Sorcerer! Kill them both!" the Governor screamed, pushing as far back into the green leather of his chair as he could, eyes wide and brow creased heavily in concern.

"Tyra! Tygreyn!" Witchson bellowed as the guards began to quickly close in on him and Ewan with swords in hand.

They hesitated at his shout, worried that he had ensorcelled them somehow, but it was not the guards at whom the young Sorcerer shouted. As the sitting prisoner finished bellowing the four syllables, a supernatural fire sprang up in front of him, blocking him from the Governor's view, crackling loudly, violent red in colour and so tall and insurmountable that the rafters were blackened by its caress.

Suddenly, a beast came hurtling through the arcane flames towards the guards. A snarling snout and scarlet eyes were all that was visible before two of the guards lay dead, their jugulars ripped out in fountains of blood. The hall echoed with gasps and shouts of terror.

The remaining guards backed away from the creature slowly, sword-hands trembling like leaves in a tempest before the majesty of the Netherhound, Tyra. A second skinless, spike-ridden, fiery hound – Tygreyn – leapt through the fire a moment later, its malefic eyes mirroring those of the first.

The flames against which the great hounds were limned slowly died away, crackling loudly as they receded, until they vanished back into the floor from whence they came, leaving burn marks on the rugs, stone flagging and high beams. Again, all could see Nighan Witchson sitting in his chair like it was a throne with five-foot Netherhounds by his sides and Ewan, the blood-drenched turncoat guard, at his back.

The Governor shrank back, seemingly paralyzed in his chair, his expensive clothes darkened by sweat. His eyes bulged, and his mouth flapped like that of a landed fish. For some of the guards – and certainly for the young serving boy and the yellow-bellied toadies that occupied the court – the sight of the huge, otherworldly hounds of death and their comrades' lifeless bodies was all that they could withstand.

More than half the guards turned tail and scarpered as fast as they could out the back of the Hall, screaming for their lives, along with the young boy and the whole gaudily dressed court. Sunlight streamed in through the wooden double doors flung wide open. The Netherhounds, however, did not give chase. They stood obediently on either side of their master, Witchson. Those guards brave enough to remain arrayed themselves with blades still drawn on either side of their Governor.

"Hehehehe," Witchson chuckled his slow, abrasive chuckle.

He regarded the wary guards closely with his odd eyes while the two Netherhounds carefully manoeuvred themselves closer to the armrests of the chair to which he was bound. After only a few moments, the prisoner stood from his binding chair, while the irons that had chained him melted like butter and dripped from the metal armrests thanks to the heat of the unholy fire surrounding his hounds. The bone-spike was gripped loosely in the Sorcerer's right hand, and the guard Ewan stood behind him, his gore-ridden sword held at the ready.

"I have looked into your minds, soldiers of Crossroads," Witchson growled, his eyes slowly passing over the group of guards before him, "and I find you wanting."

The Netherhounds advanced a pace with bloodcurdling snarls that iced the guards' veins with terror.

"Tyra, Tygreyn, kill them all, except for the Governor," Witchson commanded, his violet eye dancing madly beneath his wild, dark locks of tangled hair.

One guard dropped his sword without a word and half-ran, half-staggered away. He did not get far. None escaped the Netherhounds' flashing claws and deadly snapping jaws. The great flaming beasts ripped through armour like it was kindling, tore apart flesh like wet parchment and guzzled gouts of blood like the finest dark wine.

With supernatural speed they lunged this way and that, their encompassing fires burning, their body-spikes impaling, their claws rending, their enormous teeth gouging through bone and flesh alike, never missing their victim. Eventually, the malevolent beasts were still, their prey extinct. Their skinless flanks heaved, their fires flickered, their great teeth remained bared, and their blood-red eyes pulsed with demonic fury. The guards' innards glazed the High Hall like a splotchy coat of paint.

With all the guards having fled or been torn asunder like so many fish by a bear, only Witchson, Ewan, the Netherhounds and Bartholomew Peakes remained.

The Governor squeaked like a cornered mouse as he stared at them from his luxurious seat; apparently the only noise he could make. Drool dripped from his gaping mouth, snot hung from his left nostril, his weeping eyes had a crazed quality to them, and his tearstained face twitched like he was having a seizure.

"Bartholomew Peakes," Witchson began with a sinister smile, while his Netherhounds closed in on the Governor until all the ageing man could see was their flame-wreathed, toothy maws. "It is time to discuss *your* execution. Your crimes: murder of a guilt-free woman and an innocent baby girl. Oh, and attempted murder of me, too, I guess," he added, coolly counting fingers. "Confess to these crimes and I will grant you a quick and painless death. Deny your guilt and I will allow my hounds to eat you from the feet up."

One look at the evil, fiery dogs converging on him was enough for Peakes. "I confess! I confess! Just do not let them eat me!" he pleaded piteously.

"Very well, Peakes. Your punishment for these crimes," Witchson spoke slowly and deliberately, rubbing his stubbly chin, "will now be decided by a tribunal of your superior: me. And I can think of no more fitting punishment for the crime of destroying my family and murdering my kin than death. And, since I promised you it would be quick and painless, it will be – as quick and painless as *you* make it. Ewan, your knife, please."

The guard took his knife from its sheath on his belt and handed it to the Sorcerer mutely.

The Netherhounds stepped aside to allow the Governor to witness the young man who had brought him to his knees. Witchson tossed the knife on top of the mahogany desk. It clattered, bounced and rolled onto Peakes' lap, where it lay, begging fate.

Bartholomew Peakes slowly looked from the knife to the burning, slobbering beasts that eyed him so hungrily. Finally, he looked up to regard the rebel that stood before him, horror etched deep in his sunken eyes.

Just as Witchson had been given a prison of choices in the Nether, so now he – Bartholomew Peakes – too was given a choice: of how to die. Nighan Witchson, who had effectively brought down the system of government for a third of the country in an afternoon, watched the imprisoned Governor wordlessly, though his violet eye blazed bright enough to light the hall without the sun's assistance.

Peakes picked up the knife, his hand trembling. He touched the gleaming tip of the weapon. It was razor-sharp. His voice was smoother at the end, like he was resigned to his fate at last.

"I must ask you one more question," he said, looking up to stare his doom in the eyes once more. "Why did you permit this interrogation, boy? If all you wanted was my death, why not kill me at the beginning and be done with it?"

Nighan leant forwards, his neck snaking out so he could stare closely into the soul of the man who had ordered the deaths of his family. His purple eye blazed like a supernatural furnace, lighting up his intense observation, whilst its blue counterpart was like an abyss, deep, dark and hollow.

"Because I wanted you to know *why,*" answered the young Sorcerer softly, his voice the antithesis of his gaze. "I wanted you to know *why* I am killing you, and I wanted *the world* to know why I killed you. I did not kill everybody here, Peakes. Those who fled this place – those who survived to fight another day and tell another tale – they will all tell a tale of me and of what I have done here, and so my legend will begin."

So, under the scrutiny of Demon Eye – as some would come to call him – Bartholomew Peakes, Governor of Westshield, sighed deeply and heavily; his last sigh.

He lunged for Nighan with the knife over the desk, but was rent by Tyra's snapping jaws before he could get near. Blood fountained out of his savaged shoulder to hiss, crackle and burn in the fires of the Netherhounds and stain the wood of his beloved, mahogany desk. He screaked and dropped the knife with a clang. When the hound released him, he slumped back into his chair, whimpering and staining the leather with gore.

"From the feet up it is, then," snarled Witchson, his eyes alight with joy or insanity – Peakes thought it might be both.

"No! No!" he shrieked, but his remonstrations fell on deaf ears, seed on infertile ground. Seed on rock, thought the Governor, frantic with fright as the hounds converged on him.

In his desperate struggles to get away, he rocked his chair over backwards, sprawled out of it, rolled and tried to crawl and scamper on his hands and feet towards the open doors. Like the guards, he did not get far, and – when the Netherhounds started to gorge on his boots, toes and feet – they flipped him over so that he was forced to look up, screaming like a banshee, into the half-smiling visage of his killer while he was eaten. He felt every shred of flesh torn like fire, he felt every bone crack like a lightning strike, and – even after his feet were eaten, and they moved on to his legs – he could still feel the phantom pain of his lost limbs along with the fresh surges of agony that spasmed his whole body like a seizure.

"Rot in the Nether, Bartholomew Peakes," Witchson rasped as he watched him die.

40

Escape from the City of Gold

Palasia Bab emerged, blinking, from the blackness of the secret passage into scorching late afternoon sunlight, which caressed her red skin and gave it a metallic quality, made it shine like rust beneath her midnight-black hair.

Shielding her tawny eyes and looking around, she saw the slums of the lower city; tightly packed tall houses, shady, narrow, winding alleyways, and the usual fetid stench of human filth. No, she realised, the stench was different now; it had a new texture as if another, stronger scent overlay that of defecation, sweat, urine and disease. It reeked of despair and death; of carrion, maggots, guts and decay.

The city had been sundered, sullied by the mere presence of the *Thakshir*. Everywhere Palasia looked, she saw evidence of it. The walls of every home and the dirt paving of every street were no longer sandy, but had been blackened as if they had been afire, juxtaposing oddly with the bright glare of the sun. Looking at the blackness, she could tell – without touching it, for she could think of nothing she wanted to do less – that it had a slick texture, as if it were blood and bodies decomposed and turned to an oil-like slime. There were no bodies, though – the Princess knew where they had all gone, what they had all become. None had survived. Lord and lady, thief and whore; none had been spared.

Riton and Eli stepped into the light at her back to join her in the strangely sunny, black charnel house that had once accommodated thousands, but which now lay bare as a ghost town, empty and silent save for a moaning wind. Eli walked past Palasia without a word, red-eyed. The servants, maids and cooks of the Bab Palace trotted out of the secret passageway next, darting glances around warily like frightened rabbits leaving their warren.

Following the serfs, a stumbling Amril and his rescuers emerged, shading their eyes against the sudden glare after so long underground.

Fyrstsvard supported and murmured reassuringly to Kamilah, who was weak-kneed and tearstained.

"He's gone! He's gone!" she kept moaning, tearing at her hair.

"Shh, it's going to be okay, I'm so sorry for your loss," Fyrstsvard said repeatedly, pulling her along with her arm slung over his shoulders.

A sweating Jumal dragged a gory Ratnik out of the tunnel after them, the latter barely able to stand with the pain coursing through his face. Finally, Karth and his few remaining Palace Guard stepped out exhaustedly, looking like they had swum through the black blood of the *Thakshir* to escape.

Karth clapped a hand to Riton's broad shoulder in sympathy once clear of the passage, for they had both been involved in raising the Ogre, Gug, from birth.

"I'm so sorry, Rite," Karth said thickly. "I know you must hate me for what I did … ordering Gug to stay behind to cover our escape …" He sniffed. "But he did his job. And so did we. The Babs are safe – and we will keep them safe. They will be his legacy."

"Thank you, brother," said Riton gruffly, "for your kind words. I do not hate you. I am pleased at the fashion of Gug's end. All his life, he was pent up. He died in freedom, in joy."

Karth nodded, gulping hard, but seeing Riton's wisdom in the matter. Gug would have preferred no other way to go.

"Gaia's arse, dat was a close one!" Jumal muttered to Ratnik, still feeling shaken by his scrape with death. "Tought we were goners for sure when dat dome came down … Lucky for us, da Wizard knew what he was doing."

As the Chilpaean weakened and Ratnik started to slump, Fyrstsvard spotted them, apologised to Kamilah and hurried to help prop up the injured buccaneer.

"By the Prophet! What happened here?" the Knight asked, round-eyed.

"We ran into some choppy surf," Jumal explained.

"You can say that again! Tar Feng! Tar Feng, come and take a look at this, will you, old chum?"

The wizened Wizard hobbled over, his golden skin blemished all over by a singed net pattern that looked to be browning and healing already.

"My goodness!" he exclaimed upon seeing the young pirate's ruined face. He glanced apologetically toward Jumal before saying to Ratnik, "The eye is perhaps the most complicated organ in the body, yes it is … I am afraid I do not have the skill to heal it …" Ratnik groaned loudly in despair, and Tar Feng hastened on, "But, but I can heal the rest of your wound and … and, once we have removed the eyeball," he said, speaking louder and quicker over the buccaneer's inarticulate yelping, "I will be able to heal the socket and take away your pain."

He stared sorrowfully at the pirate as the young man kept making distressed sounds. "Well, I am sorry, Ratnik, but that eye has to come out. It cannot be left in there like that to fester. It will kill you, my boy. I will deal with it as soon as I can, I promise. For now, though – if you can still walk – I think we should put some distance between us and this cursed city, don't you?"

"He's right," Fyrstsvard agreed, his voice dripping with sadness. "We have to get out of here, or you'll die regardless."

Jumal scowled and made a noise like he might disagree, but then slumped tiredly and nodded. "Let us get out of here fast, den." Despite his words, he could not resist asking the question in his heart, twisted with inextricable passion though it was. "Do you tink … da *Takshir* leader could have survived dat crushing?"

Fyrstsvard looked his comrade in the eyes dolefully. "No, my friend, I don't."

Tar Feng contradicted him cheerily, "Oh, I very much doubt we've seen the last of them, boys, teehee!"

Jumal frowned at the old man, unsure what to make of his words or his mood.

"Hsst! Come!" hissed Karth, scanning the city alertly. He knew that any of the few stables in the slums would no longer be an option; they would surely be as dead and blackened as the rest of the city by now, he thought. They would have to run. "We must keep moving!"

The large company moved quickly, not quietly, through the stained black alleys. Fortunately, though, they did not spot a single speck of life; not even a bug, a flower or a green leaf. All was dark and soulless. Even the blue skies were empty of birds as if they shunned the place.

"What has happened to this place?" Bala whispered at one point, but none knew how to answer him.

When they reached the corner of a large open space – the plaza in which Bala had been thieving earlier that day, on the other side of which was the sandy-walled exit from the slums through which the *Thakshir* had entered – Fyrstsvard, who was running vanguard, ordered a halt with a clenched fist.

He looked around warily for a moment, but could see little to the left thanks to jutting houses and decrepit porticoes. They would be exposed in the open space of the blackened bazaar, but it would take time to go around, and they might be ambushed in the narrow alleys. He quickly elected speed over caution; they needed to get out of the city as fast as possible, and he could see the egress from where he stood. With a beckoning gesture, the Knight led them from the shadows of the alleys into blazing sunlight.

The radiance flared in the Knight's vision as he stepped into it, blinding him for a moment. He swiftly sought to cover his eyes and look around. As he stepped forward once more and swung his head around to the left, where the plaza continued for a hundred yards unabated, he saw that it was already too late.

The bazaar to the left was thronged with the undead, many of whom spotted him as he did them and moaned lustily at the sight of fresh flesh. The drone alerted the others to the nearby feast, and they all began lumbering and lurching at the group in an eerie stampede that started off slow, but quickened fast.

"Run!" shouted Fyrstsvard, breaking into a sprint straight ahead.

The others, hearing and spotting the danger as they too evacuated the alleyway, did not hesitate to follow. The *Thakshir* moved rapidly once their bloodlust had set in, but jerkily and clumsily, like they were ill used to their own husks – which may well have been the case, thought Fyrstsvard as he ran toward the far end of the bazaar, arms pumping hard, through the narrowing open space between sandy walls and closing undead warriors. Those risen from the grave appeared to have lost their initial identities, their minds, and now all followed the same objective as if they shared a hive mind.

Their objective seemed clear to the Knight now: to hunt down and kill the Prophet and any that got in their way. If that was the case, he wondered fleetingly – tasting blood, his vision wobbling – then who controlled the swarm? If such a queen was killed, would the hive ever stop?

"Mind the frontrunners!" he advised.

Ripping his sword awkwardly free of its scabbard as he ran, he bashed back a leering rotting face to his left with his shield and then let loose a savage swing in the same direction that clove a one-armed Nomad *Thakshir*'s skull in two diagonally across the bridge of the nose. Fyrstsvard could see the corpse's dark, mouldy brain wriggling inside the bone for a heartbeat, jostled by black blood, and the reek it gave off stung his nostrils. By the time the body collapsed, the Knight was far past it.

"Push them back and keep moving!" Fyrstsvard roared over his shoulder as he smashed another *Thakshir* in its red-eyed, black-toothed face with his shield, knocking it down.

From the corner of his eye, he saw that Amril was wheezing down his neck, his pale face flushed with effort. Behind the Elf, Stein was close at hand to knock back any corpses that approached.

Once past the ravening undead, at the opposite side of the bazaar,

Fyrstsvard paused and spun. Stein and Amril flashed past him, followed by Eli and Palasia, on whose heels were Tar Feng, Kamilah, Ratnik and Jumal.

The pirates staggered as fast as they could – surprisingly fast, thought Fyrstsvard, considering the Chilpaean was all but carrying the younger man – but still, they lagged behind. Tar Feng had to stop, turn and shoot down a few of the undead with sizzling globs of energy so that they could finish squeezing through the gap between the sandy wall and the mass of corpses just before it closed.

Bala had made it through and past Fyrstsvard too, although the Knight had not noticed him, small as he was. The Justiquan was intent on watching Karth, Riton and the mass of guards and servants who had not yet left the shadow of the alley.

"Come on!" he hollered to them.

Karth had his back to the Knight and the *Thakshir,* who were only steps away from the Calyprians now, and he appeared to be addressing the servants arrayed before him. Riton and the remnants of the Palace Guard, meanwhile, had seen the danger approaching and trotted forward to keep the undead from the living, decimating any corpse that wandered too near with bone-crunching blows of their bloodstained weapons. Karth did not turn, but kept his severe eyes on the serfs, trusting in his comrade and the guards to defend him for a moment.

Listening closely over the howl of the *Thakshir* and dodging backwards every other second to avoid a lunging grey hand or two, Fyrstsvard heard Karth's words drift to him vaguely on the wind.

"Palace Guard, servants of Bab!" Karth called out peremptorily. "I must demand of you one further trial, one further honour. Hold back these evil creatures for as long as you can that we may make our escape! Will you do this to protect the honoured Bab name, to protect the legacy of our city, to protect the heirs to the throne?" he asked, laying his hand on the hilt of his mighty scimitar.

The servants looked at one another doubtfully; even the guards were unsure.

"Piss on that, Karth!" one of the servants broke out, almost laughing. "We're not turning back now! There isn't even a throne to go back to! It's overrun! We have to get out of here! I say, fuck these Bab whelps, it's every man for himself from now –" Karth's sword flashed in the sun to smash the offending man's skull to red dust. The serf's body crumpled like damp parchment and hit the floor with thudding finality.

"Anyone else desperate to disobey?" Karth snapped.

A bald man – tattooed from head to toe, wearing only mucky trousers – stepped out of the masses, and Karth raised his blade again, but the man turned his back on the bodyguard and faced the crowd. He raised his arms – his blue-inked face beaming with incongruous rapture – and shouted in a high, impassioned voice, so loud that Fyrstsvard could hear him even over the ubiquitous throat rattling.

"Fear not, good people; fear not, my friends! For we stand in the presence of the divine! The Prophet has returned to us – as we always knew he would! And he has brought with him our salvation! As it is written in the Word, so shall it be: 'Fervour will sweep the land like a fever, and the righteous will be swept up in the storm, carried to paradise on the backs of the unworthy.' Look, my friends!" He swung away, pointed at the undead and spun back to the gathering, a crazed look of incredulous bliss on his face. "*There* is our immortality! *There* is our life after death! *There* is our *Citta Pacia!"*

Karth blinked in surprise and lowered his scimitar as the painted man rushed past him, Riton and the guards and ran unhesitatingly into the arms of the nearest walking corpse; a man with mottled grey and black skin, whose big belly had been opened up like a cave or a tree hollow, scooped out by flesh-hungry hands. The large *Thakshir* took the tattooed man into his arms almost tenderly, but then its flabby arms started crushing him and it bit his face, tearing off his nose amid a red shower while he keened like a shot bird.

Strangely, thought Karth, despite his fate, the inked man's words and display seemed to have struck a chord with the rest of the servants. Not a heartbeat later, they followed in his footsteps, sprinting forward with cries of "*Citta Pacia!*" and "Immortality!" and "Freedom!" and cast themselves voluntarily into the embraces of the closest veiny carcasses. Fyrstsvard could not believe his eyes as he witnessed the willing sacrifice.

The *Thakshir* set upon the serfs like a pack of wolves, all red eyes turning on the nearest meal and closing in on it in a tight knot, hands scrabbling at flesh from every angle, blood spraying, people screaming, the undead moaning. Not only the serfs, but the guards too were succumbing now, having waited too long to flee. More and more of the undead swarmed them, and they became stuck in place, unable to leave or move without becoming exposed and getting bitten. More than one guard tried to turn and run, but none made it past a step before they were borne to the ground, and the subsequent hole in the line was filled only with supreme effort by the next unlucky warrior.

The remnants of the Palace Guard and the servants formed a human wall against the putrefaction which scourged the city, distracting the undead with their sacrifices, recreating at great and bloody cost the narrow passage down the side of the bazaar through which the others had escaped.

The royal bodyguards, Karth and Riton, pounded the black dirt with their tread as they hurtled through the gap before it could close again, sprinting so fast that they skidded often on the slick darkness coating the floor as they fled after the Prince and Princess, the Prophet and his rescuers.

"Fight on, brothers! You will be remembered!" Karth cried over his shoulder as he ran.

"You heard him!" The bodyguard heard one of the guards, a man he knew well named Qetric, shouting from behind him as he pelted away. "Let's hold off these monsters as long as we can, boys! Let's show 'em what the Calyprians are made of! They may have taken our city, but by the Prophet they will not take us all! The Bab heirs will live on to tell our story and to bring glory to our names!"

"Huzzah!" the guards responded, cleaving decaying flesh with fresh zeal.

"What we do now will echo through time! Now, we fight!" Qetric rallied them.

"Huzzah!"

"On me! For Bab!" Qetric yelled out, but after that Karth heard no more from the man.

Fyrstsvard watched the bodyguards hurtle past him in incredulity, disgusted by the guards' forced sacrifice, revolted by the servants' ignorant end and repulsed by himself for being grateful for the valuable extra minute the loss of their lives bought him and his comrades. Seeing the guards and servants drowning in blackened flesh, the Knight turned and headed after the bodyguards.

"I'm not sure that's what the Prophet had in mind when he wrote that particular passage in the Word!" he shouted when he caught up with them.

Karth spared him a glance, huffing heavily. "The man was a fanatic," he replied dismissively. "The lower city was full of 'em. Did you see his tattoos?"

"Yes."

"Well, I don't know if you were close enough to make out any details, but those were religious symbols painted across his whole body, along with quotes and passages of scripture from the Word. He must have overheard us talking about the return of the Prophet and thought his day of deliverance had come. For many in the slums, *Citta Pacia* is the only light at the end of a long, dark tunnel, you know? So some can't help racing towards it."

Behind them, they heard shouts of battle and encouragement devolve into screams and wailing with frightening quickness, and then they heard only the low drone of ravenous corpses.

Pelting down the passage between the blackened, once-sandy walls, the group made it out of the slums to the south, out of the city entirely. The way was littered with blood, but no bodies, other than an occasional legless, carious crawler trying to drag itself through the slime with its arms, spitting and snarling in perpetual fury.

Outside, they were greeted by undulating fields of green and gold under a red sunset, like the horizon was vomiting blood. Far-off in the distance in front of them, beyond the fields, a tangle of forest was cast in shadow.

"Where will we go?" Palasia asked Karth quietly.

Her tearstained face was strained and tense as she looked back at her blackened, golden city, rising above her on the hilltop, and then out at the dusky landscape that stretched away before them to the south like a crumpled quilt.

Karth looked around and noticed that Fyrstsvard had overheard. "Any ideas, Knight?" he grunted.

"We must travel west to return the Prophet to Justiqua," Fyrstsvard began ruminatively, unsurely, "but we will never outrun that horde out here on open plains and hills, and I do not think they will give up chasing us just yet. Their leader seemed intent on getting his rotten hands on the Elf … No, we cannot just run west. We need cover …"

"You are thinking of using Shala'Hyddin?" Karth asked, anxious that this foreigner did not comprehend the dangers of what he proposed.

When the Knight met his eyes, however, the bodyguard saw that he understood only too well and that he picked the lesser of two evils.

"Yes," Fyrstsvard responded slowly, as if testing out the word. "Yes, we will travel south to Shala'Hyddin. Once in the jungle, we will journey west through its northern border, without venturing too deep, and eventually we will reach Jungleside. There, we can find a ship to get us away from here.

"I think it is the best plan for us all, my friend," the Knight added carefully, gauging Karth's reaction. "Will you come with us? That horde seems to want you, too." He gave the Bab siblings a meaningful look.

Karth sighed, regarding the infamous rainforest on the horizon. The Knight was right, he thought. It was the best course of action at this point.

"We will go with you to Jungleside."

Epilogue
Kraken

Nighan Witchson watched the sea through a porthole; it would not rest, could find no peace. He knew he was really the one who could find no peace, but it comforted him to imagine that the sea, too, knew troubles that would not let it sleep.

His stowaway spot was ideal; on the lower deck of an unknown ship, in amongst dozens of heavy barrels of fish. He did not even have to cling on to stop from being thrown all about deck by the monstrous waves that threatened the ship, for the barrels enclosed him on every side, trapping him safely in place.

He felt numb after what had happened at Port-Hav'n and Crossroads. He would be pleased to put those memories and his old life behind him. Apoplexy still bubbled to the surface occasionally, but apathy had gripped him of late. He knew not where he was going and did not care.

With his revenge found and the Dread Lord, Gastar, in control of his soul, what was the purpose to his living? He would be a wretch, a champion of evil, a plague upon the living, a stain upon the land, for as long as he continued to draw breath.

Even as tentacles hundreds of yards long with person-sized suckers reared up above the ship, Nighan could find no will to move, to live. The tentacles crashed down, and the sad sea crushed the Sorcerer in its dolorous depths.

Secrets of the Ashlands

Book 2 of the Convent Series

Coming soon

45963469R00214

Printed in Poland
by Amazon Fulfillment
Poland Sp. z o.o., Wrocław